SUNRISE ON THE MEDITERRANEAN

Also by Suzanne Frank

Reflections in the Nile
Shadows on the Aegean

SUNRISE ON THE MEDITERRANEAN

SUZANNE FRANK

WARNER BOOKS

A Time Warner Company

Warner Books, Inc., 1271 Avenue of the Americas, New York, NY 10020
Visit our Web site at www.warnerbooks.com

 A Time Warner Company

Printed in the United States of America
First Printing: August 1999
10 9 8 7 6 5 4 3 2 1

Library of Congress Cataloging-in-Publication Data
Frank, J. Suzanne.
    Sunrise on the Mediterranean / Suzanne Frank.
        p.   cm.
    ISBN 0-446-52091-8
    I. Title.
PS3556.R33413S86   1999
813'.54—dc21   99-19766
                                                                    CIP

Book design by Giorgetta Bell McRee

To Dan

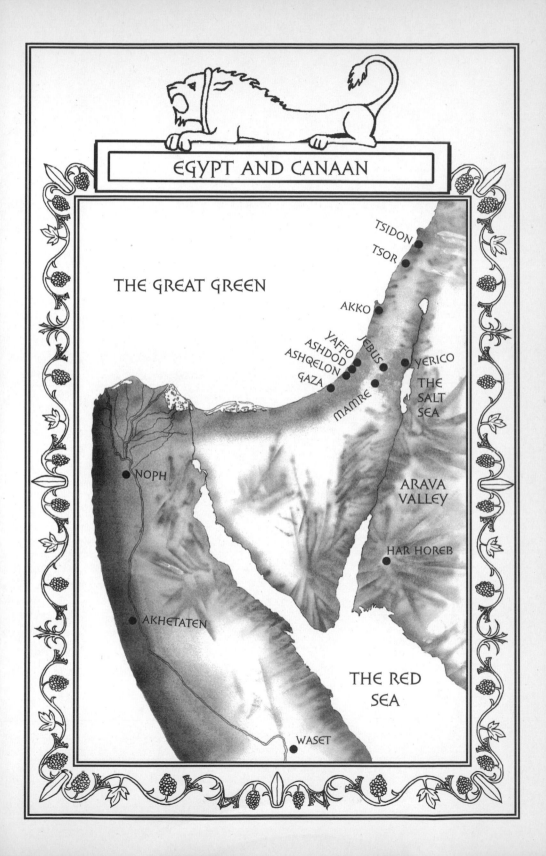

EGYPT AND CANAAN

THE GREAT GREEN

TSIDON
TSOR
AKKO
YAFFO
ASHDOD
JEBUS
ASHQELON
YERICO
GAZA
MAMRE
THE SALT SEA

ARAVA VALLEY

NOPH

HAR HOREB

AKHETATEN

THE RED SEA

WASET

GLOSSARY

adon/adoni (ad-o-nee)—man, sir, dear sir

akchav (ahk-shahv)—Hebrew for emphatic "now"

Ashdod (ash-dohd)—Philistine city

Ashqelon (ásh-ki-lawn)—Philistine city

Ashterty (ash-téar-tee)—consort of Ba'al and fertility goddess in the ancient Near East

avayra goreret avayra (áh-vay-rah gore-er-et áh-vay-rah)—transgression begets transgression

Ba'al (bah'ahl)—Near Eastern god of thunderstorms, among other things

Bereshet (b'ray-shéet)—the first word in the Hebrew Bible, meaning "In the beginning"

b'rith (breet)—covenant

b'seder (bí-say-der)—Hebrew term of agreement

b'vakasha (bih-vak-ah-shah)—Hebrew for "please"

chalev v'd'vash (ha-lev-oo-di-vash)—milk and honey

chesed (hés-said)—lovingkindness

Dagon (day-gone)—fishtailed god of the Pelesti (Philistines)

Derkato (dér-kay-toe)—mythological consort of Dagon

echad (áy-had)—one

el—god

elohim (el-o-heém)—angelic warriors and divine courtiers

Gaza (gáh-zah)—Philistine city, also known as Aza

giborim (gíb-or-eem)—David's private guards

guf—body/flesh

g'vret (give-rett)—Lady

ha—the

hakol b'seder (há-coal bih-say-der)—Everything is all right

hal (hall)—biblical term for devoting something to God through utter destruction

Hamishah (hám-i-shah)—term for the five Philistine cities of the plain

har—mountain

henti—an Egyptian measure of distance, similar to stadia

herim (háir-eem)—holy war

I AM—the name of God

isha (eé-shah)—woman

Keftiu (kéf-too)—Crete and the Cyclades islands

Kemt—Egyptian for Egypt

ken—Hebrew for "yes"

kinor (kéen-or)—ten-stringed harp

laylah (lié-lah)—night

Levim (lév-eem)—the Tribes' priests

lifnay (leáf-nay)—Hebrew for "before" in the chronological sense

lo—Hebrew for "no"

mah—what

melekh (meh-lehch)—king

Moshe—biblical Moses

nachon (náh-hohn)—enthusiastic Hebrew agreement

nasi (nah-sée)—prince

nefesh (néf-ish)—soul

nishmat ha hayyim (neesh-máht-ha-há-yeem)—the divine breath of God that starts life

Pelesti (páy-lee-stee)—ancient term for the Philistines

qiryat (kir-ee-yáht)—city

Qiselee (kí-see-lee)—Philistine city

Rosh Tsor haHagana (rosh tsore ha-hahg-ah-nah)—leader of the army

sela (sáy-lah)—amen

serenim (sáre-i-neem)—the Philistine leaders

Shabat—Hebrew for the Sabbath, sundown on Friday to sundown on Saturday

shalosh (shá-losh)——three
shtyme (shtai-yeem)——two
tani'n (tán-in)——pre-battle pep talk and dance
teraphim (téar-ah-feem)——totem statues
Thummim (thóom-eem)——oracular stone
todah (tóe-dah)——thank you
tov (to-ev)——good
Tsidon (sí-don)——modern Sidon
Tsor (sore)——modern Tyre
tzadik (zá-dick)——holy man/prophet
Urim (érr-eem)——oracular stone
Yaffa (yah-fah)——ancient Jaffa
yam (yahm)——Hebrew for "sea"
yelad/im (yéll-ah-deem)——child/children
Zakar Ba'al——the official title of the ruler of Tsor
zekenim (z'káy-neem)——the seventy leaders of the Tribes

FOREWORD

History is known, illuminated. Details that elude the historical record sculpt it from the shadows. How does this darkness shade what we already know?
What of things that aren't documented?
What of wars that aren't fought? What of plagues that are conquered before they become epidemics? What of leaders who escape assassination?
Are the things that are not transcribed, the truths that are never told, the events, good and bad, whose potential is never realized, equally vital?
As negative space in art delineates the structure of a shape, does what has not happened
lend line, form, and credence to that which has?
Ultimately, the truths on which we base our lives are half-known, because we see only what we are told exists.

PART

I

CHAPTER I

I WAS DROWNING IN SPACE; then space became water.

Okay, at least drowning in water was logical.

Of course, logical wouldn't matter much if I were dead.

Dead?

I opened my mouth to scream in protest, only to gag on the aforementioned water. Light surrounded me, blue to one side, pink from the other. Which direction was up? I kicked reflexively, propelling myself toward the pink, away from the blue.

I broke through a salmon-tinted glass ceiling, gasping for air, swallowing huge lungfuls of it. All around I saw rosy water, ruddy sky. What on earth? Then I felt it, throbbing through my bones and blood: recognition.

There are few places one knows instinctively; this was one of mine. I had played in these waters on almost every coast: Turkey, Greece, Italy, Israel, Lebanon, Morocco. The colors were unmistakable, the taste unforgettable.

I was in the Mediterranean. Sunrise was embracing the now blue black sea with fingers of rose, gold, and lavender.

I wasn't drowning.

Nor was I comforted to find myself in the middle of the Med, with neither land nor ship from horizon to horizon. My legs hadn't stopped moving, keeping me afloat. Shivering, I moved through the water, looking for a warm current. I passed through one, then turned around to return to it.

"*Dagon be exalted!*" I saw them at the same time I heard them. Before I could kick away, a wide, flat thing flew at me, covering my head, my arms, imprisoning my movements. I flailed, tried to get free, but I was caught. I cursed as I went under, able to use only my legs to surface again. In the back of my consciousness I heard a chant, "*Dagon, Lord of the Sea, we bow to thee.*" My brain was refiring the image I'd seen: a canoe carrying four bearded men in dresses. The thing tightened around me, slipping lower, stopping my legs from paddling.

I really was going to drown.

"*Dagon, Lord Dagon, we bring—*" The rest of it was submerged with my ears. Water burned in my nostrils, familiar briny Mediterranean seawater. How could I have ever known it would be my last—my thought was interrupted as someone yanked my head above water, his hands in my hair, half ripping it from the roots.

"*She is beautiful as benefits thee. Take her, Dagon—*" The chorus continued as I shrieked, then inhaled, desperately forcing myself to not fight off my pseudorescuers. Some factoid in my military training reminded me that more people drowned while being rescued. *Don't struggle, Chloe. Don't.* I was coughing up water, my eyes streaming, blurring the world around me.

Arms grabbed me as I was going under for the third time. A hand covered my mouth, another voice crooned for me to be quiet and still, they had caught me so that I could be honored. I didn't want to be honored, I wanted to be free!

It took every ounce of effort not to scream as they pulled my head again, using my hair as a handle. Then they grasped me around the elbows and hefted me into the canoe.

"*Ha der-kay-toe glows with the beauty of Lord Dagon's love,*" they sang. The vibrations of landing hard on the wood resonated through my body, knocked the wind out of me, left me motionless for a moment. I couldn't see because my hair, wet and heavy, covered my face.

"HaDerkato delights the heart of the Lord of Corn." I coughed up more water, spewing it through the—net?—I was caught in. I was outraged. I was snared in a net? Like a fish? *"Dagon, Master of the Sea . . ."* I fought to catch my breath. I twisted within my bonds, then stopped for a moment. Nearly drowning was hard work. I was exhausted.

I sneezed.

"HaDerkato blesses us," they said. *"Lord Dagon embraces her."* Quickly I did a body inventory. Everything seemed to work—arms, legs, torso, neck. Though my head felt disconnected, still I understood the words of the . . . sailors?

"Dagon, Lord of Corn, this gift we bring to thee. . . ."

Daybreak had turned the sky blue, with misty clouds above us. Through squinted eyes I saw that I was dumped in the back of the canoe—but it wasn't really a canoe, it was more like a skiff—and I was lying across a plank in the back, my feet trailing an inch above the water. Strapped as I was in the net, I saw only my legs, the sky, and the odd sandaled foot.

Sandals, dresses on men.

"We implore thee to accept this propitiation."

My eyes popped open at that.

"She's waking!" someone shouted.

"Where is her tail?" another male voice asked.

"Get her before she returns!" The net was ripped off, my wrists and ankles tied, despite my silent struggling.

Too much of a battle and I would find myself overboard, definitely drowning. "Don't look in her eyes," one of them said. I opened my mouth to scream.

"Silence her before she calls to Dagon," someone said. They gagged me with salty rags.

"Keep your ears blocked, beware of her gaze!" said another, the chanting to Dagon uninterrupted throughout.

"Why does she have legs?" one of them asked. "As a consort of Dagon, should she not have a flipper, or fins, or a tail?"

A tail? I stopped struggling and trying to gnaw through my gag, I looked around, wincing as the gag tugged at my hair. I saw them, upside down.

Men in dresses, colored and embroidered dresses with sandals. Short hair. Beards. Swords at their sides.

Okay, men in dresses. However, my mental processes didn't say, "Okay," they said, "*B'seder.*" Were they equivalent?

"*Dagon, Progenitor of the Fields . . .*"

Who was that? Where was Cheftu, my beloved husband, the reason I was here to begin with? I was here with men in dresses. I sneezed— no mean trick with a gag—then looked up again, bewildered.

The sky was suddenly tinted red; when I looked down at my legs, the water beyond them, it was also red. Then I realized my hair, which was framing everything I saw, was red.

"*Dagon, Rapist of the Rivers, creator of the seamaids . . .*"

My hair was red?

My world rocked, canted at a definite forty-five-degree angle. My hair was red! Omigod.

A shudder coursed through me as I tried to look at my clothes, at my body. Then I felt them—signs of the twentieth century in this ob- viously ancient world: the rayon miniskirt drying in the December breeze, the edge of a push-up bra digging into my ribs. Straps around my ankles attached to a ridiculous pair of sandals. The edge of a Day- Glo necklace gleamed spectrally in the morning light.

Around my neck! On *my* body!

I forced myself to breathe slowly, tried to still the racing of my pulse. I was a redhead with parchment pale skin—again—dressed like a cheap hooker. And only *my* thoughts were in my brain!

Another Dagon verse. Dagon. Dagon. A king? A god? A priest? I was drawing total blanks. Fear bottled in my throat.

Where was Cheftu?

The skiff began cutting through the water at a fast clip. I get the world's worst motion sickness on small vessels. Being petrified didn't help my stomach, either. Dagon's praises continued, like Muzak. I took a firm grip on my mind.

No Cheftu and you're a redhead: the rules have changed.

I bit back panic again and reasoned with myself. One, you woke up in the Mediterranean. Literally *in* the Mediterranean. Then it struck me: They hadn't been surprised to find me, they'd apparently been looking for me.

"*Dagon, Showerer of the Plains, thy—*"

Dagon. Dagon. My thoughts derailed as we pulled up to a big ship, complete with sails, oars, and cast of hundreds. More men in dresses. More Dagon verses. I'd been rescued by some type of sailor. An ancient sailor. I was thrown over a man's shoulder like a catch of tuna, and I bumped against him as he braced himself in the skiff. My head was pounding with all the blood flowing to it. After a few shouts, a rope was thrown down.

"Is *haDerkato* secure?" one of them asked.

The oaf carrying me patted my thigh and shouted back, "*Ken!* She is secure, but if she falls, *haYam* will provide another."

The muscles beneath my stomach shifted as the man began climbing up the rope hand over hand. "You are a weighty goddess, *haDerkato*," he huffed.

I had gone stiff as a board to stay over his shoulder: he certainly wasn't holding me! I tensed my legs and tried desperately to keep from swinging out. He grunted and groaned as he pulled us up the ship's side. Beneath me, the sea, the sailors, and the boat grew smaller and smaller. Suddenly a cold breeze blew across me.

"Watch out for her gaze," the climber gasped out as he tossed me down on yet another wooden deck.

When next I opened my eyes, they were grouped around me. Men in dresses, with hairy knees and fish cologne.

"*HaDerkato*," one of them said slowly, as if speaking to a foreigner. "Welcome aboard *Dawn's Battle*."

I insulted his heritage beneath my gag; my head was killing me.

"She curses you," one of them said.

I looked at him immediately and they all stepped back, averting their eyes.

What the hell was going on?

"Where's her tail?" one of them whispered, staring at my bare white legs. Thanks to my streetwalker attire, there was plenty to see. Why was everyone concerned about my tail? How many people actually had—

Oh, duh, I thought. They pulled me from the sea, they are scared of my voice, they think I'm a mermaid? I couldn't help it; I started laughing, drooling around my gag as I realized they thought I was a sea siren. I doubled over, howling, deaf to their reactions.

A mermaid? Oh, this was rich. Priestesses and oracles I have been. Never been a mermaid before.

Then I sobered.

Why were they pulling me out of the sea, and who was Dagon?

And what was this about propitiation?

As another verse of the Dagon song trickled through my understanding, I remembered. Before I stepped through the red sandstone portal, its lintel inscribed with the words of passage, the words of my final prayer in 1996 were, "Please God, let me find Cheftu. Give me everything I need, especially language, to be with him again."

"Dagon, Lord of Corn and Sea . . ." I understood! My body ran hot, then cold. So if that part of the prayer came true, then Cheftu was here? Somewhere?

With a shout, we set sail. Still trussed up like a Cornish hen, I watched the sails fill with wind. I heard the slow beat of the timekeeper as the oars creaked and groaned, speeding up. Big ships, square sails, and men in dresses—it was all vaguely familiar.

But who was Dagon?

The rhythm of the ship rocked me quietly, even though I was spinning with confusion and discomfort—gags are not comfortable. Then I heard the whispers. They must have thought I was asleep.

"I don't understand. Where is her tail?" one man hissed.

"She only has it when she's in the water. How else would Dagon be able to stump her?"

The first man grunted, "Are you certain she is *ha* Find?" Although I'd never heard *ha* before today, somewhere between hearing it and understanding it, I learned that it was "the." In this case the "the" was a term of honor, as in "the Big Kahuna."

"She answered to *haDerkato*, did she not? Besides, who else would be in the middle of *haYam* on the day of the Find, if not Dagon's intended?"

Ha, the big "the," and *Yam? Yam* was sea. Again, the translation was taking place somewhere between my ear and my brain. This time the internal translator wasn't only explaining the words, but giving me a cultural context as well. To these people the Mediterranean needed no other name, for there was no competition. It was the Sea.

"Look at her jewelry; do you think she is less than that? No one save the bride of the king of the seas would have such a thing as that. It glows with the light of the moon."

"Colorful, too," the other man mused.

They must have been talking about my neon jewelry. I fought not to smile.

"She is very pretty," the suspicious one said.

"*Ken.*"

I tried not to blush.

"Pity she will die."

What?

"*Ach*, well, the desires of Dagon."

"*B'seder.*"

They walked away, discussing ropes, as I lay there trying to still my racing heart. Pity about me dying? What was going on? I grappled against my bonds for a moment, irrationally trying to get free, though there was nowhere to go.

I opened my eyes when it got quiet and was surprised to see that it was dark, yet we were still sailing. Did these people sail all night? Ancient Egyptians were notorious for tying up their ships at dusk, I knew this from personal experience. The Nile was treacherous enough without compounding the problem with a lack of visibility. But the Egyptians didn't have ships like this.

A low buzz of activity came from over my shoulders and behind my back. The sailors were moving around the ship quickly, shouting orders—drop sail, double time, then the anticipated drop anchor.

Stars were sprayed across the blackness of the night. The temperature had dropped too, so now I was freezing. The bonds I wore were almost warming. I lay there shivering as the men ran to and fro. The sound of a skiff falling to the water below startled me. Just seconds later I was hoisted across another man's shoulder and carried down another rope ladder. I kept my eyes closed. What was unnerving going up in daylight was petrifying going down in the dark with a sailor whose odor of alcohol mingled disagreeably with his aroma of fish guts.

They stood in the skiff, sailing into the harbor. Consequently my first view of the city, of this time, was upside down between a set of hairy knees. Lights sprinkled the hills, lending the scene a sense of being 2-D, like a matte painting for a stage production. Again blood rushed into my head, giving me a headache that throbbed in time with his step. Between my head pounding, his bony shoulder digging into my stomach, and being in a small boat on a rocky sea, *upside down,* I felt way sick.

As the revolting taste of hot bile filled my mouth, *thump,* we were docked. I was handled with the tenderness of a ton of potatoes. I could barely hear the surrounding sailors and merchants compliment the men who had captured me. My ears were ringing as I was dumped into the back of a cart. My hair once again covered my face, and the smell and taste of near vomit stayed on my gag. I was lying on my side, unable to pull myself upright. The cart moved slowly, dragging across rutted dirt paths. Cats, no surprise with our fishy odor, trailed us, swatting at my hair hanging over the edge of the cart.

Cart. *Think, Chloe, you could be figuring out where you are.* Why the hell should that matter? I groused back at myself. Cheftu isn't here, at least not yet, and I'm in my own body with no mental tour guide to wherever I am. Moreover, I think I'm scheduled to be some kind of sacrifice.

The word *propitiation* haunted me. I'd spent too many summers attending vacation Bible school to not be nervous. Propitiation was compensating for doing something wrong, trying to work your way back into someone's good graces.

I noticed, despite myself, that I was in the back of a two-person, chariot-style cart. I couldn't tell how many horses it had, I couldn't see them. All the elements were here, though. Men in dresses, sandals, gods, and horse-drawn chariots.

I was back in ancient times.

Cheftu had to be here. He had to be. I just needed to keep my eyes—

The vehicle stopped so suddenly that I was pitched out, into the dirt. I felt the abrasion on my face, my shoulder. I wanted to cry; I'd been here less than twenty-four hours and already I was bruised. Not to mention tired, hungry, and confused.

Another man threw me over his shoulder—my stomach was getting sore from this treatment—and carried me from the cart into a building. Suddenly the flooring was different, as was the lighting, the smell, and the sound. He tossed me down, cracking my head against the floor so loudly that I heard the echo.

The sounds around me slowly unfolded into decipherable words. I heard a woman's voice. "You're supposed to set her down gently!" she shouted at him. "She isn't a catch!"

"I *was* being gentle," he said defensively.

"I hope you didn't kill her, then we'll be in worse trouble than we are now!"

He mumbled something, but I couldn't discern the words beyond the aching of my head. She told him to get out, he was a lug and an oaf. Cool hands touched me, "Sea-Mistress, he shall be punished. He is a sailor; sea urchins have been his parents! Please do not hold him against us."

A pillow was slipped beneath my head—which hurt. My hair was brushed from my eyes—which also hurt. My bonds were cut, and as the blood flowed back into my limbs, they hurt, too. My face and shoulder were cleaned off and a salve put on them—which hurt. I felt tears squeeze from beneath my lashes.

Silence fell, blessed peace. When the throbbing in my body had settled down, I cautiously opened one eye.

Holy Isis, here we go again!

All I had wanted to do was find Cheftu, to be with him. Instead I was in a temple, not like any I'd seen before, but identifiable by the smell, the layout, and . . . the twenty-foot-tall statue of a merman with food, gold, and jewels strewn at his, uh, tail.

This was not Egyptian artwork. Not Aztlantu. Neither Greek nor Roman. Pillars rose up on all sides of me, providing the studs for a wall that went up only seven or so feet. Incense clouded the air, filled it with the cloying odor of . . . coriander? Burned coriander? The acrid smell took me back to my childhood in Morocco. Definitely coriander.

The colors were the tints of the sea and sky, blues and greens that blended like watercolors from one into another. A braid pattern wrapped around the columns and edged the ceiling. The floor was a mosaic of shells and colored sand. The room was pretty, very gentle and soothing.

Where was this temple? My head still throbbed, but the nausea had passed. I was lying on my back, on the top part of a set of stairs. To my left was the idol.

He was carved from one piece of marble. It had been broken at least three times around his waist and each arm. Stone must be very expensive, I thought as I looked at him. Why else would they use such a blatantly flawed piece? He was kind of clunky and block shaped, recognizable as a merman but nothing that would set the art world on fire.

Marks had been pressed into the base of the statue. An ancient language. Then, before my eyes, the duck foot—looking wedges re-formed into letters that I understood. *Dagon, Lord of Thunder, King of the Sea, Ruler of the Cornfield, Father of Ba'al, Beloved of Derkato.*

Dagon was the merman?

How did this relate to reuniting with Cheftu? Why else would I be here, in my own skin, unless my prayer had been answered? I'd been looking for him. Instead of finding him, though, I'd been fished out of the Mediterranean and left in a temple. Maybe Cheftu was a fisherman; or a priest?

However, that would be odd. Cheftu had always been an Egyptian. Always arriving from Egypt. Then again, I'd always been someone else, and now I was myself. In my experiences—of which I'd had two, vivid, life-changing ones, when I went back in time, when I stepped into history—I had stepped into another person, her body, her voice, her life; I would put on some ancient woman's skin like a cloak.

I felt dazed, because suddenly everything was new—even the rules seemed different. But I'd time-traveled again, despite these differences.

I noticed the red hair falling over my white-skinned shoulder; I was cloakless. *Hello?* I asked my echoing cranium. *Anybody in there? Yoo-hoo?*

Would Cheftu look the same? He always had before. Now it would be up to me to identify him, for he'd never seen me in my own twentieth-century "cloak."

"Sea-Mistress *Derkato*, would you care for refreshing?"

Glancing up, I saw a young girl, her head bowed, her robe covered in fabric scales. "Water," I said, suspicious of anything else. I didn't think they would try to poison me, but I wasn't positive about that.

She looked up at me, then ducked her head and backed away. Unlike the citizens of both other cultures I'd lived in, where black hair and dark eyes were the norm, this girl was honey colored. Though she was on the tall side, she was slightly built. Long, straight gilded brown hair that matched her eyes hung in elaborate braids to her waist. She gleamed like well-polished wood.

"Please," I called after her. While I thought "Please," what came from my mouth was *b'vakasha*. Was that "please" in this language? I lay back down on the mosaic floor, staring up at the ceiling. Flat roof with clerestory windows; it was good to be in a place with an architecture I knew.

I was in the Mediterranean. In a temple of Dagon. As a mermaid/goddess who was going to die. When I raised a hand to tuck my hair behind my ear, I saw the neon on my arm. I glowed.

Neon. The priestess RaEmhetepet, who had had my body for the past two years, had been on her way to a Ramadan/Christmas party in 1996, dressed with her customary bad taste, which I was now wearing, when she had wandered by the portal and gotten sucked back. Or something like that, I guessed. In modern times RaEm had become obsessed with neon and electricity and things that glittered, which is why I now glowed like some B-film alien.

"Sea-Mistress, your water." The girl slunk forward, placed a seashell precariously on the floor, and backed away, watching expectantly. Was I supposed to lap up the water? Raise the shell to my lips and drink it all?

This was an etiquette question. I could use an "other" right now.

In each of my previous time-travel experiences, I'd moved into someone else's body in that time period, complete with her knowledge of the culture, the language, and some memories. The liaison between the actual owner's mind and my own, I'd called the "other." Now, I was otherless.

I was on my own. What did that mean?

When in doubt fake it, Chloe.

I lifted the seashell to drink it.

Instead I spewed it. Salt water? "Fresh water," I clarified, wiping my mouth with the back of my hand.

"Sea-Mistress, forgive me!" the girl wailed, falling to her knees and beating her chest. "Find mercy! Please don't curse us! I thought you had to have salt water! Please, take your fury out on me, but spare the people!"

Her eyelashes were about two feet long and curly. She still had babyish innocence in her face, but her body was almost a woman's. "Who are you?" I asked.

"Tamera is how the goddess named me."

"Which goddess?" Was there more than one?

"The great goddess, Sea-Mistress. Ashterty." She looked up. "*B'vakasha,* do not curse us." She looked as though she might start beating her chest again.

Curse her? Over water? "I, I won't," I said. She crawled to me on her belly, kissing the mosaic floor by my feet. They could bind and gag me, but now they were worried about my cursing them over water? Where was the logic in that? "Find me fresh water," I said. "Then tell me of your people, the ones you seek to save." It sounded imperious enough without being rude.

Mumbling thanks, she backed away from me and ran from the room.

Tamera returned in seconds, this time with a clay bowl. It was wide, shallow, and decorated with stylized birds, squares, circles, and fish, reminiscent of Aegean designs. The water was cold, refreshing. I sipped it and wondered if they had an equivalent of aspirin. My head was killing me.

"*HaDerkato* is to be honored, so what does she require of me?" Tamera asked, her head bowed once more.

"The men who, uh, I let catch me, where were they sailing?"

She looked at me, frowning slightly. "It is the day of the Find, *haDerkato*. They set sail from Gaza. Throughout the way they prayed for a worthy consort for Dagon. A *Derkato* for him to love. They were sailing to us here in Ashqelon, since the festival takes place here." Tamera smiled a little. "Dagon must be pleased because *haYam* gave us you!"

Words were flying at me as I strove for comprehension. "Did you find anyone else out there?" I asked. Maybe Cheftu had arrived the same way. Then her other words penetrated my mind. "Did you say Gaza? Ashqelon?"

"Ken, haDerkato."

Gaza—as in Gaza Strip? Ashqelon—that was a famous Philistine site in Israel! My mother had worked in Ashqelon, long ago and far away.

"Sea-Mistress, *haYam* gave only you to us." Tamera frowned slightly.

The pieces were falling into place in my brain, knowledge firing at me: Was I in Israel? Were these Philistines? Cheftu hadn't been netted? "And this temple here is . . . where?"

"We are in Ashqelon, Sea-Mistress."

"Why were these men finding someone for Dagon?" I asked, sipping my water, hoping that the last sea-mistress they netted had been as inquisitive. As the object of this ritual, should I already know why?

Again she frowned. "It is the tradition, Sea-Mistress." Tamera looked down at her hands in her lap, twisting at the "scales" of cloth on her skirt. "Dagon has been very angry with us."

Hence the term *propitiation*, I reasoned. "Why do you say that?"

"The seas are as blood, Sea-Mistress. We think it is because in our last battle with the highlanders they took our *teraphim* and burned them." She looked back up at me. "Without the proper sacrifice, we fear Dagon will not bless the corn harvest."

Sacrifice. The word made the hair on the back of my neck stiffen. "How, exactly, does, uh, Dagon accept his sacrifice?"

Tamera smiled. "Sea-Mistress, it is not your worry! You are our beloved lady!" She rose up, beaming. "Would you care for food? Drink? Would you like to spend time with Dagon, alone?"

I thought of the marble statue looming above us. What did they expect would happen if Dagon and I spent time alone? "That isn't necessary," I said. "Tell me, when is the corn harvest?"

Tamera frowned again; her face had two expressions. Frown or smile. "The harvest is not for months, Sea-Mistress. But we must select the seeds, and for that we need the counsel of Dagon, Progenitor of the Field."

A few more questions later I realized that good seed meant good corn. If Dagon's wisdom didn't prevail, they could plant bad corn, then starve all year. "At least you have fish," I said, feeling the merman's stony stare on me.

Tamera's honey brown eyes grew round; she was appalled. "Sea-Mistress, how can we eat sacred food? We would rather die! The creatures of the deep are for you, Dagon, the gods and goddesses! We are only mortals, we would not dare."

"You dared to take me from the sea," I pointed out.

She fell to her knees; this kid was going to have seriously bruised kneecaps. "You are a gift from the sea. Only you will be able to intercede with Dagon."

Did they bind and gag all the gifts from the sea? How could I intercede if I were sacrificed? Did they realize how illogical their religion was? "Is Dagon, uh, difficult?" I asked, wondering what else I could learn about him. The man was a merman, so a lot of the expected problems between man and woman were pretty much null and void.

Change from happy face to frowning face. "He and his son Ba'al have battled often this winter," she said. "They destroy us in their pathway."

Bah All? Dagon's son? I pressed a hand to my head, trying to understand through my blinding headache. "How is that?"

She sighed, a little exasperated with my lack of divine knowledge. "Ba'al throws his bolts of lightning, catching the fields of Dagon afire." Stripping religion out of her language, I gathered there had been massive electrical storms, sea storms, and widespread crop failure. The people were compounding the problem by not eating fish.

"The sea churns," she continued, "crushing our boats, leaving us open for destruction by the Kemti, the Kefti, and the Tsidoni."

My heart thudded. Kemt was Egyptian for Egypt. I'd learned that on my first time-travel voyage. However, I'd not known the Egyptians to be destructive.

Another thought hit me, almost as hard as my head had hit the mosaic floor: If I was close to Gaza—and Ashqelon, in modern times, was—then Egypt was to my south. Cheftu had always been an Egyptian. Did this mean I needed to head south? Could I find him there? Of course, this was all based on the theory that Cheftu actually was in this time period.

But I'd arrived here and I spoke the language, so it seemed to follow reasonably. Please God.

I also knew that Kefti was the Egyptian/Aztlantu word for people from Caphtor. Crete. They were across the Mediterranean from where the Philistines were, archaeologically speaking. If the Kefti still inhabited Crete, then had I gone forward or backward in time? When I'd left the last time period, the one in which I was an oracle, their culture was pretty much going to hell in a handbasket, complete with fire and brimstone.

The name Tsidoni, however, left me blank. She'd named south, west. If we were on the Mediterranean, close to modern-day Gaza, where were the Tsidoni from?

"The highlanders desecrated Ba'al, offended Dagon." Tamera glanced toward the merman. "He punishes us for it. We were not strong enough against them. We trusted their words, like fools."

"Highlanders?" I repeated. Just the term threw my whole theory out the door. Highlanders? Men in kilts with bagpipes? On the Mediterranean? The pieces just were not fitting together. Was my understanding of history, of the spread of cultures, that skewed? I mean, I knew I'd grown up with a better understanding of Lawrence of Arabia than, say, George III, but was I that ignorant? I rubbed my face; I'd trade the lot of them for Excedrin right now.

Tamera's look was bleak. "For decades we have fought with them. Now spring approaches, and with it the season for renewing war battles."

This was all terribly sad, but what did it have to do with me? Ashqelon was a place I'd never seen, even in modern times. Whether it was ancient Palestine or Israel made no difference to me. My purpose here was to find my husband and . . . what? That was the part of the equation Cheftu and I had never actually discussed. What did life hold for us, together? That answer could wait. I had to get out of here. War and propitiation were good reasons to hit the road.

"Sea-Mistress, do you see now why it is essential you are here? Why it is such a blessing that we found you? You can intervene for us."

"How can I," I said, wondering if I was supposed to be mortal or goddess, wondering how many goddesses they found per year, wondering what unlucky swimmer had been netted last time, "intervene with a god?"

"You are the favored of his sea maidens, a goddess, are you not? For you he gives the wealth of the sea, such treasures as I've never seen. You must be his most beloved concubine."

I looked down at my still glowing neon bracelet, then noticed I was still wearing the necklace, lengths and lengths of it wrapped around my throat. It passed through the spectrum of green to blue to purple to pink to orange. The glow had faded a little, but it was still flashy.

That was confusing. I had been pulled from the sea to ask Dagon to give these people a break; in fact, I was a gift to him, yet I already knew him? "A-am I a hostage?" I stuttered. Her expression froze as we heard a shout from the front of the temple.

"I want to see her!" the person repeated. "I insist!" The voice brooked no disagreement. It was followed by a body, a large woman bearing down on me like a steamship on a wooden raft. Tamera—the wimp—fled, leaving me to face this apparition alone.

What an apparition.

She was almost as wide as she was tall, with black hair elaborately woven and curled, piercing eyes set like Kalamata olives in a pan of saffron-tinted dough, from which only a beak of a nose and a bump of a chin stood out. She gleamed with gold, smelled like a vegetable garden, and wore the absolute worst shade of cinnamon that I'd ever seen.

But she had presence.

I raised my chin; I'd seen powerful women in action. I was Dagon's main squeeze. I was a goddess. I could do this. I was a hostage?

"What do you mean by—," the woman began.

"On your knees, mortal," I intoned in my best deep sea-mistress voice. She glared at me, then lumbered to her knees. Slaves came running in behind her, fluffing pillows for each kneecap, holding her by her wrists as she lowered herself. It was a production—but she was obeying me.

What was that phrase about power? Power corrupts, but absolute power corrupts absolutely. I'd been a goddess for less than two minutes and already I was abusing my authority.

"Sea-Mistress," she said, though her tone was only slightly more respectful. I gestured for her to continue. "Highlanders approach us from the east, yet Dagon is silent, Ba'al removed from our sorrows! We have begged mercy for the destruction of the *teraphim!* What does it take to get you to act?"

"And who," I said imperiously, "are you?"

She bristled. "Takala-dagon, the queen of the Pelesti, the royal dowager."

Oh. I smiled weakly.

"How many more of my sons do I have to lose before your mother's heart hears my prayers?"

An interpreter would be handy. What in the world was a ter-ah-feem? Why was the queen asking me questions? "Which son rules now?" I asked. "Being royal is hard on your family?"

"My sons have died defending us because Ba'al and Dagon won't!" she stormed.

"And"—I need some help here, I protested to the universe—"the highlanders are attacking from the east?" East of the Med—modern-day Jordan?

My brain suddenly became a classroom: the lights went down and an overhead projected clicked on. A picture of the city, whitewashed, mostly square and built around a dock, suddenly became 3-D as the point of view rose into the air, giving me an eagle's, or maybe an astronaut's, view of the coastline.

Wedge-shaped letters melted into names. Egypt to the south; Gaza, Ashdod, Ashqelon, Yaffo, and Qiselee on the coastline. Farther north, a small island off the shore named Tsor and another city named Tsidon.

"Yamir-dagon is a fine ruler," she said, "but I would like to see him be a father before he dies! What is Dagon doing? What does he want? Why does he ignore us?"

My brain was in overdrive, trying to assimilate the split-second map images. I was stumbling for recognition when two names appeared on the map, putting it all into perspective.

They also made me break into a cold sweat.

The Jordan River. The Dead Sea.

Holy, holy, holy shit! I *was* in Israel! Or was it Palestine yet? Were these people the Philistines? The city's names hadn't changed ever, so I could be in any time. Any ancient time.

Oh God, where is Cheftu? I don't want to know more, I just want to get him and get out of here.

"Have you never lost sons?" the portly woman before me asked. I stared at her, spinning mentally: did the when and where matter? I shook my head. Takala-dagon dropped her hands and bowed her head, her whole attitude suddenly hopeless.

Immediately I felt guilty. She was a human being, for all her pomposity. She'd lost sons. She mistakenly thought I could do some good. How was she to know that I was a barely twenty-six-year-old English American time traveler, whose sole mission was to find my husband and get on with my life? I was not a sea-mistress who could intervene with the gods. "I cannot imagine your pain," I said, trying to soften how I'd blown her off.

She raised her head. Her deep-set olive eyes were heavily made up, tear filled. "The highlanders approach again," she said. "How many missives have we written to Egypt, begging for Pharaoh to speak for us, I do not know. The king, my son, is adamant that we will fight them again. We must regain face for the destruction of our *teraphim.*" She sighed, expanding her already voluminous chest. The chains on her skin danced at the movement, catching in the trickles of winter sunlight cast down from the clerestory windows.

My ears had perked up at the word *Egypt.* Was this the way to get to Cheftu? "Perhaps Pharaoh will send an envoy?" I asked.

"For years we have petitioned. Egypt cares nothing for what transpires outside her borders."

Having lived as an Egyptian, I knew this was true. "Can we replace the *teraphim?* That way no one would need to return to battle. Perhaps negotiate something with them?" Since I was here, I might as well make suggestions.

She shook her head. "There is little possibility of negotiation. Their mountain god feasts on blood. The highlanders take no prisoners; they take no living booty. For them war is *herim.* Death to all and everything; it is *hal.*"

Hair-ream? Hall?

Across a chalkboard in my brain, the word was spelled; h-a-l. However, it was spelled first in wedge letters, then in chicken scratchings I couldn't identify before it became English. What was *hal?*

As though a page of a dictionary were being copied, words were quickly written on the chalkboard: *Hal* = *The utter giving over of something to God through destruction in a holy war, which is* herim. *Those who survive the* herim *are* hal.

"Those" . . . the word sank slowly into my brain. Even people?

Hal = *people & possessions.*

Yikes!

The silence stretched out. Takala's beady eyes bored into me. People and possessions? I looked at her again, "What do you want me to do? What can I do?" I clarified.

"Intervene," she said.

"With, uh, Dagon?"

Her glance was the type one reserves for misbehaving children and blithering idiots. One got the impression that in her perspective, few people escaped both those categories. *"Lo,* intervene with the highlander's ruler, when he arrives."

Intervene? Like Mata Hari would or like Winston Churchill?

"He is said to be arrogant, though brilliant," Takala said. "He has an eye for women in general." She looked me over from head to toe. "A good thing you don't have a tail," she murmured. "It is rumored that his hair is the same color as yours, so perhaps he will be drawn to you as to a sister."

Sister, in the Egyptian sense of the word, which was a lover? Or sister because we had the same hair color? My head was starting to pound again. "You just want me to meet with him?"

She waved her hands, gesturing for her slaves to haul her upright. Takala planted her fists on either side of her broad hips. "You seem to me no more than a mortal," she said. "But if you are a goddess, or a sea-mistress, then use your wiles on this Dadua of the Highlanders. If not, there will be no one to worship you or your fishtailed lover, either, because the Pelesti will have been wiped from the land!" She turned and stomped off. Slaves in her wake left gifts for me, clothing, vials of perfume, sandals, a small set of scrolls, and fruit.

Not bad for someone who arrived in a net.

Tamera scurried in, carrying trays of steaming corn products. Corn cakes, corn patties, corn on the cob, corn salad with vinegar, creamed corn, corn with yogurt, corn with cucumber.

They had shellfish nearby, and all they ate was corn? Could a goddess change a culture's eating habits? I was ravenous, so I ate corn. More corn. The wine was good; the beer tasted predictably like corn.

While I ate, priests came and sang to me: verses 342–768 of the Dagon song. *"Dagon of the mighty thews; Dagon, Rapist of the Rivers; Dagon, beloved of Ursinnahal; Dagon, spewer of salt . . ."* Dagon this and Dagon that.

Apparently he was a real "catch" in this mythology.

Ugh, life is bad when you are wincing at your own awful puns. I waved away the corn meal, the beer, got refills on wine, and proceeded to plan my escape.

I'd go to Egypt. My lower pyramid of needs had just been met: food, shelter, clothes. Then how would I get out of here? Was I a hostage or a guest? Either way, my time was limited. The words of the sailor haunted me: *Pity about her dying.*

I'd go to Egypt. Though my husband's whereabouts were a mystery, it had been only one day. I'd rest tonight, gather more supplies tomorrow, then head out at night. We'd find each other. We always had in the past.

Of course, I'd always been someone else in the past. Never nameless, never in my own skin. Never before like now.

As the afternoon floated by, silence settled on the temple. The priests took a siesta, the singers went to write more verses about Dagon, the sun drifted in on motes above me. While I rested in preparation for my journey out of here, I revisited the journey that had gotten me in here.

Just twenty-four hours ago I had been lying with my sister, Cammy, on her bed in the Hurghada Hilton. I'd realized pretty quickly that she would never really believe that I had time-traveled or traded bodies with RaEmhetepet, that sadistic ancient Egyptian priestess.

Could I blame Cammy for her skepticism? Would I have believed her if she had come to me with the same story? Even with the questions I raised, which seemed to me to be facts that couldn't be interpreted any other way, she had alternative explanations.

According to Cammy, I had been kidnapped two years ago. Doctors said that the trauma of the experience had changed my eye color, from (my) green to (RaEm's) brown. Then "I" had refused to leave Egypt and had moved in with an Egyptian playboy no one had ever heard of: Phaemon.

Except I, as in me, had heard of Phaemon before. That had been the name of RaEm's lover in ancient Egypt. A lover who had gone missing and was presumed murdered, a man born on the twenty-third of Phamenoth, just like RaEm, Cheftu, and me. A person chosen by destiny—or whatever—to time-travel. Had he traveled, trading with someone else's body. If so, who? If not, then why had the rest of us played a two-year cosmic game of musical bodies and he hadn't?

Sometimes I had the feeling I was seeing only half of the big picture. The feeling grew every time I woke up in another world. My glance fell on the merman. A very different world.

After we had traded bodies, it had taken months before "I"—that is, RaEm—was recovered enough to speak, and then she spoke only gibberish. One night in July of 1995, she'd crept out of her hospital room. The next day she'd been found almost dead at the Karnak Temple in Luxor.

Better than that, she'd been found by a bunch of tourists, which resulted in lurid headlines in Egypt. AMBASSADOR'S DAUGHTER ATTEMPTS SUICIDE OVER MIDDLE EAST PEACE, DRUG OVERDOSE FOR PRIVILEGED AMERICAN, SPOILED U.S. SLUT DISGRACES FAMILY . . . the slant of the story really depended on the politics at origin.

The second year, RaEm had settled down. She'd divided her time, or rather my time, among various functions in Cairo with boyfriend Phaemon and watching television. RaEm had become a TV junkie. She watched the tube incessantly, a habit from her time in the hospital. She would watch anything from Greek soap operas to dubbed Discovery Channel programs. Anything at all, until the wee hours of the morning. She never turned off Sky TV, Cammy said.

Based on what I knew from inhabiting her body for a year, RaEm wasn't inquisitive enough or intelligent enough to be interested in anything outside herself, even something as inactive as watching TV. Then again, all I had were her nonemotional memories. Maybe she just needed to be in a different century to appreciate living? Cammy said she'd also been "well-known" in Cairo. By a lot of men.

My father must have wanted to kill her. I knew I certainly did—in two years she'd done an impressive amount of damage to my relationships with my parents, my sister, my advertising clients, and the U.S. government. Apparently RaEm had obliterated a lifetime of my good behavior in two years of her being herself in my body. I eyed my body nervously. I hoped she hadn't caught anything. . . .

More priests came in, jarring my thoughts back to the present. They'd found the next verses to the Dagon song. I wondered how long I, as a supernatural girlfriend of Dagon and divine bargaining chip, was supposed to suffer through this chanting. There wasn't even much of a melody, just antiphonal recitation of the many, many, many traits of this particular merman-god.

Dusk came and with it the women of the city. They gifted me with little things, from a circlet of flowers or a perfectly whole shell to more elaborate gifts like a carved box that was small enough to fit in the palm of my hand or a twist of gold that formed a ring for my toe. Each woman had a different concern, a request for insight or wisdom, though most of them were domestic and more than a few were related to sexual matters.

Sex.

I ground my teeth, trying desperately not to let my thoughts go down that pathway. No Cheftu. . . . Though we'd been married for two years now, we had yet to live anything resembling a normal life. At this point I'd settle for just being in the same chronology and the same city.

After they left, I stared up at the stars. My fear, when I'd woken up in modern times, was that I had been cast from Cheftu's life. Then, my annoyingly positive side had suggested Cheftu would show up in modern Egypt. On that premise I'd raced off to the hotel telephone and called my father to try to mend the multitudes of bridges that RaEm had burned, so that if Cheftu arrived in modern times, we would be able to get him a passport, Social Security number, all the necessary paraphernalia.

But Cheftu hadn't gotten there before me, or I would have seen him or his tracks in the sand, and he didn't appear after me, because I had not left the site for more than ten minutes. That was when I'd made my phone calls and lain on Cammy's bed. Wow, how good a mattress felt.

When I'd realized that Cheftu hadn't turned up and probably wasn't going to, I'd concluded the only way for us to be together was for me to go find him. Here. Wherever, in the grand scheme of things, here really was. Israel? Palestine? Jordan? Philistine land?

Canaan, my internal lexicon corrected.

Cheftu, are you here? I wondered, ignoring the lexicon. Do you sleep close to me and I don't even know it? I touched my hair, still matted but red. I was in my own skin. Be safe, beloved, I thought as my eyes closed. I'm coming for you, so wherever you are, be safe.

SHE WASN'T SAFE with him, Cheftu thought. Never had he been so persuaded that homicide was a valid consideration. If she complained once more, if she whined even one more time, he would take great delight in silencing her forever. With his bare hands.

What had he done to deserve being trapped with this witch? Which god had he offended? What circle of hell was he condemned to?

"Are you listening, Cheftu?"

RaEmhetepet. Dear gods, how did he end up confined on a plot of land not big enough to be called an island with RaEm? He glanced at the sky, gray and hazy, and wondered if this was his punishment for some heinous sin he didn't recall committing.

I'm sorry, he said to the clouds. I beg for mercy.

They'd been here for a day. For a full day RaEm had complained. First about her burned body, then about the weather, then about him, then about how dirty she was, then about how hungry she was, then that she was cold, then starving to death. Her thoughts came full circle, and she'd started complaining about him again. Next she began describing meals she had eaten. Cheftu had decided to do something at that point.

Now he tugged at the line dangling in the water, hoping that RaEm's ear bauble would pass as bait. *Please*, le bon Dieu, *let there be fish.* Already his mouth was watering at the thought of food.

It had been days since he'd had a real meal. Days since he'd not been fleeing destruction and death. The time portal had opened while he was holding Chloe's hands, promising her fidelity. Her fingers had slipped from his handhold as she had vanished from his sight.

Then light had encapsulated him, pulling him upward through fire and water, wind, and the very earth on which he awoke. The lintel that was the indicator for where a time portal was, the lintel that had cast its shadow across their bodies then, was broken now. It was a statement to the passage of time. Although for him it had seemed a moment, he knew he'd flown through centuries—forward or backward, he wasn't certain.

A shout, then a gurgle from the sea, had startled him. Scrambling to his knees, he thought he'd seen Chloe. But the creature who emerged had been RaEm, his former betrothed, a woman so vile and unfeeling that by her own testimony she'd tried to kill her lover. While he was yet within her. Cheftu's skin crawled at the thought.

RaEm's stay in Chloe's modern times did not seem to have improved her.

"Can't you at least catch a fish?" she asked in her flat interpretation of Chloe's American accent. He hated her voice as much as he loved Chloe's. Nor could he ascertain why she would speak English to him—even he and Chloe spoke in ancient tongues when they were together.

For hours he had dangled the line in the water, waiting, hardly breathing. His arm ached, and RaEm's snide comments were no assistance. While she had slept, he'd rested his arm, sore, hungry, and discouraged. He now massaged his muscles for a few moments, then dunked the line again.

"You might as well be masturbating for all the good you are doing me," she said from behind him. The demon was awake.

If his belly weren't also empty, Cheftu would have thrown in the line. He'd formed it painstakingly by stripping thread after thread from the edge of RaEm's skirt, then tying them together. That had been a battle, too, just to get her to let him have a strip of the cloth.

He turned to see her, her hair burned and standing on end, her eyes brown. Crocodile brown. Cheftu looked back at the water. He assumed they were still in the Aegean. That's where he and Chloe had been standing when the portal beneath this lintel had opened. When they were now, neither he nor RaEm could guess. Why was also a mystery. Where was Chloe? RaEm said they had "passed" each other on the way here. Was Chloe now in her home time and world?

Cheftu would swallow, except his throat was painfully dry. His skin was nearly blue from the wind. He was wearing only a sash, and though it did little in the way of protection for his body, it safely held the two oracular stones he'd taken from the ruined civilization of Aztlan. All told, he was likely to catch his death of pneumonia—though was that still possible?

The fish line tugged, focusing Cheftu's thoughts on getting the fish, even as his stomach rumbled at the thought of eating it. RaEm assisted in her own way, alternately complimenting and insulting him.

"How are you going to cut it? How are we going to cook it?" RaEm asked. "It's not even dead yet! What kind of fisherman are you? Are we supposed to eat it raw?"

He was hungry enough to bite through the scales but knew he had to cut it open. After a moment he found a sharp enough rock to hack through the slippery skin. His stomach cramped as he wondered if Chloe had eaten, if she was warm. Where she was.

They'd vowed to be together again, somehow, some way. *Remember your vow, beloved.*

"Are you going to cut it or just stare at it?" RaEm inquired. Cheftu sawed through the fish, filleting it clumsily while his mouth watered in anticipation. "So we're having sushi?" she said, sitting on the rock. Night engulfed them suddenly and, with it, more wind, cooler temperatures.

"What is sushi?"

"Raw fish."

"Uncooked?"

"Wrapped in seaweed and served in little bundles with saki."

Cheftu peered through the darkness at RaEm. "I'd always thought Chloe came from a titled, landed family." He shook his head. "It must be awful being poor in her time."

RaEm snorted again. Cheftu didn't remember this being one of her habits, and it certainly wasn't Chloe's. "The poor? Nay, only the wealthy can afford sushi. They eat it in dark bars and discuss business so they can write it off."

Cheftu handed her a slab of slippery, raw meat. "Regard this as sushi, this rock as your 'dark bar,' and tell me what 'write off' means." He cut a slab of fish for himself and bit into it. Maybe he could get her to talk about Chloe's world instead of complaining.

His stomach protested the temperature of the fish, his tongue rebelled at the taste, but at least it was food. The nutrition would help to keep him warm. Cheftu was growing concerned about freezing off his privates. RaEm chewed silently. "Does it taste like sushi?" he asked.

"I don't know," she admitted. "All I have are the woman's emotional memories, only her impressions of America. She left me ignorant in her body, so I didn't dare leave Egypt."

"There is no sushi in Egypt?"

She laughed. "Nay. Except for the neon signs and the cars, Egypt is almost the same as during Pharaoh's time. Feluccas still ply the Nile, children still beg in the streets." He heard her awe in the darkness. "But the power there!"

Cheftu shivered, then hacked another slab of fish. "Whose power?"

"The electricity!"

"Eee-lek-trih-city? Who is the Eee-lek-trih- of the city?"

RaEm stared at him, the whites of her eyes visible through the darkness. "You are an idiot." Her tone was flat, dismissive.

Cheftu stifled his rage. How dare the ignorant, loudmouthed little witch ridicule him? "Then please," he said, coldly, "Educate me."

"They have harnessed the power of the lightning to use in their cities. It can be as bright as day in the middle of the night."

For the first time in Cheftu's recollection, RaEm sounded excited, enthusiastic. Her ennui was replaced with a childlike wonder.

It was appealing, though he knew it was only one small side in a multifaceted woman whose other traits he loathed. "How do they harness eee-lek-trih-city? You say it is lightning?" He took another slab of fish. Fishy liquid dripped down his arms, sticky and cooling rapidly. At least his stomach was filling up. Now they needed to find a source for fresh water.

Also, a way to get off this island.

"The Benjamin Franklin unlocked the key to lightning on a kite."

"A kite? The birds that fly over the delta?"

She sounded a little defensive. "Of course! You ignorant fool, what else could it be?"

"How did he do that?"

"Well," she said in a confidential tone, "he tied the kite to a string, with the key."

"A bird, a string, and a key?"

"To unlock the door to lightning," she said. "Honestly, you must pay attention."

Cheftu glowered.

"The kite flew into the heavens, unlocked the door, and then the Benjamin Franklin was able to capture it and use it at his will. He colored the lightning, and he boxed it. Even the hieroglyphs of these people are formed of lightning." He heard her scraping for more fish. "But," she said, swallowing loudly, "he makes it last."

Snippets of conversation from his nineteenth-century childhood, before his fateful trip to Egypt with his brother, Jean-Jacques, were falling into place. These were mentions of people he'd known only through recent history. Franklin and the American Revolution had been inspiration for France's own revolution. How did the esteemed and eccentric statesmen figure in with lightning? And a key to unlock it? Cheftu's mind was switching madly from English to French to ancient Egyptian, trying to understand. Perhaps RaEm's trip through time had addled her wits. "It lasts?" he asked, completely bewildered.

"It doesn't flash on and off, but it is a steady light. He must be very powerful to have captured lightning. I wonder what he looked like, what kind of lover he was. . . ."

Cheftu rolled his eyes—definitely the same RaEm. Franklin was deceased before Cheftu was even born. Her words still made no sense. Apparently she didn't realize that Cheftu was also a time traveler. How else would he recognize the word *city* in English? How else would he understand her English?

"What magic he had." She sighed. "So powerful."

Cheftu was fairly certain science was the cause, but to RaEm magic was the only explanation. "Apparently his magic did not die with him?"

"No. It lives in the streets, on the boats that sail the Nile. It is a magic that anyone can hold in their hand."

Cheftu frowned into the darkness. "This magic has been given to everyone?"

"No. Well, yes and no," she said, sounding confused. "Through the TV I learned all about it. The TV uses it, too." The confusion faded from her voice, replaced by RaEm-style arrogance. "*I* could control lightning if I wanted to."

Cheftu refrained from asking about the tee-vee. He'd heard Chloe mention it occasionally, though with her it was usually in a derisive tone. His beloved did not seem as appreciative of her century as RaEm was. Nor had she ever mentioned this story of a bird flying into the heavens with a key and unlocking lightning. It made no sense. There was a missing element here, he was sure of it. What interpretation would be so apparent to Chloe? He wanted to ask her, to hold her while she thought, to touch her while she spoke. Aii, *Chloe, where are you?* "What else about Chloe's world fascinated you?" he asked.

"Rameses," RaEm said promptly around her full mouth. "Serve me some more sushi and I'll tell you."

Because this was as close as RaEm came to being pleasant, Cheftu handed her another slab of fish. All that was left were scales and head. Should he try to catch another? But it was night now, they needed to rest. Tomorrow he would get more food and ask the oracular stones what they should do to survive—he didn't want to reveal them to RaEm.

Chances of rescue were limited to the miraculous. It was wintertime; no one sailed the Aegean now. The waters were deadly. Everyone from Odysseus to Saint Paul had tales of woe from trying to cross in this season. How many more had shipwrecked and been forgotten?

He looked out at the limitless sea. Was Chloe out there somewhere? They'd always found each other, though this time Cheftu feared it would be more challenging. RaEm was in the skin Chloe had been wearing. So what did his beloved look like? Apparently the two women had traded bodies again, leaving RaEm with him and Chloe in 1996—Cheftu still felt a little awed at the date—on the stretch of sand where RaEm claimed she'd been strolling.

Except Cheftu knew RaEm. It had been her natal day. He doubted her celebration had been walking alone on a stretch of sand. She was lying to him, a reaction that was as natural and common to her as breathing. Nothing she said was to be trusted. Nothing.

"Rameses was glorious!" RaEm gushed. Again her voice was filled with excitement. Perhaps modern times had been the making of RaEm. Was he judging her too harshly?

He bit back telling her that he had heard of Rameses—she obviously didn't realize Cheftu was from her future, from Chloe's past, that according to Chloe Cheftu's real name was well-known in her world. He knew of Rameses. Indeed, in his own century Cheftu had walked through many a temple the smiling pharaoh had built.

RaEm's voice was warm. "Many reigns after Pharaoh Hatshepsut, life! health! prosperity! there was a pharaoh named Rameses," she explained. "*Aii*, Cheftu, he was such a man, so magnificent! Egypt was magnificent with him! He built a huge temple before the Second Cataract, where he paid homage to his wife. In Chloe's childhood, the Nile was redirected, so that it wouldn't hurt the temple Rameses had built, the Abu Simbel."

Cheftu froze. "They redirected the Nile?"

"Yep. They took this huge temple, this Abu Simbel, and moved it up."

"Where? How?" He'd seen Abu Simbel, the monstrosity of it. How could it be moved, ever, save by the hand of *le bon Dieu* himself?

"Much funding came Frum-A-roundthwerld," RaEm said. "I saw it on TV."

It took a moment for her words to sink in. Did she even have a concept of the world being round? Did she know all the peoples who inhabited the planet? She spoke as though the phrases were memorized. How lost she must have been in Chloe's fast-paced world of eating raw fish. "What exactly did you see?" Cheftu asked. She didn't know what she was talking about, but the concept was fascinating. Moving the temple of Abu Simbel?

"They took Rameses' temple apart and rebuilt it on the cliff overlooking the lake they'd made from the Nile." She sucked one finger dry. "To have been in Rameses' time, to be loved and honored in the shape of that temple! Imagine the jewelry his wife had; the slaves, the power."

He should have known her fervor stemmed from customary greed. However, he wouldn't let her smallness bother him; RaEm was but a temporary companion.

Chloe would keep her vow. Cheftu needed to keep alert for the green-eyed women who strayed across his path. "More sushi?" He offered RaEm the head.

"Nay," she said, recoiling. "You feed me offal?"

Cheftu sighed as he tossed the remnants in the water. RaEm spoke after a moment, her tone meditative. "Though I think there is more to sushi than just seaweed and raw fish. An avocado."

"What is that?"

"I don't know, something you eat. I told you: I don't know things, or facts outside language. I just know how she felt about them. Avocado must be an emotional memory."

"Chloe was emotional over avocado?"

"I want to be a consort, worshiped and adored by a powerful man," RaEm said, changing the subject back to herself. "I want to be remembered throughout history. Do you know how those moderns worship us? The Amazing Ancients, they say. They are in wonder over how we built the pyramids, over why we mummified our dead. They live narrow, dark lives yet think we are fascinated with death." She shivered. "It is eerie how much they do not know, how unreal we are to them."

"Did you think it was easier for you to understand them?"

She fell silent, giving Cheftu a moment to marvel that he was having a reasonable conversation with this woman. Of course, there was nothing to gain right now, nothing to barter for or with. Only because she didn't know about the stones. He shuddered to think of RaEm with that kind of power.

"Egypt is ruled by a tribe called Arabs, who have a celibate, childless god. I cannot find my roots in their eyes. They are merchants and artisans, with no trace of Amun-Ra in their souls."

Cheftu opened his mouth to agree with her, to relay his wonder when he'd arrived from nineteenth-century France and into the people and culture he'd devoted his life to studying.

"If I had had the power, I would have wiped them all away," she said. "Start all over again. Even with neon and electricity, they were nothing special."

He was stunned. "They are a people," he said. "An entire nation."

"They are groundskeepers," she said. "They know nothing of real Egypt. Worshiping just one god, a god they can't even see, how could they?"

She didn't know what she was talking about, Cheftu reasoned. She couldn't.

"Phaemon, when he first woke, thought he was in the afterworld, so he fought the demons."

Cheftu felt the blood leave his face. "But—"

"But he wasn't," RaEm said. "Of course, he killed half a dozen of them, gutting them as one would do to a demon, before he realized it."

He felt her shrug. "Phaemon was distraught, but they were nothing but peasants."

"How can you be so removed?" Cheftu whispered, horrified.

He felt RaEm's gaze on his face. "Power is what matters. They had none, so they were of no consequence. They carried no talismans, they knew no magic, they were nothing except fodder."

The stones against his waist, his talismans, heated through his skin. Their warmth combated the chill this woman was giving him. An icy bite greater than the winter wind. "They were human beings."

"*Haii!* They were as pebbles."

Suddenly Cheftu was grateful he was here with RaEm and Chloe was safely gone. RaEm was a demon. He would stay awake, guard against her. He hoped someone, preferably ugly and aged, though competent, was guarding Chloe in this Egypt that RaEm would gladly destroy. *Be safe, beloved.*

CHAPTER 2

M Y INTERNAL LEXICON woke me up with the definition for *teraphim*. Images of statuettes—Lladros, Precious Moments, Hummels, and anything from the Franklin Mint—flashed in a slide show before my eyes.

B'seder, so they were the dustables, the collectibles, of this day and age. No, the lexicon said, they were more. They were little personal gods, good-luck charms, and the wealth of the household, all wrapped into one easily transportable object.

The Pelesti *teraphim* that had been burned by the highlanders were not only the little gods the soldiers had brought to the battlefield for good fortune, but also the enormous totem statues the priests took into battle. These images were positioned on a hill overlooking the field of engagement to serve as encouragement for the soldiers. At the end of the day, or battle, the statues were loaded on their palanquins and carted back to the temple.

What a way to wake up, bashed over the head with an encyclopedia.

You ask, I tell. You wanted to know, it scribbled on the blackboard in my brain.

Yep, I did. But did you have to tell me so early? I rolled over for a few hours' more sleep.

The rest of the day had passed uneventfully in perfect safety. Uneventful because people kept showing up; in perfect safety because there were priests everywhere, carrying swords. I'd checked them all out, but not a one was Cheftu. Unless, of course, he had stepped into someone else's body this time. But no one even had amber eyes.

The Egyptians believed our eyes were the windows to our souls. Perhaps that was why I always had my own eyes? To not have them would be not to be myself? On this theory, Cheftu would be here, possibly in another body but definitely with his bronzy brown eyes.

Additionally, I was learning that escape wasn't going to be easy. Each time I thought I was alone, another person would come in, seeking my wisdom and words, leaving me little gifts. I've played the part of oracle before, so I just played it again.

The overriding concern was when Dagon would get over being mad at them. Would I intercede. The answer was always yes, though I had no idea to what I was agreeing. It didn't matter, since I was leaving during naptime.

My, or rather RaEm's, cheap rayon clothing had dried stiff with salt water. My skin felt like scales, and my hair was grimy. I wanted a bath before my escape. The little handmaiden brought me a bath, then washed my hair. She seemed mystified that I had legs. So I spun some elaborate story about needing salt water in order to regain my fishtail. It seemed to comfort her, but now I really had to leave. I didn't want her to throw me back, just as a test.

She massaged my back and neck while I thought.

I'd come through water, just as the lintel had predicted. Terrified that I'd misunderstood some part of it and wouldn't be able to get back to Cheftu, I had memorized the passage during my few hours in modern times:

A portal for those of the twenty-third power, those who serve in the priesthood of the Unknown. For those, the power exists on earth, mentored by the heavens and directed through the waves. The waters will guide, they will purify, they will offer salvation. From the twenty-third decan to the twenty-third decan this doorway remains.

So was the actual portal beneath the sea in some way? Was that the only way in and out of this time period? Just how many of us were floating around in the ether of chronology, displaced?

Chronologically challenged, I amended, coining the phrase. I was drifting to sleep under the mastery of Tamera's strong hands, enveloped in the perfume of singed coriander.

"Sea-Mistress, are you ready to dress?" I woke with a jolt and looked over my shoulder. Immediately I noticed the day was almost gone. Shit! I was here for one more evening? Could I leave tonight? "If the Sea-Mistress would care to dress as we do, we could clothe her?" the girl said. The garments I'd had, a blue miniskirt, silver velvet V-neck shirt, and sandals, were cleaned and ready for me to wear. However, those clothes were small and good only for a discotheque. My necklace, sadly, had faded.

"Sea-Mistress, *haDerkato*, what would you like to wear?"

I sat up, covering myself with the linen sheet. My mind was sluggish, my heart still pounding from waking so abruptly. "To what?" I asked.

"The evening's feast, *haDerkato.*"

Hadn't they had one last night? One thing about ancient people, they never let a workday get in the way of a feast. "I'm attending?"

"*Ken, haDerkato.* First there is a small ritual at sea, then the feast will be at the palace." Her honey eyes were bright.

"You dress me," I said. This was wonderful! I would get out of the temple with them and mingle in with the masses before I made my getaway to Egypt. Or perhaps I would run into Cheftu here, in Ashqelon. Maybe he wasn't serving in the temple, which was why we hadn't found each other yet.

"Dress me like you," I said, smiling. She plucked at her dress. It was a simple, fitted sheath in a dark green. A sash of gold, rust, and green stripes encircled her waist, delineating the curve to her hips. An armband of bronze emblazoned with swirls matched her necklace and drop earrings. Around her head she wore a headband, whose tassels brushed her shoulders. She was barefoot, tiny feet with shell pink nails. She was lovely and elegant.

And a Philistine?

If I were in Ashqelon, if these were the Philistines, then I knew only a few things about them. They had lived in five cities—Ashqelon being one of them, Gaza another—and they were supposed to be pretty. Delilah, the woman who had nagged Samson to death, had wooed him first with her beauty. Looking at Tamera, I considered for the first time that maybe the story hadn't been a fable.

"Ach, ken," she said. I recognized "Ah yes," but as the words entered my ears, the lexicon changed them from the language she spoke, using visuals. I saw a Barbie, then a Ken doll. The Barbie exploded, but Ken remained, shaking his head up and down. *Ken,* I surmised hesitantly, was actually "yes"? The Ken doll smiled. The *ach* was a guttural I'd heard throughout my life in Arabic. What language did the Philistines speak?

"When is your birthday?" I asked.

"I was born under the sign of the crab," she said.

I didn't know the zodiac that well, but I was surprised it was in usage already. "And what year were you born?"

"Year?" she repeated.

"How old are you?"

"Old? How old?"

I rephrased again, striving for clarity. "What year is it now?"

"The year of the red sea," she answered eagerly.

Red sea. That was right, I'd seen how the waters looked like blood. Red tide, I thought. Wasn't that a band or a football team? Wasn't it a natural phenomenon, due to some plant or animal in the water? "Is the sea often red?"

"Only when we have angered Dagon," she said. "Then the sea is bloody, the crops fail, and we die." She looked perfectly cheerful discussing the annihilation of her people. "Now you must dress."

She raced away while I peeled myself off the massage table. I looked out the narrow window. This tiny room was adjacent to the main temple. We were high on a point overlooking the rest of the town, the port, and the sea. Crenellated walls embraced the city, the two wings extending into the water, so the harbor, filled with ships, seemed to be in the very arms of Ashqelon.

They were strange-looking vessels, with narrow-faced creatures on either end. Was that the kind of ship I'd arrived in? I didn't know. They had the same square sails, though, huge sails to carry hundreds of men across the waters and oars to speed the journey.

The city itself reminded me of Greece, with two- and three-storied homes, plain rectangular windows, and attached porches. I saw trees in courtyards, flat roofs, and straight streets. Straight anything was an anomaly in the Middle East I had known. I heard a noise behind me and turned, expecting Tamera.

It wasn't Tamera. It was a soldier.

Only total fear kept me from hiding my nakedness and cowering. If I showed fear, he might realize I was a fraud. That, I couldn't have. He, on the other hand, blushed the color of a pomegranate. I couldn't see his hair because he wore a headdress of feathers, in addition to a breastplate of leather and brass over an A-line kilt that came to a point between his knees.

He was clean-shaven and wore no kohl.

Though it sounds strange, it was the first time I'd seen a man in a dress without makeup. In Aztlan and Egypt, both men and women wore kohl, lipstick, eyeshadow, the whole nine yards. This guy looked almost naked without it.

I reached for my sea-mistress voice again. "You enter without being bidden . . . mortal?"

He didn't know where to look, so he stared at the ground. "My orders, were, are, were to, to come get you," he said. I guessed he was maybe sixteen. His voice had deepened, he'd gotten his height, but he still had the goofiness of a puppy that has yet to grow into his paw size.

"El'i!" Tamera screeched from the doorway. "What are you doing here?"

The girl knew him? But then why should that surprise me?

"Following orders," he said without looking at her for more than a second.

"She is a *haDerkato!* You don't just barge in on a goddess! She could turn you into a snail!" Just a snail? Tamera didn't have much faith in me, did she? "Now go, before she changes her mind," Tamera said, hustling him out.

In the doorway El'i paused. "I will await you outside, Sea-Mistress.

Forgive my bad manners." It was a hint of the man he would become: competent, serious, respectful. Before I could respond, even with a gracious Queen Elizabeth wave, Tamera shut the door in his face.

She fussed and fumed about El'i while we clothed me. My dress was blue, with a sash of greens, blue, and silver. I wore my neon jewelry, which I'd dunked in cold water to revive it, and she'd fixed a band of silver in my hair. I looked at the sandals I'd brought with me. They were sexy, strappy, and probably cost at least a month's salary.

Another reason to kill RaEm. What had she been doing out there that night? According to Cammy, RaEm had gone for a walk in the middle of a very lax Ramadan party that had become her birthday party. Had she just stumbled on the portal? What had happened to Phaemon?

I slipped on the sandals and suddenly grew three inches. Mimi had once told me that men liked the look of high heels because it appeared we couldn't run away as quickly. As I wobbled in these shoes, I realized she might be right.

Tamera first smoothed color on my eyelids, then decorated with color around my face, swoops and swirls on my temples and forehead, my cheeks and chin. I would have to wash my face before I tried melting into the crowd. Finally, at my request, she lined my eyes with kohl.

After coating me in the scents of cinnamon and mint, Tamera called for El'i. In the moments she had her back to me, I grabbed my little parcel of essentials. With a nod to Dagon, I was escorted out of the temple by El'i.

Though the building was functionally pretty, it had not been fashioned by a race of artists. It had been designed by engineers for a minimal amount of fuss.

Painting was perfunctory; there was no gilding, no precious stones. Whitewashed mud-brick walls and stone pillars supported a roof of straw and wooden beams. Plain brass incense bowls were attended by a few people wearing fish-head masks. The temple was useful, but hardly majestic.

I stepped into the short Mediterranean dusk and climbed into an ox-drawn cart. El'i led the team, their horns decorated with shells and bells. It was heavy, slow, giving me time to look around as we lumbered through the city. Apparently everyone was going to this ritual. People lined the sides of the streets, whispering at first, chanting—yet more Dagon verses!—then shouting that I was going to save them. Dagon was ready to forgive them! I would bring Egypt to the Pelesti! We would get the *teraphim* back! The crops would never fail!

Ritual. Damn. I started getting nervous as we drove through the straight streets, drawing closer and closer to the sea. I could smell the salt, feel a sting of spray in the air. Before we hit the boulevard that ran parallel to the beach, we headed south. How could I get away? No matter what they wanted, I couldn't do it. I knew nothing about farming. I knew less about fishing. There was no way a happy ending would come of this. I glanced behind me.

They were grouped five deep, trailing the cart.

I looked ahead.

A mass of people sat on the sand, looking out at the water. Between a rocky outcrop on the shore and a huge rock in the Med was a shadowy line, lit from below by men in skiffs with lifted torches. Within the rock-formed pool, I saw shapes of creatures I associated with Egypt: crocodiles. I didn't think crocodiles liked salt water. Was it a freshwater pool? Why were they there?

Why was I here?

I wiped nervous sweat from my forehead. The crowd began shouting a name: *"HaDerkato! HaDerkato!"* Tamera had called me *haDerkato*, but what did it mean? Should I have asked that earlier? Did the lexicon know?

We were approaching a canopied chair set on a plateau above the rock. Women wearing fish cloaks swarmed the scene. The ritual by the sea; I had a feeling that I was going to be center stage. My nervousness threatened to choke me. What did this mean? *Hello, lexicon?*

Time was getting short.

The images were instant, a montage of videos, animation, and artwork from my lifetime. A girl, a handmaid of Dagon, is stolen from the sea. Then, after Dagon is notified she's missing, she is offered back to it. In a rather final fashion.

If she survives, she is believed to be the adored of Dagon, who will then restore the crops. The handmaid will live with the people throughout the year, to assure them of Dagon's favor. If she does not survive, then she is devoured by the sacred fish, the crocodile, and returned to Dagon that way.

Survive what? I asked nervously.

A tightrope.

That was the shadowy line I saw? A tightrope, suspended between the two rocks? How did I get out of here? Surely they didn't expect me to cross the tightrope? A tightrope? I didn't know ancients even had tightropes!

We'd arrived, parking the cart inside a solid wall of people. My only hope of escape was to be airlifted out of here. El'i helped me from the cart, then up the worn stone stairwell. Help! I cried silently. Cheftu, if you are here, now is the time.

The pause button clicked off on the lexicon. There was more? Like the opening of *Star Wars*, words started scrolling across the screen in my mind.

During the red tide there is a caveat to the normal procedure.

The so-called normal procedure being a woman falling to her death and being eaten by crocodiles?

I had reached the pinnacle of the rock. Hundreds of people crowded the beach, torches raised, their eyes on me. From where I stood to where the rock in the harbor was a straight distance of about sixty feet, approximately fifteen feet above a pit of crocodiles. What was this—I was living a video game?

I could see a pool at ground level about twenty feet off to my left-hand side. There was no guessing at its depth, but it was big. The wind blew fiercely, whipping my hair in my face. We were listening to the nine hundredth verse about Dagon.

Really, my choices were narrowing. I couldn't make it sixty feet on a tightrope. So I would die as crocodile bait? I looked over at the pool again, apparently some type of sacred lake within the temple enclosure. Could I land in it without killing myself? How would I get from here, this stupid rope, to over there? Would a jump kill me? God, what had I done to deserve this?

The song stopped. Tamera came forward, her mouth moving, but her words were swept away by the wind. She knelt before me, then gestured to the platform. It was less than eight inches deep, about twelve wide. How many brides of Dagon had died this way?

They were extinguishing the torches beneath me.

Tamera's hand on my shoulder scared me. "Wait, haDerkato. The story must first be told."

"Take your time," I said. Surely it wasn't my destiny to die in some lame proto—circus show? Was Cheftu here, in the crowd, watching? Was this how he would identify me? My palms were slick with sweat. Tamera climbed a few steps above me, telling the story in song. It was a lovely, lyrical siren's tune.

Somehow I would have to swing on the tightrope in order to get to the pool. I looked down at the water. Maybe the crocodiles were full? Not hungry? The wind was turning my sweat cold as I listened and tried to find a way out.

When the gods of the mountains warred with the gods of the sea,
        Our families were cast out, the progenitors of you and me.
        Across haYam we fled their wrath, to settle here where it is peaceful and flat.
        Yet the god of the sea, to him we still owe, both life and livelihood, war battle and soul.
        Dagon's lusts are bottomless, he seduces those he wants. In the form of Mexos, from across haYam, he came to take a maiden to woo her, wed her from among his mother's people, to win her hand.
        She was Derkato, the fairest of the fair. Her voice was high, like the sea at dawn, like the sea at night was her hair. Mexos-dagon sought her, through vineyard, field, and vale. At last he trapped her on this rock; her choices were few.
        Her cries to the mother-goddess were unheeded, she could walk to the rock through air or throw herself to Dagon or embrace Mexos as her lover fair.
        While he wept for her love, she fled seeking the virgin embrace of the sea. Yet when she awoke beneath the waves, her lover was there.
        Dagon won the body of the fair Derkato, though her soul was already dead.

Tamera finished, the last note floating away to the stars, rising to the full moon.

This was the legend I was named after? This doomed woman? Sixty feet, could I make it? But then what would happen? Ancient people and their farming solutions. Shit.

I had to get across. Somehow I had to get across. If I could just tie myself . . . tie myself! With what? Tamera was still speaking or singing or something, as I ran quick hands over my body. There was nothing in my parcel pack. My sash was fragile fabric, my dress useless. I slipped off my sandals because they were death traps.

What? What? I looked down at my body and saw the solution.

Neon!

The neon necklace was a chemical in a plastic casing—about four feet of it. It wouldn't hold forever, but maybe it would be enough to help me regain my balance if I slipped? Could they see me? Was I breaking rules?

Damn, who cared. With trembling fingers I unfastened the necklace, then dropped into a crouch, one foot on the rope—which was about three inches wide—the other still on the platform. I had to tie my ankle so that I had enough of a stride.

This was harebrained, but dying as a crocodile crudité wasn't an option. I had a promise to keep to Cheftu. My vow in our last ancient time had been the same as his: I would go anywhere, any time, just to find him. I kept my promises: I was a Kingsley.

Tamera fell silent. Most of the torches were gone. She touched my shoulder. My cue?

The only problem with my theory is that the plastic didn't tie tightly. I'd wrapped it around my ankles again and again, but it didn't hold a tight, satisfactory knot. So close. Tamera nudged me again. My thoughts were racing. What could I use? I reached up: earrings. Posts and backs!

"Call my lover for me," I instructed her. "Dagon needs to feel our, uh, desire and love for him."

"Sea-Mistress—," she started.

"Do it!" I commanded. A moment later I heard her voice above me again. It was a choral piece, with the assembled Pelesti all singing along.

I pulled the earrings out of my ears, then knelt, jamming the post through the plastic coil after the final knot. As a backup measure—I couldn't have enough of them—I stripped off my sash and wrapped it around the plastic knots, reinforcing them with the fabric.

"*HaDerkato!*" Tamera shouted. The last torch extinguished below me. The neon had faded again, just enough of a glow that I could see a step before me. "Oh God, oh God, oh God," I whispered, almost in tears.

They began chanting my name. I stepped out and realized my dress was going to kill me. Without thought, I stripped it off. The wind was like ice, but I had movement. One step and I felt the rope beneath my feet. When one foot felt secure, I slowly brought my other leg from the platform.

Remember being on a balance beam, I told myself. This is just a balance beam, it's just a balance beam. Focus on your goal, look straight ahead. I did. Into darkness. Oh God, omigod.

Balance beam, Chloe. Think back, remember being a kid? Remember that base in southern Spain? You loved gymnastics. You took them for . . . I moved my first leg forward, feeling the tightening of the neon tube around my ankle. My toes touched, then gripped the rope.

For a split second I wobbled, then felt my center of gravity settle. I was comfortable, balanced. The next few steps were easy, more a question of stride and timing than anything else. Then a gust of wind unbalanced me. I heard my catch of breath, felt the fear grabbing me again. *Balance, Chloe. Slowly, move slowly.*

Before we'd left Spain, I'd gone from being five four to five eight in a matter of weeks.

I made it a few more steps. My nipples were so cold, they felt like attachments. My legs were trembling from the effort. My hair was wet with sweat, and I still couldn't see squat through the darkness. Keep moving forward, I told myself. Remember that summer? I'd returned to Texas, to my grandmother Mimi. She'd taken one look at me and enrolled me in other classes. Ballet. Modeling. Dancing. She'd made me walk with a book on my head, she'd watched me do endless *tendus, demi-pliés,* and *relevés;* she'd even had a barre installed on the sleeping porch.

A few more steps; it was coming easier now. A few more. I was almost halfway! The sweeping feeling of extending my leg, then moving forward slowly, was instantly remembered. The air was still; the crowd was silent. Teeth gritted, I unclenched the sole of my foot and brought it around gently, only a little in front of me. I didn't want to shift my weight from my hips and thighs, so no reaching. Another step, my body was hot with sweat. My arms were out to the sides, helping me balance.

By the time I'd left Texas to return to my family, who had since moved to Turkey, I had control of my limbs. I'd grown another inch or so, but I knew how to move. When Mimi took me to the airport, to fly to Rome for my connecting flight, she'd hugged me. I thanked her. In the middle of my gratitude speech—

The rope wobbled. The people screamed. I fell.

Because of the way I was tied, my feet were still on the rope; also, I'd caught myself with my hands. But my body was hanging down. Crocodiles were snapping beneath me. There was no thought; I pulled myself onto the top side of the rope, my hands stinging, one shoulder either dislocated or close to it.

The rope was between my shaking thighs. The neon cording was twisted so that I was now in the position to walk backward. The people were hissing.

Words that would have caused Mimi to roll in her grave shot out of my mouth. Lying there, fighting tears, I wondered how to get up. Shit! Shit! Could I hand over hand it all the way to the end? The people below me were not sounding sympathetic. Shit! After a time-out that lasted until the sweat on my hands dried and I got my ankle ropes untangled, I rose.

Careful not to jar my center of balance, I got out of a fetal position and into a crouch. This was water-skiing all over again. Rise up slowly, slowly. My legs were shaking again, but I was standing.

Below me they broke into cheers.

I looked ahead; still darkness, but only half as much.

After two more falls, I felt the edge of rock. My shoulder was completely dislocated. I collapsed on the solid stone, tearing at the neon cording with my good hand. I needed to get rid of it, because I didn't think they would allow cheating like that.

Hands touched me, wine wet my lips, and for moments I heard nothing except the adrenaline rush of having made it. Oh God, I survived! Thank you, petrochemical companies! Thank you, God! My hands were shaking too badly to wipe my own face. My shoulder was becoming unbearable.

I hoped I wouldn't have to walk down the rock. I didn't think I could even stand.

"HaDerkato?" Tamera said. Someone pulled at my wrenched arm; I heard my scream as the world turned black.

ONLY BECAUSE RAEM SPOKE OF Chloe's world was she bearable. She told Cheftu of Chloe's sister, the Egyptologist Camille; about Chloe's clothing, which was mostly black and bias cut; and Chloe's boyfriends, who were stolen only from his beloved's distant memories but still rankled; and Chloe's occupation as an artist. RaEm considered art to be a task for slaves and servants and thus far beneath her.

From what Cheftu gathered, after spending a few months protesting her experience, RaEm had decided to play along at being Chloe. He mused that each of them, he, RaEm, and Chloe, had pretended when they'd first arrived. Was that due to a fear of discovery? Or just the realization that if one didn't go along, one would be profoundly alone in a new world?

However, RaEm's facade was foiled almost from the start, for she had no talent. She hadn't touched any of Chloe's artists' tools, a choice that had apparently raised many an eyebrow in modern times. However, to say or do anything else would be to place herself outside of physical comfort and companionship. RaEm would never do that.

But it had irked her that she was unimportant in Chloe's day and time; he knew this now. Of course, he knew everything now. He knew how she loved neon and "Day-Glo" and things that were visible in the dark. He knew who shot J.R. He knew every menu the Cairo Hilton served.

The knowledge would have been good, entertaining even, if it weren't sprinkled with the other stuff. The complaining, the sniping, her way of viewing the world. Six days on this rock with this woman—his sins had been expiated through this sentence!

Dehydration had set in, and they both had splitting headaches. Inhaling salt water only burned their nostrils, and the little bit of water they could lick made them ill. The situation was growing desperate.

He still had the oracular stones, the Urim and Thummim that he and Chloe had rescued from Aztlan, but he didn't want to let RaEm know he had them. Since the islet was slightly wider than he was long, he hadn't had any privacy whatever. If she knew he had the capacity to tell the future, or at least converse with the One God, she would probably kill him.

The thought of RaEm being able to see the future was terrifying. How would she manipulate that knowledge for herself . . . it was a thought he daren't contemplate.

He rolled onto his side. It was nearly dusk of the sixth day. The fishing had worked for three days, but these past three there had been nothing. Nothing, save RaEm's derisive nagging and distorted perspective.

Finally Cheftu had snapped at her. She had screamed obscenities at him, then sat facing the water for the rest of the day. Actually it had been quite pleasant, drifting in and out of sleep in silence.

Had that been yesterday or the day before? He couldn't recall, couldn't fathom any time other than the one they were in. He had stared at the horizon for so long that his eyeballs were imprinted with the image; morning, noon, or dusk, it didn't matter. Once again he was staring across the water, but wait! Was that a shadow? Slowly he sat up and watched the shadow gain substance. It was getting darker, but he was certain it was a ship! How could they get its attention?

What was it doing here?

All night long Cheftu watched that spot, praying that he hadn't hallucinated, praying it would be there with the dawn. When light fell across his face he woke with a jolt, staring out across the waters. No ship. The disappointment was so sharp he could taste it. They would die soon of thirst while surrounded by water. Maybe he should use the stones; what would it matter now? He looked over his shoulder, just in case he'd gotten confused about the direction.

The ship was bearing down on them! They were rescued. It was a miracle! "RaEm, look! Look!"

She sat up, rubbing her eyes. "Do they see us?"

"They must," Cheftu said. "They are coming our direction." He looked at the vessel, trying to place when they were. The sail was not Egyptian style, yet it displayed an Egyptian design on the topsail. "What is that symbol?" he asked.

"The disk with the hands?" RaEm said, squinting up at the cloth swollen tight with wind. "Is it a hieroglyph?"

"Nay, I think not."

The ship was still heading straight for them, but it was not losing speed. In fact, it was gaining momentum, using both sails and oars. "Are you sure they see us?" RaEm asked. They were both standing, hope having given them strength.

It was going to crash on the islet! "They don't," Cheftu realized. "They don't see us! Scream, shout, warn them."

Suddenly the ship veered, heading away from them, from the islet. "What in the name of Horus are they doing?" RaEm shouted, her hands on her hips. At the angle the ship was moving, it would completely bypass them.

Bypass them and *leave* them. Cheftu cupped his mouth, shouting across the water. Would they hear him over the beat of the timekeeper's drum? Again the oarsmen halted, the sails wilted. The ship stopped.

RaEm and Cheftu stood, watching as the sun rose. They heard the sound of conversation, but nothing distinctive. "What are they doing?" RaEm asked, her voice hoarse from shouting.

"I cannot fathom," Cheftu said, squinting at the ship. Suddenly the oars started again, almost backing the ship up.

"They are going to miss us!" RaEm shouted, leaping into the water and swimming toward the ship, which was now sailing away from them.

Cheftu watched in horror. This was a farce! This could not be happening! Slipping his fingers into his mouth, he blew over them, a shrieking whistle that should be heard in Crete.

The ship stopped.

"Man overboard!" someone shouted. Cheftu sagged in relief when he saw a skiff lowered over the side, heading toward RaEm.

Grâce à Dieu! What kind of idiot had been navigating?

He saw the skiff approach the islet, amazed that RaEm remembered him. As the boat grew larger Cheftu saw that it held three men. Two were rowing and one was hanging his head over the side. What caliber of sailor was that?

The vessel touched the edge of the islet. The two sailors ignored RaEm and helped the third man, a small, spindly Egyptian, onto land. With precise, extravagant gestures the man mopped his face and turned to Cheftu.

"Aii, you fool! What in the name of the great god Aten were you doing, standing in the middle of the sea? Speak!"

Cheftu stared into the man's face, utterly taken aback by his vehemence.

"Speak! Or are you some unwashed foreigner who doesn't even know a civilized language?"

"He is often mute in the presence of such an esteemed traveler," RaEm said in a tone of voice that managed to be both sultry and respectful. The man dismissed her with a glance, and Cheftu saw RaEm's nostrils flare in anger.

"Is that your slave?" the man asked Cheftu, jabbing a thumb toward RaEm. "If so, you need to make more gold, buy a healthier one. He looks about to die."

"He?" RaEm repeated, outraged. *"He?"*

The man ignored her, speaking to Cheftu. "Are you a farmer? An artisan?" He looked over their shoulders. "Don't even have a roof for your heads! What gods have cast you into a place as dismal as this?"

"The one god," RaEm said.

"Your pardon," Cheftu said in his most diplomatic tone, "but who are you?"

"Wenamun—*aii*, nay, I'm Wenaten. Lord Wenaten. Ambassador Wenaten."

Cheftu and RaEm exchanged glances. He didn't know his own name?

"I've been Wenamun for about twenty-five Inundations, then that fop snatched the throne, outlawed Amun-Ra, and we've all had to change our names," he groused.

"Outlawed the king of the gods?" RaEm said, her voice rising in horror.

"Silence, man!" he barked. "It's a crime even to mention his name."

"I'm a woman," RaEm hissed. "Can't you tell?"

Wenaten glanced at her breasts, her skirt. *"Aii,* I guess you are." He turned back to Cheftu. "The Aten has confused us all—men, women, everyone looks alike these days."

"Who, or what, is the Aten?" Cheftu asked.

Wenaten turned around and pointed at the sail, hanging lax from the mast. "See that disk with the hands?" Both Cheftu and RaEm nodded. "That's the Aten. Those little hands are sun rays he puts out, touches us on our heads." He lowered his voice again. "Has downright touched Pharaoh in the head, if you catch my meaning."

Again Cheftu and RaEm exchanged glances. "What are you doing here, my lord?" Cheftu asked.

"Coming home from Tsor. That useless son of a goat trader, Zakar Ba'al, made me wait for two seasons before he fulfilled Pharaoh's wishes to export some wood."

"Wood?" Cheftu felt like a parrot, repeating every other word, but it was so much to take in, to absorb. He was light-headed, thirsty; that must be part of it.

"Aye. Pharaoh, His High Foppishness, is building yet another addition to that cookpot he calls a palace in Akhetaten."

"Why not mud brick?"

"Well, this Aten"—Wenaten glanced toward the sun and made the motion against the Evil Eye—"he is pretty cursed hot in Akhetaten.

The mud brick is far too hot to walk on, so we need wood for the floors in the palace and temple."

"Why would the floor of the temple get hot?"

"Because the sun beats down, fool!" Wenaten shouted. "Are you a peasant? Do you not understand how the sun's heat falls to the earth?"

"The temple has a roof to protect its patrons from the heat," Cheftu said slowly, keeping a rein on his temper.

"Nay."

"Nay?" Now RaEm was repeating, her eyes so wide that Cheftu could see the whites on all sides.

"Nay," Wenaten said. "It has no roof."

"What idiot built that?" RaEm asked. For once Cheftu agreed with her.

Wenaten shook his head. "I know not, but Pharaoh designed it. Amun-Ra, who doesn't want his priests to bake what little of the brains they have, his temple had a roof. It's even cool inside, if you have ever been inside." He looked at Cheftu, at his long, curling hair.

"You obviously haven't," Wenaten said to him. "Anyhow, the Aten wants to rain his light down on us. All day. Every day. From dawn to dusk. Hot, blistering heat." Wenaten touched his forehead. "Being at sea has healed my sunburns, but you should have seen them! Peeling skin like an Ashqeloni onion! A great tribute to the Aten."

"That's disgusting," RaEm said haughtily.

"It is a part of the new court attire. A sunburn. Burns testify that one is a good Egyptian and devout in his worship of the Aten." Wenaten hesitated a moment, seeming less ridiculous and more meditative. "The envoys from other lands are convinced Pharaoh is mad," he said ruefully. "Most of Egypt's nobility has already disavowed him."

RaEm was watching the little man, openmouthed. She'd probably never heard of discontent with the ruling class, certainly not in Egypt. Cheftu smothered a smile. What would she think if he told her that his countrymen had not only overridden their monarch, Louis, but chopped off his head also?

Rebellion was not an ancient Egyptian concept, for Pharaoh was god incarnate. At least, rebellion *hadn't* been an Egyptian concept. "Who is Pharaoh?" Cheftu asked carefully.

The small man drew to his full height and extended his hand upward, palm flat. "Pharaoh, living in Aten forever! is Akhenaten."

Ak-nah-ten, Cheftu repeated mentally. He lives in Ak-het-ah-ten, obviously named after himself.

"Who is consort?" RaEm asked.

Cheftu could see the wheels of her greed spinning.

"*Aii*, used to be Nerfertiti. What a woman. . . ." Wenaten drifted off, a dazed expression on his face. "She even looked like a woman. Alas, she was banished. Even shipped across the Great Green, I think. Her face was lovely enough to inspire a thousand ships to set sail." He sighed again.

Cheftu's skin prickled. When would these men share water? His tongue was swollen.

"If she is gone, then who rules beside Akhenaten?" RaEm purred at the spindly ambassador.

"No one for long. Pharaoh has married each of his daughters, attempting to whelp a son, an heir to the throne." The little Egyptian wiped his nose on his palm. "It's been two Inundations since I set foot in Egypt. I will know nothing more until we arrive in the Delta."

A shout made them turn, and Wenaten crowed with delight that the ship was now in the waters beside the islet. "*Aii*, I appreciate your allowing me to rest in your home," Wenaten said, bowing. "The Aten blesses you."

"Wait!" RaEm shouted. "You cannot leave us here! We have nothing!"

"You should have considered that when you married this longhaired fop. What do you do?" Wenaten asked Cheftu.

"We're not married," Cheftu said through gritted teeth. "And I'm a . . . royal adviser," he said, ignoring RaEm's snort.

Wenaten stopped and glared at him. "Then why are you naked? Sitting out here, with your bride, and not even married! What kind of adviser are you when there is no king around!" He looked over Cheftu's shoulder. "Is there a king around?"

"I didn't—there isn't—," Cheftu began, then gave up, chasing after Wenaten as the small man boarded the skiff. "My lord, we are not married. We do not live here. We are stranded."

"Take us home to Egypt," RaEm wailed. "Please, for the love of the gods. We are Egyptians!"

Wenaten stopped, looking from one to the other. "Why did you not say so at the start? Fool thing to move here, middle of nowhere, nothing to plant," he muttered. He shouted to a sailor, told him to prepare two more sleeping pallets, threw Cheftu a cloak, then sat down in the skiff.

"I hope he remembers to send it back for us," Cheftu murmured, watching the smaller vessel, feeling the warmth of heavy linen around his body again. The little Egyptian was hauled up the side of the ship like a parcel, then the boat was rowed back to Cheftu and RaEm.

They exchanged a relieved smile when they were both aboard— probably the first noncombative action of the past week. Cheftu looked around at the full daylight. It was a miracle that they had been rescued.

They arrived beside the ship and waited for the rope to be dropped down. Then they waited longer. The cry to weigh anchor floated above them and RaEm launched herself at the ship, banging on it, screaming.

The two sailors shook their heads at each other. Neither had spoken, and Cheftu noted they were not Egyptians, nor were they dressed as Egyptians. If Akhenaten was the disavowed pharaoh of Egypt, who was his father? How had he come to worship the Aten? The three men watched RaEm wage battle with the side of the ship.

"What's all that caterwauling?" Wenaten bellowed, looking over the side.

"My lord! Please, take us to Egypt!" Cheftu shouted up, over RaEm's head and vocals.

A rope tumbled down, and Cheftu tugged against it, starting to pull himself up. RaEm draped herself across his back, and he almost lost his balance. "Don't think you are getting rid of me this easily," she said quickly. "I'm right here."

"Aye," Cheftu said through gritted teeth. Being with RaEm made his jaw ache. Perpetually. "You are on my back. I can't climb with the extra weight, RaEm."

"You think I'm too fat?" she said, the pouting audible in her tone.

In fact, she was skeletally thin, her body stripped of all femininity. "Not too—"

"Come along, you fop!" Wenaten called from above. "Quit cuddling that doxy and climb up here like a man!"

The sailors were laughing, smothering their guffaws beneath their hands. Wishing both RaEm and Wenaten at the bottom of the sea, Cheftu hauled himself and RaEm up the side of the ship. He fell onto the deck, gasping for water.

The next morning, after a small meal with fruit and a limited supply of water, so as not to make them ill, Cheftu watched the waves lap against the hull. This was a Tsori ship, built by Zakar Ba'al himself, Wenaten claimed.

The ambassador had been on a mission for Pharaoh and was returning to court two years later than anticipated. Cheftu watched as RaEm licked her healing lips at the thought of gold, court, and nobles. Wenaten's ship's navigator had died a month after setting sail, and they had been trying to find their way back to Egypt ever since.

None of the men agreed on which direction to go, hence the type of sailing Cheftu and RaEm had seen: moving first in one direction for half a mile, then rethinking and going back to where they'd started, but not ever being sure. Cheftu had a decent idea where they were, so he suggested they sail southeast.

After much pursing of his lips and frowning, Wenaten gave the order. The Tsori exchanged glances with each other, then reluctantly raised the sails and repeated the order in their own language: "The old fool has figured how to get home. Set sail while we come up with another plan."

Suddenly furious, Cheftu called out in their tongue, "Setting sail, southeast to Egypt, is your sole plan." The sailors froze, staring at him in shock. "We should arrive in Egypt by dusk of the third day."

Wenaten and RaEm were watching him and the sailors as though it were a tennis match. Cheftu's gaze homed in on the boatswain. "My lord," said the wily Tsori, "we are far at sea; it has taken us months to get here. I fear it will take months to return us to the Nile, even knowing which direction to go."

Cheftu crossed the deck to the man, until they were standing nose to nose. "What takes weeks and months of travel going north, takes only three days moving southward," he stated flatly. "I know. I've done it before."

The Tsori blanched, dropping his gaze.

"You have deceived the ambassador," Cheftu said in the boatswain's language. "Do not think you will do so with me." My wife awaits me, he thought. Your plotting will not prevent my seeing her. "Test me on this, and you will know my wrath." Cheftu stared into the man's eyes, challenging him. "The appropriate response is, 'Aye, my lord.' "

The man said nothing, but insurrection gleamed in his eyes.

Cheftu stepped back, calling to two of the men, strapping fellows with dark, quick eyes and beaky noses. "Relieve this man of his duty," he instructed them. "Confine him to the ship's hold until we arrive in Kemt."

"My lord—," the boatswain protested.

"Now," Cheftu commanded.

Sheepishly the sailors took their superior below deck. Cheftu beckoned to RaEm. She crossed the deck, her body brazenly displayed. Cheftu spoke to her in a whisper. "We cannot trust that the boatswain is safely locked away," he said. "Follow them to be certain." She nodded once. "Remember, RaEm, if they mutiny, you will never see Egypt again, nor will you meet Pharaoh."

"Can I beat him?" she asked, her lips parted.

Cheftu looked out at the water, while his blood ran cold. "Don't leave him in need of medical care. I have no desire to nurse him to health." Her breath was heavy, her pupils dilating. "Don't betray me, RaEm," he said. "Or I will teach you the true meaning of pain. Now go," he said, not looking at her again.

The sailors were frozen, staring at him. One by one Cheftu met their gazes. "This ship is Lord Wenaten's. You are also his, a gift from your own king." His voice carried up into the waiting silence. "You have played my lord for a fool, but no more." He licked his lips, hat-ing that he had to threaten them. However, they would not yield. Perhaps they had been told to lose the ambassador at sea? "We will arrive in Egypt within this week, which allows for foul weather, or you will begin to pay for these poor directions with your very lives."

They squirmed. Good, Cheftu thought. "Already your boatswain is enduring discipline. It would be a pity for more of you to experience that." Especially since RaEm would whip them until she was frenzied. Cheftu shuddered. "Sail southwest to Egypt. Now!"

The Tsori ran, releasing sails, starting the beat for the oarsmen, scrambling up the ropes, and moving down the deck. Within moments the ship was under way, the sails fat with air, the oarsmen keeping a pleasant, productive pace. Wenaten met Cheftu in the middle of the deck.

"Masterfully done, my lord," he said without preamble. "I am honored to have you aboard."

Cheftu bowed his head, his anger dissipated. "It is vital to me to arrive in Egypt soon."

"Does Pharaoh expect you? Are you a gift to the throne? How did you come to be in the sea like that? And what is your name?" Wenaten was more respectful, but also showing more wit than Cheftu had credited him.

"It is a long tale," he said. *And I have yet to form it.* "I am weary, actually." *And I fear to give you my real name.* "Chavsha," Cheftu said, "is how you can call me." The names were close enough in meaning that there was not much deception.

Wenaten clapped his hands, summoning slaves. "Rest in my chambers, my lord Chavsha. I will wake you to eat."

A scream rose from beneath the deck. The sailors paused for a moment, then moved even faster. Cheftu allowed himself to be guided to Wenaten's chamber. No sooner had the door closed than it opened again, admitting RaEm. Had Wenaten forgotten they were not married? Another chance for Cheftu to ask the stones what to do was ruined.

Did they still work in this time period?

Would they give him the answers he wanted?

Aii, *Chloe, where are you, my love?* Could he travel forward to her time?

Learn to ride an airplane? Watch the tee-vee? Eat at McDonald's? Each nugget of information he'd learned about Chloe's world fed his hunger for her and staved off the maddening fear that maybe their last farewell had been the final one.

When Cheftu awoke the next day, he saw the sails were swollen with wind, the sailors sleeping, playing dice with each other, or attending to the busywork of being shipboard. Inside the covered cabin, Cheftu saw the shadow of Wenaten bent over a desk. Was he preparing the papyri documents that would grant them entrance to sail up the Nile to Akhetaten? RaEm had left their couch already; he saw her sitting by the prow, the wind blowing her burned hair. She made quite a picture for the sailors.

Akhenaten. The name meant nothing to Cheftu. Did Wenaten know of Pharaoh Hatshepsut, the wise leader under whom Cheftu had been a courtier? Or had her successor Thutmosis kept his vow and stricken her from all records? What of the-Most-Splendid, her mortuary temple on the west bank of the Nile? It had survived until Chloe's time; was it just ignored now? The sun began to rise, and Cheftu's mind raced faster. Pharaoh sounded quite mad. Was Chloe in that court?

"Dreaming of your lover again?" RaEm asked. She'd crept up on him; he must still be exhausted not to have heard her.

He ignored her query. "What will you do when we arrive?" he asked, noting that most of the damage sustained in the eruption to the black-haired, copper-skinned body she wore was healing. At least nothing had happened to the face she was wearing.

"A pharaoh currently without wife, and you ask that?" RaEm laughed, and Cheftu noticed the sailors glance her way. Though they were beneath her notice, she was not beneath theirs. However, the lashing she had given their senior tinted those gazes with fear and respect, in addition to lust. They followed her with their eyes as she slinked along the deck, her shoulders brazenly displayed even in the winter weather. It was acceptable dress and behavior in Egypt; alas, the oarsmen were Tsori. To them she was less clothed than their whores. Cheftu had suggested a cloak, but RaEm had laughed at him, grateful to be out of Levi's and Vic's Secret contraptions she said.

"What will you do?" she asked, " 'Adviser to royalty'? When did you learn to speak the tongue of these people? How can you take these things so calmly?" Though her tone was teasing, Cheftu felt wary. RaEm was self-centered to a fault; she was also vain. But he must never forget that she was clever, wickedly so.

"Offer my services to Pharaoh, of course." Perhaps he could win a position high enough that he could find Chloe? Or she could find him? That assumed she had left her twentieth-century world again. Could she do that? Had she?

He must ask the stones at the earliest possible moment.

"Aye, I forget you are the nobleman who is so noble, he cannot bear to spend time with anyone other than the rich and titled," RaEm said to his silence.

He opened his mouth to protest, then shut it. What value to argue with RaEm? Maybe if he said nothing, he would be allowed to enjoy the sunrise in peace. Would he see Chloe in days? Was she in this Akhetaten?

Wenaten bustled through to them. "*Aii*, greetings of the morning goddess to you." He slapped a hand over his mouth. "May Aten forgive me! Greetings of the one god Aten to you," he said. "I really must recall the proper way to greet people! Isis—umm, Aten help me!" He walked over to the timekeeper.

"What do you make of this worshiping this Aten?" RaEm asked in a whisper.

"Given our host's nervousness, I am uncertain," Cheftu said. "Is he exaggerating the situation? I cannot imagine Egypt without the gods and goddesses. Just one god seems so little for such a rich land."

"Modern Egypt has only one god. A harsh, bloodthirsty god," RaEm said. "He has little sense of beauty or grandeur; he cares only to rule as many as possible."

"Allah?" Cheftu asked.

"Aye. Mohammed—"

"Is his prophet." Cheftu looked out across the water. Egypt was Mohammedan in his time also.

"How did you know that?" RaEm asked, an edge of suspicion in her voice. "How did you know it was me in this body? How did you know Chloe's language?" She laid a hand on his arm. "You travel through the portals also? You are of the twenty-third power?"

Wenaten's approach saved Cheftu from having to answer. "We will be in the blessed two lands by Ra—Aten's zenith," he said. "I have called for baths, razors, so we should be ready to present ourselves to the guard as Egyptians. Home again!" he sang, walking past them.

"This man, he makes me dizzy," RaEm said. The phrase sounded so much like Chloe that Cheftu almost laughed. He ran a hand over his bearded chin, noted that his hair still flowed down his back in the style of Aztlan. It was no wonder that Wenaten had dismissed him initially. *I look about as Egyptian as a Philistine.*

"I will go first," he said. "If that is well with you." He didn't know how to answer her questions. Information was a dangerous thing for this woman to have, for she had no limits. She wanted everything for herself. That, Cheftu thought, might be the deadliest ambition of any soul.

RaEm looked him up and down. "Please do. I tire of looking at you that way. Also shave and perfume yourself. First impressions, you know."

He frowned and walked into the shaded area. A bath would be good, as would a shave. As would being back in Egypt. As would being back in Chloe. *Aii!* gods! However, he had another purpose in bathing.

Once inside the tub, the cold water rinsing away the salt, he slipped the oracular stones into his palms. Each was an oblong, one black and one white, inscribed on both sides with letters. The carved scratches were painted in gold and silver, forming letters that would someday be recognized as most ancient Hebrew. The Urim and Thummim. The convoluted path that had followed to end in his ownership astounded Cheftu, but he knew their value.

Even as he held them, one in each hand, he felt their life.

Glancing over his shoulder nervously, he phrased his question. "Where am I?"

He tossed the stones and they danced in the air, each spin illuminating a different character etched in their sides. "I-n w-a-t-e-r."

Cheftu snatched them apart. Of course, how could he have forgotten how very literal these stones were.

"Are you finished yet?" RaEm asked, not too far behind him.

"Cannot a man have some privacy to bathe!" he bellowed, hiding the stones in his palms.

Swearing at him, she stomped away. Cheftu waited until all was quiet again, then whispered the question of his heart to the stones. "How do I find Chloe?"

"F-o-l-l-o-w."

Follow what? Follow where? Follow whom? Maybe he should start at the beginning. "Is Chloe here?"

They were silent, an indication that the question wasn't phrased properly. Cheftu had forgotten how irritating it was to deal with their oracular powers. "Is Chloe here, in this time period?"

"A-y-e."

Joy surged through Cheftu. She was here! She was here! All he had to do was—

"Don't dirty the bath," RaEm called.

Cursing her, Cheftu bundled the stones away, tempted to urinate childishly in the water just because RaEm was such an annoyance. Instead he rose, dried himself, dressed, and strode off to meet with the barber. The stones were tucked safely in his waist sash once more: one on his left side, the other on his right.

Chloe was here, somewhere in this time period. To get to her he needed only to figure out the first message. If he followed, he would find Chloe. Gratefully he submitted to the hot, steamy face clothes as he pondered the answer to his question. The stones were never wrong, but also they were rarely clear. He needed more direction in that response.

However, she was here. The world wasn't so big that he couldn't find her. Remember your vow, he thought. I remember mine.

Egypt. She stretched before them like a multifaceted jewel. The fields were green with growing grain, and the waters of the Nile reflected the blue sky. Cheftu touched his newly shaven chin, felt the winter wind whip at his legs, shielded by a long, heavily woven kilt. The tight dryness of kohl surrounded his eyes, and his neck was once more naked to the sun.

The Tsori ship, with its wary sailors, had been traded for a Nile vessel. Shallow bottomed, with no keel, it was easier to move over rocks and through the sometimes dangerous twists in the river. Wenaten and his staff had easily passed inspection by the lazy officials on the Delta; now they moved toward Akhetaten.

Temples that once stood proud and regal along the river were now swamped with weeds, serving as homes for rodents. Many of the statues to other gods and goddesses had been defaced, leaving only the orb with its extended hands, the Aten, where an animal's visage once was. Cat-headed Bastet, ibis-headed Thoth, falcon-headed Horus, all were defaced in favor of the handed disk.

Obelisks had been knocked over, and fields lay fallow with no priests to work them. What other industry had absorbed the discharge of tens of thousands of priests?

"What has he done to Egypt?" RaEm said beside him. "It is . . . an embarrassment!"

Cheftu watched the waters slide by, felt the timelessness of the Nile, the sadness of the decay around them. "He seems a destroyer, not a creator," he said. Though these temples were dilapidated, there didn't appear to be new ones to take their places. "What are the people doing?" he wondered aloud.

RaEm watched for a few more moments, then announced it was making her unwell and she was returning to her couch. Wenaten's couch, Cheftu thought, which she had commandeered, casting Wenaten from it.

A few minutes later the ambassador joined Cheftu by the railing, drumming his fingers on the wood.

"What bothers you, my lord?" Cheftu asked lazily. Where was Chloe? Was she in Egypt? Follow what, follow whom, follow how . . . The words chased each other in his head like a dog with its tail.

"I spoke briefly to an acquaintance of mine at the border. Pharaoh, umm, living forever! has allowed three uprisings in Kush to go unchecked." Wenaten had donned a new wig, short and curled. "Even though Canaan boils with trouble, the entire eastern outpost has been dissolved, save one old diplomat."

"Egypt is the most powerful entity in the world," Cheftu said, wondering if those words were still true. "Surely we have nothing to fear from Canaan?"

"All the land that Thutmosis the Great One gathered for us, is gone."

Which means I am now after the time of Thut, Cheftu thought, and before the time of Rameses. I know nothing of this history. *Merde!*

"One by one we have lost our vassals." Wenaten slapped his wig straight, irritated. "This time we stand to lose the King's Highway."

"That is where?" Cheftu asked. This was not a phrase or term he recalled.

"Runs from the Salt Sea up to Mitanni and Assyria. Straight across the plateau in the center of Canani land, so we don't have to worry about those conniving Tsidoni thieves on the seaboard. They have no respect for Egypt," he muttered. "Uncircumcised sons of jackals!"

"How can we lose the King's Highway?" How could Egypt lose anything? Cheftu stared at the abandoned villages, haunted roadways; he would not have believed this had he not seen it. How the people must be suffering.

Wenaten began picking at a loose thread in his sash, his short, skinny fingers working at its edge, tugging it free. "The fool lost it through passivity. The same way he lost us the Sea Road that runs from Sais to Gaza." The thread broke off in his hand, so with a shake of his head, he started picking around for another one to pull. "Already they are calling it the Way of the Pelesti. Passivity," he muttered. "Now the Pelesti have renamed it, as though it didn't belong to Egypt for generations and generations." The second thread broke. "It was the Way of the Sea, named by the Egyptians, before those sea raiders cursed our land with their invasions."

Cheftu nodded, as though this were common knowledge to him. Pelesti; who were these people? Were they sea raiders, or were the Tsidoni the sea raiders? Had everyone taken to stealing rights-of-way from Egypt? "One of the petty mountain lords in central Canaan has overtaken the others' lands," Wenaten said. "The *seren*, how the Pelesti call their king, plead with Egypt to intervene."

"The Pelesti are our vassals?"

Wenaten glared at him. "What part haven't you heard, fool? The Pelesti are our vassals, but they have forgotten! *Haii*, that fop on the throne, instead of reminding them of their allegiances by sending a few soldiers their way, he withdraws the one competent idiot still there!"

"Egypt rules an empire. Part of accepting their tribute is to protect them, whether they have forgotten or not. It is the covenant of suzerain," Cheftu said.

Wenaten glared at him. "You must be a royal adviser; you sound just like one."

Cheftu gathered from his tone that Wenaten wasn't complimenting him. "Aye, well," the ambassador continued, "Inundations have been poor, our priests are dying like lotus without water. Even the court is dwindling, though every noble who leaves Akhetaten is immediately declared an enemy of the state. It's hardly an empire, sad to say."

"Do you have to return?" Cheftu asked. "I could take the ship to court with a message from you."

Wenaten pursed his lips. "I've seen much of the world outside Egypt. Even if Pharaoh, living forever! is foaming mad, still our land is more peaceful, beautiful, and soothing than anything on earth. Look at this," he said, stretching his hand toward the horizon. "You can see for *henti*. No mountains, no trees to obstruct the view and weary the eye." Wenaten sighed. "*Aii*, Egypt, the garden of the gods. Err, god."

"When will we be in Akhetaten?"

"With this current? In two weeks."

A few days later they dined beneath the stars. Wenaten had stopped again at the mouth of the Delta, picked up a scroll from a friend of his, another envoy. As he ate fish, fowl, and fruit, he chuckled over the contents of the papyrus.

Cheftu and RaEm exchanged glances. He was being rude, but also he had been traveling for two years. It must be good to be home.

RaEm, per Egyptian fashion, had shaved her head and wore a new wig, called "the Kushite" with the same angled cut and curl as Wenaten's. It was the trendiest thing in court, she'd been told, further testimony of how androgyny was the rule in this new regime. After a few tries she'd given up explaining to Cheftu what "trendy" meant since the Egyptian language they spoke to each other had no equivalent for the term.

Trendy, or *au courant*, went against the Egyptian concept of perfection, of Ma'at. In Ma'at, nothing changed. All things dwelt in a universal sense of balance—Pharaoh ruling from above, commoners in the fields, nobles feasting on the Nile—throughout this life and into the next. This divine stability was what the rational, devout Egyptian sought.

New fashion was change. New wig styles were change. The new artistic style was an even greater change. The Egyptian whom Cheftu had been for seventeen years balked; this was not the Egypt he knew and understood. The Frenchman who had wholeheartedly believed in *Liberté, Fraternité, Égalité,* saw change as progress. Most changes, at least. Cheftu looked back at RaEm.

Pleated linen sleeves covered her from clavicle to wrists, another new style, while the skirt of her gown was layered over a solid underskirt. RaEm declared she was delighted to be back into a black-haired and copper-skinned body, even if it belonged to another person; she didn't care about anything else. Praise the gods, Cheftu thought, the body she was in had emerged from the eruption of Aztlan free of permanent scars, though RaEm was still boyishly frail. Without her wig or dress, one would almost wonder at her gender.

The promiscuous priestess of HatHor appearing asexual: it was an interesting, ironic twist.

Wenaten rolled up the scroll, then drank his beer in one gulp. *"Aii,* well, shall you hear the news?"

RaEm nodded, smiling at him. Did the little man realize she would bed him just for the control of it? Cheftu wondered. He leaned back with his own cup of beer to listen.

"Rumors fly thick and fast that Akhetaten has sent for his cousin," Wenaten said.

Cheftu knew that the term *cousin* essentially meant anyone with a drop of royal blood. As the pharaohs of Egypt were known for generously spreading their seed, it was possible that half of Egypt was a cousin of Pharaoh.

"Where is his cousin?" RaEm asked.

"Aii, well, beyond the cataracts," Wenaten said, lowering his voice. "Queen Tiye the Kushi was married before she became the consort of Amenhotep Osiris, Akhenaten's father. Tiye's brother is Ay."

Cheftu tried to recall any of these names. Amenhotep had been Hatshepsut's father's name, though it was Egyptian custom for royalty to bear almost all of their ancestors' names. Each pharaoh had his prenomen and his secret name, then a list of lineage names.

"Ay is fan bearer to Pharaoh." Wenaten hunched closer to them. "Tiye's husband in Kushi gave her a child, before it was recognized that she bore the throne right."

Aye, the royal blood of Egypt coursed through the veins of the women, Cheftu knew. So even if Tiye were wed to someone else, if she were the only royal woman left, it would be Ma'at that she wed again to serve the throne.

"She was brought to Amenhotep Osiris, leaving her child and husband in Kush."

"A son?" RaEm said.

Wenaten shrugged. "No one has ever seen him, so it is assumed he is a son." Wenaten muttered the rest. "Pharaoh needs a co-regent so that while Pharaoh focuses on prayers and sacrifices to his hot god, someone else will handle with the details of ruling an empire." He stared into the distance for a moment. "Some of the envoys have waited years for intervention from Pharaoh. Their lands await rescue by Egypt."

"How many Amenhoteps have there been?" Cheftu asked, trying to grasp the chronology, narrow down when they were.

Wenaten stared at him. "Amenhoteps have always ruled Egypt," he said, his tone confused.

Aye, and it was the Westerners who broke the reigns of Egypt into dynasties, for the Egyptians had no sense of individual rule. Even if Wenaten gave Cheftu a chronology, he wouldn't recognize it, Cheftu thought.

"No one has ever seen this cousin?" RaEm asked, drawing Wenaten's attention back to her. "He is an heir to the Egyptian throne? I thought all the heirs were raised together?"

The envoy picked at some skin loose on his arm. "*Aii!* Thutmose was Akhenaten's brother, but he died young. There was another brother who had died while he was yet in the cradle. It seemed wise to hide any other heirs. Akhenaten, while he was called Amenhotep, ruled with his father, Amenhotep. Though, truth be known, Tiye ruled them both," he said in an undertone.

RaEm's eyes gleamed. "Powerful women are still admired in Egypt?"

Wenaten pursed his lips. "She is more than a woman, she is a general!" He shivered. "Many a career soldier or diplomat has been reduced to tears in her presence."

"Does the queen mother live in Ak—the town where Pharaoh does?" Cheftu asked.

"What of this unknown son?" RaEm asked, glancing at Cheftu.

"Smenkhare is the third son—"

"Smenkhare could as easily be a woman's name," RaEm interrupted.

Wenaten answered RaEm. "I guess it is possible that maybe he is a she. Who knows? The point is that someone, anyone of royal blood, will be ruling Egypt instead of just letting her run to ruin."

"Tell us about Akhetaten," Cheftu said, glancing at RaEm, who had fallen silent, her gaze on the horizon, a slight frown on her brow. He could almost smell the brimstone and sulfur from the workings of her mind. "Does the queen mother live there?"

"It's a new city, barely built when I left," Wenaten said. "Most of the court still lived in Waset, though Akhetaten was becoming populated." He closed his eyes, as though summoning the image. "The city has very large buildings and very few roofs. We're all supposed to bake our brains in service to the Aten."

"Does the Aten take sacrifices?" RaEm asked, pushing herself back into the conversation.

"Nay," Wenaten said, shaking his head. "The only person who knows what the Aten wants, or when, or why, is Akhenaten."

"He has no priests?" Cheftu asked.

Wenaten filled their cups again. "Priests aplenty, but none of them speak to the Aten. Or he doesn't speak to them," he said, waving a hand before his face. "I'm not sure. I never considered myself a religious man. The gods were the gods, we wore amulets to protect ourselves, we sacrificed when we needed something. They stayed in the heavens, we stayed on earth. Now, now . . ." He sighed and drained another beer.

RaEm looked uneasy. "Is that Aten really Allah?" she whispered to Cheftu. "He is so rigid a god." To Wenaten she said, "What of the other gods?"

"Banished," he answered shortly. "Gone."

How could one man do away with the Egyptian pantheon? "Surely they have just become minor deities?" Cheftu said. "Much in the same way that Amun-Ra—"

"Are you a fool?" Wenaten interrupted in a hissing whisper, glancing around. "That name is death! Death, I tell you! There is one god in Egypt! One! His name is Aten!" Wenaten leaned back, calmer, his tone normal again. "It is a punishable offense to speak the name of another god. Worship is daily, in the Temple of the Rising of the Aten, as a group. No one is excused. Punishments are levied if one is late or misses." He rose abruptly. "I must piss," he said as he staggered off.

Cheftu sipped his beer. "Was the Aten not just a minor element of Amun-Ra?" he whispered to RaEm.

She glared at him for saying the name of Egypt's god; then, when she saw that no one was watching them, she shrugged. "I have never heard of this god, this Aten. What a strange thing, Egypt without her gods. What of HatHor? Isis? Neith? Bastet?" She looked at him. "Are there no goddesses at all?" She gestured to the topsail, hanging limp above them. "This god doesn't even have a face! How can we worship something that has no eyes to see us, no ears to hear us?"

Cheftu looked at the symbol: a disk, with rays extended, each ending in an open-palmed hand. How had this pharaoh turned his people against what they had known and worshiped for so many millennia? It made no sense. "I am for my couch," he said, rising, finishing his beer.

RaEm looked away. "I think I will stay up awhile longer," she said.

You think you will seduce Wenaten, Cheftu realized. However, he nodded and walked away. Once inside the tent enclosure, stretched out on his pallet, he withdrew the stones again. "What land is Chloe in?" he whispered to them.

"I-n-t-h-e l-a-n-d-o-f-y-o-u-r-d-e-s-t-i-n-a-t-i-o-n."

Cheftu blew out the lamp. *"Zut alors."*

I CURSED, ROLLING OVER. My shoulder was still extremely tender, but at least it was back in place. How the hell I'd survived that insane Batmanesque tightrope torture wasn't abundantly clear.

At least I was alive. I could walk. Also, for better or worse, I was the local goddess. I wasn't sure exactly how it worked, but by making it across, I had outwitted the lover Mexos, I hadn't embraced Dagon, and I was one with the mother-goddess. Like many ancient people— and I felt as though I were becoming an authority on ancient peoples—not every last thing they believed had to agree with every other thing they believed. In fact, stories could contradict each other but not be viewed as inconsistencies.

To a Western linear thought pattern, it was bewildering. But to the Eastern mind, which I'd spent a lot of time with both here and in my childhood, it made a strange, convoluted, and quirky kind of sense.

Consequently I was the local goddess, a facet of the great goddess Ashterty. They had given me a house, Tamera as my handmaid, food, clothing, and power. I'd been invited to sit with the *serenim*, the city elders, when they listened to cases and dispensed justice. I was to attend every dinner, every event, of which there were many. The bad news was I was escorted everywhere, waited on by everyone, and my chances for slipping into the crowd and hitchhiking to Egypt were nil.

Especially since I still couldn't use my left shoulder, arm, and hand. I wasn't healed yet. Though it was back in place, the swelling wasn't completely gone. I looked up at Dagon, since I was living at the base of his tail until I took possession of my new, goddess-worthy dwelling. "Heya," I whispered to the idol. Groaning, very un-sea-mistress-like, I sat up. What I wouldn't give for coffee! Or a painkiller.

"*HaDerkato?*"

I motioned for Tamera to enter. She left me a breakfast of fish grilled with tiny little sweet onions. Scallions? The meal was delicious, though it hurt to hold the plate after a moment. I set it down and looked around, trying to orient myself.

Who, what, when, where, and why were my questions, and I hadn't a single answer. Had these people come from the ashes of the time period I'd lived in before, in Aztlan? Had I moved forward in time? No one seemed to know the name of Pharaoh, so that checkpoint was ineffective. All in all, I was firmly adrift, waiting for Cheftu to chance across my pathway. I shifted and saw a priest wielding a spear poke his head around the corner.

My chains were figurative but effective. They hadn't even given me shoes!

Tamera mixed me some concoction involving salt water, a raw egg, coriander leaf, and something else. Whatever it was, it eased some of my aching. Gingerly I climbed into a bath, then submitted to having my hair brushed and oiled while my legs were waxed.

The Pelesti were not as conscious about hygiene as either the Egyptians or the Azlantu. However, I was. Plucking and shaving and waxing had become a way of life for me, one I wasn't anxious to give up. However, it was agony with bruises. I settled for a minimum of service because I'm a wimp when it comes to pain.

Even bathing, I wasn't alone.

By noon I was clothed, jeweled, coiffed, and painted. I was eating some raisins and bread when Tamera came in, a contingency of priest-esses behind her. They were all wearing fish masks and fish body cloaks. Tamera handed me the same garment, telling me that I was now one of their order, a goddess to serve Dagon as they each served him while mortal.

Again, more of the incongruous story thinking. No one seemed to find it odd that I didn't know what to do, that I didn't know what prayers to say or even what the ritual was. They must have assumed I was a stupid goddess, but all were so agog at my passing the tightrope ritual that they were willing to overlook some things. Thank the god-dess!

This fish garb was definitely a fashion don't; however, I had no choice. I put it on, slipped the mask over my head, then went out to wait for El'i, my chauffeur.

The Pelesti were between growing seasons and had nothing to do. Therefore the *serenim* had created mass entertainment to keep the peo-ple happy. Today there were gladiator teams. That wasn't the term they used, but my lexicon had shown enough pictures of matinee movie stars in short dresses and helmets that I'd gotten the idea.

Rather than stay in the sheltered comfort of the Temple of Dagon, we sat outside, grouped around a central stage beneath the trees. As *haDerkato* I had a throne next to Takala and Yamir. The youngest son, Wadia, who was about fourteen years old, sat at my feet, passing grapes and olives back to me as though they were popcorn.

Six men emerged from one side of the sandy pit, six from the other side. A priest, wearing his official fish robe, invoked the gods and god-desses to observe this challenge. Then he bowed away, and the teams attacked.

Slicing, hacking, stabbing, and jabbing, they tried, with a passion, to kill each other. I clenched my teeth, letting my vision fuzz so that I didn't actually see anything but also didn't raise questions by cowering beneath my chair, which I would have very much liked to do.

First blood brought a roar from the audience, compounding the intensity. Men and women spectators were equally involved. I didn't doubt some bookie waited outside the gates for the tallies.

By midafternoon the sand was bloody, everyone was dead, and we were headed home. I felt sick to my stomach; I'd just seen eleven men slaughter each other. What had happened to my soul? What had possessed me to stay?

Fear. Fear of being alone, fear of being lonely. It was a scary, unknown world. By playing along, I survived. At least that was my rationalization.

We mounted our sturdy carts and trundled back to the palace. I was ushered into the feast along with everyone else. Dinner was served, a mash of corn with patties of corn shaped into fish. We were halfway through when I heard a shout.

"*HaDerkato*, for you!" Tamera declared.

I looked up, horrified. The surviving gladiator beamed at me, holding a tray in his outstretched arms. A tray with the open, staring eyes, the scream-gaped mouth, and the severed neck of the final combatant. The man's head was being delivered to me on a platter!

Corn refilled my mouth; what could I do? *Dear God, please help me!*

I looked away, into the gaze of the gladiator.

His bronze-eyed gaze. Black hair fell over his broad shoulders. He gleamed with oils from his postslaughter bath. He was dressed in the pointed kilt of the Pelesti, the lower half of his face obscured by beard. I looked back into his luminescent eyes, my heart racing.

Could it be?

"Sea-Mistress," the king Yamir said, "it is customary to reward the winner with a kiss."

The gladiator slid the tray with the head onto my table, next to my dinner. I raised my face, knowing that if it were Cheftu, if he had stepped into the body of this person, I would recognize his kiss.

First the gladiator brushed my lips with his, then he seized me in a bear hug, pulling me across the table. He was rough, stabbing his tongue into my mouth repeatedly, crushing my shoulders, and pressing my lips so hard that I felt the impressions of his teeth. I saw stars from the pain of my shoulder.

This was not Cheftu.

The oaf released me and I fell back, stunned.

The Pelesti cheered; they were a cheery sort. The gladiator grinned, revealing that the teeth he'd pressed against my mouth were the only four he had. I suppressed a shudder. My gaze fell on the tray, into the muddy gaze of the unfortunate man. I told myself it was all wax. Just a reproduction. Not real. Not real, Chloe.

Wadia was examining the head, lifting its hair, looking in its ears, with the transchronological fascination that teenage boys have for the gruesome. The blood had left my cheeks. I felt horrible. Please don't let me throw up, I pleaded with the universe. "Take it to Dagon," I whispered. "Offer it to the sea," I told Tamera.

They loved the idea, so a group, dancing and singing, trooped off to the shore, the head held like a banner above them.

They left the bloodstained tray for me. I gestured for Tamera. "Get rid of it," I said. "I return to the temple."

"May the goddess bless your sleep."

May the goddess keep me from having nightmares, I thought as I climbed into the cart.

I WOKE UP IN ANOTHER TOWN. Not a physical change in location, but the cheeriness and playfulness of the city had been replaced overnight with somber faces and battle readiness. Highlanders had been sighted, peering down from their mountainous strongholds. It was the first sign of spring, I was told.

"They fear to meet us on the plains," Wadia bragged later. We'd eaten dinner together; now we sat outside beneath the stars. More than anyone else, Wadia and I got along. He was a teenager; they were universal. "If they met with us on the plains, our chariots could beat them."

"They don't have chariots?"

"*Lo*, not even horses."

"How do they move about, then?" I asked, plucking a fig from the bowl. It was the season for figs, a welcome change from the corn-and-scallion diet.

I got seafood only for breakfast.

"They swarm like bees," he said, his hands moving parallel to each other, imitating the swarm. "Then bzzzz, down from the forests of their god, swooping on our men! Bzzzz! They sting us again and again."

"But they don't have horses?"

"In the hills, it's deadlier to have horses," he explained to me slowly. "They get stuck, they can't get good footing. They can't move like bees. The highlanders don't even have good weaponry."

"So why be fearful?" I asked as I sucked the seeds from my fig.

He looked at me with an expression I recalled giving my parents when they were being too obtuse for words. "Bees can kill, even when they are little, even when their stingers are small, because they are fierce."

"Bees? Are fierce?"

"Have you ever tried to take anything from a bee?" he asked me.

No, I actually hadn't. I tried to avoid bees. "So they swarm and sting you," I said.

"They also have a powerful god, so that they win battles, through divine intervention. Their god is mighty, he's vicious."

"Then why don't you, I don't know, worship him instead? If he's more powerful than Dagon?" Halfway through my statement I realized that what I was saying approximated blasphemy. I held my breath.

"Their god only lets the highlanders worship him. He doesn't want any other people."

A god who wasn't interested in proselytizing? This was new.

"So we try to stay away from their highlands, they keep out of our lowlands." He looked away. His profile was like his brother's, with a prominent nose. Unlike Yamir, though, he had a matching chin that already fit his face. He was a teen, but he had none of the awkwardness of youth. His voice was low. "They are so unspeakable, they are so much refuse, that they even burned our *teraphim*."

Here we go with the statuettes, I thought. I wonder if I could just make some from the local clay, save us all a lot of pain and suffering. "Their god doesn't want you to worship him, so what kind of divine intervention did he use? What's the point?"

Wadia grinned. He loved telling stories. Though he was next in line for the throne, he had the spirit of a scholar. Or a stand-up comic. He began, *"Lifnay . . ."*

My lexicon held up a card that said " 'Before' or 'Once upon a time.' "

". . . the lion who now roams the mountains was but a cub."

Why couldn't anyone with a Middle Eastern street address ever speak directly? They would be mute if it weren't for metaphors. I nodded for Wadia to continue.

"There was another rule, Labayu. He was the first king to unite the highlanders. He was really big," Wadia said. "Even taller than you. He brought battle against us, agreeing to have a champion fight for the honor of the highlands, versus a champion for our honor." He sucked the seeds from his fig, then continued.

I tried to reconcile my idea of Lancelot jousting, with the image of a man in a kilt.

"It is an accepted way," Wadia said. "If every time there was a war we sent out the entire army, then there would be no one to wed the women or plow the fields. The Pelesti would die out." He shrugged, his thin shoulders jabbing through the wool of his cloak.

That made sense. My biggest, baddest guy fights yours, and everyone else watches. Less muss, less fuss. But what did the rest of the soldiers do? "So what happened?" I asked.

"We picked the largest of our men, the champion, a giant. Five times undefeated!" he said, holding up his hand. "Five times!"

"Their champion was better?"

"Ach! They sent a child! A little boy, no older than I am now! Smaller than me. It was embarrassing. Labayu wanted to ridicule us."

The hair on the back of my neck started to stiffen. A child and a giant?

"He was not even a soldier, just a kid, a scrawny little runt at that!"

"Maybe, maybe they had no one else better?" I offered, knowing that I was lying.

Wadia gave me another of those looks. I think he'd learned them from his mother, the wide Takala-dagon. "Sending a child to fight our champion was a horrible insult. Not only to us, but to our families, to our god, and especially to the *serenim*." He paused, a storyteller in the middle of his tale. "No one was angrier than the champion, though." He lowered his voice. "Now the champion isn't the tallest tree in the forest, anyway. He rages, he fumes. He breaks furniture, rips off the legs of a nearby cat, he's so furious."

He ripped the legs off a cat? Was that a figure of speech? I grimaced.

"He calls to the heavens, protesting this dishonor." Wadia frowned. "We were trying to be honorable, pitting champion against champion. It's fair." He shook his head, picking at the stem of a fig. "Our honor is diminished by their behavior." He sighed deeply. "Highlanders are a wild, uncivilized bunch." He suddenly sounded so mature—but he should—he was going to be the next king. It was a weird paradigm.

"Did your champion fight this boy, despite the dishonor?"

Wadia sucked the last bit of fig juice from his fingertips. "It was over with one blow. One divine gust of their god's breath and That One, that little boy, had felled our champion. It was a disgrace."

My fig suddenly had the flavor of a golf ball. I could barely find my voice. "Was, uh, Goliath your champion's name?"

He raised his head sharply. "Gol'i'at, *ken*. How did you know?"

Omigod, omigod. I swallowed hard. Go-lee-at. "I'm a goddess, remember?"

"That little boy slew our giant Gol'i'at, then he went on to fight for his ruler, Labayu. That One was dismissed from Labayu's court, so for a while he was a mercenary for our brother *seren*, Akshish of Gath. When Labayu died in battle with Akshish and the other *serenim*, That One turned against us. Now he rules the highlands, but he is wily, untrustworthy." Wadia leaned in. "He has no honor, he doesn't respect the laws of the land, or the heavens. He slights the other gods and he tramples our people and traditions. He looks to the sea, to the cities we trade with, for conquest." He leaned closer to me, his voice barely above a whisper. "He wants our smelting secrets."

My lexicon was working so fast, I was afraid it was going to short out. Pictures from Sunday school, of men in robes with beards and crowns: the older man Labayu I knew as Saul. The part of Gol'i'at was played by Goliath.

"Why do you call him 'That One'?" I asked, chewing my golf-ball fig.

"My mother has forbidden his name to be spoken," Wadia repeated. "But it's Dadua."

The lexicon flashed another picture: the young, harp-playing teen with curling hair and slingshot was Dadua.

David.

I was afraid I was going to fall over. This was unbelievable! David and Goliath? Was everything in the Bible, the "Hebrew mythology" that I'd thought was only slightly more real than fairy tales, fact?

"HaDerkato, are you well?"

"I need a drink," I muttered.

Wadia commanded slaves to get me a drink. Yes, Pelesti wine, that might be strong enough. "So," I said, coughing, trying to focus my mind, "That One is now the king of the highlanders?"

In my mind the plaid kilts were now replaced with yarmulkes and the bagpipes with the ram's horn. I now knew we were discussing . . . omigod . . . the children of Israel. I was in Israel. In Ashqelon. In Israel. In ancient times with Bible characters. In Israel. Jews. I didn't know anything about the Jews. I was practically an honorary Muslim. Yet I was here, now? This was the Bible; what would happen if I screwed up?

Where on earth was Cheftu? We had to get out of here!

CHAPTER 3

Akhetaten was on the horizon by afternoon the next day. Cheftu didn't recognize a thing about it; it wasn't a city that had been known in Hatshepsut's time, nor had he known it by this name in his own nineteenth-century journeys in Egypt. The sun was hot even though it was winter, but it was nothing like it would be in the summertime. He wiped the sweat from his smooth upper lip and squinted against Ra's—the Aten's—light.

It was a flat, white city, with pockets of greenery cradled against the Nile, in a semicircular plain surrounded by cliffs. Sunlight radiated onto the wide, empty boulevards. The harbor was silent, a few ships were docked, but there was no activity, no bustling about.

No people.

Cheftu brushed the oracular stones with his fingertips. This was not how the seat of a prosperous—living—empire should look.

Because Inundation had been so poor this year, the Nile hadn't overflowed its banks, making the waterway farther from the city than usual. So they disembarked the ship for small rowboats. Amid swarms of mosquitoes they cut across the river to the docks. A few slovenly laborers were hoisting Wenaten's many parcels into a light chariot pulled by an old nag.

No delegation had arrived to greet the returning envoy. Save for the workers, no one was there at all.

"Has Egypt been stripped of people as well as gods?" RaEm asked in an undertone.

"I know not." At least it would be easy to find Chloe, since there was no crowd.

"Greetings of the Aten to you," said one of the dockworkers. "Join He Who Reigns on High with Akhenaten, living glorious in the light of the Aten forever! in the Chamber of the Apex to the west side of the Hall of Foreign Tributes." The words were rattled off, a formula repeated to every visitor, Cheftu guessed.

"We are travel stained—," Cheftu began.

"It is no matter," the dockworker interrupted. "All that matters to the Aten is your presence so that he may bless you with his light."

"I would like a bath first," RaEm said. Pleasantly, for her.

"The Aten loves his children as they are, especially returning from the corruption of foreign shores. Please join Akhenaten, living glorious in the light of the Aten forever! as he worships the maker of all Egypt."

"We are tired. We are hungry. We want to rest," Wenaten said. He glanced at Cheftu and RaEm. "However, we know how vital it is to worship the Aten."

"My lord is wise," the worker said. "Your belongings will meet you in the palace. The chariot is awaiting your journey to the Aten." The man's smile was polite but cold.

Stinking of journey and hungry because the ship's stores had been emptied two days ago, they climbed reluctantly into the chariot. It was a short journey down the empty, drought-stricken streets of Akhetaten.

Trees withered in the soil, dust flew from the bare yards of new nobility's homes. Not a soul, a child, a slave, or a foreigner, was on the street. No one, save themselves. The chariot drew even with an enormous building, which Cheftu thought looked like an elaborate fence. Voices, thousands strong, rose from its interior.

The dockworker escorted them to the very doors, allowing no pause in their steps. Cheftu's discomfort grew. Another man, a priest carrying both sword and spear, ushered them through a long, bare hallway. The sound of voices grew louder.

RaEm slipped her hand into the crook of Cheftu's arm. He didn't recoil because he too needed the comfort. What madness possessed Egypt? One could not bathe before attending the temple? Or, surprisingly enough, one attended the temple rather than worship in the intimacy of one's home with family and a personal statue of the god? Egypt had never been a place of corporate worship before; indeed, no ancient culture was. Cheftu shook his head, exhausted, exasperated, and feeling off-kilter.

Rather than disturb those who were in the throes of worship, the guard-priest explained, they would slip in unnoticed. He took them down a flight of stairs into darkness. "Go through that door and up the stairwell," he said.

Wenaten nodded, leading the way. The darkness was cool, refreshing. Above them the floors vibrated from the force of the recitation. Wenaten opened a door and they followed him up, stepping out into the temple.

The heat was staggering, the warmth of the day compounded by the body heat of thousands of people. It stole their breath, sucked the life from them.

The room was easily the size of the *place des Vosges*, Cheftu thought. Ten thousand people or more stood with their faces raised, eyes open, arms outstretched, swaying to the rhythm of the speaker. All around them people had fallen to the ground. They lay as they fell, arms akimbo. Cheftu noted that some of them had soiled themselves, but those standing ignored them; it was not an Egypt that Cheftu recognized.

The man was evil, Cheftu thought instantly. Akhenaten was a fiend. Half of these people were going to go blind from staring into the sun. Another eighth had heat stroke. The rest seemed to be drugged, complacent. What kind of ruler did this to his people? Cheftu wondered, stifling his rage.

Wenaten pushed forward through the crowd. The stink of sweat, human refuse, sour milk, and vomit coated them, tinged with the heavy myrrh of Egyptian religion.

Once they found a place to stand comfortably, Cheftu peered through the crowd, wanting to glimpse the madman who so abused his people's welfare.

Reclining on a golden couch, wearing only a kilt and the blue crown of warriors, was Pharaoh. He was stoop shouldered, lantern jawed, full lipped, potbellied, his skin burned black from the sun. As Cheftu watched, the king stirred, then sat up, as though to enfold the light.

Cheftu suffered his second great shock.

The man had a voice like an angel! As misshapen as his body seemed to be, as perverse as his ideologies, his voice was perfection. Commanding, strong, musical, the timbre was so exquisite, it was almost hard to discern the words.

When he did, Cheftu suffered his third and greatest shock: They were words he knew. They were words he'd read and copied time and again.

"Praise the Aten, my ka within me. The Aten is a great god, clothed with splendor and majesty. He is wrapped in light like a garment, sitting beneath the heavens as his tent. The beams of his house are on the waters in the sky. He rides in a chariot of clouds, lightning gives him flight. The four winds serve as his messengers, fire is his servant."

Cheftu looked around at the faithful, swaying to the sound of Akhenaten's voice, and understood why they were here. There was a charisma, a sense of depth, in the sound—even if the words were stolen.

"He set the columns of the earth into their foundations, unmovable. The Great Green was laid across it, waters raised above the cliffs. With one word, the waters fled the soil, at the roar of your voice, the River ran from the plains into the valley, to rest in fertility in the breast of the red and black lands."

These words weren't written for this place, where rain, lightning, and thunder were rare, almost nonexistent occurrences. Neither was it written for a flat land with no mountains, no columns of the earth; nor was it written for a people whose sole comprehension of a large body of water was a river, the Nile.

Change the words, the name of the god, Cheftu thought . . . and it is a psalm!

Pharaoh had stolen the Bible! *Mon Dieu!*

RaEm had felt liquid desire pool in her body the moment Akhenaten began to speak. As his words rolled over her, undeciphered and sensual, her legs grew wet with her lust. He gestured with his hands, long fingers that she longed to have explore her. His body writhed on the couch in the midst of his prayers, as though the sun's rays were taking him as a man took a woman.

RaEm wanted him. Aye, he was Pharaoh. He had gotten girl children from his own girl children; he had no son. She had also learned that, unlike many of his predecessors, he refused to bed someone who was not a relative, for the seed of the Sun could not be cast on just any field.

RaEm had learned early that her beauty, whether it was in this body or another, had little to do with seduction. Men were a learned skill, and much practice had made RaEm a magus.

Pharaoh thought he had eyes only for those in his own family. He hadn't counted on her.

He was the son of the Sun. Hatshepsut had declared herself the child of Amun-Ra, but it had been a political move. Now, RaEm knew Akhenaten truly was the offspring of the immortal orb. His voice was liquid fire, set to burn them all, awake them all. Consume them all.

As she stared into the sun, her thoughts grew more feverish. Light merged with light, and she swayed to the lilt of his voice, the throbbing penetration of it. She raised her hands in surrender, opening to him and the Aten, wanting to be one with them. A little moan escaped her lips. Around her she heard another. Then another. Akhenaten's voice rose, deeper, stronger, more forceful. She no longer tried to smother her cries.

Unable to take the torture, she undid the clasp of her gown, felt the heat of the sun on her flat, naked breasts. Pinching her nipples, she offered herself to the sun, standing braced in the light.

A hand cupped her from behind, slipped beneath her dress. In the press of people she didn't know, she didn't look. In her mind it was Akhenaten, his long fingers on her, in her, his voice rippling across her back and neck, his tongue in her hair, her ear. The thousands of people moved as one now, swaying, throbbing, sweating to the heated rhythm of Pharaoh's prayers.

Hands above his head, bare to his god, enlivened by the sunlight on his body, Akhenaten thrashed through his prayers, begging Aten for more mercy, asking for more wisdom, pleading for the pleasure of serving the sun. His final plea was a wild, low groan, drowned in the ecstatic cries of his people.

RaEm's thighs shook so strongly that she barely caught herself before hitting the ground. Around her people were falling to the temple floor. She was exhausted, sweating, and completely sated, more so than ever before in her life.

Pharaoh lay like Osiris, still, arms crossing his chest, his erection reaching toward the sun. RaEm had never seen a more beautiful sight. She needed to be with him, she needed to touch him, to have him touch her.

She needed to become his family; she needed to have this man.

She would.

RaEm walked home at dusk with Wenaten. He was strangely quiet; Cheftu was also silent. "Tell me more of Smenkhare?" RaEm asked.

"No one knows," Wenaten said.

"About?" she prompted.

"More about Smenkhare, save he—"

"Or she," she said, ignoring Cheftu's glance.

"Or she," Wenaten said, "comes from Kush."

"When will Smenkhare arrive?"

"He comes directly here, so perhaps a week. Maybe more or less." They walked the rest of the way to the palace in silence. RaEm didn't notice her surroundings, save to see that Akhenaten had broken Ma'at in art. The figures no longer stood in pure profile, with their faces and bodies perfection. Instead they looked . . . natural, though everyone's face and appearance was like that of her beloved Akhenaten. What magic was this?

Cheftu disappeared into a room, and RaEm pulled Wenaten aside, running her hands over his scrawny shoulders, smiling at him from beneath her lashes. A week, RaEm thought. In ten days can I claim this destiny? "Where would I get a really strong blade?" she asked.

"Why would you need a blade, safely here with Cheftu and me?"

"You know how weak Cheftu is," she said confidingly. "He is the greatest fop alive. Not anything like you." Wenaten squinted at her, not exactly the response she'd hoped for. "Therefore, as a woman alone, it is of great concern to me." She caressed him on the arm as she spoke.

"You aren't alone," he said, placing his hand over hers on his arm. RaEm felt a moment of panic, then relaxed.

"You have a wife, a family, responsibilities," she said. "And I, *aii*, I am not cut out to be anything save first wife."

"Most wives wouldn't care for that," Wenaten said slowly.

Thank the gods, RaEm thought. "You see my confusion? No matter how strong and clever you are, it wouldn't work, alas." She looked away, her face pinched with just enough sorrow at the missed opportunity of taking Wenaten to her couch. "Therefore I must be brave. So where can I get a blade?"

"You aren't alone, because there are soldiers everywhere," Wenaten said. "That is what I meant. Everywhere. You probably can't walk through the garden without stumbling on one."

RaEm wanted to strike him, the dense man. Had he been playing with her? She crossed her arms over her chest. "Where can I get a blade?"

Wenaten shrugged, then referred her to a smithy in the Pelesti quarter. "The Pelesti are the only ones with iron," he said. "But nothing cuts better. Straight through leather, wool, any manner of protection. Bronze doesn't even dull it."

She thanked him, though her words were said to his back since he just walked off. The idiot, she thought, slipping into her room. But he would be a useful idiot; he knew the court, the nobles. She'd have to work on him more, learn about this strange country where even the language sounded a bit different from the Egypt she'd known. Once the door was closed behind her, RaEm bellowed for slaves. She needed a bath, food, and clothing, in that order.

He couldn't resist her; no one ever had.

Cheftu lay on his couch, exhausted but unable to sleep. RaEm was up to something, but he didn't know what and didn't have the energy to ponder the perversions of her mind right now.

What had he seen this afternoon?

Pharaoh leading his people in the mass climax simply by reading to them the words of the 104th Psalm? Where had Pharaoh gotten it? Were the words of David, the author of the Psalms, not original? Had David reworked an old Egyptian hymn? Was it blasphemy even to think such a thing? When was David in relation to this time period? Impossible; David was God's favorite—he couldn't be a thief. Pharaoh must have stolen the words, though where had he gotten them? Cheftu's thoughts had chased each other almost into sleep, when he sat up with a jolt.

He was alone. He could ask the stones! Stumbling from the couch, he walked to the window, letting moonlight shine onto the Urim and Thummim. His hands were trembling as he asked the question most pressing in his mind. "Is Chloe safe?"

"N-o-w."

Now? Did that mean she hadn't been before? Did it mean she wouldn't be in the future?

"Where is she?"

"W-i-t-h D-a-g-o-n."

Dagon? Who was Dagon? Was there a man in court named Dagon? Was he a god? A priest? A country? A ship? "How do I get to her?"

"D-o-n-o-t-w-a-t-c-h-t-h-e-i-d-o-l!"

The idol? "What idol?" Cheftu asked, but the stones lay motionless, mute. Frustrated and exhausted, he put them away. Obviously they had answered all they could, or would, for the day. He'd try again tomorrow.

Tomorrow yielded no answers, or rather, the same answers. Cheftu gritted his teeth as he went through his day. He asked Wenaten if he knew anyone named Dagon. "Sounds like a foreigner to me," Wenaten blustered. Then he edged around questions concerning RaEm. Cheftu recognized the signs: Wenaten was entranced with the time-traveling priestess. Consequently he was no longer trustworthy.

Cheftu should know, since once he had been that bewitched. He'd neglected his responsibilities and ignored his head, listening only to his heart, his lust. When RaEm smiled, it was as if the door to all potential for pleasure cracked open, allowing a glimpse into anything a man could desire.

He'd been a fool. Only Hatshepsut, with her understanding of her friend RaEm and her sympathy for Cheftu—and her irritation at his sloppy execution of his duties—had communicated to him what RaEm was truly like. He'd ignored his liege, only to have his ego trampled, his heart bruised, and his soul screaming "Fool!"

Then he'd listened to Hat. "RaEm is a crocodile," she'd said. "A crocodile has no knowledge of a world outside what it sees. It is not a family animal, nor does it care for the continuation of its dynasty. Its concerns are its belly, its comfort, and nothing else has any significance." Hat had sipped from a golden goblet. "RaEm is a great priestess because her needs are synonymous with HatHor's. She will do anything necessary, even take a life, to maintain her comfort."

"I wanted her to be comfortable," Cheftu had protested. "I would build her a house, on the Nile—" He had fallen silent when Hat raised her hand.

"Comfort for RaEm means not only the ease of her flesh, but a constant source of new conquests."

Cheftu had stiffened. RaEm had gone off with a new "conquest" while a household of guests awaited their marriage ceremony.

"A crocodile," Hat had said, "is interested only in live bait, fresh blood. After the initial kill, the crocodile loses interest. She wants fresher meat." Hat's dark eyes had met his. "One man will never sate RaEm. She must consume what she can, then leave his husk behind her as she moves toward the next, *aii*, kill, shall we say?"

Cheftu's *amour propre* was bent; it hurt worse that RaEm hadn't even paused in her behavior, that he was that insignificant to her. Then he'd realized that while his self-respect was wounded, his heart hadn't been fully engaged.

"You were lucky to escape," Hat had said. "The gods smiled on you." She had set down her goblet and motioned for a slave. "Now be a man, a lord of Egypt, and do as your liege demands. Forget this woman!" Then she had assigned him to the court of Mitanni, to do just that.

Now, however, he recognized the same glazed, crazed look in Wenaten's eyes. The expression that said he would do anything, tell any lie, go to any length, for a smile for RaEm. How was it that she did this to men? After she'd left Cheftu, he'd watched her work her way through the ranks of the army and the court. She was an enchantress, as deadly as any Circe, leaving a swath of broken hearts and mangled men behind her.

She was up to something now. He knew it. He especially knew it when Wenaten coldly refused to answer his questions, denying help to Cheftu in any way. The stones were silent, his host was abrupt. Chloe was not in danger now, but who knew when that circumstance would change? What did the words of the stones mean? "Don't watch the idol?" What idol? How would that help him protect Chloe, get him to her side? Have faith, he admonished himself. *Le bon Dieu* had never failed them. Never.

As the days and weeks passed he didn't see RaEm or Wenaten. Cheftu attended Aten's worship services along with the rest of the populace. He was almost frantic with concern for Chloe, but at a loss as to what to do. Time was moving too fast and too slowly at the same time. The inactivity was about to drive him mad, but his terror of doing something wrong was even stronger.

He was standing on the step to Wenaten's palace home when the door was wrenched open before him. Chaos greeted his gaze: barbers stood at attention, brandishing the tools of their trade; slaves, draped with gold jewelry, held pressed kilts at the ready; women were shrieking for baths, for cosmetics. In the middle stood Wenaten, his shoulders stooped, wringing his hands.

One glance and Cheftu knew that Wenaten had just realized he'd been deceived by RaEm.

"Pharaoh has agreed to see the ambassador!" the housekeeper said breathlessly. "Lady RaEm is missing, I fear."

Cheftu's eyes narrowed. "For how long?"

"I do not know how long he—"

"How long has RaEm been missing?" Cheftu clarified.

The woman shrugged. "Almost a week?"

Cheftu pushed through the slaves, the barbers, and the frantic women. He put a hand on Wenaten's arm. "What happened?"

"She's taken everything," he whispered. "She took my wife's jewelry, she took my family's funerary objects, the ones we'd had made before I left." His tone was dazed, his gaze flat.

She's done worse to better men than you, Cheftu thought. He refrained from saying anything. "We go to court?"

"Aye, aye. Pharaoh will see us now."

Perhaps this was his chance to see Chloe? Was she there, in the power of someone named Dagon? A foreigner? An envoy? "I will escort you," Cheftu said.

Wenaten, still distracted, agreed, allowing Cheftu to take charge of getting everything ready for the presentation.

He was waiting with Wenaten by the time Pharaoh sent a chariot for them. They boarded the vehicle, crammed in behind the driver. Wenaten held on to his wig as they moved up the boulevard.

The ambassador fretted that he hadn't seen his family in two years. He'd not even seen his own father's tomb, for the man had died while he was at sea. Now RaEm had stolen the most valuable things that went into it. Wenaten trembled at the thought of telling his wife her jewelry had been stolen. Cheftu murmured his condolences, wondering who might bear the name Dagon.

The Great State Palace's audience chamber was open to the sun's rays, too, the rays of the Aten. Each little hand pounded on those assembled. Almost every country was represented in Akhenaten's court. Mutterings confirmed that some of these envoys had been waiting for years to meet with Pharaoh. Some had been forbidden to return home without Egyptian escort. Wenaten was right; the empire was slipping away.

The walls of the palace were strange for Egypt. No representations of Pharaoh vanquishing sand crossers, or reigning with the gods. Instead Pharaoh cavorted with his children, his head misshapen, his body curved and full hipped like a woman's. He even had breasts!

Cheftu had to hide his amused surprise when he noticed that most of the courtiers wore padding beneath their kilts to effect Akhenaten's body shape. Flabby bellies hung over long kilts, and stubby false beards imitated Pharaoh's lantern-jawed face. Headclothes were padded to copy Akhenaten's elongated head. The women were emaciated, their breasts flattened to resemble Pharaoh's, their hips draped to resemble the king's, wearing the "Kushite" short wig. Which was which? Men and women were hard to discern. The Egyptian court, male and female, looked like misfits.

All to match the leading misfit, Pharaoh.

"All hail he who speaks to the Aten, he who praises the Aten, he who is one with the Aten, the most high, most glorious, Akhenaten!" the chamberlain cried. Every head touched the floor in obeisance, Cheftu's included.

"Rise, rise." Akhenaten's voice had the power to melt bones. His were the tones of a siren. Listening would be the path to self-destruction, with no remorse. "Speak your business so I can continue the business of praise."

An older man, his kilt and headcloth painfully dated, stood. "My Majesty, I have received more cries from Canaan. The lion Labayu is dead, they say, but a new cub has risen to take his place. They fear—"

"What have they to fear when the Aten loves us and dwells with us? What is fear next to the heat, the power, of the Aten?" Pharaoh's voice was so calming, so melodious, that his insane drivel on the matter of international defense seemed reasonable. Except to an envoy whose people were going to die. Soon.

"My Majesty—"

"Embracing the Aten, melting into his power, the glory of his fire, is the only way battles will truly be won."

The nobleman made several more attempts, but each was interrupted and expanded into a praise of the Aten. The man finally gave up, stiffly bowing his way out.

"Continue," Akhenaten said to the court, the waiting ambassadors and lords whose initial enthusiasm had greatly waned. "Whom did I call on to report to me?"

Wenaten rose, bowing.

"*Haii!* Of course! Wenaten, tell me of your journey! Where are my cedars?" Akhenaten looked around, as though he expected Wenaten to have thrown a few over his shoulder and carried them in.

"*Aii*, My Majesty, they are, unavoidably, delayed."

"How is that? Already you are years late." The peaceful, gentle pharaoh vanished. Akhenaten sat forward, glaring. "I knew you were incompetent!"

"They will be here in three weeks, My Majesty," Wenaten said, though he wasn't cowering as Cheftu would have expected.

"A long time," Pharaoh said curtly.

"Many a setback I encountered," Wenaten said. "All for the love of my country and liege." He bowed.

"Yet you do not return with the gold I sent, or with the cedars for the House of the Rejoicing to the Aten. Why is this?" Pharaoh demanded.

Cheftu found himself under the gaze of penetrating, intensely dark eyes. Pharaoh might be mad, but he was intelligent. Akhenaten's glance moved over Cheftu's body, then returned to Wenaten.

"I left with the blessings of A-Aten," Wenaten said. "It was a simple enough journey, sailing from here to the land of the Pelesti, then on to Tsor for the cedars."

"A simple journey for a simpleton," Akhenaten said, shifting on his throne.

Cheftu's gaze moved over the court, the women. Did he see Chloe? Would he recognize her if he did? He thought he looked the same, but then, he always had. Why was that? Why did she change bodies? RaEm said she was truly red haired and fair skinned. A quick glance showed him that if she were a redhead, she wasn't here.

I will know her, he thought. I will. My bones, my blood, will recognize her. Many a dark-eyed maid met his inquiring gaze, but no green-eyed ones.

"Well, we landed in Ashqelon, and at some point in the night, one of the sailors took the gold you had given us for the lumber," Wenaten continued in his explanation.

"You were robbed by a Pelesti!" Akhenaten roared. "Where is Horemheb? We will sack this ungrateful city—"

"Majesty, Majesty," Wenaten soothed. "It was an Egyptian sailor who stole the gold."

Akhenaten was silent a moment. "You are certain?"

"Quite." Wenaten straightened his kilt and continued his story. "Naturally, I went to the ruler of the city, one Yamir-dagon, demanding to receive my gold back. After all, it was stolen while in a Pelesti harbor."

Dagon! Cheftu's attention was fully captured. Yamir-dagon? Was that where Chloe was? Had he heard correctly?

"I thought you said an Egyptian sailor stole it?"

"He did."

Akhenaten frowned. "Did this Yamir give you the gold?"

"Nay. He said that had a Pelesti done it, he would have compensated me for the loss. As it was, he would help me look for the thief, but he could not pay me back since I was robbed by a kinsmen."

Dagon? Pelesti? Ashqelon? Was that where she was? Cheftu found himself craning forward for more of the story.

"For nine days I tarried there, awaiting news from the ruler of the city about the search for the gold and the thieving sailor. Alas, none came. I prayed for a sign whether to go on or whether to return. That morning, during my prayers, a hawk with three wings flew over my head, then northward."

Cheftu's heart was pounding in his throat. This must be why he'd been rescued by Wenaten! In order to find this *dagon*, this Yamir! When would the audience be over so that he could ask questions? Why had not Wenaten recognized the name *dagon* when Cheftu had asked?

"This seemed a sign to continue onward," Wenaten said. "Since I had the image, the gracious image, My Majesty, of the Aten with me, I knew I would be safe. Perhaps those people who were more civilized in other lands would listen and hear my tale. Perhaps they would be more willing to give credence to me, not to mention extend me credit, if they saw the majesty of the one god."

"But you had no gold." Akhenaten wriggled on the throne. "Because you hired disloyal fools who took it from you."

Wenaten colored but answered only part of the query. "I had no gold, nothing. However, the god provided me a chance, while docked in Yaffo, to regain silver in place of the gold that had been stolen."

Though Cheftu flinched at the idea of stealing, the rest of the court shrugged along. Foreigners were foreigners. Unwashed, uncivilized, uncouth. The god would not condemn a man for taking from a foreigner.

"I arrived in Tsor, that miserable little island kingdom. The king refused to see me. In fact, daily he sent a slave to bid me good journey home. For fifteen days and nights I pleaded with him for an audience. I have come to buy cedar for the god! I say. But will he see me? Nay!" Wenaten shook his head, discouraged.

"Can you blame him?" Pharaoh asked, drawing a titter from the crowd. He was biting, Cheftu thought. What happened to the "love your neighbor" philosophy from a moment before?

"There is no help for it; I load the idol and my belongings to return to Egypt. By this time, since you know I left two months before the flooding, I have less than a month to get home before the winds are impossible and I am stranded with foreigners until spring."

Akhenaten was listening, as was the court.

"The day I am boarding the ship to come home—that very day!— this king sends a man to me, to take me to audience. I remonstrate with the servant, for I am certain he is sent to distract me so they can steal the statue I have and the rest of my meager belongings. I express my concerns, and the king bids the ship to stay in port. When I open audience with the king, who to his own people is Zakar Ba'al, master of all, I ask why he has taken so long and why today, of all days, he has deigned to see me."

Wenaten spoke in a deep voice, imitating Zakar Ba'al. " 'A Canani *tzadik,* a holy man, told me to bring you up here,' he said, gesturing to his palace. It stands on a cliff overlooking the Great Green, which that far north is even greener. The hills of the mainland are covered in cedars, some bigger than an ox is wide, others with no more substance than my arm. He asks abruptly how long I have been gone from Egypt's shores. Five months, I say." Wenaten paused, refreshing himself with a beer.

"I tell him I am anxious to return home. I share with him the curse this journey has been."

Cheftu listened as Wenaten told Pharaoh how Zakar Ba'al had demanded proof of his mission in the form of letters, letters that Wenaten had erroneously left in Egypt for safekeeping. Then the Tsori king had derided Egyptian seamanship. "He told me of two Egyptian envoys who had traveled to see him years before, told me he could show me their graves. I was sore afraid. I begged him, on the basis of honor, integrity, a worshipful heart, honesty, graciousness, hospitality, all of these things, to let me have the cedars for the house of the god."

Wenaten looked down, shoulders sagging. "Alas, only when I mentioned returning and sending ships back filled with the fripperies he deemed important, did he reason with me."

Akhenaten's nostrils flared in anger, but he gestured for Wenaten to continue. After a moment Wenaten told how he had set sail from Tsor, but the ship had been wrecked on the isle of the Kefti.

Akhenaten suddenly rose, cocked his head, and left the room. No words, no dismissal, nothing. The crowd hurriedly dropped to their faces until the door slammed shut.

Cheftu leaned against a shaded column, listening to the envoys and the nobles pour out frustration over the situation, waiting for Wenaten to finish talking to the scribe. According to the gossip in this chamber, whole sections of the country were without food—the local priesthood had been disbanded—leaving too many fields for the small villages to harvest. Yet now the villagers had new shrines to the Aten and new priests who demanded their attendance. Priest-soldiers, a new invention of Pharaoh, searched the peasants' homes, to check and see if any other gods or goddesses were being honored. The penalty could range from slavery to death.

In similar circumstances France had revolted against her king, eliminated the aristocracy, and made men equal.

The Egyptians had no concept of equality, nor did they have the rigid social structure of eighteenth-century France. One thing was immutable, though: Theology told them Pharaoh was king, the god divine; to go against his word was to break the balance of Ma'at.

Cheftu's heart grew heavy; Egypt was dying. Neglect was as certain an assassin as invasion—perhaps more devastating because it also tore at the soul of the country. The people's faith in their gods, their king, was put to the test.

Cheftu feared Akhenaten was failing that test. He was assisting in the destruction of his people, just as surely as if he ripped their beating hearts from their chests. How Hatshepsut would mourn if she knew.

They were ushered out of the room like so much cattle, then herded to the walkway to the Temple of the Rising of the Aten, with no chance of independent thought or action. Despite the heat and his concerns about Egypt, his heart felt lighter. Soon he would talk to Wenaten, find out more about this *dagon*, where he was, how to get there. Chloe, I come for you, he thought.

Perhaps the "follow" was to follow Wenaten's original journey and sail for Tsor?

Once they were inside the temple, joining thousands upon thousands of people, soldier-priests closed the doors. They were trapped in the heat of the afternoon to worship. Egyptian and foreigner alike raised their bared heads to the sun in adoration until dusk.

Cheftu stared into the sun, closing his eyes when they began to burn. His thoughts were on Chloe, lulled by Akhenaten's remarkable voice intoning the wonders of peace, love, and the power of the sun.

Hands grabbed him, while another hand muffled his protests. Cheftu was dragged backward through the crowd, the people parting to make way for him, never glancing at him. He was thrown into a pit, the sun blazing on him, beating off the walls of the enclosure, scorching his feet through his new sandals.

"Who are you?" a voice asked. Cheftu looked up but could see noth-

ing besides the glare of the Aten. Two figures stood at the edge of the
pit, visible only in silhouette.

"Ch-Chavsha, scribe of Wenaten," he responded quickly. It
wouldn't do to give these men his real name. With one's actual name,
evil could be wrought. This was as true in France as it was in Egypt.

"You closed your eyes to the glory of the Aten," the other man said.
"You have broken the law."

It was against the law to close one's eyes? "I did not want to go
blind," Cheftu said. "I was merely . . . taking a while to blink."

"Blindness gives us true sight," the first man said. "Only when we
are not distracted by vision do we see what we really are, what we really
have. Blindness is a gift of the Aten."

Cheftu was speechless. They *wanted* him to go blind? Staring up at
them this way, he might be able to grant their wish, and soon. Sweat
trickled down Cheftu's back, sticking clothing to skin. "Your penalty is
to worship from now until you are freed. Close your eyes for more than
a moment and we will remove them. Blindness brings true clarity."

Sweet Isis, Cheftu thought. Someone, help me.

THE PALACE OF TSOR STOOD ON A wave-washed hill, tiers of stairs linking
the white cubed blocks together. Atop the mass was an enormous mosaic floor, sometimes sheltered, other times not. Banners of a blue so vibrant that it hurt the viewers' eyes waved in the wild winds above the
crenellated walls.

Below the floor, whose curious tiled figures rotated in a twelve-part
circle, were chambers and hallways, staircases and lightwells. Men and
women lived here: women who wove and men who sailed.

The lower floors were partitioned into audience halls and gathering
chambers. The walls were plain, only inlaid with seashells or washed

with color. Outside the many squared-off doors were gardens with cedars and bougainvillea growing side by side. In the waters beside the gardens, dozens, hundreds, sometimes thousands of ships anchored. The dock ran the length of the island; in fact, the dock was the island. The only part that was not dock was palace.

On the island of Tsor there was no need for family housing. Each man was gone the six sailing months of the year, each woman spun and wove for six; then together they walked to the lowest level of the palace, the pits, and dyed for the winter six.

It was said that even the sea in Tsor was a darker blue.

On the mainland, the residents lived in carved-out caves overshadowed by trees that grew so tall, they almost blocked out the sun. The men there were craftsmen, whittling at wood to shape the winged lions Zakar Ba'al, the master of Tsor, so greatly loved.

They carved Ashterty trees, symbols of the goddess's fertility. They built temples far and wide. Each three-chambered building was hewn of wood already prepared in Tsor, then attached to the local stone with the master's *shamir*—a wondrous, magical tool—in a soundless, scarless fashion. Only those sworn to the secrecy of being a *mnason* could learn the master's powers of pouring rock, shaping stone, and transforming. The others were carpenters, hewing the wood and never setting sail. In Tsor, each person wanted to own himself fully.

It was a goal they all sought. The women worked, as women always do, maintaining the home, rearing the children: however, these women were also merchants. As a body they had called on the master, petitioning that his sailors trade for food with homegrown delicacies: a drink made from pine needles; the nuts from the inside of a pinecone; their embroidered, dyed cloths; and orphaned children, to the many courts and ports the sailors visited.

The Tsori were a wealthy, wealthy people because of this merchandising. Zakar Ba'al was not alone in dining on gold plates, drinking wine from across the Sea, or playing dice with ivory-and-jade play pieces.

The master fingered his playing pieces meditatively, staring from the island to the mainland. The coast was rugged and beautiful, the sea a shade of blue matched only in Tsori cloth. Trees and mountains, these with no fire, no molten lava, rose in the distance. Zakar Ba'al looked away, bored.

He had two pathways leading from the splendors of Egypt, Kush and the jungles beyond, to the great civilizations north, Mitanni, Hattai, and hundred-gated Assyria. Beyond Assyria were the wonders of the East, with their elephants, slant-eyed men, and curiously spicy food.

One of the pathways was via the sea. Sail south to Qiselee, Yaffo, Ashdod, Ashqelon, the Delta of Egypt, then through the throat of the Nile, to Noph, Waset, Simbel, Kush . . . then beyond.

Or he could send a caravan of donkeys north, up through the Arava, mounting the hills to walk on the King's Highway all the way to Assyria.

Both thoroughfares were now blocked. Soon his people would be hungry, for the Tsori were not farmers; they traded for their foodstuffs.

Tsidoni, the imbeciles, had declared war on Tsori ships. Already the master had lost a handful of vessels. There was no way to sail south without passing Ako, a Tsidoni port. Since Tsor wasn't a battling country, she had no army. Retreat was the sole option.

Then the King's Highway, his back door of security, had been breached. Some new power prowled Canaan's hills. A monarch unwilling to share in profit.

That king just hasn't been properly approached, the Zakar Ba'al thought. No one refused him.

Then the years fell away, hundreds and hundreds of years, a millennium. One face remained forever etched in his memory. Once he had been refused, before he wore the name Hiram Zakar Ba'al, Shiva, Thor, or Dionysus. Only one man had he longed for, had he sought after to no avail. Only one man had been his equal. He had loved that way just once, giving his best, granting immortality, then letting the object of his passions leave him.

The one man he'd wanted and never known.

Cheftu sa'a Khamese. The Egyptian.

CHEFTU WANTED TO WEEP WITH RELIEF when the sun finally left the sky. His head was throbbing, he was nauseated, and the spots before his eyes concerned him. He would not last many more days of this. Not survive and keep his eyesight.

How to escape? Had anyone noticed he was missing? Wenaten probably wouldn't notice if his own body were missing, much less Cheftu's.

The temple complex all but shut down with the setting of the sun; he'd had three days to observe it. The priests bade each other good night and left. A closed temple was something he'd never seen in the courts of Amun-Ra. However, he was beginning to believe that most of this was behavior he'd never seen in the courts of Amun-Ra. When had the Egyptian religion and its practices changed from being a personal choice to being a law? What perversion of faith was this?

His eyes burned, his stomach cramped, and Cheftu wondered what he could do. Right now it was dark, so he couldn't even see the stones to learn what the future held. Leaning against the cooling wall of the pit, he closed his eyes. He would rest for a moment.

"Chavsha?" a whisper woke him.

As he opened his eyes, the memory of the past three days engulfed him. Fighting the panic in his throat, he remained motionless.

"Chavsha?" It was Wenaten's voice. "Are you there?"

"Aye," he said. Cheftu heard rustling, then felt a rope hit him on the head.

"Climb quickly. Guards will be reporting for duty in moments."

Though he was weak from hunger and heat, the very thought of being free was icy water to his soul. He jumped for the rope, checked the anchor, then pulled himself up, using the wall to speed him.

Hands, hard with calluses, grabbed his arms, hauled him over the edge; Wenaten had assistance. Cheftu couldn't see the face of his rescuer. "My undying gratitude," he said in a rush. "I am indebted to you."

"Flee now. You will become a wanted man," Wenaten said. "Egypt is not safe for you."

"Can't I hide here?" Cheftu asked. He had no valuables, no way to buy passage anywhere. He needed to check with the stones, be certain Chloe wasn't here. Or was this what he was supposed to follow?

"Nay, everyone will be looking for you. You didn't watch the sun, you turned away."

Don't watch the idol, the stones had said. The idol was the sun! "Where was Yamir-dagon?" Cheftu asked. "Tell me that."

"With the Pelesti. Go now."

"Thank you," Cheftu said again. "If I can—"

The voice cut him off. "You did, by getting me home." Wenaten gripped his shoulder. Cheftu winced as his burned skin was pressed. "No more. Go!"

Adrenaline cleared Cheftu's head as he slipped into the shadows, careful to keep an eye on the street and the *tenemos* walls of the temple. If Akhetaten was built like any other Egyptian city, the Way of the Nobles would be the large houses right on the edge of the Nile. The river was his thoroughfare out of here. Once on the other side, or on a boat, he would ask the stones how to get to Chloe. Whom or what he should follow.

Carefully he picked his way from black shadow to gray shade, for it was a full moon. Finally he stood on the dock alone. No sailors loitered around, lousy with beer. People weren't allowed on the streets after dark, for to spend time in darkness was perceived as embracing the enemy of the Aten. At the Nile's edge were boats, some awaiting a boatwright's attention, some already repaired, all bobbing in the shallow water. He slipped the stones from his sash and tossed them. "Where is Chloe?"

"G-o."

"Is she here?" he asked them, squinting to see the letters through his sore eyes.

"G-o."

"Am I going to get any other answers?" he asked angrily.

"G-o-n-o-w."

He put them back in his sash. Gritting his teeth against the necessity of stealing, Cheftu selected the smallest of the rowboats and stepped in.

Fumbling for oars at the bottom, he pushed away from shore and paddled like a madman to get away from the city before the break of dawn. He would never return to this cursed place where the prayers of God were used in manipulation of a people. Pharaoh cared nothing for the land.

As the muscles in his shoulders pulled, as his eyes teared in the dawn, as his skin burned in the morning light, he knew it didn't matter. He was leaving Egypt. Chloe was waiting for him.

He abandoned the skiff on the eastern side of the Nile, just south of Khumnu, the Middle Kingdom capital of the Hare Nome. The town had been mostly abandoned. The temple of Thoth was closed off. Even this far north Cheftu saw the stele of Akhenaten, marking the border of Akhetaten. Uncertain if priest-soldiers would be tracking him, Cheftu walked into the desert, then doubled back. For the night's stay and three days' provisions he fell back on his skills as a physician and delivered a baby. It was a boy child, whom they wanted to name after him. Impulsively Cheftu gave them the name Nacht-met. It was a good, solid name meaning "One who could see" and was completely unlinked with him. He could leave no tracks.

Cheftu walked out of town as the women of the village were tying amulets onto the infant's arms, protecting him against the many evils in the air, the night, and the water.

Those provisions kept Cheftu as he walked next to the Nile, through field after field, north. The stones were silent; all he had to go on was *dagon* and Pelesti. He walked onward. Priest-soldiers sailed up and down the river, harassing fishermen, stopping in villages to be certain the temples were closed, that only the Aten was being worshiped.

In Akoris he heard rumors of a dangerous felon who had fled Akhetaten. Cheftu was shaken to hear his own description given, quite accurately.

That night, under the cover of darkness, he crept to the ruined step pyramid where a wisewoman was rumored to dwell. From her, for the price of clearing away the mouth to a cave, he bought a drug that would disguise his appearance. Then he continued north.

In Per Medjet, where fish were worshiped in addition to the Aten, he sewed up a barber's daughter's flesh wound in exchange for provisions, a homespun kilt, and skin-darkening paste to protect against further sunburn as well as misrepresent his appearance.

The man who entered the streets of Noph was vastly different from the one who had crept out of the streets of Akhenaten. The sun—and dye—had blackened his skin, his head was bare, his long hair shaved off and burned to ash somewhere in the desert. He wore a small goatee and mustache. However, the pièce de résistance was his eyes.

Belladonna, purchased from the wisewoman, both protected his vision from the Aten's punishing rays and dilated his pupils so much that the amber color of his irises was hidden.

Cheftu didn't recognize himself when he went to the temple; his only fear was that Chloe wouldn't, either. Was she here? Still the stones said, "G-o." A quick but necessary sacrifice to the Aten, then he would find his way farther north by ship.

Due to great rejoicing throughout the kingdom, however, no ships were sailing. Smenkhare had arrived. In celebration, Egypt's remaining stores of food would be open to the people for three days of rejoicing that Pharaoh's brother—or cousin, no one was sure—had safely joined the court.

For three days Cheftu sought passage north. A letter of passage from the petitioner's local temple of the Aten was required for anyone seeking to leave Egypt. At first it seemed simple enough. Then he asked around, loosened tongues with beer, and learned that these letters were written on a special type of papyrus. A fraud would be recognized immediately.

Cheftu cursed. Every night he rolled the stones. Go, go, go, they said. "I am trying!" he protested, frustrated. The streets were alive with tales about how Smenkhare had arrived.

Some said she'd sailed up the Nile in a golden ship and was built like the old Nile god with both breasts and phallus. Others said he had appeared from the desert horizon, as fragile as mist with an entourage of children. Everyone believed she was an incarnation of the goddess, any goddess, come to woo Egypt back from the sole control of the Aten. Having been Egyptian, Cheftu understood that just because they thought Smenkhare was male did not mean he could not also be a goddess. That anyone would be ruling Egypt instead of that siren-voiced misfit was cause for rejoicing!

Did Akhenaten realize nothing of his land? Cheftu wondered as he mixed with the crowds, trying to find someone to sail him to the Great Green. Determined to get to Chloe, he bought provisions at the cost of an entire family's cataract removals, then joined the merchants' roads toward Canaan. Once across the wadi of Egypt, he would buy or barter passage to the Pelesti.

He was on the third night of his journey through the sands when brigands set upon him. He didn't hear them, didn't see them, but once they were present, he smelled them. They lived with goats. They tore through his tent for gold, for jewels, furious that he had no wealth to easily trade, so they ate his food instead.

Cheftu didn't recognize their dialect, but one of them wanted to kill him. Fortunately the one holding the knife to his throat was more reasonable. They shackled him, then threw him on the sandy floor of his tent while they looked for something else to take or destroy.

The stones! He had to hide them! But where? If they took his clothing, they would find the stones. He had no pouch, no secret location. Burying them in the sands here would be to lose them and their wisdom. He'd never find Chloe.

Could he swallow them? They were too large; he would kill himself that way. That was to say nothing of how they would have to be retrieved.

Un moment . . . Though it was distasteful, it might work.

The shackles afforded him a lot of flexibility.

When the brigands came to drag him to the rest of their captives, Cheftu was stripped bare. With quick movements they pierced his ears in the cartilage above the lobe, chaining him through those holes. Marking him forever as a slave.

They marched north.

PART

II

CHAPTER 4

A SHQELON WAS BEING OBSERVED: not overtly, but definitely someone was eyeballing us. I'd never lived in a war zone or been in danger of invasion before. The highlanders—as the Pelesti called the Israelis, or Israelites, or Jews, or whatever—roamed the perimeters of the territory. We were under surveillance.

Creepy.

Wadia, Takala, and Yamir were in discussion with the *serenim* of the city. Like most significant business, this took place at the city gates.

They weren't gates that you opened and closed, but rather rooms built into each side of a massive switchback doorway. The actual entrance was narrow, hardly the space a man and donkey needed, and definitely not wide enough for a division to invade. Soldiers stood on either side, carefully monitoring those who came and went. The Pelesti were on alert, protecting their families, their livelihoods, and their fields.

They were no different from any other people at any other time, really.

I was waiting in the opposite chamber from where the discussions were taking place. Why was I here? Being a goddess was growing old.

I couldn't go anywhere alone, I couldn't leave the city, and every action brought a wealth of questions.

Unlike my concept of how you would treat a god who lived down the street—i.e., sending flowers, candy, and poetry so she wouldn't strike you dead, then trying to stay out of her way as much as possible—they regarded me as an encyclopedia on the divine. And on almost everything else.

Movement on the far hills caught my eye. The common understanding was that the highlanders would not attack on the plains. As long as the Pelesti stayed where they were, the city and its nearby fields, they would be fine. However, at some undefined time in the spring, battle would be engaged.

After all, it was *spring*. These people couldn't just dance around a pole and fool around in the bushes like the rest of us; no, they had to go to war.

The really sobering thought was that if the leader of those highlanders was David, the sweet psalmist of Israel I'd heard so much about, then I was backing the wrong horse. The wrong horse and chariot.

How was I supposed to get out of this alive?

A ruckus outside drew my attention, so that I caught the very end of the epithet "—always have before!"

"Well, not while I have been on duty," the Pelesti soldier said.

He was denying entry to this particular group of people, apparently. I looked beyond, instantly repelled. Men and women, shackled to each other, burned and peeling, stood in the shadow of the crenellated wall. They were slaves, immediately identifiable by the chains that ran through their upper ears. One yank and yeow!

My ears ached in sympathy.

"Sea-Mistress," the guard said, seeing me. "Please, cast your eyes not on these unclean and unfortunate creatures." He looked upset to see me there. "This man has been reprimanded for petitioning *ha Hamishah*, the five Pelesti cities of the plain." He looked back at the trader, a thin man with greasy skin and grime-encrusted cloak.

He wasn't recognizable as any particular race, other than maybe the fraternity of crooks and two-legged roaches. The guard told him again to leave, that he wouldn't be admitted. I looked back over the people, probably thirty in all, who were panting, sweating, and sunburned. They must have come through the desert, because the weather on the seaboard was balmy and beautiful.

One of the men was helping a young woman. She was pregnant, her belly swollen, though the rest of her was rail thin. He dabbed at her forehead, whispered to her. Was he her husband?

He looked up, straight at me, as though he felt my gaze.

No, Chloe, he's not her husband.

He's yours.

"Do you see something you like, Sea-Mistress?" the slimy trader asked. I couldn't look away. That was Cheftu: filthy, skinny, sunburned, and bearded, but it was Cheftu. My chest ached with the strength of my heart's pounding.

I was a late-twentieth-century American—slavery was only a theory to me. I'd grown up with servants all my life as part of the diplomatic package for living in other countries, but they weren't slaves. Waking up in Egypt, I'd stepped into a world of slaves, but I'd always tried to treat them with respect. Especially since in the two ancient cultures I'd been in, slavery was more of a class rank. No one human owned another human in the fashion of plantations; in ancient times the slaves had simply been the lowest class of society.

"Go on, leave this place," the guard said to the trader. "Quit bothering the goddess with your questions."

"I see her eyes," the trader said. He turned and looked at the group. They were slightly better than a chain of skeletons. "A young lady, perhaps? To fan you and ease the heat of these sultry nights?"

My glance, I hoped, was vicious. Cheftu had turned back to help the young woman; didn't he recognize me? "That man. How much?" The words coated my tongue like bile. How could I even ask?

"*Aii*, the young man?"

Did he have more than one? "The one with that girl."

"*Aii*, my apology, Sea-Mistress, but he is her husband."

For a moment my vision went snow white. Her husband? I dug my fingernails into my palm; chill, Chloe. You know that is impossible.

The trader pointed to a small boy, probably not more than four, who was standing in the shade, docile and healthy. "That is one of his, a good boy. I really can't let such a profitable stud go at the price of an ordinary male slave."

"He's the, the father?" I stuttered out, livid at how this piece of trash was lying. About *my* husband?

"Aye. Breeds them strong."

Turning to the guard, I excused him back to his duties. Though it repelled me, I took the slimy trader's arm, breathing through my mouth as I smiled at him. "As a goddess, I have need of a stud from time to time," I said. "However, I would need to know if such a one were worthy of my attention." I paused a moment, pressing my breast into his arm. "And my coin." I wondered if the Pelesti had coins.

His eyes narrowed to slits. "You honor me with your patronage," he said. "If you were to, say, need an inspection in private, for an afternoon or so—"

"An afternoon-long inspection will not make this sale," I said. "Give me a day with him."

"A day?" he repeated, his eyes open again.

"*Ken.* Should he please me, I will take his wife and child also. One would abhor his being lonely." *C'mon, you weasel, for the cost of one day you stand to make three sales!* I had no idea where I would find the money or what form of currency these people had, but it didn't matter. Cheftu, Cheftu alone mattered.

The trader bowed. "Where shall I send him?"

Send him? I want him now! "*HaDerkato*," one of the priests called from the gate's room, "we await your judgment."

I looked back at the trader. "We make deliveries," he said. "It would give me a chance to clean and shave him."

I glanced over at Cheftu, who was still focused on the woman. He hadn't looked up once. He was so thin, so beat-up. "If there is one more mark on him, even a feather's mark, I will have your head," I said. "He is mine."

The trader bowed his head quickly. How could I be sure he wouldn't vanish, taking Cheftu with him? With trembling hands I took off my earrings, stones of some sort with gold wiring. "This is a down payment."

He bowed from his waist, taking my jewelry in his dirty palm. I stepped backward, unwilling to look away from Cheftu. Would he still be here? I called the guard. "Under no circumstances, even if the high-landers pour from the hills like water, under no circumstances is this trader and his"—I choked on the word—"merchandise, to leave."

The guard watched me solemnly. I looked in his brown eyes. "Swear to me."

"By Ba'al," he said, nervous.

"It's your head if they aren't there when I get back," I said. The priest had been calling for me. Now he came up to me, irritation on his face. "I'm coming," I said, then followed him through the gate and into the room.

Please let Cheftu still be there, I thought. Please, please, please. Though I was trembling, fighting the urge to attack Cheftu here and now, despite any possible consequences, I had walked away. Tell me that was the right thing to do?

EGYPT

RaEm stretched, feeling the aches and pains of Akhenaten's lovemak-ing as he whispered in her ear. "You satisfy me, sister-brother Smenkhare. Open for me again."

For a moment RaEm considered telling him she was exhausted, sore, that she wanted a bath and food. However, he was Pharaoh. He could give her all the power and gold she had ever dreamed of. He would continue to worship her with his body, speak to her in his voice, if only she never said no.

Though her arms throbbed, she rose up. He filled her instantly, fully, his hands tight on her waist, his nails digging into the bruised skin of her belly. The greater his tension grew, the harder he moved in-side her. Tears streamed from her eyes as pleasure became pain. "I adore you," he panted in a voice that brought her physical pleasure. "I love that you appear beside me as a man. But," he said, emphasizing each word by striking her bottom, "I love that in my couch I rule you as a man."

The royal seed rushed through her, finding no home, no possibility of life. Akhenaten crushed down on her, instantly asleep, his handmarks on her body, her blood on his. She looked through the fence of his arms to the cartouche on his chair, the gold walls of his chamber, the linens so sheer they were as mist, and finally the crown of Pharaoh at war. The blue crown.

She would wear that. She, RaEmhetepet, whose parents had never known her; whose sister-priestesses had never liked her; whose lovers had never sated her; she would rule Egypt.

Akhenaten snored in her ear as his flaccid penis finally slipped from her body. She was right where she wanted to be: touched by this man, trusted by him. She would rule Akhenaten by the very crook and flail he had used to rule her. All it would take was time.

TIME WAS A COMMODITY Zakar Ba'al never lacked. He could take what he wanted, he could wait out anything, for time was eternally his to manipulate. Others were not so fortunate, which was why the Tsori would one day rule the seas and the land.

Zakar Ba'al didn't do it for the gold, the spices, or the minerals, but rather because it broke the monotony. He'd realized hundreds of years ago that when there was no sense of urgency, much of the sweetness of living was missing. He'd probably spent a lifetime or two chewing poppy pods, until even that state grew tedious.

Power was the only constant. Those who knew their time was limited fought him, and in that battle of wits, or brawn, or weaponry,

Zakar Ba'al drained the life from them, slurped from their bowl of enthusiasm, then threw away the husk.

A new challenge had arisen. A bold young man who was both poet and warrior thought to rule over the Way of the kings. Abdiheba, the doddering idiot, was shaking in his Tsori-dyed shoes, pleading with anyone to come vanquish this threat.

Zakar Ba'al smiled. He would present himself, but he would do it solely for the pleasure of watching youth and guile outwit the old paranoid sheep stumper. As always, Zakar Ba'al wondered where Cheftu was. They should have crossed paths at least a hundred times in the past thousand years; Cheftu could not be dead, for no wise-woman had ever found his soul among the shades.

It was a mystery, the only mystery that Zakar Ba'al hadn't unraveled. He turned to the ship's captain, who stood at his elbow. The light of dawn rose from behind the honeycombed hills of Tsor. Dion longed for change, for vitality, for something and someone to stimulate his brain and will, to challenge him.

What was the gift of immortality without the desire to live?

He gestured, the captain shouted, the ship set sail.

Let me live fully or kill me, Dion asked the gods.

I WAS NERVOUS. Cheftu was standing just the other side of the curtain—Cheftu, who was my dearest friend, my companion, and the lover who lived in my very soul.

My gaze flickered back to my image in the water mirror. He'd never seen me this way. I was tall and pale, and my green sheath made my eyes greener. Kohl rimmed them, and I'd stained my lips with pomegranate juice. The round neck of the dress was reemphasized with a gold necklace. I wore matching drop earrings. A headband of green, gold, and brown held back my straight, copper-colored hair.

My hands began to tremble when I heard Tamera's voice. "Sea-Mistress, your slave awaits."

I could barely croak out a response. Instinctively I moved between two of the lamps. I would have the advantage, make absolutely positive it was Cheftu. My blood recognized him even as it careened through my body; I just wanted to verify it with my brain.

Suddenly he was standing before me, so proud and beautiful that I wanted to weep. He said nothing, looked at nothing in particular, merely stood there. My gaze caressed the muscles of his shoulders where they knit together over bone, the cords of veins that ran up his arms from his beautiful hands.

Tomorrow I was going to paint his hands—I'd been planning on doing it for two years!

His stomach was hollowed out, the lines of his ribs showing through. My poor beloved had been starved. His gaze remained fixed on my knee, or the lamp, or something low. I was panting; it seemed an eternity had passed in these short moments. Was I scared?

Well, yeah. He'd never seen me in this body before. He'd never been a slave before. Would he believe it was me? Stupid thoughts, but niggling. What could I say? What could I do? I felt my eyes welling with tears. "Ch-Cheftu?" I whispered, stepping forward.

His face went slack when he heard my voice, his eyes snapped to mine. *"Mon Dieu,"* he whispered, wide-eyed as he looked me over from head to toes. "Chloe?"

I nodded, unable to step forward, shaking.

He dropped to his knees. *"Grâce à Dieu,"* he whispered, hands upraised. Then I was in his arms, learning again what my body seemed to know but my mind and heart so quickly forgot: the heat, the passion, the homecoming of being within his scent, his touch, his taste.

My heart unlocked, freeing all the thoughts and fears and emotions I'd held in such check. It was a wonder to hold him, to feel his heart beating against mine, the heat of his blood beneath my hands. We stood, locked together, reacquainting ourselves with the feeling of the other person.

His hands were trembling also; he too was panting. "I feared," he said, "I didn't know—"

I pulled back, turning his face toward me. His amber eyes were liquid. "It's okay," I said in English. "We're together."

He closed his eyes as tears ran down his cheeks. *"Grâce à Dieu,"* he whispered again and again in my hair. When our bodies steadied, we pulled back to look at each other again. His gaze traveled over my hair, my face; he touched my cheek and ear with his finger. "You are beautiful," he said. "How I have missed seeing your pretty face."

My smile was melted by his kiss. I didn't know to whom the tears I tasted belonged as we clung together. His hands moved gently in my hair as my hands touched his back, feeling the scabbed whip marks, the line of his ribs. He pulled me closer, so that I felt the jut of his hipbones, the need of his body. I held him close, the ribbed edges of his abdomen inside my elbows, my hands gripping his narrow waist as he pressed into me, groaning against my mouth.

I don't know what language I spoke, but I know the gist of it. Yes. Yes. Yes.

The slide of flesh on flesh, the wonder of it, brought me both extreme pleasure and tore me into tears. Cheftu held me, caressing my hair, kissing my eyelids, my cheeks, my mouth, telling me the many ways he loved me. Telling me how he had ached for me, wept for me, prayed for me.

He called out for me, his hands in my hair, his forehead against mine, as we climaxed together. Unwilling to move, he cradled me against his chest as our breathing returned to normal.

The lamps had burned out, and the sky was still dark. We had fallen asleep. I kissed his chest, just as a confirmation that I could. He caught me tightly against him, shaking suddenly as though he were being chased by demons.

I lay quiescent, reveling in his touch. Slowly he calmed down, his grip loosened, and I wriggled my way to his face. "Tell me," I said.

"Are you going to purchase me, Sea-Mistress?" he asked, his eyes smiling in the faint light from the windows.

"Well," I said, tracing the lines of his nose and cheeks, "you do seem to have many talents."

His face became somber, his voice tender. "I had not dared believe this day would come," he said. "When the brigands took me, I feared never to see you again. I thought I had erred and the capture was my discipline."

It hurt me to think of all he had suffered. The lines on his back would remain imprinted on my palms forever. "What were your thoughts coming here, to the temple?"

"I had none," he said. "I knew I wouldn't be able to please another woman. I just hoped that whoever this goddess was that she needed me to garden for her instead." He focused on me again. "Thank God you are here, *chérie.* Thank you, God," he said, pulling my mouth to his.

We loved each other slowly, exploring, talking, remembering, discovering, sometimes just staring at each other. Finally we collapsed in sleep, peacefully unconscious until Tamera shouted to another slave, "I will see what the sea-mistress advises."

I woke up with a jolt, my heart pounding. Cheftu slept on, snoring softly. In moments I was dressed. The sheath was crumpled, my hair bedraggled, but I rinsed my face, donned my jewelry, and covered up the gorgeous body of my husband.

My husband. Here. I giggled to myself. God had brought us together, again. Now all we had to do was blow this Popsicle stand!

Tamera awaited me in the hallway. Her face was pinched. "Yamir has chosen to lead a group of warriors into the Refa'im valley. Takala wants your presence on the battlefield. You are the *teraphim.*"

I opened my mouth, but she continued speaking. "Also, the trader outside the city walls is causing quite a fuss, claiming that you have bought the male slave, plus his wife, his son, his four daughters, his mother, and her slave."

"A slave with a slave?" I said.

She shrugged. "He is Amaleki."

That explained everything? I closed the door behind me, speaking to Tamera in a normal voice. "Pay the trader for everyone," I said. "Then free them."

She frowned at me. Was there a problem? Did I not have money?

"Ken?" I prompted her.

"What is 'free them'?" she asked as we walked into the main chamber to greet Dagon.

"What is the opposite of being a slave?" I asked, trying a different angle.

"To be a landowner," she said, assisting me with my fish cloak. The other priestesses came in, greeted us, and left again.

Slave or landowner? I rubbed my face with my hand. I didn't know how to communicate my concept, so I'd settle the immediate problem. "Buy the slaves. Can you do that?"

She nodded as we entered to sing the god awake.

After the morning prayers Tamera asked if I needed anything else. After ordering a seafood breakfast for two, I dismissed her and returned to Cheftu.

As I stepped back into the room, I saw that Cheftu was up and dressed, his hair slicked back with water, revealing his mutilated ears. "Does it hurt?" I asked, pointing to the chain.

He shrugged. "No more than not having one's freedom."

"It doesn't matter. You're here. We'll be leaving soon."

Cheftu looked at me, then slowly crossed his arms. "Going where?" I opened my mouth to answer, but he continued speaking. "Chloe, I have been marked a slave for life. I was purchased to be your slave. This is not our world, one cannot change this."

"It won't matter once we're out of here."

He crossed to me, gently taking my hands in his. I was getting a very bad feeling; he was way too resigned. So I started babbling. "It will be easy. I've been given all these gifts, all we have to do is get out of the city, then hop a ship—somewhere. We can be free, we can be together—"

He laid a finger on my lips, silencing me. "What are you here?"

I glanced away, a little embarrassed. "The local goddess."

"You think they will let you just walk away?"

"I don't care what they want. I came back after you. I have you. Now—"

"Do you think you are here solely for—"

Tamera opened the door, directing slaves to set the food on the low table, then shooing them out. Her gaze moved from me to Cheftu, then she squared her shoulders. "Takala wants you in her audience chamber right now."

We had plans to make; I didn't have time to wait on Takala. My short-lived job as goddess was drawing to a close. I needed some more time with Cheftu. "She must come here," I said, stalling.

Tamera ducked her head. "As you will it, Sea-Mistress. The king Yamir-dagon has gone into battle, I just learned."

Spring had arrived. "When did they leave?"

"The division left for the Refa'im valley at the second watch, Sea-Mistress."

"I need a bath before I can do anything," I said, buying more time.

Tamera's gaze was measured. I was certainly being more abrupt with her than ever before. Did she know what I was thinking? "I will hurry with the water."

Cheftu chuckled when the door closed. "Keeping noble company these days?"

I kissed his shoulder. "Forget that. What is our plan?"

"Look at my ears, *chérie*. I am slave in this time."

"Well—can't I just travel with you as your, your owner?"

His face changed subtly, hardening. "You aren't a slave to me," I whispered. "This just seems so unbelievable, I—" As I spoke, my fingers found the rips in his skin. It *was* believable; he had been beaten. He had been wounded. He had been treated as a slave. "To me you are my beloved, my equal, my partner, my lover, my best friend."

"*Merci*," he said quietly.

The slaves brought in a tub, and we washed quickly, silently. "We need to leave," I said again.

He looked at me. "You aren't here for me alone."

"Well, who else am I chasing through time?" I asked, suddenly tense. "You are being far too accepting of this unacceptable situation!" I gripped his forearms. "Why are you giving in so easily?" He stared at me, his gaze unreadable. "Don't you want to be with me?" I asked in a scared whisper. I thought I knew the answer, but also I would have never guessed that he would react this way. He was so . . . passive.

"Where is she?" Takala's voice boomed from outside. We sprang apart, throwing on clothes. I had just gotten a comb through my hair when Tamera announced Takala was here.

"There you are!" she said, wheezing up to me in the corridor. "What kind of goddess are you? We need you on the battlefield immediately!"

I looked at her face. Her makeup had been applied with a heavy hand, but her eyes were rheumy, shadowed. As bossy as she could be, she was also a loving mother and good queen. For a moment I felt guilty, since my plan was to bug out ASAP. She stared at me, her eyes piercing through me. She shifted her gaze for a moment to Cheftu, and I knew she realized what he was to me. With a gesture she dismissed everyone.

"Who are they against?" I finally asked. I didn't want to know. I wanted to leave. I had my husband. I had my own body, surely there was somewhere we could go and live happily ever after? Wasn't the third time the charm?

Takala sighed deeply, the chains and fetishes around her neck shimmering and jingling with the movement. "The highlanders. They are planning to take the city of Jebus."

"Jebus?" The name was vaguely familiar; where had I heard it? "What do the Jebusi have to do with you. Us?"

"Abdiheba, the king of this city on a hill, married my daughter. He killed her immediately afterward—"

I looked at her in shock.

"She cuckolded him with a sheep. It was deserved," Takala explained.

Maybe I should rethink my concept of "loving mother"? I nodded numbly.

"However, we have a suzerain covenant with them. Should anyone attack, we are sworn to defend."

"Have the, uh, highlanders attacked?"

"Not yet. They circle the city, keeping to the hills like a pack of wild dogs looking for the weak lamb."

"Where is the Refa'im valley?" I asked. I'd been following her, and suddenly I found myself halfway to the palace.

"East of the city. We will ride to Lakshish tonight, await news, then join the battle tomorrow."

"Wait," I said. This was not part of my plan. "I cannot leave as yet."

Takala turned on me. "The *serenim* of Ashqelon have housed you, fed you, given you gold, jewelry, and position. You have lived better than I! Your intercession with Dagon changed the sea back into clear water. However, we have asked nothing else of you than this. Come to battle. Be our totem."

I looked around me. Soldiers on every side. Walled city. Guards. Slaves. Calculated escape routes? None.

She swallowed, humbling herself more than I'd ever seen. "You are a goddess, I cannot force you. But I ask you, you know my sons. You've dined with us, you've served with us. They are good boys, they love this land, they honor the gods. If you do not come, the Pelesti will be no more."

Pelesti, a word I'd rarely heard. Philistines, vanquished by the Jews; that much I recalled. I had no business being here, I wasn't part of Bible history.

Yes, I'd seen the Exodus, but I hadn't been a part of it. Moses and I hadn't had a tête-à-tête. I needed to get out of here before I screwed something up. After all, these Philistines were against the Jews. They didn't survive, only the name Palestine did.

I knew from my father's work that renaming this stretch of land "Palestine" was a Roman attempt to remove the Jews from the history books, from the maps, from, ultimately, the world. It was the only word that remained of the Philistines. But the people who had donated the name didn't last.

I really didn't want to see that, or know any of this. What a horrible thing to be thus doomed. However, in the here and now, her pain was as real as Cheftu's whip marks. Would it hurt to just go stand there for a while? I wouldn't be on the field, and I wouldn't have to do anything. It might help the morale of the people.

Not to mention that it would get me away from all these guards and walls. It would be easier to escape. I licked my lips. "I will need my slave," I said.

"It is done. He will join us at the battlefield."

I smiled inwardly. This woman would have made a helluva colonel. I tried to think of anything else I could get, without causing too much fuss. "Also, my jewelry, my clothes."

She watched me with black eyes. "It is done."

"Provisions."

"Done."

What else could I ask for? The clothes would keep us warm, the jewels would buy our way, provisions would keep us fed—what more was there? "Then let us go," I said resignedly.

The chariots she summoned, the speed with which they were ready, let me know that she'd planned on my going whether I'd agreed or not. I mentally bumped her rank to general.

Unlike the carts I had seen around Ashqelon, these chariots were light, fleet. They had spokes in their wheels instead of solid wood rounds. Fortunately Takala had her own, since I wasn't sure the horses would bear our combined weight. No sooner had I stepped into the back of the vehicle than we were off.

I held on for dear life, watching the world fly by. We were on the coastal plain, which was covered in flowers: pink, yellow, and white. Stalks with red-and-purple blossoms grew on both sides of this glorified goat path, but we were moving fast, so I couldn't see them closely. The wind blew my hair, and I understood immediately why we all wore headbands: so we could see.

After a few miles the tension in my body lessened. I'd gotten used to the swaying, jouncing motion and was no longer so afraid of falling out the back. The chariot had a great suspension system. My grip loosened as I began to relax, make plans. Giddiness bubbled inside me; Cheftu had arrived!

Just hours ago we had held each other. And we would again tonight. And every night from now on. But where could we go? How could we get there? Thank you for bringing him to me, I said to God. You've been great, thanks.

By late afternoon Lakshish came into view. It was a city nestled beneath a higher slope, the surrounding hills terraced and planted with slumbering grapevines. The walls surrounding it were formidable. To the east I saw the tents of the encamped soldiers. Watchtowers stretched to the north, three visible to the naked eye.

We slowed down. Our horses were tired from the trip. My bones seemed to ache, and I could still feel the rhythm of the journey in my skin. We waited for Takala. At the moment I looked away, she swooped out of nowhere. Unlike me, she was doing the driving. Her horses were lathered. She flew past us, heading down the hill to the army camp. The soldier driving me did not wait for instruction, but followed her.

We arrived at the camp at dusk.

There is something instantly recognizable about being on military alert, whether as a whatever-century Philistine or a twentieth-century American: that jazzed, edgy feeling is the same. The Pelesti soldiers looked like professionals. Everywhere I looked there were men in pointed and piped kilts, with bare faces and feathered helmets. Quite a few wore an upper-body armor that resembled leather and metal ribs. They carried long spears tipped with dark blades in addition to swords and round shields.

As I watched them sparring, I rephrased my statement: They *were* professionals. Our horses were unbridled and led away, the chariots taken into line with the others. I watched with amazement as our light vehicle became an armored one, simply by soldiers fitting it with bronze greave-style scales.

Yamir-dagon was easy to find. His feathered headdress was red and blue, his cloak red. Amid the brown, green, and gold kilts, he stuck out like a poppy in a cornfield. Takala pushed forward. I was astounded to see that she had donned both feathered headdress and a battle dress like the soldiers. As we passed through the camp the men bowed to her. Yamir embraced his mother, inclined his head to me, then gestured for us to follow him into his tent.

I'd never seen action as an officer in the air force, but I've been in plenty of meetings. This was obviously a council of war. I recognized the *serenim* and a few of the soldiers. Wadia, in a headdress and cloak just like his brother's, winked at me. I sat down beside Takala.

The general in charge outlined the plan.

The highlanders were stalking around the city of Jebus. Therefore the Pelesti would sneak up behind them, trap them against the wooded foothills below the city, and slaughter them there. It was well-known that Dadua was too clever to send all his men to any one location, so the battle would not be definitive. However, the lesson would be taught and face would be regained after the burning of the *teraphim*.

"Why do we not just steal their *teraphim?*" I asked. Any talk of going against Dadua sounded like suicide. After all, I'd heard the Bible stories. The knowledge made me feel sick. I wanted to get out of here, desperately.

The council was appalled. Wadia told me that he would share that story later but that even their totem was deceitful. Never again would the Pelesti trust the honor of the highlanders, not after the way they had humiliated the champion Gol'i'at with magic. Not after the destruction their *teraphim* had wrought.

My head was spinning. I'd always thought the Israelites, the highlanders, were the underdog. Wasn't that how the Bible portrayed it?

Yet to hear the Pelesti point of view, the highlanders were unprincipled ruffians. There was no standing army, just a group of Apiru wanderers who had been hired by Dadua, who fought with scythes and rakes if necessary. They ignored the accepted etiquette, they showed no mercy, and worst of all, they did not respect other gods.

The things the First Methodist Church of Reglim, Texas, had never told me. . . .

Since the totems of Dagon and Ba'al had been stolen and destroyed, I was, as the local goddess, attending the battle in the totem's place. My job would be to stand on the hill and watch the engagement, asking for the intervention of Dagon—since they had chosen to fight near a stream for his powers—and Ba'al, the thrower of thunderbolts, should it be necessary. As a safeguard against the wily highlanders, the Pelesti would not go past a certain point in the valley because the chariots and horses could not maneuver in the hills with rocky ground and trees.

Takala and I lodged in the same tent, which wasn't much more than a goatskin awning over a few branches. It didn't matter; between re-

uniting the night away with Cheftu and riding for hours in the chariot, I could have slept in the backseat of a race car during the Indy
500. However, I was nervous that Cheftu wouldn't show up. She pla-
cated me as I collapsed into sleep.

I woke in the deepest blackness of night, the hair on my arms
standing on end. I heard nothing else in the tent, not even Takala's
breathing.

Then the words floated in, confusing me momentarily.

I rose up, slipping out from under my blanket, going to the edge of
camp, then beyond. Slightly above us, about forty feet away, the highlanders reveled. From my perspective the plateau served as a prosce-
nium stage with natural acoustics.

The music began, a wild thumping that set my blood racing. A
huge bonfire burned behind them, the black figures dancing around it
lit by orange and red and gold flame. It looked like All Hallows' Eve.

"We ask for so little," Takala said from behind me, her voice soft
for once. "Our land for our own. Dagon gave us *ha Hamishah*, why
doesn't he help us protect it?"

When she said "Hamishah" the slide show zoomed back to show
me the five cities the Pelesti considered their own: Gaza, Ashdod,
Ashqelon, Ekron, and Qisilee.

I said nothing, just looked up between the trees. Now standing before the bonfire, in silhouette, was a solitary figure, his hands raised
over his head. His voice carried as though he had a Bose stereo system,
the curve of the cliff acting as an amphitheater.

"We meet our old allies"—the group of highlanders chuckled—
"and our present enemies in battle tomorrow." The sole figure paced
the edge of the fire, his head bowed, every action casting shadows
across the trees and plateau. Shadows of a giant man in prayer or deep
thought. As he turned, the man within the shadow, a glitter of gold
glinted on his brow.

His soldiers were motionless humps of black in the gold-tinted
light. "What do we say on this eve of battle?" he asked in the same
language the Pelesti spoke. "What questions stream through our
blood? What hidden grief will keep us from sleep tonight?"

This scene was designed to send fear pulsing through the veins of the Pelesti. Even though I knew it, it worked. The men's voices rose in one titanic response, as if the very valley were crying its answers. As though the heavens were on his side, we heard all around us, "May Shaday answer you in your distress! May *el sh'Yacov* protect you! May he send you help from the outposts and grant you support from Qiryat Yerim! May he remember the blood you have offered in sacrifice and accept your burnt offerings!"

El was "god"; this I knew, from my mother the archaeologist and because I understood the language. Yacov was Jacob . . . as in Jacob and Esau. I didn't recall the details of the story, but I knew Jacob was a big deal. The "sh" sound was the scariest. It meant that Shaday was the god of Jacob. This same god of Jacob was into blood sacrifices and burnt offerings.

The one who demanded *hal* from *herim*.

"Is that Dadua?" I asked Takala.

"*Ken*. That One is Dadua. *Ach*, for the days That One was ours. How many seasons did he protect and feed us? How many seasons did we treat him as son, only to have him turn on us like a mongoose?"

The highlanders continued with rote responses, seemingly offering assurances to the man now limned by fire. "May he give you the desire of your heart and make your strategies fruitful. We shout for joy at victory and lift our standards to honor Shady. May *El* grant your requests!"

Then a lone voice, a different voice, shouted through the valley for all to hear. "The Immutable One saves his anointed; He answers he who was selected, from the high heavens, with the strength of his right hand."

The man by the fire spoke again. "Some trust foolishly in chariots and horses. They believe that speed and armament can win the day. But we . . ." He paused. "But *we*, what do we believe in?"

"We trust in the name of our God!"

"The others, they are humbled!" he cried.

The crowd groaned.

"They drop to their knees—" Enacting his part, the man fell to his knees as though too weak to stand.

The highlanders laughed.

"They perish, they fall." His words fell into quiet, an expectant silence. "We, chosen by *el ha*Shaday, we who march the length of Canaan, we rise and we stand!"

Chaos! The men leapt to their feet, frenzied, dancing, singing, crying. An antiphonal chant overlaid the activity. "Shaday, save Dadua. Answer his calls! Shaday, save Dadua! Answer his calls! Shaday, save Dadua! Answer his calls!"

I watched the man glowing with fire. Eyes closed, he too danced. Dervishes would envy his movements. Glancing around me, I saw the Pelesti soldiers, kilted, but unhelmeted, staring up at the plateau.

Defeat was written in their faces already.

Psychological warfare apparently was in use long before I realized.

"His god gives him all he asks," one of them commented. "Even should we win on the morrow, we cannot defend the Jebusi forever. He is making the valley his own."

"He could never capture Jebus," someone else said. "We tried for decades and failed."

"I wish he would die," Takala spat. "Then Pelesti mothers wouldn't lose more sons. Yamir will fight That One until our hopes of children lay in their father's blood."

Though I was listening, I was watching the men on the hill. All of a sudden they rushed toward the speaker and lifted him onto their shoulders. It looked like the winning side of a football game, until I heard their words, their cries, echoing across the valley, into the hearts of those who were now already beaten, already conquered, half-dead. "A blessing he has given! The blessing of the land and *chesed!*"

The minute Cheftu showed up, we were hitting the road! I'd gotten what I came for; now it was time to go home. Whatever or whenever that was, at least it wasn't here.

"Thus they complete another *tan'in,*" the soldier closest to me said. He was older, his hair faded to gray, though his brows were still dark and bushy. "Before every battle they work themselves into a frenzy of blood." The rest of his statement hung unsaid in the fire-scented air: *they make themselves invincible through it.*

We returned, silent, to our beds. Before I closed my eyes I realized the highlanders had been successful on two counts. One, they had

psyched out the enemy through this elaborate show; two, they had caused the entire camp to lose at least three hours of sleep, knowing that the remaining two hours until dawn would be filled with anxious thoughts.

Tomorrow morning I was gone. My thoughts of going to stand on the hillside had melted in Dadua's bonfire. Nothing good would come of this. We had to leave.

Where was Cheftu?

RaEm TURNED TO THE SIDE, allowing the artist to view her profile, though she knew he would add some of Akhenaten's features to her face. Smenkhare, in truth, did not exist. Then again, neither did Ma'at. Both were reinterpreted through Akhenaten's desires.

The term and goddess that formerly referred to the balance of the universe now meant "candor" and "individualism." Smenkhare, a bow-legged, dirt-skinned adolescent had been buried, while the new Smenkhare arose: RaEm.

"It is enough, my, uh, Smenkhare," the artisan said, backing from the room. RaEm dismissed him with a wave.

"Pharaoh's daughter Meryaten requests an audience," RaEm's chamberlain said.

"Which one is she?"

"Ankhenespa'aten's sister. The selfsame one who has visited you before, my, my Smenkhare."

RaEm wished someone would just guess at her gender and be done with it. Sometimes she doubted it herself. Was she woman or man? Did it matter? Either way she had Pharaoh's heart and body, at least for today. "Anyone else? I have no wish to see Meryaten right now."

The chamberlain, a stuffy old man whose wig was always askew, coughed. "The queen mother, Tiye, your mother, requests you attend her."

It was silent for a moment. "I will see Meryaten."

The girl was admitted later, a fragile thing, with such bad eyesight that she couldn't tell RaEm was really a female. Then again, in Akhenaten's court, where even Pharaoh had both breasts and a phallus, no one could tell.

"The great god Aten's blessings on you this morning, cousin Smenkhare," the wispy thing said, her melodious voice only a breath above a whisper. It was a wonder that such a vibrant man as Akhenaten had birthed such colorless worms as his daughters.

"Likewise on you, Meryaten," RaEm said, rising from her chair. "Would you care to perfume your mouth, cousin?"

Meryaten glanced up, her big brown eyes blank. "Aye. That is very considerate of you, my lord."

RaEm smothered a smile, eyeing the chamberlain. "You are too delicate a lotus for less," she said soothingly. With a glance, food was delivered to them. Watered wine, flaky pastries, and sickly fruit. RaEm would have thrown it out, save she knew it was the best the kitchen had to offer. The thought gave her pause.

She sat beside a leopard-headed table, beckoning for a stool to be brought for Meryaten. The girl sat down, barely brushing against RaEm. Up close she was lovely in a dainty way. Her eyes were round, her chin pointed like her father's. The short wig she wore emphasized how frail her neck was.

How easy to snap, RaEm thought. She poured the girl some wine.

"Have you seen your mother yet?" Meryaten asked softly.

"Not yet," RaEm said. She had been diligently avoiding Tiye while she worked on binding Akhenaten to her, body and soul. It was a wonder she could walk after the nights they spent together. Soon, however, the woman must be faced. Would she know?

Per current fashion, RaEm, as Smenkhare, wore a shirt and a kilt, an androgynous wig, gold jewelry. The three weeks she'd spent in the desert, nearly dying to make her plan work, had made her even more boyishly thin. Her breasts were smaller, her hips not so womanly.

She looked just like Akhenaten.

Which was why he couldn't resist her. He believed she was the mirror image of him, the male and female of the same soul, created to be in harmony with the Aten. No one else knew what to make of her, even how to address her.

And this poor girl child at RaEm's side wished to be her bride.

More interestingly, RaEm was contemplating how to pull off such a fiction. She wanted to rule Egypt; alas, a woman would not be allowed to, not again. How could she persuade Akhenaten to let her be co-regent?

"I . . . I am nearing my second year of womanhood," Meryaten said shyly. "Father has mentioned marrying me. I . . ."

If she didn't speak faster, RaEm might well choke her. "All your sisters married your father," she said.

"They all died, too."

"What of Akhenespa'aten?"

"She's little, intended for Tuti." Meryaten looked up, stricken. "Do you like her better?"

RaEm caressed the girl's face. "Of course not, she is a child. You are a lovely young woman."

Meryaten blushed, her brown eyes darting away. *I was never this much a fool,* RaEm thought. "I . . . I would very much like to have babies," Meryaten said.

That, my dumb lotus blossom, is exactly the problem. "Sons for the Aten?" RaEm asked, still stroking Meryaten's hair.

"Aye." The girl looked up, staring straight into RaEm's eyes. "You are so pretty, almost prettier than I am." She smiled. "I, I also want sons for me. To hold them. I hope they will be pretty."

RaEm removed her hand. "Any children you have will be beautiful, Meryaten."

"I want yours."

RaEm stared, half impressed by the girl's gumption, half repulsed. In that moment of silence, Meryaten leaned forward and kissed her on the lips. Her mouth was soft, yielding, and RaEm responded despite herself.

When they separated, both were surprised at their ardor.

"Will you speak to my father?" Meryaten asked, her small hand on RaEm's thigh.

RaEm's eyes narrowed. She had misjudged this girl. These little morning visits had been planned as though they were on papyrus, with RaEm as the dupe. The hand moved higher. RaEm stood abruptly. "I will."

Meryaten jumped to her feet, once again staring at the ground. "May your day be blessed with the Aten," she said, her cheeks ruddy, her hands trembling. She stood as high as RaEm's breast, a child of barely thirteen Inundations.

Who thought cousin Smenkhare was a boy of seventeen Inundations.

Meryaten looked up again as RaEm sighed heavily. As Chloe's people would say, What the hell. She kissed the girl again, thoroughly enjoying the control she had over the child. "Go to your gardens," she said. "I will speak to your father tonight."

The door closed behind Meryaten, and RaEm threw herself on the couch. With a clap of her hands she summoned the chamberlain. "Inform Queen Mother Tiye that I will dine with her tonight. Then see if My Majesty Akhenaten is alone after dusk."

Aye, indeed. She would rule Egypt.

PELESTI

Wind whipped at us, standing on the rise's edge looking onto the battlefield. My God, I was at a battlefield. I'd stood on Omaha, Utah, beaches; I'd walked through the Shenandoah Valley; hell, I'd even seen the plain of Troy—but never before with people.

In armor.

With weapons.

I tugged at my piped and pointed battle dress, adjusted the feather headdress they'd given me. I looked like a giant statue, which I was supposed to since I was the totem. Acid burned in my stomach. Cheftu had not arrived yet, or I would have gotten out of here. Just do this and he'll be here this afternoon, I thought. Then we could both leave.

Takala was seated on a chair, sipping wine in a semblance of calm. Wadia stood beside her, frowning. "She won't let me go, Sea-Mistress," he said, his voice slightly whiny. "Tell her I am a man, that I can serve Dagon this way."

He was fifteen? Fourteen? Even soldiers in the Civil War weren't that young, at least not at first. "She needs your strength beside her," I said. He gave me a look that said I'd betrayed him, so I motioned him closer, whispered to him. "It is a hard thing for you, I know, but if something should, Dagon forbid, happen to Yamir, then you are the crown prince of Ashqelon. You are too valuable to risk."

He looked at me reproachfully but must have realized the truth of the statement. "I will pray that Dagon watch over my brother," he said. "That way in the next battle *he* can sit up here and *I* can fight in the valley."

Would there be a tomorrow? I wondered. Another battle? Didn't it take the Jews a long time, like centuries, to vanquish the Philistines? I just didn't know where we were on that time line. David. King David. Holy shit.

Takala stayed focused on the valley, but I was certain she had heard every word. With reluctant steps I walked to the edge of the cliff. Below us by a hundred feet, the Pelesti walked in orderly rows, each platoon surrounding one of the team-drawn chariots. The sun glinted off their spear handles and shields. They looked invincible. It was hard to reconcile these Philistines with the term that had come to mean barbarians. They had mosaic floors, for crying out loud!

The sun beat down on us, though a breeze kept us comfortable. It must have been much warmer in the valley. "A wind sweeps across the Refa'im from *haYam* about zenith," Takala said. "It is a good time for an attack."

I saw the band of highlanders approaching from the north. They carried rounded helmets and wore metal caps. "They do not have strong weapons," Takala said. "We alone know the secrets of smelting. Their weapons bend and break with ease." Compared with the Pelesti, who wore only a breastplate, the highlanders had almost full armor.

Then again, if the Pelesti were expecting bronze weapons—the bronze age of weaponry was before the iron, another useful tidbit from being an archaeologist's daughter—they didn't need a lot of protection. The highlanders, however, were up against iron.

But the highlanders were Jews. I couldn't get the ultimate result out of my mind. No Philistines remained. I really wanted some Pepto-Bismol.

The highlanders' dresses gave them a scaly appearance. Nothing matched, the weapons didn't gleam, and the men seemed to walk with very little energy. Was this the same group as the night before?

"Perhaps they wearied themselves at the *tani'n* last night," Takala said cheerfully. "We will smite them and be in Lakshish by dusk."

I was not so easily persuaded. They were clever, last night proved it. Who knew what they were up to now? They marched more slowly than the Pelesti, as they were coming down from the forest.

"What are they doing, Sea-Mistress?" Wadia asked, confused.

I couldn't tell what they were doing. Getting ready for a picnic, maybe? I stared at the highlanders. They'd all sat down.

These were the children of Israel? What was going on? Surely they knew we were watching? Yet before us, they sat down as though they couldn't walk a step farther. Were they taking a nap?

The Pelesti were almost upon them. It was going to be a slaughter. I had been concerned about the poor Pelesti being defeated by these morons? I couldn't watch; it was going to be awful. Couldn't we just call a draw?

"They aren't even fighting," Wadia said, his voice trembling. I didn't have to uncover my eyes; I heard the cries, the fear, the horror. Clashing metal against metal, screams of men and horses.

"Dagon be praised," Takala shouted. "We are winning!"

I looked down, forcing myself to watch. Was I wrong about history? Was history changing?

The valley was deep, a wadi that had been shaped by millennia of flowing waters, carving this channel from the stone walls. Trees ranged both sides, with a greater forest at the foot of the mountain where the valley abutted it.

With horses, chariots, uniforms, and feathered headdresses that made them seem even taller and broader, the Pelesti looked like an army. The highlanders looked like farmers who'd been given swords ten minutes ago.

They backed up, half the number fading into the forest at their back, the other half getting into rough columns. Blood pounded in my ears, and my hand was slick against the lance. The highlanders seemed surprised to see the Pelesti, but then at a call, a weird whining call, *a shofar*—the lexicon whispered—half of them rose and half of them crouched.

We heard low, faint whistles as we saw the Pelesti dropping to the ground. What had felled them? Then I saw the arrows and spears flying through the air. Green uniforms were suddenly stained red. Feathered headdresses were hitting the dirt.

Yet the highlanders kept backing up.

"We are pushing them into the forest," Takala said joyfully. "We will have sent That One and his troops back to Mamre by dusk!"

The lexicon whipped out the map again. Mamre was Hebron. Neither of those names meant a thing to me. The highlanders were vanishing into the woods, but not as men who were being chased. They were sneaking away.

"It's a trap," I whispered, suddenly realizing what they had done. "Get them out!" I cried, turning to Takala.

"We are winning," she said, unwilling to look away.

I grabbed her arm. "We have been lured in! Get out! It's a trap!" I pointed down to the battle. The heel of the valley had become too narrow and too steep for the chariots and horses, the main Pelesti weapons. In their enthusiasm they had progressed beyond the safety zone.

The color drained from her face. "They can't turn around," she whispered. "They can't back up!"

The fighting grew more intense, two Pelesti for every Israelite, as I watched. My heart was in my throat as I wondered what to do. Was I right or wrong? The forest seemed empty, but waiting. I held Wadia's hand on one side, while I held my spear with the other, grinding it into the ground with the force of my fear. There were fewer and fewer highlanders. Some appeared to be on the ground, slain. But not many. The Pelesti started backing away from the forest, returning to where the chariots and horses had bottlenecked.

A breeze blew over us, the same breeze Takala had talked about. Then a sound rustled in the trees, the sound of heavy machinery moving.

The soldiers heard it, too; then the triumphant cry, "Shaday rides ahead of the *elohim!*" Loudly. Again and again.

In my mental lexicon *elohim* brought to mind countless, endless divisions of angelic beings. Not fluffy little cherubs with bows and arrows, but fearful specters with bloodstained swords and the wingspans of pterodactyls.

"Shaday with the *elohim!*"

Highlanders suddenly poured from the trees, escalating this skirmish into a battle royal. Adrenaline rushed through me with such force that for a moment I was deaf. My God, no. *No!*

The first headdress down was that of Yamir. Takala screamed her denial while Wadia watched, tears flowing down his cheeks. Her son was dead. I was shocked; this was a man I'd known. Now dead.

I wanted to hide my face, to turn away. That seemed a shameful reaction, though. Blood flowed in my veins, warrior's blood from Cromwell's time to the Vietnam fiasco. These soldiers deserved to have someone watch and to bear witness to their bravery.

In that moment I became Pelesti. The people I'd eaten with, the smiles we'd shared, the laughter; they became my people.

After a while I grew numb. Takala and Wadia stood beside me, watching. The mingled odors of blood and excrement wafted up to us. We held hands as we observed the pride of the Pelesti, their horses and chariots, become their death sentence.

The remaining Pelesti soldiers tried to scramble over the mess of wood and horseflesh that trapped them in the valley. The horses, terrified by the scent of blood, spooked by the sound of metal and men's cries, bucked and reared, trying to free themselves. At the end, they probably killed as many Pelesti as the highlanders. Those who managed to get across the bottleneck fled toward Lakshish.

"We need to go," Takala said. "Take Wadia to Ashdod or Gaza."

I turned to her, and everything became surreal. The "za" had just left her mouth when her body jerked. Her eyes widened, then her body twitched again. As I watched, a red stain darkened the blue of her dress; her eyes lost focus but didn't close. I shouted for Wadia, and we slowed her fall to the ground.

Two snaps and she screamed. She was bleeding profusely, her skin clammy as the pain began. *"Derkato,"* she gasped out, "you must take Wadia. You must leave." She'd been shot twice in the back: when she fell down the shafts broke, burying the heads deep in her flesh.

"We cannot leave you," I said, wrapping up a cloak and tucking it beneath her neck.

"He is the crown prince," she said.

My words that had been so flippant, so manipulative, earlier came back to me. They were true. He was the only prince left.

"You must get him to Gaza or to Ashdod," she said.

"What about—"

"I'm dying, you worthless goddess!" she gasped out. "Leave me with my soldiers! Go! Now!"

Wadia was holding her hand, weeping. She squeezed it and smiled at him. "Be wise, my son. Go now."

"I can't leave—"

"You are king, Wadia. You owe it to your people." Takala stared him down, sweat beading her forehead. Someone tugged on my arm, and I watched my hand reach out for Wadia's.

"You," Takala gasped, glaring at me. "You are responsible for the city—you are our goddess—" Her words ended on a scream as the pain increased. I pulled Wadia along with me, following blindly.

Another roar of humanity surrounded us as we walked away. Wadia ran back to the edge of the cliff, tugging me after him. Those soldiers who had fought so bravely to get over the obstacles, to make it safely home, now were being cut down ruthlessly. Another contingency of highlanders poured from the hills below us, falling on the tired, terrified Pelesti. The Philistines turned and fought, but they were already beaten. "No," I whispered, too appalled to check my language. "Please, God, no."

A soldier wrenched my arm, dragging me down the mountain. I pulled Wadia along in turn. He threw Wadia and me inside a chariot. "Ride for Ashdod," he said. "Tell them we need reinforcements!"

He'd already lashed the horses; we were rambling across the uneven ground with no one at the wheel. Soldiers surrounded us, highlanders with their battle-lusting eyes, beards, gleaming helmets, and constant cries of "Shaday rides with the *elohim!*"

I grabbed the reins, trying clumsily to control the frantic horses. Wadia pushed me aside and shouted at me to get down. He lashed the horses again, throwing me to the floor as we bounced and jounced in a wild ride down the hillside. My bones were jabbing out of my body, my teeth rattling loose.

We careened down the mountain to where the terrain flattened out, but our speed did not change. I braced myself and stood up.

His eyes were blank; the poor kid was in serious shock. He'd seen his brother killed, his mother shot, his people massacred. I couldn't imagine his pain, but I didn't want him to fall apart. There was still too much to do. "Tell me about the time the Pelesti took the highlanders' *teraphim*," I shouted over the sound of the horses. Anything to bring life back into his eyes.

"It was in battle," he said, as though he were reading a Tele-PrompTer. "We won the battle, so we took their totem as a trophy."

"Why?" I asked. "What was the point?"

"We would take it through *ha Hamishah,* so that all the people could know that Dagon was superior, that we had captured the god of the highlanders."

"Why didn't that work?" My questions were as rote as his responses.

A little more color was tingeing his skin, and we were slowing down. "Their totem was deadly. When people touched it, they died. When they got close to it, they became sick with tumors, then they died."

"The highlanders had it booby-trapped?" I asked. Obviously

"booby-trapped" didn't work in this language. It came out as "rigged for evil."

He shrugged. "The king of Ashdod sent the totem to Gaza. It killed more people there. Then they sent it to Lakshish. The king there didn't want it, for almost twenty thousand Pelesti had died in five months." His gaze finally focused on me. "They cheated. When you capture the totem of a people, he is supposed to work for you, not against you."

I nodded.

"Then the king of Lakshish guessed it was lethal because it was angry with our actions. It had not received the proper, holy treatment that a totem of a god would deserve and expect. So we sent it to the Temple of Dagon in Ashqelon. It is the holiest place in Pelesti."

"What happened?"

"After the first night, the priests found the statue of Dagon lying on the floor, broken at the waist. The totem of the highlanders had been laid opposite it."

"That must have bewildered the priests," I said, realizing that the breaks I'd seen in the statue were not from lousy craftsmanship, but from the totem. What was the totem of the Jews?

"It did. It happened the next night, breaking off Dagon's hands this time."

A mergod with no hands would be like a screen door on a submarine, utterly useless.

"Immediately the citizens of Ashqelon sent it back to Lakshish. The priests there, those who had survived it the first time, said, '*lo lo lo!*' and put it in a cart aimed toward the highlands." His eyes began to gleam. "However, when it got there, according to the spies who followed, it was still mad, because it killed the highlanders, too."

We reached another rise; somehow we'd stumbled onto another battlefield.

The sun was setting, but still we could clearly see the bodies, beautifully hewn of copper and bronze flesh, cut with muscle, graceful and strong. Now they were laid in unnatural positions. Masses of blood had soaked the grass brown, splattered the trees. It lay pooled and congealed beneath bodies.

Had we moved backward, or had the battle been here before? "Apparently the highlanders"—Wadia spat to show his disgust—"are chasing us back to Gezer." He looked over his shoulder, back the way we'd come. "I guess they went around Lakshish."

"We're supposed to go to Ashdod."

Wadia looked at me, his eyes as haunted as a sixty-year-old man's. "*Lo*, only me."

Takala's words floated over me. The city was my responsibility. I looked southward. "Ashqelon is down there?"

"*Ken.*"

Though my legs were shaking, I dismounted. "If they are there, how do I get in?"

After instructing me how to invade the city, should I need to, Wadia drove off to Ashdod, to gather more defenses. The boy had become a man.

I'd realized that just walking away was no longer possible. Alternately cursing Takala and glaring at God, I made my way toward the sea. I should reach it, and Ashqelon, by morning.

Stars scattered the sky above. It was hard to believe this was the same universe as this morning. I felt different, yet nothing had been moved. Trees still grew upward, dark still concealed, and boys still missed their mothers. The impact of the day felled me.

I'd seen a battle. A war, complete with death and maiming. I'd done nothing but watch.

I had no idea of time, only that I was tired. Bone tired. Had all of this taken just one twenty-four-hour period? Only this morning we were setting off, thinking ourselves the victors. Oh God, I thought. But are you the God of the opposing team? Does that mean the Pelesti were doomed before they even began? It seemed terribly unfair to have the deck stacked so.

These were men killing men. The men who wrote the Bible, the "thou shalt not kill" part, killing men. "I'm going to become a Hindu," I whispered.

CHAPTER 5

EVEN THIS FAR AWAY from the city of Ashqelon I could hear the cries, the clash and clatter, of ancient war. The Pelesti and highlanders were still fighting?

My steps hastened as I thought of Cheftu. Was he safe? Had he been hurt? Why hadn't he showed up in Lakshish?

When I stepped through the treeline, I saw men at each other's throats. Still. This was why there was yet a Middle East peace knot, I realized. These people, even in all these intervening centuries, never learned how to get along. Maybe we should just let them kill themselves now and save history and the rest of the planet a lot of grief? I couldn't recall ever feeling so disgusted with the human condition before.

I skirted around the battlefield, into the growing shadows of the valley. Men's cries, horses' screams, and the incessant banging of metal on metal rang in my eardrums. Thousands of men fought, amid the remains of their comrades. It was ghastly chaos.

The Pelesti wielding swords were old men, their weapons too heavy, their armor in disrepair. These were the reinforcements for those slain in battle? My despair grew.

The columns and order were gone. Now it was simply feather-headed man fighting bearded man. The crenellated walls of the city were lined with Pelesti, waiting for the battle to get close enough so that the arrows, spears, and hot oil they had prepared would have effect.

On the horizon I saw the sun was rising, bloodstained colors on a bloodstained land. The light peeked over the beach, climbing quickly, throwing the shadows of man killing man on the ground, black and gray against the reddish brown grass. The shadows of dawn were dispersing, the sounds of battle, of screaming and dying, fading away.

In a matter of hours the Pelesti would be no more. Not in Ashqelon. I backtracked to the shore, then edged through the sacred lake enclosure. The crocodiles were sunning themselves in the morning light.

The Temple of Dagon was empty, for the male priests had donned headdresses to go defend their lives and way of life. The priestesses were, presumably, standing on the city walls with the people.

I let myself into the room where Cheftu and I had made love. Cheftu was there, chained through his ears to the wall, huddled up. Asleep? Dead?

"Cheftu," I called, running to him. His skin was warm, but he was out cold. Drugged? I was furious with Takala; she must have done this! I knelt beside my husband, looking at his face. The lines around his eyes were sharper, deeper creases. His skin was so dark, he could pass as East Indian. And those holes—they had healed, but still they were enormous, as though they'd been made with nails or an awl. Instinctively I reached for my ears. God, that must have hurt.

He would be out for hours to come.

I sat on the edge of the bed. The sounds of battle were gone. Soon the sounds of invasion would begin. I looked down and saw that blood covered me. It was layered on my skin like latex. I put my head in my hands.

The city was my responsibility. How did this happen? Though I didn't want to, I forced myself up, out the door, into the main chamber.

Tamera's face was stained with tears; she was panting, sobbing at the feet of Dagon. When she saw me she screamed, then threw herself at my tail. "You, my Sea-Mistress! You are all we have! Takala-dagon is dead. Wadia is lost to us—"

"He's safely in Ashdod," I said.

"Already Yamir-dagon has been sent to the heavens by ash."

It took a moment to process her words. "He has been cremated?"

"It is our way, *haDerkato*," she said with great dignity.

I nodded numbly. My mouth opened of its own accord. "What can I do?" Shit! I didn't want to get involved! We were on the losing side of a battle with God's team! But Takala had died speaking to me, Yamir had always smiled at me, and Wadia was too young to bear all this alone.

"The highlanders will soon send us their terms," she said tearfully. "They are camped outside the city, but I understand it is their holy day. So they will not move or do work or battle until dusk tomorrow. Our men are gone, most of them. Only women and children remain in the city."

"We have another day," I said.

She tried to smile.

"What did you do to my slave?" I asked. I needed Cheftu—I needed his mind. He could help me figure out what, if anything, could be done.

"He will awaken soon," she said.

"Do the highlanders treat their captives well?" I asked, trying to get a sense of what my options were. A whole city was my responsibility. Tamera's face crumpled.

"They do not, Sea-Mistress." She said it softly, resignedly, then I remembered the lexicon.

Hal and *herim*. I closed my eyes as the world turned white for a moment. "They take no prisoners," I said, hoping she wouldn't confirm it.

"None, Sea-Mistress."

I turned abruptly, staring at the useless, poorly mended statue. There was no more time to guess why I was here, if it was by accident or design, if it was blessing—very well disguised—or punishment. Now was the time to deal with it.

For hours I stood in silence, staring into space. Outside, it had become black, Sabbath night. Into it the highlanders sang a ghostly, minor-key tune. My breath sounded loud to me.

After a while noises came from within the temple: Cheftu-waking-up noises. I ran back to the room, threw open the door. *"Mon Dieu! You are here! You are safe!"* he said, staring at me bleary-eyed.

"Yes," I answered. "How do I get you off the wall?"

He turned his head slightly, his eyes going opaque when he saw the chain. "Cut it."

A search of the temple produced two priests getting drunk in one room and an iron dagger in another. I struck at the chain, channeling my fury into cutting the metal. Once he was free I gave him some bread and a little wine and spent twenty minutes and a bath assuring him I wasn't wounded, that none of the blood was mine.

"What happened?" he asked.

"What happened to you?"

"I woke up chained," he said. "I guess from the way my head aches, they drugged me."

I sighed, sick of the images that lived behind my eyelids whether they were opened or closed. "The Pelesti are the Philistines."

"Oui?"

"The highlanders, who they are in battle with, who they were just slaughtered by, are the Jews. The Israelites."

Cheftu's eyes bugged. "From the Holy Word?" he asked. "Samson? Saul? David?"

The man was a biblical encyclopedia. "David is Dadua."

"We are in Dadua's time? We are knowing these holy people?" His English sounded awed.

I saw nothing holy in these people. They slaughtered like professionals. I continued in English. "The bad news is that we are, and we are on opposite sides of the fence. The royal family is gone, and I"— I licked my lips—"I am in charge."

He searched my face, my eyes. "They made a wise selection."

My eyes filled with tears. "Thank you."

"How can I assist you?" he asked after a moment of staring at me. How my soul thrilled with him, even now.

"Do you have any idea who I will be talking to?"

"Joab was David's general," Cheftu answered promptly. "Nathan was his prophet."

"Do we know anything about them?"

He frowned. "Joab seems to have been a brute. Bloodthirsty. He was David's, how do you say? Assassin?"

"Henchman?"

"*Oui.* Henchman. He did for David what David did not want to soil his hands with."

"What about Nathan?"

"He was a prophet."

"Anything else?"

"*Ach*, well, Nathan's prophecies changed from time to time. He reversed on himself because of dreams or something. He wasn't a very confident prophet."

"What kind of intercession do you think Tamera expected me to manage?"

Cheftu's tone was flat. "Painless, fast deaths."

"Are you just exercising a positive attitude, or do you know for sure?" I snapped. Dawn was approaching; I was getting really scared. These people were depending on me.

"It is in the Bible, though there were times when the Israelites were allowed to take spoils," he explained.

"So death or slavery?"

He nodded once.

"Holy shit," I whispered. After a moment I asked, "Uh, what kind of death options are there? I mean, do they have firing squads? Do they shoot a volley of arrows at us?"

He got up, pacing the room angrily. "How should I know, Chloe? When I read the Bible I wasn't seeing what adventurous and vile ways the people of God had of killing their enemies! Why must you be so ghoulish, wanting to know details?"

I felt myself bristle at his outburst. "I was just trying to get the whole story," I said defensively. "You aren't the one who is supposed to barter for people's lives or deaths. You aren't the one who is supposed to know what is the more or less painful way to go. I don't even bargain well for sandals!" The weight of it all came pouring down on me. "This is for people's lives! It's on my shoulders!"

"*Ach, chérie,*" he said, instantly contrite, hugging me, touching my wind-ravaged hair. He pulled me close so that I felt his words as I heard them. "Are you fearful?"

"Petrified. Are you?"

He took a moment to respond, and I closed my eyes as his fingers ran through my hair, massaging my scalp. "I worry for you, but that is not the source of my fear."

"Is it because this is the Bible?" I asked after a moment.

He sighed deeply. "For me these are holy times. Seeing David and Joab as they are, it is almost impossible to believe."

"Because they don't act holy?"

Tamera appeared in the doorway, her hair arranged, her dress elaborate. "The priests wish to cleanse and adorn you for the morrow," she said. "Please come with me."

Cheftu squeezed my hand. "I will pray for you."

"Don't be afraid," I whispered.

As the local goddess, I was bathed, made up, prayed over, fasted, feasted, and eventually allowed to sleep. When I woke up it was the day to meet with the highlanders: the Israelites. I had not a clue what to say.

Tamera came in with the fish cloak. As a representative of all of Ashqelon, it was my job to wear it. So much for feeling confident in one's clothing. "Are they entering the city?" I asked.

"*Lo, haDerkato.* We meet at the city gate."

"*Lo,* not at the city gate," I said, trying to recall all the things my father had said about diplomacy, about winning an argument, about negotiating. Oh God. "We will meet them on the beach, by the sacred fishpond." That seemed neutral ground.

She bowed and backed out. I called after her to make sure there was wine and food—something other than corn. And no shellfish or pork, because just like Muslims, they would be offended by that. Not for nothin' have I been an ambassador's daughter.

That thought struck me cold. Was it possible I was here for a reason beyond finding Cheftu?

My fish cloak was on and my body was painted, though without the elaborate kohl markings on my face. I knew that part of successful negotiating comes from looking as much like the other side as possible. Help them see what you had in common. I hoped it would work.

Cheftu was by my side through all of it, and no one said a word about his presence, how *haDerkato* suddenly had this slave in attendance. We proceeded silently down the beach. Everywhere I looked I saw the faces of the Pelesti. Eyes that were honey brown, blue, green, and black beseeched me to save them. The fate of the city of Gezer had been dreadful. The highlanders had killed everything that had breath, then burned everything that would kindle.

The good news was that the troops waiting outside our city walls were sated with their destruction. Piles of gold, jars of oil, and stores of food had been wheeled into camp from the wreckage of Gezer. But no captives.

Under my direction Tamera had arranged for the meeting space to have two covered chairs, with a small table in between. Servants stood on both sides with fans, wine, and sweets in hand. The breeze was mild this morning, a sign that we were that much farther into spring. The season of war.

"When the negotiator arrives, I want everyone to leave except my slave," I instructed the attending priests, priestesses, and slaves. "My slave alone will serve us." When Tamera started to protest I told her that the envoy's entourage needed to be entertained as a distraction. I would do better speaking to the negotiator alone.

The highlanders waited until the heat of the day to arrive. I spotted them coming down the beach. Five men, gleaming with armor.

Okay, Chloe. Showtime.

"*Chérie,* try to barter with the prophet," Cheftu suddenly said. "I have an idea."

I turned to him, eyes bulging. "They are fifteen steps away and *now* you have an idea?" He slipped his waist sash down a little. I saw an oblong of white. "You still have the stones? How is that?"

"I hid them," he said. "They still work. Get the holy man."

The group was almost within hearing distance. I met and held the gaze of the leader, while speaking from the side of my mouth. "Weren't you robbed? Beaten? How do you still have them?"

"You don't," he said firmly, "want the details."

I didn't have time to consider it; the highlanders were here.

Our two groups stared at each other. There were five of them versus the three of us. The odds alone should make them feel better. Of the five, one looked like a Klingon, straight out of Cammy's newer *Star Trek* series. Two of them were twins. Another wore a white robe beneath his breastplate. The fifth was the leader. He had green eyes and curling black hair. Although he wasn't tall, he was beautifully proportionate. All the men had beards and curls that fell over their ears and down their chests.

The scaled bronze armor must have been extremely hot, even over the kilts and shirts they wore. They were definitely dressed for the mountains, not the beach. I rose to my feet, extending a hand to the leader. Touch was important, my father always said. Touch and perspective.

Pray God I would use both well.

"Welcome to Ashqelon," I heard myself say in our common language. "*B'vakasha,* seat yourself. There is entertainment and refreshments for your men in that tent." I gestured to a pitched tent just out of earshot. I motioned for Cheftu to bring an extra chair for one of them. The leader would have to choose which man would stay with him. That choice should reveal a lot about him and how flexible he was willing to be on this matter.

"Yoav ben Zerui'a is my name," the black-haired one said. "Ashqelon is a doomed city, *isha.* Your god Dagon is weak."

I opened my mouth to say, "I am *haDerkato.*" However, what came out was, "The *Derkato* is my name." I couldn't say "I am"? How weird. "Would you like wine? Beer?"

"I do not enter *b'rith* with the uncircumcised."

I looked up at him. "Would you really want me to be circumcised?"

His lips twitched, but I thought he was trying to keep from laughing. I felt slightly encouraged.

"*B'vakasha*," I said, "sit."

Cheftu returned with a chair for the other man. The one in white took it. He had the look of an ascetic, dark and lean, nervous. He twisted his beard, watching as Yoav—Joab in the Western rendering—and I spoke. This was David's henchman? He seemed quite civilized.

Reluctantly the two men sat, perched on the edges of their chairs. I would guess Yoav to be in his late thirties, early forties. The other man was probably not yet thirty. The twins and Klingon strode away, escorted by Tamera. They kept an eye on us.

I hoped that Yoav would be reasonable now. Perhaps without an audience, no preening male egos, the bartering would go better.

"The battle in the Refa'im was cleverly fought," I said. "The use of natural phenomena, the wind through the trees, to make it sound as though a war machine were moving through the forest, was quite brilliant."

"It was the plan of our God."

"Which your army enacted well," I concluded. We sat in silence. My father always said that silence worked like a corkscrew. Over time it would open even the tightest lips. So we sat and stared at each other. Yoav was bold, his eyes moving over my body with lustful intent. It's just another way to psych me out, I thought. I refused to blush, just let him make a fool of himself.

Cheftu was cool, standing at the edge of the tent, pitcher in hand. The muscles of his upper body were tense. I had no doubt that even one second of distress from me would lead to the murder of Yoav. It was kind of a nice feeling, because I really was intimidated. The wind blew, and we stared at each other. Occasionally, just because this had grown so ridiculous, I would smile at them.

Yoav looked away first. Ha! Score for the chick in the fish suit!

The other man, who still hadn't been introduced, smiled back. He looked like an overbred hunting dog. Lean and pointed. And somehow familiar in the angles of his face, the set of his shoulders. Had I seen him before? His fingers never left his beard alone, and side curls covered his ears, down to his chest.

Sweat dripped down my back. It must be sometime in March, I guessed. Already it was hot. Finally Yoav sat forward. "The Pelesti are done," he said. "Your god is weak, you have no more soldiers, you are no longer a threat to us."

"Then go on your way and leave us in peace," I said. "You won."

He blinked. I guessed that capitulation was not the accustomed response. After a quick glance at the man in white, he spoke again. "I cannot do that. It is *herim;* therefore all who have breath are *hal.*"

"Is this move against Ashqelon your decision or your king's?"

"Mine."

"Therefore, you are the king of this battlefield?"

His eyes narrowed. He spoke more slowly. "*Ken.*"

"Gezer is destroyed, is it not?"

"*Ken.* Razed to the ground. It was *hal.*"

"What cities of my people remain?"

"Lakshish, Qisilee, Yaffo, Ashdod, and Ashqelon."

"How many men of fighting age do you think remain?"

He tugged at his sidelock, musing. "The men from Lakshish and Ashdod served with the *seren* Yamir, *nachon?*"

The lexicon jumped in with a flashcard. *Nachon* meant everything from "exactly" to "this is correct?" to "bingo!" I gathered he was using the middle term. I nodded. "Yaffo and Qisilee are mostly fishing towns," I said. "From there we import the very luxury items that your king and people desire." Now I leaned forward. "Your people are highlanders. You are farmers, husbandmen with fields, cattle, and vineyards."

He leaned back, not a good sign. "*B'seder.*"

"Without us, you will not have the finely dyed cloth you wear now," I said, indicating the red tunic he wore beneath his armor. "Without us, your temples and high places will stink, for there will be no myrrh, no incenses, no spices. These are things we bring from far shores."

His eyes were opaque, like green beach glass.

"Most important," I said, leaning back, "we have iron."

"We will wipe you from the face of the land, then iron will not matter."

"Eventually Pharaoh will awaken from his slumbers," I said.

"Those who live north, in Tsor and Tsidon, will cast an eye your way. Our cousins from across *haYam* will lust after your fields. They all have iron.

"Between their seagoing ships, which will land on your shores—because if you 'wipe us from the face of the land,' then they will *be* your shores—their chariots, which can invade right up to the hills of your kingdom, their never-ending supply of men, food, and horses, for they are nations, not some petty kingdom whose mountain god fights for them, they will splinter your bronze swords with one hand, while they take your land, your women, and your totems with the other.

"We are your security zone, protecting you from marauders going east. We are your armory, and we are your merchants. We have your harbors in Ashqelon, Yaffo, and Qisilee; we have your weapons in Lak-shish, Ashqelon, and Ashdod. You don't have the skills or the man-power to replace us."

The man in white leapt to his feet. "She insults us!" he shouted. "She parades her god before us, shames *el ha*Shaday! We must not lis-ten to this!"

"Seat yourself, N'tan," Yoav barked. "She speaks economic truths." He glowered at me.

Sweat was dripping down my spine. I didn't dare look at Cheftu or out to sea. I stared at Yoav fixedly. Give us a break, I thought. Please!

He was silent for a long time. It was torture. Should I have said something else? Should I not have been so snide? Should I have begged for mercy? I was growing to know his features as well as my own, I'd been looking at him so long. If he'd had fewer scars, he would have been kind of handsome. As it was, he just looked rakish, a little pirat-ical. "It is a matter of face," he said. "The Pelesti have attacked us again and again."

"You said yourself, there are no men left."

"If all the women are like you, I wonder if men are necessary for a war," he muttered.

I chose to be complimented.

"What do you want?" he said. "What do you hope to get from me, from my tribesmen?"

"Our lives," I said simply. "Our cities and our lives. Already you have taken our husbands, brothers, and fathers. Our *seren* and his mother were also slain by you. Allow us to live here, that is all."

His gaze shifted off me to the walled city behind me. The white buildings were stacked like blocks, the sunlight casting blue shadows from the windows and doors. Flowers had just started to bloom, cascading from window boxes, trees, and pots. "It is a beautiful place," he said. "To the south you have a safe harbor."

"*Ken.* But it is useless to a people who terrace their hills and know nothing of ships."

"I want the secret of smelting. Teach us how to make iron."

Never say no. My father's words echoed through my head. No is the end of any negotiation. Lie if you must, twist the truth, but never say no. I licked my dry lips. "What would stop you from learning our secrets, then killing us anyway?"

He twisted one of the curls before his ears. "Nothing." His focus was on me again, laser beam eyes in green. "You must trust us."

"You must swear by your god," I said.

"That is an abomination to use the name of our god in swearing!"

I shrugged. "It is the only thing you hold dear. It is the only proof that you will keep your bargain."

"That's not all I want," he said.

I was afraid of that. "What else?"

"Your princeling must die."

Not Wadia, he was a boy! I had to bite back my emphatic no. "You have killed all his brothers, his father and mother, why not let the boy be? He is a child."

"He can piss against the wall; he is a man. He will grow to lead the Pelesti against us again." His eyes spoke honestly. "My lord king Dadua has more to do than battle the Pelesti, as one swats at mosquitoes, every spring."

"If Wadia swears not to attack?" I said. I heard the edge of desperation in my voice and cursed it.

"What is to keep him from breaking his word? What assurance have I?" Yoav asked.

"Because, though he is young, he is a man of honor."

Yoav leaned back, stretching his legs out, close to mine. Was that on purpose or accident? "I will take that wine now," he said. Cheftu was pouring it before he had finished his request. Yoav took it from Cheftu and handed it to me. "Drink first, as a courtesy."

Knowing it wasn't poisoned, I took a sip. It was tart, refreshing, and completely safe. I handed it to him. "Unlike you, we observe the laws of hospitality."

He downed the cup, then wiped his mouth with the back of his hand. "Unlike you, we offer it only to those who are kin and can be trusted."

This man was getting to me. *Calm down, Chloe.* Cheftu handed me a cup, and I drank it as quickly as Yoav, though more neatly. I set down my cup, my challenge clear. "What are your terms, Yoav?"

"The secrets of smelting. Your continued service as purveyors and merchants. Decampment of the valleys. We will man those watchtowers instead. Only the towns of Ashqelon, Ashdod, and Yaffo will remain whole."

They would take the countryside? "What of Lakshish? Qisilee?"

"My tribesmen will move in with the Pelesti in those cities. We will have our own temples, worship our god, and learn from your people the skills of smelting, pottery, dyeing . . . these frivolous details that are significant to a nation of any size."

A peaceful invasion. "What of Wadia?"

His gaze narrowed on me, then moved to the water behind me, the waves washing onto the shore. "I'll take you instead."

Adrenaline flooded me, leaving me suddenly cold, almost shivering. "Me?"

"You are the leader of Ashqelon. If you are removed, then they will have no one to follow. Moreover, if you are our hostage, then young Wadia will be held in check with his actions."

"That will not matter if you kill me," I said. My voice still sounded okay, which was a miracle. I was reeling.

He smiled. "I do not want you dead, I want your arrogant hands serving me."

Somewhere a pitcher dropped, shattered.

"What?"

"You, *haDerkato*, will be the ultimate trophy," he said with a wolfish smile. "A goddess serving as a slave in my household."

"My husband . . . ," I whispered, stunned.

He shrugged. "You are of an uncircumcised race. I will be no Samson to be led astray by Pelesti charms." His look was derisive. "Your husband can be as easily enslaved. You can mate and give me more slaves, I care not." He turned his cup over, a signal of completion. "But you will serve me."

It was me or Wadia? How did I get in this mess? This wasn't my problem! Shit, shit, shit. "What of the city, the people?" The few who were still alive.

"For the sake of my face, my pride, I must kill the remaining men."

I opened my mouth to protest, then shut it. "Go on."

"I will take half the population into slavery, in addition to taking all your slaves."

Half the remaining women, I thought, and Cheftu among others. "Go on."

"We will burn half your fields, but leave the city untouched."

I swallowed. "Go on."

"Lakshish will be untouched, but I will move my men into the fields between here and there."

I was right! He was going to take over the countryside, hole up the Pelesti in their cities like ghettos. Comfortable, nice ghettos, but the same idea.

"Lakshish will offer us homes in time for harvest. It will be the same with Qisilee. Ashdod, well, I think the lesson of Ashqelon—"

"You mean the destruction of Ashqelon."

He glanced at me. "The conquering of Ashqelon will be enough to teach your other cities that we are now masters of the land." He rubbed his thighs. "My men are tired, they are hungry for their wives and the cool of the hills. This should be enough for honor on both sides."

Could I kill him right now? Could I both do it and get away with it? "Swear you will not kill or rape the women," I demanded, my voice low. I knew the men, the few old and young men still alive, were a lost cause.

For the first time, he got offended. "We are holy men, *isha*. We do not rape. The seed of the tribes is not to be scattered about like that of idolaters! War in the land is a commission of *el ha*Shaday, not for the pollution of the body." He looked as though he might spit.

My breath was shallow. Should I agree to these terms? Or was there a better future for my, these, people? For the first time, I looked over Yoav's shoulder to Cheftu. His eyes were dark, his face immobile. *Death was the alternative, Chloe. It doesn't look that bad in comparison.*

Only in comparison—otherwise it was horrible!

Yoav rose. "Think on this, *haDerkato.* I will await your response." He glanced at the sky. "You have until dusk."

"How shall I contact you?"

"I will know your choice by your actions. If I see half of the remaining population file out of the gates, you in the lead, then I will know. If I don't, then I will raze Ashqelon to the ground. As you said, both Yaffo and Qisilee are ports, too. We don't need your city standing."

He turned around and walked off.

The twins and Klingon hurried to Yoav's side, with N'tan trailing behind. Once again the five walked down the beach.

I collapsed back on my chair, trembling all over. What had I done? What could I do? Why was this my job? Why had Takala cursed me like this? Why couldn't I just walk away?

Tamera appeared, with a cold yogurt-and-cucumber drink in her hand. It eased my stomach as I pondered my options. "How many boats are in the harbor? Enough to sail us all to Qisilee?"

"*Lo,* Sea-Mistress. They are still in dry dock for winter repairs." She adjusted her own fish cloak. "There is no sailing in this season."

So much for escaping. I slammed the rest of my beverage.

"What transpired?" she asked. "The *serenim* of the remaining cities in *ha Hamishah* beg to know."

Would they really do as I suggested? I was a goddess to them, but surely they didn't believe I was divine? The idea seemed preposterous. Then again, the whole tightrope incident was pretty unbelievable, and they had chosen me through that. I took a deep breath and destroyed her world with my words.

"The days of, uh, our supremacy are over," I said. "By dusk, half of us must be ready to become slaves. Half of the fields will burn. Wadia can return from Ashdod and rule, but he will be under the eye of the highlanders, for they are moving to the fields between here and Lakshish."

She sat down, cross-legged. "What of you?"

My hands were shaking. "I go to become a slave."

Tamera's eyes filled with tears, so I dismissed her.

When Tamera left, Cheftu's hands touched my shoulders. "We will slave together," he said.

"I can't ask that of you," I said. "You should stay here, teach Wadia how to rule."

"*Lo.* This time is not mine. This boy Wadia loves you, not your slave. My vow was to be with you. Also, Israelite slavery only lasts seven years."

"That's supposed to encourage me?" I burst out.

"We have less than a year here," he said. "The portal will open, then we will be freed."

"I don't know where a portal is. I came through water."

His hands tensed on my shoulders, then relaxed. "I will be with you. I thank God for that."

"The family that slaves together stays together?"

Only silence met my joke. I didn't blame him; it wasn't funny.

At dusk we opened the gates of the city. The sound of weeping and wailing was a constant whip to my conscience. Was there something else I could have done? Why had this been my job? God forgive me, but I didn't know what I was doing!

Like condemned ducks they followed me, a ragtag collection of mostly older women and a few teenage girls. The city had held tightly to the few boys who were left, who would be marriageable in a matter of months, and to the women whose wombs were fertile.

Ashqelon must keep her means of repopulating.

Cheftu walked beside me, proud and beautiful despite the chains in his ears. The same chains that I would have soon. Of all of this, that was the scariest thought—for it seemed the most real. I'd seen the scars on his ears. It was a beacon that didn't fade away. I straightened my shoulders and walked on.

We had thrown the Urim and Thummim, but the answer had been vague, frustrating. "Service is to serve." What the hell did that mean? When that was the same answer, time and again, we gave up. Cheftu excused himself to rehide the stones—and I finally understood where his secret hiding place was, that could pass through being naked. His cleverness was disgusting at times.

Outside the city a line of highlanders stretched from horizon to horizon. They were standing at attention like the Rockettes, immobile, the wind tugging their skirts, the setting sun blinding on their shields and dome-shaped helmets.

Impressive.

Yoav stood at the front, resplendent in red and green. I smelled my fear over the cinnamon and mint I'd bathed in before leaving the city. If I represented Ashqelon, Tamera said as she dressed me up, the highlanders would recall forever the beauty and majesty of the city.

My gown was finely woven, dyed, and embroidered. Gold hung from my neck, my shoulders, and my ears. Tamera had tied a sash of woven gold around my head, the colors of gold, blue, and green picked up in the striped sash around my waist. Attached to the back of my dress was an elaborate fish cloak, this one covered with fabric "scales" and "fins." My face, my shoulders and clavicle, all were adorned with gold dust in patterns of magic protection.

Was this how Cleopatra felt, getting decked out before she did herself in?

Shoulders back, my kohled gaze on Yoav, I walked to within four feet of him.

"You seek the subjugation of the Ashqeloni," I said. "By your very words, you have half her fields, half her people, and their goddess, *ha*Derkato. Swear, Yoav ben Zerui'a, in holy *b'rith*, that you will treat these captives with justice and honor, that the maids will remain pure, that the mothers will not be beaten. Swear that Ashdod will remain untouched, that *seren* Wadia will live, that Qisilee, Yaffo, and Lakshish will not suffer the sword or the torch. Swear to these things, and the ownership of these Pelesti is yours."

"I will not swear by the name of my god," he said.

"Then swear by his footstool, your totem."

He glared at me, ground his teeth for a moment, then shouted, "By the Seat of Mercy, I swear to these statements! By the footstool of *el ha*Shaday, these professions are true!"

Cheftu's hand clenched in my sash. Yoav looked at me, smug. "Subjugate yourself, goddess."

As gracefully as I could, I got to my knees. One highlander moved to stand behind me, another two stood at my sides. Yoav accepted a mallet and an awl from N'tan. I began to tremble violently; I prayed Cheftu would watch quietly.

We had discussed this. It wouldn't be much worse than getting my ears pierced, I hoped.

One man pulled my hair back, then another removed my earrings, handing them to me. The two men at my sides pressed my shoulders down, holding me still, firm against the soil.

Yoav, strangely enough, didn't look as though he were enjoying this. I blinked furiously against tears. I was grateful I'd emptied my bladder. He handed me a leaf. "Artemisia," he said. I accepted it, chewing furiously. I felt a block of wood press against the curve of cartilage in my ear above my lobe.

The prick of the awl.

"Breathe from your belly," he said, then pounded the awl through my ear.

The pain was sudden and consuming. While I was slumped, dizzy and sick from the first piercing, he did my other ear. The block holder and Yoav stepped away, shouting up to the Pelesti. "As I have enslaved your goddess, so are the people of the sea enslaved. You will serve the tribes, even as you are allowed life!"

The two men helped me up, turning me toward the city. I felt the

tug on raw skin as the chain was linked through. It pulled; I didn't have words for how it felt. I was light-headed and feared I was going to be sick. As I looked up, feeling the chain in my hair, the weight of it tugging at my tender ears, the people before me, the remaining Pelesti, knelt. I couldn't focus on any one face; I couldn't see that far.

From the walls of the city I heard, "Bless *haDerkato*, for she has given herself for Ashqelon." The highlanders set off toward the city, ready to kill the remaining, the very few remaining, men. The cries of pride turned into shrieks of fear. The chain moving through my ear suddenly seemed nothing. Perhaps it had saved a few lives?

Cheftu picked me up gently, easing the pull of the metal. He slipped something into my mouth, another leaf. "Chew and sleep," he said. "It will ease you."

My last thoughts were that the fear-struck screams had turned into wails of agonizing loss. Wails that followed me into blackness.

"THAT MEANS I WILL leave your side?" RaEm asked, focusing on Akhenaten through the blackness of the night.

His hand found her thigh, smoothing over her skin, soothing her *ka*. "It is a short visit, just to establish that the reign of the Aten will continue. Besides, you need a bridal voyage."

RaEm sighed, adjusting the headrest beneath her head, letting the warm breeze cool her body. "Your daughter is a joy, but a whole month of her may drive me mad."

He chuckled, kissing where his hands had been. "She loves you desperately, Smenkhare; she would do anything to please you."

This RaEm knew. Ever since she had wedded the girl, she had had almost no peace. Meryaten was desperately in love with her, always seeking to touch her, to kiss her, to be with her. RaEm sat up, bracing her head on her elbow. "I need to get her with child."

"*Aii*, well, that will take more magic than any priest I know has," Akhenaten said. "Besides, she will not be plowed with any save a royal tool." His voice brooked no disagreement.

But she will drive me insane until she is pregnant, RaEm thought. Between Tiye, who was suspicious but going blind, and Meryaten, who was blind but sweet, RaEm was paying too dearly for too little power. "Your mother—"

"Yours too—"

"Aye, well, she wishes to build a temple in Waset."

Akhenaten rose from the couch. "I will not speak of this," he said firmly. "Though I owe her respect for bearing me, still she has the heart of a . . . a nonbeliever."

"The temple matters nothing to me," RaEm said, following him to stand on the balcony, beneath the moon. "Meryaten I will keep happy. You, My Majesty, you are all I want." She pressed her lips together to keep from begging more. "Please don't send me away, away from your fire." She kissed his shoulder. "I will be so cold."

Akhenaten was on her, in her, immediately. "You want heat, you want to burn?"

"Aye, My . . . Majesty," she gasped out.

"You want my fire to flow through you?"

"Aye! Aye!"

He was violent, tearing her open to get deeper inside. "You will melt for no one but me. However you please my daughter, only I will feel your heat, Smenkhare. Never again will another person hear you gasp, you moan. Those belong to me." He slapped her hard, his hand around her throat. "I am your deity. You will have no other. I am the Aten."

He pulled away, raining liquid fire on her, salt from his depths that mingled with the tears torn from her deepest heart. Pharaoh walked away, pausing at the door. "Spend a month with your bride. Return to Akhetaten as my co-regent."

The door shut as RaEm curled up, wrapped in the cooling fire of her god.

PART

III

CHAPTER 6

Y FIRST WEEK OF SLAVERY passed in a drug-induced blur. Some-how we made it from Ashqelon to Mamre. The only points of clarity for me were each night when Cheftu made me shift the chains through the holes in my ears. I would cry and complain, but he was right. If I left them still, then as the piercing healed, the chains would be sealed into position. This way, at least, though the scars might be permanent, the chains would not be.

"Keep thinking of the future, *chérie*," he said. "This will not last for-ever."

As I was enduring the rawness and ache that resulted in a never-ending headache, I had a hard time thinking of the future.

One night, as the hundreds of us from Ashqelon were gathered by firelight, a small, bent man stood before us. "*Shalom*, welcome to the tribes Y'srael."

Cheftu and I exchanged glances, startled. It was one thing to know you are part of history and the Bible. It was entirely another to have someone greet you and confirm it!

"You are slaves because of war," the bent man said. "However, among the tribes we do not treat slaves as you pagans do." He coughed and spat into the fire. "Here, any person may become a slave. Maybe because he cannot pay his landlord? Or perhaps when the husband died, there were no brothers for the widow to marry, no home for her? So she sells herself and her children into slavery. It is common enough."

Was this Slavery 101?

"For seven years you will belong to the tribes. You will be slaves to the land, to the people and to our God, Shaday. You are pagans, so it is assumed you will worship the gods you brought with you. But you will obey our feasts and fasts."

He started counting on his fingers. "*Echad:* Every seventh day is a day of rest. No working, no cooking, no walking or lifting. No work. To defy this law is to draw a death of stoning upon yourself. No work."

Cheftu's hand tightened around mine.

"*Shtyme:* For a week in the spring there is no yeast. Nowhere. For any reason. *Shalosh:* No sacrificing babies. It is an abomination. Anyone found doing so will be stoned to death."

He continued. "At the end of seven years, it is the year of rest. The *Shabat* year. You will be set free, though any children you have will still be slaves until they are ransomed back." His black gaze flickered over us. "Tomorrow we arrive in Mamre. Some of you have been chosen for palace duty; others for the fields surrounding the city. It is the end of the barley harvest. Because *adoni* Yoav led this attack on Ashqelon, and because you surrendered to him, he is ultimately responsible for you." He paused, looking us over. "Have you anything to say?"

Were we supposed to ask questions? Cheftu glanced at me warningly. I swallowed my queries. That night the men and women were separated, then chained for the walk into the city; it was a matter of the tribesmen gaining face.

I didn't sleep well: images of black girls being raped by white owners, of strong men being beaten, of a section of the populace sweating on fields not their own, haunted me.

Was this what my life was supposed to be? Yesterday a goddess, today a slave? Had I done something majorly wrong? No, it wasn't personal, just a freak circumstance. The bigger question I had was, how could people of the Bible permit slavery?

The lexicon scribbled on the chalkboard of my mind: *Slaves here aren't personal property. As in Roman times, or Byzantine times, slaves are an entire class within the society.*

Great, so I'm at the bottom of the food chain?

It's your responsibility to bring in the food chain, but yes. You're a drone. Not a slave in southern plantation style, for you have far more rights than any of those poor souls.

I touched my ears as I pondered that: I'm a drone.

My first impression of Mamre was noise, confusion, and children.

They were everywhere, running in the streets, tugging at cloaks, laughing as they played, working with their parents, climbing up trees, and scampering down alleys. Children galore.

To someone with a splitting headache who hadn't bathed in a week, Mamre was hell. Most of the slaves had been left to the families in the fields to help with the barley harvest.

I'd never even eaten barley, much less harvested it.

Cheftu and I were going into the city, because we would be palace slaves. Apparently all the *giborim,* as Dadua's top men were called, lived communally. Though we were slaves, at least we were going to be together. That in itself would be worth a lot. We'd rarely had that experience.

Because Mamre was uphill, it made sense that the tribesmen—as they called themselves—would be called highlanders by everyone else. It was an old city. The buildings were heaped together, misshapen and crumbling. Even the city gates were unimpressive. But this site had been sacred to the tribesmen since *lifnay,* which meant "before" in the same way that "Once upon a time . . ." meant "before."

When you got up the hill, however, the view of terraced slopes and green fields was stupendous.

We arrived at the palace, walking around the front of the dilapidated building to the muddy track in back. After all, we were slaves now. Children raced through our party pell-mell, shrieking and laughing. My dress, which had been beautiful at the gates of Ashqelon, was now stained with blood, mud, garbage, wine—it was hideous, I hated even wearing it. But I had nothing else.

Three men stood inside the small, crowded courtyard. One introduced himself as the overseer. There were three levels of slaves, he said. The youngest children were body slaves, mostly from among the tribes. The next group were also tribesmen, adults who were in slavery for some reason like poverty or homelessness. Then there was us, the lowest of the low because we were among the uncircumcised. We would fill in wherever necessary.

"You," said a man standing by a barred door, pointing to Cheftu. "Report to the fields."

"We were told we would be living in the same place," I said. "Where is that?"

"You are the wedded pair?" the man asked, eyeing us both.

"*Ken*," we said in unison.

He shrugged. "There are plenty of watch houses you can occupy."

"But—," I protested but he'd already turned away.

"I will find you, *chérie*," Cheftu said as he was hustled away.

More children, these older and wearing nicer clothes, chased each other through the hallways and gardens. As I followed another person into another courtyard, I noticed the former were dark and narrow and reminded me of rabbit burrows; the latter needed someone to care for them.

From morning till afternoon I sat on a step in the courtyard, waiting. Every time I moved, someone would show up and say that another someone would be right out. I almost smiled, because this was so typically Middle Eastern. Or military, for that matter: Hurry up and wait.

I was starving by the time the fourth, fifth, and sixth stars were coming visible in the night sky, but I'd been told not to move.

Suddenly a tiny, faded red-haired woman barreled at me. "You!" she said, pointing at me. "What are you doing sitting here?" I opened my mouth to explain, but she yanked me up and pushed me out of the courtyard. "Help there," she said.

It was a kitchen, built apart from the main house so the heat and smells wouldn't bother any residents. Once I stepped over the threshold I was handed a jug of wine and told to go upstairs, on the main roof, and fill cups.

This was not a petite jug. It was about thirty-two inches tall, with a mouth four inches wide and two handles. My handy lexicon showed me a picture of a jug, a container that would hold a liter or so. Then it wrote the "=" sign to the word *jar*. Apparently, in this day and age, a jug was a jar. Either way, it held a whole river of wine. I followed other slaves, lugging my jar upstairs.

Again, modern Middle Eastern architecture held true here. The flat roof was the venue for entertaining. Lean-tos were pitched on all four sides of the roof, providing shelter from the chilly night wind. It was springtime on the coast, but not here.

I filled all of the clay cups—about fifty—then traipsed downstairs for another jug of wine. People had begun arriving, men and women with swords sheathed, worn more as insignia than weaponry.

The red-haired woman, who identified herself as the king's sister, Shana, glared at my clothes and bade me follow her. "Here," she said, throwing a bundle of fabric at me. "Dress well."

After she left, I unrolled the bundle. It was a straight sheath in harvest gold, with a sash of red, gold, and brown. I stripped off my current tattered ensemble and put it on. The dress was sleeveless with an asymmetrical shoulder, but it was long enough. With quick fingers I braided my hair, which RaEm had let grow very long, then replaced the gold headband. It helped keep my hair out of my face.

I hustled back to the kitchen, got my jar of wine, and ran back to the roof.

The *giborim*, what the Israelites called their soldiers, literally "mighty men," consisted of both men and women. They reclined around the low, long table. Embroidered cloths in red, black, blue, and saffron lay beneath clay dishes of Pelesti design, glazed in black and red. Bowls of grain, garnished with spices and herbs, served as decoration. Meat steamed on bronze dishes, while loaves of bread made a yeasty wall down the center of the table.

For this first time in my ancient travels, I wasn't invited to sit down. I was nobody—or less. I was invisible.

The music began, with Canani girls blowing on Egyptian-style double-reed flutes, playing the tambourine, and palming the drums. A blind *kinor*—my lexicon held up a picture of a harp and another "=" sign—player sat above them as they jammed. It was a pleasing, festive backdrop.

Women floated up from the stairs, their hair in braids, their bodies revealingly draped in brilliantly patterned clothes. Who were they? Lounging on cushions and leaning against each other, the *giborim* exchanged jests and challenged each other to drinking contests.

I was still amazed that I understood every word.

My task tonight was simple: Keep the watered wine cups full. The large, double-handled jug rested on my shoulder as I looked from man to woman, gauging their cup levels. Shana told us that *G'vret,* which meant "Lady," Ahino'am, the king's second wife, would be serving Dadua and his private army, with the help of his concubines.

They were the aforementioned floating women. One man to at least twelve women.

Spying an empty cup, I strode through the crowd, dodging Dadua's concubines, trying to keep from spilling. A female *gibor* held up her cup, not even glancing at me.

This would be my first time of pouring with an audience.

Fearful of spilling, I tipped the jar gently, feeling the weight of the wine inside shift. It was all in the timing. A stream poured over my shoulder, filling her cup. As it reached the top, I twisted the jug, causing the final drop to run along the rim and back inside.

No thanks, certainly no tip. I raised my head, looking for another empty cup. As I recrossed the room, I noticed it had grown silent, expectant. Even the musicians had quieted. I turned around slowly, trying to keep the jar from overbalancing.

Only because I was gritting my teeth did my mouth not fall open. Three people had entered the dining area. One was Yoav, looking impressive in a long, fringed robe that glittered as he moved. Another was a dark, petite woman dressed entirely in blue with an opaque stone the size of a baseball on her wrist.

The third man was dressed in a long, one-sleeved wrap dress, but his clothes faded to insignificance beside his beauty. Mahogany red hair hung in ringlets to his shoulders. Black eyes gleamed from beneath russet brows. His surprisingly white smile was framed by russet beard, mustache, and side curls that hung to nearly his waist. He looked like a mythological hero rendered by Dante Rossetti, the nineteenth-century artist.

He raised his hand and offered a blessing to Shaday as I was having a mini–heart attack. This was Dadua? David? I looked around for Cheftu, catching his gaze across the room. Was it my imagination, or was he as shell-shocked?

When the prayer was over, the feasting began. After being on a diet of either corn or scallions or figs, I found it tantalizing to see the massive variety these people were consuming. First a soup of yogurt with raisins and grain for garnish, then the meats: lamb, poultry, and fish. Barley was piled in hills on copper dishes, flavored with oil and herbs. And bread, tons of bread.

They needed lots of wine, so I was busy trying to not spill, moving through the crowd gracefully and fast so I wouldn't hear, "Slave!" shouted out.

Finally the dishes were removed, the drinking had slowed, and people grew quieter. Dadua reached for a *kinor*.

I could not believe I was here.

The room fell silent. He flexed and relaxed his hand, then stroked the strings to test the sound.

Who can stand on the mountain of Shaday? Who can dwell on his sacred hill?
Walk uprightly, walk righteously, speak truth from your heart
Slander not anyone in whole or in part.
Work well with your neighbor, lift up your tribesmen
Despise those who curse Shaday, and honor those who trust in him.
Truth keepers through pain, freelenders all.
Stand up and walk through Shaday's holy hall.

It was a pretty melody, embedding itself into one's brain. As the last note died away I glanced at the *giborim*. Tears streaked every face. Dadua lifted his head, looking out on their expectant expressions.

"I speak of a place that is not yet ours," he said. "It is a place where my *nefesh* cries *el ha*Shaday must dwell."

My lexicon held up a sign: *Nefesh = ka = psyche = soul.*

"There," he said, "I will build a palace for us, and a palace for the God of our fathers. No longer will he live in a tent, like a pagan deity on a journey. He will have a home, with his people."

They were stunned.

"You, my faithful thirty, my *giborim*, will be given homes on border properties. You and you," he said, pointing to two bearded younger men, "will be on the south side, protecting us against the marauders of the Negev. You and you," he said to two others, "will go north, between the tribes of Zebulon and Asher against the Tsori, Tsidoni, and Mitanni." In this way he parceled out homes to his men. Homes that cost him nothing but provided him with border patrols. The men would be fighting not only for their liege, but for their own homes and families.

I looked over at Cheftu. He was agog.

"We will build a fleet," Dadua continued. "Thus the land will stretch from the desert to the cedars!"

The men cheered; they liked being in control; they liked their victorious God. Dadua sang the song again, teaching it to us until we were all singing. Not exactly a drinking song, though that didn't put off anyone's efforts.

I was pouring from my fourth jar by now.

Dadua talked about a library he wanted to build. Also a residence for students of Shaday's words and a section of town where foreign artisans and craftsmen could share their skills with the highlanders. All of this was to be built on a hill.

A hill? I felt razor-stubble goose bumps against the fabric of my skirt. Not that hill; surely I wasn't here for that? I clenched the jar to steady my trembling.

"This hill lies just beyond our reach," Dadua said. "However, I offer a challenge of the ages to you, my best, my most sacred brothers.

We who were outlaws together in the caves of Abdullum, we shall rule together."

Enthusiastic shouting drowned him out.

"For the commission of this one act, I will offer the greatest reward."

"Learned from Labayu, did you?" a *gibori* suggested laughingly.

Dadua smiled. "*Ken.* I learned a man will do a lot to bed a woman!"

They all laughed. Cheftu whispered in my ear, startling me since I didn't know he was standing that close. "According to Holy Writ, David gave his king Saul the foreskins of two hundred Pelesti to take Saul's daughter Mik'el to wife." He kissed my ear as he moved through the crowd.

"*Lo,*" Dadua said. "This is not for the bed of any woman, who can choose to deny you even that pleasure when it suits her," he said in an undertone. The men hooted as I wondered what woman ever had refused him. He was gorgeous, charismatic . . . heck, he was even a musician. None of my friends would have refused him. I glanced at the woman beside him, *G'vret* Avgay'el. She was his second wife, exquisite and looking at him with pure adoration, even after that comment.

Dadua continued. "For this feat, if he should survive, Shaday willing, he will become, for now and ever after, the *Rosh Tsor haHagana.*"

The lexicon in my head threw out visuals. I saw a picture of George Washington as general; then MacArthur saying, "I shall return"; finally Colin Powell. Dadua was giving an open call for the highest-ranked officer.

"He must give me Jebus."

Silence fell like a stage curtain, straight down and blacked out. Dadua smiled at them. "Abdiheba, king of Jebus, claims that only the blind and lame can defeat his mountain citadel. Moreover, he claims that any man who invades will become blind and lame. I fear I don't understand this logic." Dadua chuckled, and the *giborim* joined him. "So here is the challenge: I want, and Shaday wants, to celebrate the Feast of Weeks in Jebus! As my city!"

Jebus? Why Jebus?

The lexicon showed me the map again, marked with the cities of the Philistines. To the east of them, high in the mountains I read the word *Jebus.* Then the letters melted into English, into modern English, revealing Dadua's desire. I was braced, but imagination is nothing like reality.

Jerusalem.

David and Jerusalem. I didn't know much about the Bible, but I'd heard a lot about Jerusalem. My father had spent the latter part of his career on Jerusalem. Still, I hadn't a clue as to chronology. Did David conquer it now? Or was there a period of waiting or siege?

Cheftu moved behind me. As I turned to trade my empty jug for his full one, I whispered, "Our children are going to memorize their history books." That way, if they happened to stumble into a time-traveling career, they'd be better equipped than their clueless mother.

"*Nachon,*" he said as I moved off, a fresh jar on my shoulder.

Would Cheftu know the timing here? If it was in the Bible, he would. Was it in the Bible, though?

"Get me the city and the *haHagana* is yours," Dadua said to the *giborim.* "The first man to open the doors to Jebus is forever my first in command." This position wasn't already taken? I glanced at Yoav, sitting motionless, his eyes like green glass. Was his job up for grabs here?

In a single voice they responded, "Thy will be done."

I poured cup after cup of wine as I listened to the men's mutterings, while dancers and jugglers entertained, in addition to the many musicians. *HaMelekh* Dadua, King David, reclined, a satisfied smile on his face. He knew how to motivate his men.

The night passed on, the *giborim* fell asleep in their places, several of them staggering to their rooms, the others snoring by the doors. We slaves moved silently among them, picking up cups, plates, shooing away cats and dogs that thought it safe to dine while the soldiers rested.

Cheftu waited for me so I would know where to go to sleep tonight. I couldn't believe we'd just arrived this morning. "We are in a watch house," he said as we walked through the vineyard. The leaves had just started to grow on the vines. Unlike French vines, these weren't espaliered. They were left in little bushes, with one cord holding them in a line.

In the center of the field was a cylindrical building, with a spiral staircase to the door. "Our home," he said, squeezing my waist. We were going to live together, like a married couple. After two years of being married, we were finally going to play house. I leaned my head on his shoulder.

It looked like paradise to me.

Dawn was breaking as we mounted the steps, opened the door. It took a moment for my eyes to adjust. The interior was only slightly more luxurious than the exterior. It was dug like a pit, deep enough that I could stand and still see out, for the walls ended about two feet from the roof, giving a 360-degree view.

A cursory glance revealed a few niches in the wall stocked with a pallet; musty and torn; two blankets, both of scratchy wool; a round, unglazed clay dish; a water jar; and an oil lamp.

We made up the pallet, and Cheftu fell onto the bed. He was a fieldworker and had to be there within the hour—though the Israelites didn't have a designation for times as short as an hour. A little light fell on the blankets across his calves. His hair was growing out, and he'd decided the reason highlanders had beards was because their bronze blades were too dull. He wore scabs from his attempts to remain clean-shaven.

"Are you finished thinking?" he whispered.

"How did you know I was thinking?" I whispered back. I thought he'd fallen asleep.

"You frown."

Oh. I hadn't known that.

"Come to bed, beloved, let me remove that frown." As he spoke he leaned over, propping himself up on his arm, blinking sleepily.

"He's set his men against each other as a competition to make it into Jebus," I said as I removed my sash. "Does David wipe out Jebus at this time? I know he does somewhere along the way."

"How do you know that?" Cheftu asked, pulling back the blanket for me.

"Because it is called the city of David . . ." I paused as I slipped out of my sandals. "Unless that is Bethlehem?"

He chuckled. "Jebus is also David's city."

I unbraided my hair, running my fingers through it, finger combing through the knots. "Why are we here in this time period?" I asked. "I came back just for you. This is the big time, Cheftu. We're not in the middle of unknown history, or something most people think is fable. We are living a history that all of Western civilization inherits!" I heard the edge in my voice; I was really wired. I turned away, embarrassed at my emotion.

As I slipped my dress over my head, I suddenly felt Cheftu against me, the sleepy warmth of his body against the night-cold skin of mine. His arms embraced me, pulling me safe into the cocoon of his heat. We were almost of a height, cheek to cheek in the dawn.

"Tell me," he said. "What do you fear?" I felt his words on my neck.

"This is real," I said. "What are we doing here? What if we screw up?"

He kissed my shoulder, then picked me up and carried me to the pallet. His body followed mine down, and as I felt the familiar rush of heat at the thought of being joined with him, he spoke. "What mistakes are there to make?"

Instead of naming the millions of ways I could imagine, I drew him to me. His mouth was hot, sweet, his body growing to mine. "Look at me, *chérie*," he said. "What mistakes are there to make? You speak of history as though it is carved from stone."

"Isn't it?"

"History is daily life, beloved. History is a couple making love, making a family, laughing and crying. No one knows what history is until that couple is ash and their children's children are making love and making families."

"This is one of the reasons I love you," I whispered, raising up to feel him enter me. What a miracle to be connected like this. What a freeing paradigm shift he suggested.

"History is perspective," he breathed against my skin, his pupils wide. I held him tightly with my arms and legs, tears trickling from the corners of my eyes. For me this was prayer.

Cheftu pulled my arms over my head, holding me fixed, facing him. "Look at me, beloved. We are history. God has placed us here, who knows why. But"—he drove into me—"we will learn. Time passing will become history."

I leaned forward and licked a drop of sweat off his chin. "So are we about to make history?"

"*Lo*," he said with a devastating smile. "We are about to make ice cream." Then he began to melt me, harden me, taste me, and revel in me, his delicious treat.

From that apex, my day raced downhill; I met the millstone.

Suddenly the clichés made sense to me. Tying a millstone around your neck could easily drown you. Bad news could be just like a millstone.

And a woman's work was never done.

The basis of every ancient people's diet—on which I'd become quite an expert—was bread. Bread required dough. Dough was made of water, yeast, and flour. God made water, yeast was kept from the last batch of bread, and making flour was my task.

It was a mindless, backbreaking, two-person job.

My teammate was a girl, a homely thing with bug eyes, buckteeth, and a lisp. She was all knees and elbows. Her mother had sold her into slavery when she was ten. Now she was twelve, with barely budding breasts. However, she was the first platinum blonde I'd seen this side of Malibu Barbie. White blonde, Viking blonde, California-dreamin' blonde. She was called 'Sheva and didn't speak, even when spoken to.

Shana, the bossy redhead, showed me the millstone, which was a foot in diameter with a hole in the middle. It looked like a granite doughnut. "I need seven measures of grain," she said. "There is the storeroom. 'Sheva here will help you."

She walked off. I looked at the girl. "Do you know what to do?"

She stared at me blankly.

"Do you? I don't."

No response.

Fearful of screwing up, I ran after Shana—the woman could walk fast for having such short legs. "Forgive me, *g'vret*, but—"

She turned, hands on hips. "What now?"

"I, uh, don't know what you want me to do."

For a moment she was silent. "You don't know how to make bread?"

Hesitantly I shook my head.

"You don't know how to grind grain?" Her voice was rising. People all around the courtyard were starting to look, to see what the commotion was about.

I shook my head again, tried to smile beseechingly. My face was warm.

"You are the most useless slave I have ever known!" She turned to look at her audience. "Look at her! An adult woman! With a husband! She can't make bread! She can't even grind grain! *Ach!* Thank Shaday no children have graced you, *isha.* They would have starved!"

My face was so hot, you could've fried an egg on it. She looked back at me, as though public humiliation might have taught me how to use the millstone. I focused on her feet, waiting for the next scathing remark.

"*Ach!* So you were raised a *g'vret,* a lady. It is no wonder our god can beat yours; our women are not so delicate. Delicate women breed delicate babes." *Tch*'ing her way back, we returned to the millstone.

'Sheva, the human mushroom, was sitting motionless, staring into space.

"*Yelad*"—Shana called 'Sheva a child—"hurry and fetch some grain!" She clapped, and the mushroom ran. "You!" she said to me. "Sit here."

I was supposed to sit on the doughnut? Fumbling with my skirts, I managed to straddle it nicely.

"You will spin around, while the *yelad* pours the grain into the hole, you see?" I nodded my head. I would have agreed even if I'd had no clue. I'd been embarrassed enough for one day.

"See here," she said, gesturing to a channel that ran from beneath the millstone. Then I realized that the millstone was two pieces, and the device made sense. I was using the combined weight of myself and granite to scrape the little grain pods until they were as fine as dirt. Then the *yelad* would collect them, weigh them, and either store or use them.

"Grind seven measures," Shana said, "then I will teach you, poor Pelesti fool, how to make bread."

She left just as 'Sheva returned.

If this were ancient home ec, I would have failed. The first batch was too rough, so I had to regrind it. Then it was too fine, more like dust than flour. It looked like the stuff Mimi had used, but since I didn't know what was next in the process I was quiet. Shana had given up yelling at me. She just sighed extravagantly, then poured more grain so I could do it again.

By lunchtime I had three measures. Since I was running behind, I had to work instead of eat. 'Sheva mechanically poured grain in the hole while she picked her nose. I kept a careful watch on her two hands, just to make sure the pouring hand and the picking hand didn't overlap.

My back ached, my legs hurt, and my backside was really sore. This action reminded me of being a little kid, sitting on the playground roundabout and spinning it while seated. However, stone on stone didn't move with any great ease.

For the first time I really missed being a priestess or a princess or an oracle. Hell, even a mermaid! This was bloody hard work.

By dusk I could barely move. Shana sighed but dismissed me. Once through the vineyard, I climbed the steps slowly. Our room was dark, empty. I fell face first across the pallet—

Later Cheftu woke me. I think he tried to talk to me, but I kept falling asleep.

I awoke with the rooster crowing at dawn. I felt as though I'd been under the granite doughnut. Cheftu was already gone.

Since I'd worn my only set of clothes to grind in, then sleep in, I slipped into my old dress and hobbled through the vineyard. In the distance I could see the men working the barley fields already. Some were cutting, some were sorting grain from chaff by throwing it in the air, and some were standing around. I couldn't pick out Cheftu from this distance.

By midmorning I was through about five measures. Shana allowed me some food, then sent me back to work. Cheftu came home late, hot, and tired and we both lay on the pallet, too exhausted even to eat.

By week's end, however, we were in much better condition. In fact, we lived life so autonomously that, except for the chains, it was almost like being free. Though he was exhausted, Cheftu never complained. He said it was a nice change from medicine. That seemed an odd comment, but I didn't ask any more. He taught me a song they sang in the barley fields, a farmer's almanac set to swing.

"Two months to harvest the olives; two months of planting grain. Then two months of late planting. The month of hoeing up flax, a month to harvest the barley. Then two months of vine tending, and a month of the fruits of summer."

Israel was an exhausting, hardworking place, but the people really did whistle while they worked. We could even hear them singing in the courtyard of the palace as we gave thanks for being pampered palace slaves.

"Sing with joy to Shaday, it is fitting for his people to praise him. Praise him with harp, sing along with the ten-stringed kinor, sing to him a new song. Play skillfully and shout with joy.

"From the heavens el haShaday looks down, sees all the earthlings. From his dwelling place he watches all who live on earth. He who forms the hearts of all, who considers everything they do."

The barley fields were considered Dadua's property, which of course *haMelekh* didn't glean in person. The cutters walked in a circle as though they were oxen tied to a pivot point, for the harvest. The fields were square—and this cut a perfect round of grain for Dadua. I was out distributing water when I noticed them for the first time. The poor.

Though I was technically enslaved, I had food and shelter. Though they were technically free, they didn't. Suddenly I understood why so many people sold themselves or their children into slavery. In a way it was almost a better life. That seemed terribly perverse.

I saw them clumped in the corners, picking barley. When I asked about it, Shana said, "It is the law. Not everyone has inherited fields, so those who have are bidden to share with those who have not. They are allowed to glean whatever is left, and the corners."

When I returned to the courtyard and talked about it, 'Sheva got excited for the first time, offering to go to the fields with me. It was possibly the longest sentence she'd ever constructed. We walked there together, and then she left me, running toward some of the gleaners.

"It's her family," another of the slaves said. "They sold her because they couldn't afford two girls and a boy."

I watched as 'Sheva stood before a stoop-shouldered man and a cowering woman with a baby at her breast.

"As soon as she was sold, they had another child. A son," the slave explained. Obviously they had kept him. Poor 'Sheva.

No one touched the mushroom, and then we saw her family walk away. She bowed her head, picked up her jug, and stumbled farther into the fields. She was going the wrong way, neither toward the palace nor toward the town. We watched her in silence.

"All those corners end up being about a quarter of the harvest. That seems a lot to lose," I said conversationally.

The other slave's eyes turned cold. "They are tribesmen. Either we care for them this way, or they will have to beg or become as we are. Slaves." She moved on, leaving me standing, pondering, until I heard my cue:

"You! *Isha!* Water!"

That afternoon I tried to be sweet to the mushroom. She was in prime fungal form, bundled up and inwardly focused. There were lifetimes between us, though she wasn't much younger than Wadia and I'd bonded with him immediately. I sighed, turning the stone.

"She comes!" suddenly echoed through the courtyard. Shana came out of nowhere and pushed me off the grindstone. One of Dadua's concubines, Hag'it, gathered the flour quickly, then both women vanished through the courtyard gates.

Who was coming? Men and women began to flood through the courtyard, and no one paid me and 'Sheva any attention. "Did you see the spectacle he is making of himself over her?" I heard.

'Sheva's head rose up, like a puppet on a string. She turned to me, eyes focused. "Mik'el," she said, grabbing my hand. We ran through the courtyard, out the gate, and into the crowd.

It seemed as though every citizen of Mamre was outside, all pushing toward the gate. 'Sheva was lean and slippery, and she never let go of my hand as we squeezed through the crowds, pushed and shoved through the throng by the gates, until we stood in the front. Dadua stood at the city gate wall, dressed in his finery.

Sunlight glinted off the crown on his head. He wore a purplish blue dress edged in gold that spiraled around his legs. His beard and hair were oiled, and gold hoops hung in his ears. Even his sandals were gold. N'tan stood to his side, his official white ensemble brilliant in the afternoon light. At certain angles N'tan looked really familiar.

"Isn't he divine?" 'Sheva said, staring at the monarch.

What was going on? I glanced at Dadua. "*Ken*, he is very comely."

"He writes the most divine music," she said, entranced.

I was peering over the crowd, trying to see what we were all waiting for. The crowd had bottlenecked, so we couldn't move forward. I muttered something affirmative to 'Sheva.

"He is divine with a slingshot," she continued. The girl was a groupie, I realized. With a one-word vocabulary.

"I see the years haven't humbled her," somebody behind me said.

Through the shadows of the gateway a woman approached on a white donkey led by a finely dressed warrior. A man followed behind, ashes smeared on his head, his clothes torn so that the dingy white of his undershirt showed. Behind him trailed four small children, the eldest carrying an infant.

"It took so long to gather her because she needed to wait out her time of impurity. She just birthed her last son," another crowd member said.

"Look at her, dressed as a bride," a woman scoffed. "A virgin, by the eye of Ashterty, I think not!"

"Only those arrogant Binyami would dare send a bride who was married to another man."

"It's a wonder Dadua wants her back."

"She's a harlot!"

"She was a tool of Labayu's revenge."

Comments floated all around me, useless since I didn't know what was going on and no explanations were forthcoming. Even 'Sheva was paying no attention, just watching Dadua and sighing. This child had a major huge crush on the king of Israel. I imagined she could get in a long line on that count. Though he always had the option of adding to his collection, I doubted he'd ever look at her.

The object of all the surrounding gossip walked right in front of me. She was veiled, and gold disks hung from her headdress and the edges of her veiling and banded around her arms and legs. The woman carried at least twenty extra pounds in currency.

Who was she?

"Why is she back, then? If she was so happy?" The crowd conversation continued.

"Dadua made it part of the *b'rith* covenant when he agreed to rule over Yuda and Y'srael."

"*Ach*, so he unites the old house of Labayu with the new house of Dadua."

She was Mik'el, Saul's daughter? Dadua's first wife? The weeping of the gray-haired man following her made my heart clench. He must love her deeply to humiliate himself like that.

Mik'el didn't spare him as much as a glance.

Dadua stepped down and lifted her off the donkey, then set her beside him. A snap of his fingers produced another crown. He lifted her face veil, shielding her from the crowd with his body. As the crown touched her head, the wails of the child, forsaken by his mother, rent the air. Dadua kissed Mik'el on both cheeks, then turned her to face her subjects.

Her expression was frozen, though her face was lovely. Long brown hair fell to her waist, and huge doe eyes surveyed us all dispassionately. She stood tall and regal, the wind blowing her dress against her high breasts and soft stomach. Mik'el stepped forward, her arm linked with

Dadua's, into the city. The child cried again. They paused for a moment, then walked on.

When we got back to the kitchens, there was hell to pay. Shana yelled at us, then put us to work cleaning vegetables. My ears were still ringing with epithets when I got back to my house. I lay down next to Cheftu, who was already asleep on the pallet.

He turned to his side, slipping his arm around me. Feeling clothes on my body seemed to wake him up.

"Why are we here?" I asked sleepily. "What real significance is there to my grinding grain and you working the fields? Is this a cosmic joke?"

Cheftu frowned. "I thought you were happy. I thought you liked living here, being together. No madmen are chasing us, the ground is secure, and the waves are far away. It's nice. We can actually live instead of running from one disaster to another."

"How can you be so complacent?" I asked.

He shrugged, that Gallic movement that made my blood race. "Is it complacent to be content?"

I got up to pace, restless though I was tired. "Don't you think we should be serving a purpose, though? You're a doctor, for heaven's sake!"

"What is the purpose of life? Of love? Of living?" he asked, ignoring my last comment. "It is the end of itself," he answered. "It is the question and the answer."

"I hate it when you give those kinds of esoteric responses," I said. "It makes me feel very young and . . ." I searched for a word.

"Idealistic?" he said in English.

"I mean, why are we here?"

He sat up, adjusted the blankets, and linked his fingers behind his head. "You claim you came back for me alone."

"I did!"

"Then I alone am not enough?"

I did a double take before I realized he was teasing. "*Ach*, forget it," I said, suddenly sick of the subject. "There is a wedding feast tonight. Dadua's first wife is back. They are renewing their vows, or remarrying, or something, for political reasons."

"*Chérie*, at any point in history, it is the same. Only when we see it in a book does history appear to be happening every moment. In truth we just live, day to day, whether under the rule of Pharaoh and in court, or under the rule of David and in the fields."

I splashed some water on my face and rebraided my hair as he spoke. "Well, then I'm off to be under the rule of Shana, in the kitchens," I said on my way out.

The spirit in the palace was one of forced gaiety. Children dressed up for their father's first marriage's renewal of vows raced up and down the stairs. Shana stood at the top of the staircase, guarding the decorated roof.

"You!" she said. "Keep them from coming up here before the feast."

I played the role of cop, keeping the children away and letting the adults in. *G'vret* Avgay'el was preparing the evening's feast to honor her husband and his first wife. That must really stink.

However, she put on an impressive spread, competition or no. Grain in five forms, fruit that was steamed, stuffed, mashed, root veggies that were roasted, and a platter of dark, stringy meat passed by me. My stomach was growling as the family began to arrive. That was the amazing thing about dinner tonight: all family members would be present, including children and wives.

It was a boisterous meal, the *yeladim* singing and running around, women laughing and chattering, Dadua overseeing it all, exchanging pleasantries with the various men also considered part of his household. Mik'el, still wearing her pocket change, sat as still and exciting as a statue.

Actually, that was unfair. A statue could be exciting. Mik'el, however, made the mushroom seem vibrant.

As the moon rose, the men demanded a story. Dadua, who hadn't actually looked at his bride all night, agreed enthusiastically. Avgay'el was beseeched to tell one, as she was the best storyteller.

Charmingly hesitant, she began. "*Beresheth . . .*"

I could not breathe, from her first word. My lexicon translated, stumbled, then translated again: *In the beginning . . .*

"Yahwe created the sun, moon, and stars with a single word. Like a tent he stretched the skies over the Deep, making a place for his court, the *elohim*, upon the Higher Waters." Avgay'el gestured gracefully, showing how God lived above the rest of the planet.

"Now look: For by his creating, Yahwe rose over the Deep, which rebelled against him. Tehom, the dark queen of the Deep, tried to drown the creations of Yahwe, but in a chariot of burning flame he rode against her, his weapons hail and lightning."

The children watched, wide-eyed. I sat there, bewildered.

"Tehom set her champion Leviathan against Yahwe, but Yahwe hit his skull with lightning, then thrust a sword into the serpent Rahab's heart. The waters of the Deep fled from Yahwe's voice. Tehom, shaking with fear, surrendered. Yahwe declared the moon to partition the seasons, the sun to differentiate between day and night. In awe of Yahwe's victory, the morning stars sang together, while the *elohim* shouted for joy."

The children shouted, elated, while the adults knuckled the floor—the tribesmen's approach to applause. Avgay'el leaned forward to her audience, her voice soft. "Before a plant or a field was growing from earth, or a grain had taken root—for Yahwe had not sprinkled rain, nor peopled the land with earthlings—yet from the day that the earth had divided from the sky, a mist rose from the deep to moisten the land.

"From the *adama*—"

Red soil, my lexicon provided.

"Yahwe, with his hands, crafted an earthling."

The children gasped with surprise.

"And into his nostrils, like you have, Avshalem, or you, K'liab," she said to two of Dadua's children, "Yahwe blew *nishmat ha hayyim*."

The screen in my brain filled with the image of God and Adam touching, the Michelangelo fresco in the Sistine Chapel. Only now, instead of fingertip touching fingertip, the bearded heavenly portrait of God was breathing into an inanimate Adam: who opened his eyes and looked at his creator.

That, my lexicon said triumphantly, *is* nishmat ha hayyim. *The very divine breath of God, which gives life, a zeal for living.*

"Now look: Man has become flesh," Avgay'el said.

My hands were shaking; I hoped no one would request wine.

"So: Yahwe grew a garden; eastward of Eden he settled the man, Adama, whom he had formed of clay and his own breath. All trees that pleased the eye, pleased the stomach, grew there by Yahwe's word. The tree of life grew there, also the tree of differentiating between good and bad." Avgay'el paused to tousle one kid's hair.

"Yahwe brings the man to the garden to husband it. 'Eat from any tree,' he tells the man. 'But the tree of differentiating between good and bad, you will not know. The day you eat of it is the day death knows you.' "

"Isn't he lonely?" one of Dadua's sons asked.

Avgay'el smiled at him. "*Ken*, he is lonely. Yahwe has made all the creatures of the field, the air, and the sea, Adama names them, but none are his partner."

"But Mik'el is Dadua's partner, *nachon*?" one of the children said. The entire room stiffened, looking at the motionless woman. Avgay'el smiled at her competition and didn't miss a beat.

" 'Poor Adama,' this is what Yahwe says. So he lays Adama in a deep sleep. While he sleeps, Yahwe takes a rib, seals the wound. Starting with the rib of man, Yahwe handcrafts a woman, then returns her to Adama's side."

"What's her name? What's her name?" they shouted enthusiastically.

"You know her name," Avgay'el said, smiling. She looked like a Wedgwood cameo. "The mother of all things. Who is she?"

"Hava!" they cried in unison.

My lexicon unnecessarily provided me the name: *Eve.*

Avgay'el turned to the bride, Mik'el. "As Hava ruled Eden and Adama, so I welcome you as my sister, to rule—" She stopped speaking, then bowed gracefully. Was there going to be more?

Mik'el looked at all of us. The room leaned forward imperceptibly, curious as to what she would say, how she would graciously respond. She was silent, probably gathering her thoughts. She looked straight at us. "I would like to retire now."

A gasp. Dadua's face hardened, but he rose with her. Avgay'el stayed bowed, her face shielded. The queen Mik'el rose and walked out. Dadua was right behind her.

"*Ach*, well, she was tired after such a long day," an older *gibori* said. "She is not as young as she used to be."

She'd probably scratch his eyes out for that observation. I watched them leave, then it was time to clean up once more.

Really, my current servitude wasn't much different from being a waitress. With no tipping. But no come-ons, either. Actually, I was almost invisible. It seemed to me that slaves were wallpaper. Had I ever paid attention to the hundreds of men, women, boys, and girls in the palaces of Thebes in Egypt? Or Kallistae in Aztlan? Had I been as blind then as I was now unseen?

RaEmhetepet slapped the girl, sending her away. Some blessed time alone! Some time to breathe without fourteen handmaids, three flower-strewing children dogging her every step, five women to touch up her coiffure, her makeup, adjust her clothing. She'd had enough; enduring this was driving her crazy!

Meryaten came in almost immediately. "My lord, you struck that child?" RaEm's bride was too fragile, too damnably sweet, to strike anyone.

RaEm focused on her image in the mirror. "What of it?"

The girl glided across the room. "Are you not happy, my lord? Is there something you require?"

She laid a small hand on RaEm's shoulder, and RaEm had to fight to not flinch. It was the beginning of her cycle and her month-long banishment had expanded into two months. Never had she ached for someone the way she did for Akhenaten. She needed his body, his voice, his mind. She was cold, chilled to the bone with longing. "I abhor being here with these rebels," she finally said.

Meryaten glided to the window, looking out on the city of Waset.

She leaned on the low mud-brick wall. "I confess that I love it here. Look! It is so colorful, so vibrant."

RaEm stonily watched herself in the bronze mirror. Waset was a wreck. The temples that had once been brightly painted and emblazoned with jewels were faded, neglected. The colorful standards that had once blown from every window throughout the city were gone. It was hot, white, crowded, and noisy. The Way of the Nobles was lined with boarded-over homes. The practice fields for Hat's once great army were now overgrown pastures for field mice.

Though RaEm loved the man, she had come to loathe the ruler Akhenaten was. Where was his pride? Did he not know what these people said of him, the Son of the Sun, Pharaoh, living forever!, the god incarnate? She didn't care much for the people, either, certainly not as individuals. They were so much grain in a field. However, as a mass they were the wealth of Egypt, the throne legs on which rested the weight of the royal house.

They despised Akhenaten.

Meryaten was yet on the balcony, listing the many things she found delightful about Waset. RaEm watched coolly as her makeup was applied: kohl for her eyes, harsh lines that took away their almond-shaped curves. Her head was shaved, the night's growth removed. Did they ever wonder why her face had no need of shaving? Her stomach growled, but she ignored it. Especially in Waset she needed to stay as lean and masculine looking as possible, since they were unused to the idea of men and women being undifferentiated, save for clothing. She thanked the gods that shirts were the fashion of the moment.

Though her dresser would testify to seeing the bulge of Smenkhare's proven masculinity, still RaEm was concerned. Meryaten hadn't an idea, and RaEm wanted her secret to remain—especially in Waset. Living this closely made it all the more difficult to hide her monthly cycle.

"Queen Tiye requests you," the chamberlain said.

RaEm rose, stepping into the curved toe sandals, adjusting the heavy counterweight and collar she wore. "Where are you going, my lord?" Meryaten asked, standing beside her, brown eyes wide with rejection. "You said we were going to walk through the market today. Are we not going?" She touched RaEm again.

Smenkhare stood while the slave buckled on his jeweled dagger and sheath. "Business calls me away. I shall return late."

Meryaten looked away, blinking furiously. "Have I been too talkative? Did you not like the dinner I prepared? Why—"

Rolling her eyes, RaEm kissed her wife. "It is business. Nothing more. Take your cousin . . . one of them"—she gave up on the name— "to the market with you. Be certain to take a contingency of guards, however. These people do not respect your father's house."

"Your brother's house," Meryaten said.

"Aye. Now go, no long faces."

Meryaten smiled tearfully, her voice barely above a whisper. "Perhaps tonight when you return we could . . . try again?"

RaEm looked over her head. "Perhaps. May the Aten bless your day."

Her wife ducked her head and left the room. Thank the gods, RaEm thought.

Once loaded in her palanquin, RaEm opened the scrolls that were delivered in the dead of night while Meryaten slept off the drug that she drank each time she and "Smenkhare" made love. What a nuisance she was, RaEm thought.

For a moment she paused, seeing the seal on the papyrus. Hatshepsut, my dear friend, how I miss you, she thought. Then RaEm cracked it with her nail and unrolled it, squinting at the scribe's small, perfect writing.

The former priest had kept immaculate records of where things were kept, such as grain for a country that would soon be starving. Field after field lay fallow, with no one to plow them, seed them, for always this had been the job of the priests. The masses kept their plot of vegetables. In exchange for their taxes, in payment for their faithfulness to the gods and their shrines, they received flour to make bread.

Save there was no flour, no grain, and eventually no bread.

RaEm's finger followed the scribe's line drawing. It showed several underground silos of grain. In the intervening reigns—RaEm didn't know how many or for how long—the priests had followed this lay-out. Therefore grain should be awaiting RaEm.

She beckoned a slave. "Go to Queen Tiye," she instructed him. "Tell her that her son Smenkhare has left the city on urgent business and won't return till week's end. Ask her if she would share this information with his wife, the princess Meryaten."

The slave ducked his head and RaEm dismissed him, gesturing for another. After instructing him, she leaned forward to the palanquin carrier. "Take me to the stables, then arrange for a boat to meet me on the Nile. A small skiff, nothing large."

She didn't have a lot of power yet, but she was learning to use it.

The trip had taken twice as long as she'd thought. "Stop!" she called out to the oarsmen. Once again she looked at the map, then looked around them. She waved away more mosquitoes as she was assisted out of the rowboat. Her feet immediately sank into the marshy ground, submerged to her lower calves.

Leaving her sandals behind, RaEm squelched through what had once been a field. "The Inundation was poor, why is this field rotting?" she asked the hapless farmer they'd stumbled upon a few fields back.

"The corvée, my lord," the man said. "It broke about two Inundations ago, and there is no one to fix it."

"What do you require for the repairs?" RaEm asked, picking her way carefully. Snakes were rumored to live in places like this.

"Stone, my lord. We don't have stone, just mud brick." He sighed. "The mud brick is what we kept using to hold it, since it was better than nothing. Then one night, must have been about this time last year, old Ma'a—atenum," the man stumbled, making the name religiously acceptable, "was out here. *Aii*, he was repairing the corvée when the gods took him."

RaEm turned to face the man. "He died?"

"Aye, my lord. Never found him, because when he fell, he bashed out the overly dry mud brick, and *whoosh!* the waters came rushing in and washed the whole mess, Ma'atenum, the corvée, and the river, right into this pasture. Drowned a few animals, too."

RaEm was stepping gingerly now. She didn't want to find the remains of Ma'atenum.

"Is this it, my lord?" one of the oarsmen called. He was standing by a stone stake, more than half submerged. RaEm didn't need to consult the diagram because she knew it by heart. She nodded once as they continued plodding toward him.

Looking around, RaEm tried to picture what these fields had been like before they became a mosquito-infested pond. "Is there any way to open the silo without getting water inside?" she asked the men in general.

"You could dredge the field," the old farmer suggested. "Then you could do anything, open it as wide as you please."

And you will have your field back at the cost of Pharaoh doing it for you, RaEm thought. Still, she admired his wiliness. "How many slaves for how many days?" she asked him.

He looked like a raisin, bald, brown, and shriveled. The people were quite unattractive by adulthood, she thought dispassionately. "Twenty workers out here, from dawn to dusk, should take a week, fifteen days at most." His squinty dark eyes sized her up. "I know about twenty men who would do it, probably cheaper than slaves."

RaEm crossed her arms, feeling sweat roll over the bumps on her arms and legs from mosquitoes in this marshland. "Cheaper than slaves?"

He picked his teeth—the few still in his head, then adjusted his kilt, a grimy, coarse cloth. "Slaves have to be fed, *haii*? A few cucumbers, bread, salted fish, that is what they are due according to contract, am I right?"

"You are."

"Seeing how food is what Pharaoh, living forever!—"

"Glorious Pharaoh, living in the light of Aten forever!" RaEm corrected him automatically.

"Exactly. Seeing how food is what he doesn't have, wouldn't it be better to hire some men who can feed their own bellies, then pay them in something Egypt isn't running out of?"

"Like?" RaEm asked, swatting another mosquito.

"Stone, mayhap?"

She threw back her head and laughed. "You'll get your stone, old man. I'll be back here in seven days—"

"Seven days! Do you think I am a pagan's god to reclaim land from the waters in seven days?"

"Seven, old man, or we have no deal."

He crossed his breast in respect, an antique gesture that warmed RaEm to him even more.

"It had best be done by then, or I will use the stone to bury you."

He wiped his nose with the back of his hand, speaking slowly. "If you can't get to the grain, my lord, then no stones will be needed. Hunger will weigh us down."

Suddenly weary, desirous of a bath, a change of clothing, and a young boy, RaEm ordered the oarsmen to carry her back to the Nile.

Seven days. It was the final hope, a giant silo beneath the earth filled with grain to feed a hungry people. Seven days.

Chapter 7

THAT NIGHT AT DINNER the *tzadik* N'tan stood up as we slaves sat down, grateful for the break. It was *Yom Rishon* dinner, which actually took place the evening after the Sabbath, since the holy day went from dusk to dusk. People stopped talking to each other and reclined, as N'tan adjusted his white robe.

They were used to being entertained like this, by N'tan's sermonizing. Every week, *Yom Rishon* dinner was filled with laughter and dancing—and stories. The tribesmen would have made great subjects for a focus group on television programs; they were good spectators.

"We are to be like sheep," N'tan said, and the crowd groaned.

"If it weren't for your lovely bride, we would worry about you!" some *gibori* shouted at him.

N'tan's very pregnant, very red-faced bride threw a loaf of bread at the heckler. "He has to talk to you of sheep, so that you, Dov ben Hamah, understand!" Everyone laughed.

The *tzadik* continued speaking. "We are to have a sole shepherd to guide us, one voice to follow." He twisted his sidelocks, appearing to be in thought. "We tribes are not to worship other gods, as other peoples do. We are a nation set apart. To us, *el ha*Shaday is not part of the process of nature. He is not a season, or a weather condition, or any one thing we can touch or see. He is not the land."

He looked out at his audience. "What is this land? What did Shaday give us?"

"*Chalev oo'd'vash*, the Sages said," a young *gibori* repeated proudly.

My lexicon showed me a carton of Borden's, then a honeycomb. Milk and honey. Got it.

I was no longer amazed when what I heard jelled with what I'd been taught about the Bible. I hoped that somewhere in the darkness beyond this shelter, Cheftu listened. Standing there in the dark, beneath the stars scattered like sand on the seashore, he must be rejoicing in his heart. God was real. The Bible was true.

His faith was deep, mine less so, but then we'd always had differing levels of conviction. I know it saddened him that I didn't believe more, or more fiercely. But if I said I trusted so that he would be comfortable, it wouldn't be genuine.

He was almost in a contented awe to be here in David's Israel. I kept waiting for the proverbial other shoe to drop, but the waiting was convincing my left-brained, well-educated, totally Western mind that all the Hebrew mythology I'd ever heard was true.

"*Nachon!*" N'tan said. "We are not Pelesti, or Mizri; we do not have gods for the seasons. Shaday gave us fertile land, did he not?"

"*Sela!*" the people shouted. I'd learned that the closest equivalent to *sela* was a gospel church crying out, "Amen, brother!" It could also be used as a benediction.

"*Sela*," N'tan said. "The fertility of the soil is within the land. We, we are the ones who control how it is received. We control the productivity of the earth, the frequency of the rains, by how we behave.

"We are chastened to remember, which is why our branches are tied with red thread."

Huh?

N'tan tugged at his beard for a moment, focused elsewhere while we watched him. "All of our traditions focus on remember. Remember what Shaday did for us, leading us up out of Egypt."

Oh yeah, I remembered that. Vividly.

We all said, "*Sela*."

"Remember how he provided for us in the desert."

"*Sela!*"

"Remember how he passed over us as the death angel."

I shivered, recalling that horrifically beautiful face, the claw marks in its wake, the screams in the night as it took yet another victim.

"*Sela!*"

"Remember how he destroyed the Egyptians in the sea."

Gold and bodies afloat in white water, then the mighty rushing wind that calmed and cleaned the waters.

"*Sela!*"

"Remember, remember, remember!"

They knuckled the ground with enthusiasm. N'tan did know how to get the blood pumping. He turned to the crowd. "For generations, since we entered this land beneath the leadership of Y'shua and Ka'lib, the *tzadikim* and *kohanim* have returned to the Mount of God in Midian to give legs to their remembering. There we see the place where *ha*Moshe and the *zekenim* sat with Yahwe and ate for the *b'rith.*"

I almost dropped my jug. N'tan had just said that the leaders of the tribesmen—the prophets, the priests, and the individual tribes' rulers—sat down and ate a covenantal meal with God? This was in the *Bible?* They knew where this meeting took place?

"To remember the *b'rith*, our forefathers climbed the mountain to sit, eating in remembrance of our fathers and Yahwe."

Obviously I had been listening to the wrong Bible.

"So: Because it is tradition, because it is necessary for remembrance, I will be leaving with a group of *kohanim* to make this pilgrimage, after Shavu'ot. Those who wish to join me, to sit where their forefathers and fathers have sat, to see the mountain of our God, you are bidden to walk with me. Come to remember!"

The mental image I had was of a picnic with God on a mountain. My brain, even my useful lexicon, was having a hard time wrapping itself around this one!

"Wine!" I heard in a voice that sounded as though it had been calling for it for a while. I hustled over, poured distractedly from my jar, and actually spilled a little on the ground. The glance I received was displeased, but I didn't care. I stumbled back to slave's row, where we all stood, waiting to serve.

I was blown away. I'd grown used to knowing what to expect in this day and time. No one else seemed shocked by this pronouncement, however. This was something they all knew? Dadua sang another psalm, we all said, "*Sela*," then I was cleaning again.

By the time I got back to our watchtower, the sun was creeping across the horizon and Cheftu was walking out the door. We kissed. "Did you hear?" I asked sleepily. "Last night. Were you there?"

"*Lo*, what happened?" He glanced out at the dawn, harried. "Beloved, tell me tonight. We harvest in the far fields today." He kissed me again and left.

My dreams were bizarre, a cross between Alice in Wonderland and what I'd heard about the *zekenim*—*the seventy*, my lexicon added—sitting down with God. Only this time God was sipping tea, the seventy were white rabbits, and RaEm stood in the Queen's outfit screeching, "Off with her head!"

I woke to the sound of Shana screaming for me.

"That idiot!" she said at the top of her lungs. I joined the back of the crowd of slaves: tribesmen and children, pagans and women. "He willfully makes these choices with no concern for the upcoming festivals, the seasons. *Ach!* Men!"

I glanced at the other slaves. Kali'a, whom I saw on occasion, leaned over. "Her fit is because of N'tan's announcement last night. We have been preparing for Shavu'ot all week. Now he plans to leave the night after it."

Though the times may have changed, my Mimi and my mom had said almost those same words about the men in their lives: people were people, no matter when. I grinned at the thought.

"*Isha!* Is what I say so amusing?" Shana homed in on me.

I shook my head violently. God forbid she think I was laughing at her! She glared at me, though she didn't seem as angry as usual. She continued. "So: *haMelekh*'s fields need *b'kurim*."

My lexicon was not forthcoming.

"You and you," she said, pointing to two young boys, "will be in charge of managing the sheep and the lambs. You and you"—she pointed to two young girls, one a tribesman, the other a pagan—"will tie the branches of the orchards." She chose 'Sheva to join a group tying the grape clusters. "You," she said with her customary antagonism toward me, "will be in the kitchen."

Great, everyone else got to play outside. I felt as though I were grounded. "You are not a tribeswoman," she said. "You cannot touch the *b'kurim*." She sighed. "I can tell from your expression you don't know what it is."

I shook my head. I was Pelesti, remember?

Shana turned to us all. "Yahwe brought us into this land, with *chalev oo'd'vash*. Three times a year our men are to present themselves at the Seat of Mercy. The *b'kurim* are the first fruits of the season, *ken?* Every farmer, every vintner, when he sees the first produce of this season, instead of eating it, he ties the branch with a red thread."

Shana gestured to some slave, then turned back to us. "These fruits are to be presented as a thank offering to Shaday, with a prayer."

"What is the prayer?" some other, braver soul than I asked.

She covered her head with a scarf and raised her arms, intoning the words. *"My father was a stranger in the land of Mizra'im. There he grew into a mighty nation. The Mizri were jealous and enslaved us, afflicted us. With miracles and magic, Yahwe freed my people from their hands, and brought us into the land, rich with milk and honey. So: I bring to Yahwe the first of what he has given me."* She opened her eyes. "In this, we remember. Now go! We have much to do, and to prepare food for the seventy." She walked away, *tch'*ing.

Before I handled any food, I had to wash my hands and bind my hair. Then they showed me the dates.

A mountain of dates, an Everest of them! Each had to be seeded, then inserted with raisins or nuts. We're talking millions of dates, enough for everyone in the palace, including the thirty *giborim* and their families.

It would be Shavu'ot of next year before I finished this!

My blade was a flint, and I started splitting the dates, throwing them from one basket to another and thinking that if I were Catholic, this would be purgatory.

People bustled all around me. Wonderful smells came from the ovens, where cakes and breads were baked, then dusted with spices or decorated with fruit, then wrapped in dried palm leaves and set aside.

I limped home that night, noticing the budding vines of grapes were adorned with threads, the *b'kurim.* Cheftu had gotten dinner, a few pieces of meat and a mash of lentils, for us. "From what I recall of my friends who were married and both working, our lives aren't much different," I said, trying to sound positive. I was too tired even for love-making.

"Women work?" he asked.

I chewed, looking at him. "There really are light-years between us, at times."

"A year filled with light?" he said, bewildered.

I just kissed him, too ragged to start explaining. "Have you heard what N'tan said last night? About the seventy, the dinner with God?"

He sat back. "Indeed. It was all we talked about in the fields. Families are vying for a way to get their sons included. It is an unspoken way of declaring the new rulers of their tribes."

"There are seventy rulers of this tribe?" I asked.

"*Lo,* it is open to all the other tribes as well. They will join at Shek'im, then journey down the valley, past the Salt Sea. From there they will board a ship that will take them to Midian. Then, I hear, it is only a two days' walk."

I put aside the bones of my meal. "Is it my imagination, or do you sound wistful?"

He looked away. "Think on it, Chloe: They know where to go. They know where the mountain of God is! In my time, we think it is the Sinai. How wrong we are!"

"In my time I think we think it is the Sinai, too," I said. "If anyone knew it was in Saudi Arabia, well, there would be another war against Israel."

He sat up. "Israel is a country in your time?"

"*Ken*," I said. "My father is a diplomat, trying to establish peace between the Jewish state and the many Arab countries."

"That is why you are here," he whispered in wonder. "You know these things." He shook his head. "I marveled at the way you spoke with Yoav. You were arguing with a man from history, *chérie*! You dared to insult a Bible character."

"Don't tell me that. It's too immobilizing. I can't think of who these people are, or where I know them from." I took a quick drink of beer, spitting away the husks. As slaves we didn't have the cups with the built-in filter. "So what is this story N'tan was telling? Have you heard it before?"

He stood up, stretching, looking out over the vineyards where the leaves were just starting to show. He held a hand out to me and we climbed onto the edge of the wall, sitting in the setting sun, looking out over the prosperity of the land. "*Chalev oo'd'vash*," I whispered.

"It is," Cheftu said. "According to the Holy Writ I recall, this story of Moshe sitting down face-to-face with *le bon Dieu* is unknown. In fact, he could not see God face-to-face, but only the back of him. Even that caused him to be burned, and his face was so terrifying that the people, when he returned to the camp, begged him to cover his features."

"Why?"

"He'd been in the presence of God, and it showed on his face and scared them."

Whoa. Like radiation or something?

"I thought that to touch the Mount of God was to die," he mused. "This story N'tan told, I know nothing of this."

"Do you think it is true?" I said. The sky was streaks of lavender, pink, and gold. Cheftu's strong fingers were linked in mine. Tears welled in my eyes at how perfect this moment seemed. I didn't even feel the chains anymore. My ears had healed, and I realized that I'd probably made the whole enslaving experience worse by being so scared. Now, it was just as if they were pierced; granted, they were pierced with quarter-inch holes through cartilage, but so insignificant. I squeezed his hand, smiling. We finally had our corner of heaven.

"*Ach,*" he said. "How can I know? These people, they have kept these stories alive for generations."

"Do you think it is a legend that was expounded on, or a fact? If it is a fact, why have we never heard of it?" I asked.

"For seventy men to have climbed the mountain, to have dined with God, this seems too extraordinary to be a falsehood."

"Not a falsehood, just an exaggeration," I said.

"Is not an exaggeration a falsehood?" he asked.

I frowned at him; I didn't know. "When did they go up?" I saw Charlton Heston coming down from the mountain, as Moses, alone with the Ten Commandments. "I thought God wrote the commandments on stone with his finger."

Cheftu smiled, drawing me closer. Night had fallen, and the stars were starting to glimmer in sparkles of white, green, pink, and yellow against the night sky. It amazed me that I could actually see the color, though I knew it had always been there. Was that like the rest of my life? Had I ever been this happy? "You remember quite well for an *isha* who claims no knowledge of the Bible."

"My Mimi would be proud to hear that," I said, nuzzling his neck.

"Your *grand-mère?*"

"*Oui.*"

Cheftu laid his cheek against mine. The fuzz of his beard had finally passed from the sandpaper stage through the horsehair phase and now was a soft pelt. The curls over his ears were growing, and he had taken to wrapping the long pieces of hair around his ears just like an Israelite. "It must have been the second time Moshe climbed up," Cheftu said, rumbling in my ear, a vibration I felt through his chest. "When he took down God's words in his own hand, maybe then?"

"I love you," I whispered, pulling away to look up at him. "Your knowledge astounds me. You make me breathless with your mind."

He crooked a brow at me. "Just my mind?"

"Well," I hedged, chewing on my lip.

He took over my mouth, murmuring that perhaps he needed to remind me he was more than just wit.

Later, as we lay curved together like spoons, almost asleep, I asked a fatal question. "We are making love with no protection, *nachon?*"

Cheftu was silent so long, I thought he was already asleep. "You are," he finally said.

"Why?" I asked, half-dreaming, half-awake. "I thought you hated the thought of having a baby here?"

He kissed my jaw, pulling me tighter against him, his fingers splayed across my belly. "I feared having a baby amid the disasters we have seen," he said. "I also feared what would happen if you were not in your own body."

My eyes opened; suddenly I was completely awake. I'd never even thought of that, of me not being in my own body. Maybe because to me, wherever I was felt like my body. It was almost as though other people's skins were leotards I climbed into. They fit that well around me. A trembling started in my throat as I rolled over and looked at him. The starlight fell on his face from above, casting shadows of his lashes on his cheeks. His hair was dark against the bleached white of the pallet. "Are you saying . . . what I think you are saying?" I asked. I heard the wobble in my voice.

Mimi always used to say that there were Coca-Cola moments in life. Snippets of time, which for however long one lived, one would recall fondly over a Coca-Cola. My Mimi loved her Coca-Colas. We would sit on her screened porch in the afternoon when I was at university, and she would relate her Coca-Cola moments:

When she married her first husband; when she received word that he'd been killed and almost lost her first baby because of it. When she'd met the love of her life, my dad's stepfather. When she'd heard my father speak his first sentence of Arabic and realized he would never stay at home, that he was born to be a nomad. The first time she'd flown anywhere, which was to Greece, to see my parents married. The first time she'd seen me, with green eyes so big, she said, that no one had to tell her who was her grandbaby.

All of those were Coca-Cola moments.

Cheftu's eyes opened. "What do you think I say?"

I searched his face, felt my life turn a corner: a feeling that would stay with me always, a definite Coca-Cola moment. "Whatever it is, my answer is yes."

Then I was flat on my back, my husband looming over me. The lines of his body, the muscles hardened by wielding a scythe, by throwing sheaves of barley, by holding me, were sharply drawn. His eyes were dark, so I couldn't see them clearly. But I felt his desire, felt my body flood with my own. "My answer is also yes, *chérie*. However, it is a delayed yes. I will not have my child, children, should *le bon Dieu* bless us so well, born a slave."

I felt myself choking back disappointment, while at the same time being relieved.

"I wish to see our lives commingled in this way, but not while these chains still bind me." His voice was hard now; I knew there would be no swaying him. "However, this time, I take the prevention."

"You what?" I asked, completely startled.

"It would be foolhardy of me to love you so often, so well, if these are my desires. Therefore I inquired of a wisewoman what could prevent me from getting you with child, but allow me to love you. She gave me an herb, to lessen the potency of my seed." He pressed my face into his shoulder. "Don't cry, beloved," he said. "We will be free, somehow, soon."

His kisses were soft. I didn't know why I was crying, but the moment felt cheated. So much for Coca-Colas.

When I got to work the next morning, everyone was running behind Shana's schedule. I found myself back at the millstone, with a double order for the day. I gathered that my dates could wait. 'Sheva and I were almost finished with the flour when Shana came up to me. Immediately my mind raced: Had I broken anything? Offended anyone? Nothing came to mind, but that didn't mean much either.

"You!" she said, but it was lacking her customary virulence. "Come with me. 'Sheva, take over."

The mushroom nodded slowly as Shana yanked me up. "You will need to wash first," she said, looking me over. I tugged at the edge of my dress. I'd bathed yesterday, I'd sponged off this morning, but my hair was awful. She sighed as she commanded me to follow her.

We went inside the palace, then stepped into the women's quarters.

Once inside, Shana bellowed for water, for clothes. What was going on? Did I dare ask? "Strip," she said. "You are going before *haMelekh*. As you are now, you would offend him and reflect poorly on me."

"The king?" I repeated, stunned.

She glared at me. "*Ken.* The king."

I was stripped, submerged, washed, dried, my hair combed and braided. Then Shana reluctantly gave me another dress. It was lovely, a dark green with a band of blue. The sash matched, with tiny stripes of blue, green, and gold.

"This is yours," she said, handing me the gold jewelry I'd had when I arrived. The Pelesti stuff was beautiful, intricately worked arabesques and swirls that repeated throughout the four strands of the necklace. The earrings were heavy; in fact, they had dusted my shoulders.

It was not the attire of a slave. "*Todah,*" I said, "but these are from another life."

Her gaze touched the piercing in my ear, the length of chain that looped from one to the other. I kept the links beneath my clothing, against my skin for protection. Shana gestured to one of the women, who adjusted my hair, then tied on a blue headband to hold the arrangement in place. Why were they doing this? I was a slave!

"Would you like these?" I asked a moment later, holding out the earrings and necklace to Shana.

She blushed! The lines on her face lifted as she reverently touched the necklace. "I have never seen such fragile stuff," she said softly.

"Then take it, for yourself," I urged.

She smiled. "The days for this are in the past for me."

"*B'seder,*" I said, handing my jewelry back to her. "As they are for me."

She looked at me for a moment, then snapped back into Shana

mode. "Well, don't stand there! You!" She turned to the others, gesturing toward me. "Isn't she lovely? A vision! See? This is how well Shana takes care of the palace and her slaves. Now go," she told me. "The audience chamber."

I opened my mouth to ask where it was, but she said, "Don't worry where the room is, your husband awaits you outside the doors."

Feeling a little like Cinderella—had she felt this dazed?—I walked through the harem quickly. Cheftu was standing, as clean and starched as I was, in the hallway. His kilt was tightly wrapped and brightly colored. His hair almost touched his shoulders now, and his beard had been trimmed. His sidelocks fell beside his ears in inky black curls. He too was bewildered at this request, this treatment.

He held out his hand for me. "What does this mean?" I asked as we walked away hand in hand.

"You!" I heard before we took three steps. I turned automatically. Shana bore down on us, a determined expression on her face. "Maybe these are better for your life now," she stated, her hand outstretched.

She handed me a pair of hoop earrings. They were bulkier than the jewelry I had had, but they had been given some kind of finish that made the gold seem to glitter. "They are beautiful," I said, trying them on immediately. They didn't catch in the slave chain that went from the piercing in the center of the cartilage in the back of my ear to the other ear.

She beamed. "Shana takes care of her own," she said. "Now go! You will be late!"

Giddy, we walked down the hallways. As slaves we never saw these parts of the palace. Normally we kept to the back passages that linked the house from room to room, out of sight, to maintain the illusion of graciousness. Hauling chamber pots through the front hallways would be very uncool.

Thank God I'd never pulled that assignment.

We halted outside the doors to the audience chamber, looking for the chamberlain. No one showed up, so Cheftu knocked hesitantly.

"What is this about?" I asked.

"I have no idea. It is odd that they should want to see me." He looked at me. "I bade them send for you."

"Why is that odd? You are extremely talented, I'm surprised they haven't asked earlier."

"Beloved, by the time I came here with you I was already a slave, *nachon*?"

That's right. No one knew that Cheftu was a physician or a former lord of Egypt or a scribe or any of it. "Have you enjoyed working in the fields?" I asked.

We heard a call from inside to enter. Cheftu looked over his shoulder as he pushed open the wooden doors on their leather hinges. "Immensely." He shook his head, suddenly remote. "I do not know if I ever want to practice medicine again." Before I could respond to this extraordinary statement, the door swung open.

It was a lousy excuse for an audience chamber. Dark, low ceilinged, and small, it looked more like a room in the Bastille. N'tan lounged in his white robe. Dadua sat opposite Yoav, deep in thought over a game board. In one corner a girl rewired her *kinor*. In another corner Avgay'el wove, throwing the shuttle and comb with silent efficiency. This was the private chamber of the king of Israel? It made the rest of Mamre look nearly cosmopolitan.

"Your slave is Egyptian, *isha*?" Yoav asked me with no preamble. My slave? I was a slave. They stared at me until I remembered that technically Cheftu was my slave. Sort of. "Uh, *ken*," I said, then darted a glance at Cheftu.

"Then ask him if he has ever heard rumor of gold in the desert."

Did they think Cheftu couldn't speak their language? Did Cheftu want me to let them know he understood? He made the slightest negative movement. I didn't understand why he wouldn't want them to know, but I translated the question exactly. He answered in fluid Egyptian: "Which desert?"

They exchanged looks after I relayed his response. "The desert of Midian."

I translated, while trying not to sound so bewildered. "*Lo*, he has not heard of such a thing," I said.

"Does he know the legend of how the tribes fled his homeland?"

Were they talking about the Exodus? Would the Egyptians pass down a tale of their own defeat? Not hardly! I translated, and Cheftu responded that he, as an Egyptian, had never heard such tales. However, he had been enslaved with an Apiru man, so he'd heard the stories that way.

"Apiru!" N'tan scoffed.

Cheftu and I exchanged glances, for "Apiru" was the term the Egyptians had used for the Israelites. I licked my lips and spoke. "To the Egyptians, you are Apiru."

Yoav looked straight at me. "Apiru are a distant branch," he said. "It is a derogatory term for those who weren't part of the covenant our forefathers made with our mountain god when they were at his home."

Were they talking about God on Mount Sinai?

"They aren't really considered citizens," N'tan said. "We share Avraham as a forebear and they are circumcised, but they stayed here while Yacov and his tribe went to Egypt and became enslaved."

So they were subcitizens because they had the sense to stay out of slavery?

"Does your slave know his way through the Sinai?" Yoav asked.

The direction they were going with this was becoming clear. Sinai, Midian. I repeated the question, and Cheftu hesitated. Neither of us knew how to handle this. "A little ways," I said, translating his response.

At the game board Dadua triumphed over Yoav. With a shout of laughter he sat back. "Tell him the story, Yoav," he commanded.

As I suspected, Yoav looked straight at Cheftu and began the tale: in Egyptian.

"Before generations ago, my people were slaves to yours." He smiled unpleasantly. "Strange how the river runs back on itself, *aii*? Our God was smiting the gods of the Egyptians. Finally, your pharaoh Thutmosis agreed to let my people leave. But he did this only after much grief, many plagues and poxes were visited on your people."

Cheftu's expression was inscrutable. But for the first time I noticed that although he wore the clothes, even the hair, of the tribesmen, he still looked foreign. The man was an Egyptian, regardless of his being born a Frenchman, despite whatever costume he wore. I was in love with an ancient Egyptian. Cheftu nodded once, an acknowledgment of Yoav's words.

"Because of the great chaos and grief of our leaving, we went to our neighbors, who were Egyptians, and asked for their gold."

"After your god had poxed . . . my people?" Cheftu clarified.

"They were willing to pay anything," Yoav said, "just to have us leave. So: The descendants of every tribesman, who had entered Egypt free but poor, left four hundred years later free and wealthy." Yoav smiled again, a flash of teeth in his dark beard. I could hear the whisper and whack of Avgay'el at the loom. Dadua was scrutinizing Cheftu, not Yoav.

N'tan was watching us all. Whom did he look like?

"Loaded with this gold, we traveled down through the Sinai, then our god opened the Red Sea, so we walked across on dry land."

"You have a powerful god," Cheftu said politely. He was a good actor; you'd never guess that he worshiped this same God. Or that with his own eyes he'd seen what was merely legend to these people.

"So," Yoav said, sitting back. "Pharaoh changed his mind, sent his horses and chariots after us. They drowned there."

I remembered it well. I'd been there, rooted lichenlike to the shore. I'd been horrified, terrified. I still felt a little sick and uncertain at the recollection. This was not a calm, reasonable-style god. This was God, master of the universe, commander on high, all-cap G-O-D.

He kinda scared me.

"My people danced for joy on the opposite shores, then moved into the desert, where the leader, *ha*Moshe, had lived before. His father-in-law raised sheep there, so he took the tribes through. Well . . ." Yoav's arrogance was fading. "They camped at the foot of a mountain, Horeb, where *ha*Moshe had received communication from Shaday before. He brought all the people there, for that was his task: to go to Egypt, get the people, and bring them back."

Yoav called for wine; instinctively I jumped, but Cheftu laid a calming hand on me. I wasn't here as a slave. Don't act like one, I chided myself. Yoav sipped from his cup, then proceeded with the rest of the story.

"*Ha*Moshe went to meet with God. He took with him the seventy elders of the tribes, the *zekenim*, leaving behind his brother Aharon and his sister Miryam." Everyone in the room fell silent. He took the seventy on the first trip? Yoav's expression was troubled; he wouldn't meet our eyes.

N'tan sighed and took over the storytelling. In Aramaic, or Akkadian, or Hebrew or whatever language this was. Was this also a test? Did they expect Cheftu to know this language, too? Did he? "The people were scared. They had lived in cities, now they were in the desert. They were used to the lushness of the Nile, having water whenever they wanted it, food for the taking. Here, there was nothing but sand and the occasional palm tree. Then the leaders all disappear and are gone for days, then weeks. The people are scared."

"They went to Aharon," Dadua continued, interrupting N'tan. "They asked him to make them a statue. Something they could see, so they would know not to be afraid. With the statue they could pray, beg for the safety of *ha*Moshe and the *zekenim*.

"Aharon felt uncomfortable, so he tried to put them off by asking for all their gold. Now, when the gold had been brought from Egypt, most of it had been put into a communal storage. Small things, like earrings or bracelets, that were wearable and easily transportable, were kept by individuals. But golden images, lamps, boxes, all of these were put into one cart, kept protected in one sealed tent.

"Aharon thought the tribesmen would not part with their earrings and bracelets, thus he would not have to make this statue."

"He was wrong," N'tan said, interrupting Dadua in return. "They brought him their gold. He then tried to put them off again, but they were building an altar, then a fire to melt the gold. A few of the goldsmiths had learned their trade in Egypt.

"So: They made beer the Egyptian way, dressed as they had seen Egyptians do for generations, then proceeded to craft an image of a god. An Egyptian god."

Yoav cut N'tan off. It was a strategic move, so that the tribesmen's errors wouldn't be revealed. The general spoke in Egyptian again. "The rest of the story matters little. What is essential is that much of the gold was not used, either in the building of the idol, the subsequent punishment, or in the building of the Mercy Seat, our totem, and its implements."

"That," Dadua said, "is why N'tan goes to the desert. When he returns, we shall bring the Mercy Seat into the city, claim Jebus as its home. But we need the gold," the king said, staring at Cheftu. "I cannot spare Yoav; no one else speaks Egyptian and also understands our language. You do understand our tongue?" he asked, suddenly uncertain.

"*Ken*," Cheftu said.

Then why had I translated? They had tested me! Or had they tested Cheftu?

"Between here and there are many Egyptian outposts. Though Pharaoh seems to care nothing for what happens outside his river valley, still we should be cautious. It would be better to have an Egyptian with us, who can speak to them." Dadua's gaze was calculating. "It is obvious you have not always been a slave."

Cheftu stood motionless.

"Also, as an Egyptian, you know things about the gods of gold, the statues that we will unearth. You read and write, I have been told?"

Who had told him that? I wondered.

"Hieroglyphs, cuneiform, the language of the sea peoples," Cheftu said.

Dadua glared at Yoav. "Why have we wasted this man in the fields?" he said. "I could have used a scribe!" His dialect was different from what he usually spoke, but I understood it still. I looked at Cheftu from the corner of my eye. Had he also understood? Did he have a lexicon, too? How *did* he know these languages? All of them?

Cheftu was as expressionless as a tomb painting. And as beautiful.

"You are a slave, thus could easily be commanded to go with N'tan," Dadua continued. "But instead I say to you that you are invited to go with him. The journey will be a few months, back in time for the grape harvest, the arrival of the Seat."

Dadua's words penetrated my brain: Cheftu would be going away? For how many months? Would I get to go? We'd be apart, again? I felt tears welling in my eyes. This couldn't be happening, not when we'd come so far to be together. Not when we'd endured slavery to be together. Please, no.

Cheftu bowed his head. "*Ha-adoni* honors me, but the fields and coming home to my wife content me now."

Dadua's black eyes glittered; it was his only outward sign of irritation. I suspected he didn't hear *lo* too often. He spoke curtly, white teeth flashing in his russet beard. "Go to Midian and come back. Upon your return you will be made a free man."

Cheftu stiffened; if he'd been a dog, his ears would have perked up, his tail would have begun to wag.

A free man. His children wouldn't be slaves. He would have standing in the community. He could control his own life. I knew Cheftu, I knew this was the ultimate carrot, the seducer royale. Cheftu would have his freedom back; to get it he had only to do what he'd longed to do from the moment he'd heard about it. He would travel to the mountain of God.

"Only if my wife is freed also," he said.

Dadua glanced at me, then away. "Go, return a free man. Then, in another year, on the anniversary of your departure, she will also be freed."

"Within six months."

"By the Feast of Unleavened Bread, next year."

Cheftu did the calculations, then looked at me. "What say you?" he asked me in English.

It killed me to say this, but I knew I had to. Especially after our talk last night. "As you will. I want you to be happy, to be free."

"I will wait for him to offer six months."

"Why are you taking this at all?" I asked, trying to sound reasonable.

"Because neither of us have found a portal. I spent seventeen years in Egypt. If we were free, we could live well here. Rear our children with the One God, be safe and happy." He glanced at our audience. "Trust me, Chloe. We can craft a life this way."

"Do what you think best," I said, though I choked at the cost of these words. "I love you."

"*Ach*, but do you trust me?"

"Implicitly."

His gaze remained on my face a moment longer, then he turned to Dadua. "Thy will be done," he said. "I will go."

They offered Cheftu a chair, then dismissed me.

He's leaving, I thought in a monotone chant that played with every step of my way through the hallways, back to the women's quarters. He's leaving. He's leaving. I walked into the main women's room, thinking, He's leaving.

Shana took one look at me and hugged me. For a moment we weren't slave and owner, but two women. "They think such stupid things," she said as I cried, explaining through my tears what Dadua had offered and that Cheftu had accepted. "Always they seek glory for themselves, or their gods or their king." She patted my shoulder. "When all we really want is for them to be home, to laugh with us, to coddle our babes. Poor *isha*," she said. "This, this is what it means to be a tribeswoman."

I pulled back, sniffling. "Why?"

"Because every tribeswoman has bade farewell to her father, her brothers, and eventually her husband. It is the way. Now come, you. Change out of these clothes, wash your face, and go to the kitchen. Tell that harridan that I said you were to have some cucumber soup with honey." I tried to smile but just ended up crying at her kindness. "Go now," she said, pushing me toward the waiting slaves, who stripped me again.

After my soup with honey, Shana said it was time for me to learn how to make bread; the dates were forgotten. "Kneading is Shekina's way of relieving our anger," she said.

"Anger is not what I feel," I protested.

"Yet," she said darkly. We crossed to the opposite side of the courtyard from the millstone. "Here," she said. I was looking at another stone contraption. It was flat, rectangular, with a U-shaped ridge around it. "After 'Sheva finishes with the grain, you will mix it with water and a pinch of yesterday's bread, to make everyday bread. Then," she said, scrutinizing me, "you will cover it while you go get the water for the day."

"At the well?"

"Where else do you find water?"

I don't know, a faucet, maybe? At 7-Eleven? I was feeling a little loopy. Cheftu was choosing to leave me. For good reasons, granted. But still. Where was Midian? The fleeing Apiru had crossed at the neck of the Gulf of Aqaba, going into . . . Saudi Arabia? Giddy laughter bubbled up inside me. The Jews' gold was in the Arabs' country?

You already know that, the lexicon scribbled across the chalkboard in my mind.

I heard it, I retorted, I didn't *know* it, not like I do now.

"After that, you wait, for maybe the length of a watch," Shana said, continuing her cooking lesson. "Not too soon. Then you will put the dough down and knead it. You don't know how to knead," she said. I noticed it was not a question.

"*Ach, lo,*" I said, unnecessarily.

She *tch*'d only once, then pulled me down to show how to knead. You pounded the stuff, stretched it out flat, then rolled it back on itself. "Now you."

I managed it, but I wasn't going to be starting an ancient pizza parlor anytime soon. However, I knew how to exercise my triceps for the rest of eternity. "Do that about forty times," she said. "Then make it into rounds."

Rounds I could do.

"If you will leave them here, the kitchen slaves will come and get them."

I nodded.

"Now get back to your dates!"

She had been gone for about six rounds when I wondered, Who was Shekina?

Cheftu said nothing that night. I said nothing. What could I say? His reasoning was good; it was rational. I was the one being neurotic. We lay down in silence, not touching. We woke up in silence, still not touching. He left for the fields, I returned to my unconquerable mound of dates.

Only I was conquering them. One by one they had been moved from one pile into another. Now all I had to do was add spices and whatever stuffing, then store them in the jars. After exchanging my flint for a small spoon, I sat down on my haunches and began stuffing.

When we'd lived in Saudi, I'd had a friend who swore dates were roaches without legs. The thought grossed me out then, and it held the same power now. Putting Kafka from my mind, I stuffed them with pistachios and I stuffed them with raisins, listening to the women gossip around me.

Somewhere in the palace, a door slammed. The whole building rattled with it. In the kitchens, we all froze. Even the constant babble of children playing was silenced.

"How dare you?" we heard. The sound came from the windows, though I also could hear it closer. An irate woman, screaming at the top of her lungs.

"Dare? You say such a thing to me, the princess of the monarch of our people?" Irate woman number two, also screeching.

"You were princess until your father pissed away his right to be king!"

The voices were recognizable: Avgay'el and Mik'el. The translation in my head was of a man not only urinating, but keeping the urine as a precious commodity. Someone whose priorities were twisted. I glanced around; we were all listening avidly.

How embarrassing for these princesses and how humiliating for Dadua.

"Royalty is never lost," Mik'el said. The frost in her voice could have iced the windows. "I would not expect a person in your station to understand such a thing. You are just the proof that deep calls to deep. Or shallow to shallow."

We all gasped. Though he lived in a slummy house and ruled over a band of religious ruffians, the man was king. King! He was a man with the authority to say, "Off with her head."

"Now you dare to call Dadua shallow?"

I guess Mik'el could say that, since we all knew Dadua didn't care for her. I almost saw her shrug. "He is a commoner. Mixed blood of a Yudi farmer"—she laughed—"and an Apiru slave."

This was a grave insult, I realized now.

Mik'el laughed again. "Only his brawn has gained him the throne. It is not his right; he wasn't chosen, he snatched it!"

"*Ach*, she is a fool!" one of the kitchen slaves whispered.

"You would understand snatching," Avgay'el said, her voice sharp with disgust. "Did you not snatch at the first doddering fool willing to take you in, a rejected wife?"

"Dadua didn't reject me," Mik'el hissed, still deafeningly loud. "He knew I was too fine to live in a cave!"

"This is true," another of the slaves commented. "She wouldn't know how to change her own straw!"

I winced because that was a harsh dig: Tribeswomen sat on straw when they had their periods. I wanted to shush the slaves; we were going to miss the next part.

"Nay, he knew you were too cold to live with a man," Avgay'el shouted.

"Nay, I lived well with a man. He knew I was too much a *g'vret* to scramble for some oversexed Apiru's attentions like a rooting pig!"

Silence. Poor Avgay'el didn't have a choice except to compete with the other women in Dadua's life. It was her lot; it was the time period. But it was a taboo subject. You didn't mention it because it was tasteless and painful and there was no equal retort. It just was.

Then there was the additional insult with the pigs. In my time pork was a grave sin in both Muslim and Jewish cultures. Had that rule begun already?

"At least he offers his bed to me," Avgay'el said archly. "With me, his energy is never lagging, his passion overflows. He wants me."

"Ouch," I whispered aloud. Everyone knew that although Dadua had required the return of Mik'el, he had not bedded her. Not even on their renewal wedding night. There was nothing Mik'el could say. For the first time, I felt genuinely sorry for her.

It was one thing to endure him even though she didn't want him; it was another to be rejected and the whole court know it. Public humiliation at its most base.

Now doors slammed in stereo.

In the kitchen, none of us looked at each other. We simply contin-ued our tasks, the model of decorum when Shana showed up a little while later. Her color was high. I knew she knew we'd heard. I kept stuffing my cockroaches and adding them to the jar.

"Don't forget the almonds," she told me.

Almonds? She'd never mentioned almonds. Before I could figure out how to protest, without making a fuss, she told me that the mush-room would bring them to me and I could use them to finish out the dates. I ducked my head and continued stuffing.

By the afternoon every muscle in my body ached. My arms screamed, because I'd done nothing except stuff dates, my haunches were sore from my miserable position, and my neck ached. I was con-centrating on getting through just a few more before quitting time when another woman touched my shoulder. "*Isha*, your husband is out-side."

I looked at the dates, my hands covered in sticky goo. "Go on," she said. "I will finish for you."

"*Todah*," I expressed my thanks. "I will owe you."

She smiled. "I love dates. I can't promise I will add to your jar, but I will clean up for you."

"If you eat any," I said, "please, eat the ones that I haven't de-stoned."

She laughed and helped me up. I tried to rinse my hands, but date meat is stubborn. A few minutes later I was outside. Cheftu stood in the sunshine, his gaze fixed somewhere to the south.

"Hi," I said.

He turned to me, then touched my jaw, seizing my mouth in a ten-der kiss that turned my knees to water. Distantly I heard the cheers of the kitchen slaves. "Come with me," he said.

"Should I read a double entendre in that?" I asked, dazed, smiling.

He flashed a grin at me. "I hope so."

I looked back. "Can I just leave?"

"Trust me," he said, and took my hand, deliberately linking our fin-gers together. He was frowning slightly, intent. We walked out of the palace, down the hill into the fields. I looked around me for the first time in weeks. I was outside during the day, seeing more than a mud-brick palace and blue skies. "Will we get in trouble—?"

"*Non*," he said.

Shrugging at his response, I followed along. We took a steep goat path down the hill, bypassing our vineyard and watch house, going lower into the valley.

"Do you know that I love you?" he asked as we edged our way down a steep path. My hand was tight in his, the other one outstretched to balance myself. It was amazing how tough the soles of my feet had become.

"I, uh, of course," I said, hopping the last few feet. We were on level ground again, in an olive grove. The whisper of silver green leaves was almost as soothing as the ocean. All around us, branches were adorned with red threads. More *b'kurim*. Spangled shadows fell across us.

He took my other hand in his, turning me to face him. "Your certainty is lacking, *chérie*," he said.

I didn't know what to say. I knew that he did, I just didn't . . . feel it as much as I would have liked to.

"I brought you here, because I want you to know, as I will learn, if it is destiny for me to make this journey to Midian." He was speaking Egyptian again.

"How will you—" I began, then remembered the stones, the Urim and Thummim. "You still have them?"

He blushed, nodded. "I do."

"Are you still keeping them in your, uh . . ." I gestured vaguely toward his kilt.

"That has been the safest location," he said.

I knew as an Egyptian, especially as a physician, that the anus was a vitally important part of the body. Enemas were the aspirin of ancient Egypt. I didn't know if this were true with the Israelites; I didn't really want to know. "You'll understand if I don't toss them?" I said.

He smiled, then removed them from his waist sash. The Urim and Thummim: the oblong stones were engraved with rows of ancient Hebrew characters. If you brought them close together, they danced. He held one in each hand, and suddenly I knew what they were, what "magic" made them work.

"They're magnets!" I said.

"But of course they are," he said. "Now watch, read the signs as I ask." He stared into my eyes. "You ask why we are here, beloved. Now maybe we will learn?

"Should I, Cheftu, go into the desert, to the mountain of God?" he asked slowly. He tossed them, and I watched as they interacted with each other. The sunlight seemed to pick out a letter at a time, a letter that Cheftu read aloud.

Before my eyes the squiggles and scratches turned into letters I knew: "T-h-e w-i-l-l o-f Y-H-W-H w-i-l-l b-e d-o-n-e."

He frowned.

"Does that mean you go or not?" I asked, staring at the stones. They lay on the ground, a foot or so apart, motionless. "That seemed an awfully esoteric response."

"It ofttimes is," he said glumly.

"May I try?" I said, reaching for the white one.

"I thought you didn't want to touch them?"

I ignored him as I picked up one, then the other. When I brought my hands together I felt them vibrating in my palms. Zips of power went up and down my arms. It almost hurt. "Should I go?" I asked, throwing them.

"D-e-l-v-e i-n-t-o t-h-e w-a-t-e-r-s t-h-a-t g-u-i-d-e."

"Maybe they are broken," I said. "That makes no sense."

"*Non,* you asked the wrong question," he said. "It should be, 'Should Cheftu go?'"

"Oops!" I asked the carefully worded question, and we got "T-h-e w-i-l-l o-f Y-H-W-H w-i-l-l b-e d-o-n-e," again.

"*Ach,* well, they made no sense when they said you were with Dagon until I was in Ashqelon." He looked puzzled for a moment. "They said you weren't safe, but when I arrived you were ruling the place."

"That was probably when I was doing the tightrope," I said, amazed by the stones despite myself.

Cheftu repeated the term slowly in English. "What is that?"

"Long story. You asked them about me?" I said, still partially amazed that this wonderful, handsome, witty, and good man loved me.

"You beautiful *idiot*, but of course! However, then, five days later you were bargaining for all of our lives. They are accurate, just not in a way we understand."

"What happened to you?" I asked, "While you were with the slavers?"

He pressed his hands together, silent for a few minutes. "I will tell you once, then we will leave it here in this olive grove, forever after, *na-chon*?"

"*B'seder.*"

"They beat me," he said tonelessly. "They beat me harder than the others. They starved me. They tried to violate me, but the, uh, stones . . ."

My head was in my hands. I was embarrassed to know, sorry that I'd asked, that I'd demanded to know anything. Cheftu cleared his throat. "After that, they left me alone."

I said nothing for a while. "Why haven't you wanted to practice medicine?"

"Aztlan."

"Why?" We weren't even looking at each other.

"They all died, Chloe. No matter what we did, they died. Then I, the physician, *ach*, well, I end up extremely healthy."

"I don't follow."

"Illness." He sighed deeply. "I have lost my empathy."

I was stunned. Cheftu was easily the most empathetic soul I'd ever known. Had he just burned out? I waited in silence. If he wanted to say more, I would listen. However, I'd just learned a huge lesson about asking questions.

Cheftu sighed and sat back. "In Aztlan, no matter what we did, people died. So we searched for the reason why." He looked at his hands, turning them back and forth as though the answer might lie in their lines, in his cells. "When we learned the reason, when we tried prevention because there was no cure, still they did nothing. No one listened. No one believed. Everyone died. They died endlessly, need-lessly." He folded his hands and stared straight at me. "I find myself angry with them. They chose to die, yet I am the one who carries their deaths on my shoulder."

He flexed his jaw. "Then I thought of all the medications and cures and suggestions I'd made over the years, of how few people actually followed my advice and were healed and—" He threw his hands up. "It seems pointless. I don't care to continue working my fingers and heart until they bleed when it means nothing."

"So go to Midian," I said jocularly. "See how you feel when you return."

He shrugged.

I handed the stones back, then watched as he tucked each one into his sash, his body between them so they wouldn't dance. "When do you go?"

His gaze met mine. "Next week. After Shavu'ot."

"Do we celebrate that?" I asked. Shana had said nothing beyond mentioning the preparations.

"They go to the city of Shek'im for it," he said. "That is where their totem is. I believe we stay here, guard the fields."

The awkwardness was back. Sitting cross-legged in this olive grove, I felt strangely alone. "Where are you?" I asked bluntly.

He blinked, a little surprised. "What do you mean?"

"You. You're not here. Are you already at the Mountain of God?"

His gaze dropped. I was right.

"Cheftu, you are going on this journey. You leave next week. These are terms I begin to understand, to believe. However, while you are here, please be here." I reached over and raised his face to mine. "Tell me of your excitement, tell me what you think you will learn or the reason you want to go. Don't shut me out. Don't leave me even before you go. Please."

Spears of sunlight gilded him all over, catching lights in his black hair, accentuating the small scars on his skin. "How are you going to experience this as an 'uncircumcised' Egyptian?" I asked. "They won't let you on the mountain, they won't let you touch or do anything once they are there." I squeezed his hand to cushion my words. "They are using you."

"As I use them," he said. "*B'seder*, you want my truths? You want to hear the whole of my heart?"

"Yes!" I said in English. "Yes, of course I do! How could you even doubt it? *Ach!*" I screeched in frustration.

"We are here, Chloe, with people whose fathers sat down face-to-face with God. They ate with him, they spoke with him. This was no deity too powerful to be viewed except the back of his head. He was real, flesh and blood, sitting with them. Incarnated before we ever know of an incarnation!"

His eyes were glowing, he was animated, he was beautiful. And I didn't know what he was talking about.

"When *ha*Moshe asked for God's name, he was told an unfathomable riddle. But Moshe had already given God his name, so he was in God's power."

"Because he knew his name?"

"Names are powerful magic, *chérie.* To know someone's name is to know about them. This is why people, especially royalty, have always had secret names." He touched the side of my face, running the backs of his fingers over my cheekbones. "When first you told me your name, Chloe, I knew it was the truth of you."

I frowned slightly as the wind rustled the trees and silvery green leaves rained down on us. "How is that?"

"In the Greek, and I told you this, your name means green and verdant. More than that, it means alive, growing, hopeful." He smiled at me, a slow smile that started in his eyes and moved to his mouth. "To me, you are these things. No matter what happens, you grow beyond it. Never do you lose hope, never are you less than alive."

My face was warm and my heart was in my throat. We stared at each other for a few more minutes, content. I didn't remember what we'd been discussing. "Kiss me, *chérie,*" he said.

We melded mouths in the sun-dappled shade, then bodies, then our souls. As we lay there, staring up at the blue sky, he said, "I am a scholar, and a Catholic; that is why I want to go to this place. How much more is my life to see these things, to experience them. Even if I do not touch the mountain. I have no desire to see God; I will see him when I die."

"If you die," I corrected.

"*Ach*, Chloe," he said, turning to me, watching his brown hand on my white skin. "Our children are the only immortality I want," he whispered. "For myself, to be locked with you, living with you, is forever." He kissed me, whispering against my lips, "This is eternity to me."

WASET

RAEM GLARED at the priest who dared to present himself, uninvited, before her. Two days ago Akhenaten had sent the news throughout Egypt: His brother and son-in-law, Smenkhare, was co-regent with him in the light of the Aten forever. RaEm had not been free to leave the audience chamber in Waset since then, for many of the nobles who had escaped Akhetaten suddenly presented themselves, begging forgiveness.

And, thank the gods and goddesses, Meryaten believed herself to be pregnant, which also took Tiye's hawkishness off RaEm.

"My name is Horetamun," the priest said, bowing. "As high priest I have come to welcome you to the Temple of Amun-Ra, Lord Smenkhare."

This was the sticking point. Should Smenkhare officially welcome this priest or acknowledge his god, then Smenkhare stood to lose every bit of power afforded to him by Pharaoh, living forever! If, however, Smenkhare didn't dance to this flute song, he might well find himself escorted from Waset in a hail of rotting vegetables.

RaEm's head hurt. "Address me as Smenkhare, living forever!, Horet*aten*," RaEm said. Already it was hot. The priest blinked insolently at her. The sun shone off his bald pate, dazzled on his white kilt, glinted amber from the eyes in the leopard he wore around his shoulders. Slowly, almost more as an insult than in compliance, he bowed his head.

Through her peripheral vision she saw that his bowing to her had an effect on the courtiers standing around. It was a good thing that something had an effect on them; soon they would be starving, too, regardless of the pharaoh they supported or the gods they worshiped.

There was nothing left, no stores left untapped. In her clenched fist was the papyrus response to the infuriated message she'd sent to Akhenaten. Two weeks past a reasonable response time, she had heard back: "Aye, those stores were used at Amenhotep Osiris's last natal day celebration."

Fortunately the men who had worked the field had wanted payment in stone, which Egypt was overrun with. Pity the masses could not eat stone. She directed herself back to the priest. "My Majesty"— for some reason the thrill of saying those words wasn't as sharp as she'd thought it would be—"welcomes you to this court, though you worship an outlawed god whose name will be unmentioned."

The priest's lips tightened, but he said nothing. The silence grew longer, the rustling of the attending courtiers more pronounced. "Have you anything to say?" RaEm asked, irritated.

He looked up at her, dark brown eyes meeting hers directly. "The blessings of the season upon you, My Majesty."

RaEm rose. The audience was over.

She had just put on her robe and taken off her crown when the chamberlain poked his head around the door. "A man here to see you, My Majesty."

At least it wasn't mulish Meryaten. RaEm rubbed at her neck while she bade the man join her. A cloaked figure entered the room, then threw off his hood.

The high priest of Amun-Ra? "What are you doing here?" she asked, looking around. In moments she had bolted the doors, pulled the curtains that led onto the garden path. "It is death for either of us to be found here."

He stood, facing her bravely. "My Majesty, mistress—"

RaEm spun on her heel. "What did you call me?"

His gaze was direct, unapologetic. "Mistress, for you are, are you not?"

RaEm crossed her arms. "My name is Smenkhare, husband of Meryaten and co-regent of Egypt."

"It matters not to me, though I pity the child Meryaten," he said. "She doesn't know, does she?"

RaEm said nothing. How could he know? How did he guess? Had he told anyone else?

"It is no matter," he said again. "Save in this: We need the priest-hood of Amun-Ra restored. The fields are rotting, the people will starve without that manpower to disperse the foods."

"I can do nothing," she said. "I endanger my own life even to hear you."

Horetamun drew his hood over his head. "When you are ready to act as a pharaoh should, let me know."

He turned to unlatch the garden door.

"When the time for action is upon us, Horet," she said. "Let me know."

DURING SHAVU'OT the city emptied, with all the men required to go to Shek'im, where the Be'ma Seat, the Mercy Seat, waited. On it rested the power of Yahwe.

If Yahwe was there, why were the *zekenim* trooping out to the moun-tain to see him? I wondered. But I didn't ask. Slaves did not ask. I was becoming as silent as the mushroom.

So, I temporarily lost my husband. Then someone decided I shouldn't stay by myself, so I was reassigned to the women's quarters: Avgay'el's territory since Mik'el had moved across the street.

The men began to return from their journey, ready for the endless labor of vine tending. I was mindlessly grinding grain and sweating one afternoon when a soldier, not a *gibori*, but a normal soldier, knelt beside me. The mushroom was off somewhere. More and more often she vanished. I didn't care; her absence saved me the trouble of trying to make conversation.

"*Isha,* in the third watch, Yoav wishes to see you." I didn't notice much of him beyond crystalline blue eyes.

Then he was gone. Third watch of the day or the third watch of the night? I would certainly rather try to find Yoav in broad daylight, especially since this seemed an unorthodox way to suggest a meeting. After all, I was his slave and more or less at his beck and call. Why didn't he just call?

However, this was also an excuse to get out of the palace.

By four o'clock the sun was still shining and the courtyard was deserted. It was the third watch of the day. I stood up and poured the flour into the appropriate storage jar, while I looked around. No one observed me.

I wandered through the hallway and picked up a water jar. At least I could say I was on my way to the well, though that particular chore had never been made mine—I'd gone only once. I slipped through the courtyard, noticing that no one noticed me. Big change, that, I thought sarcastically.

Outside. Wow! I was outside! This was the city. Mamre. I'd never been on this side of the doors by myself before. The thrill made me almost giggle.

Yoav's place was attached to Dadua's, since we all lived together in some kind of commune. Did I go in the front or the back of his house?

"*Isha,* come with me." I turned, startled. It was the same soldier from this morning, only now his eyes seemed less beautiful and more robotic. He was a little too convenient. I felt suspicious. Who was this guy? Did I know for certain that he was from Yoav?

"Tell me where to go, and I will find it on my own," I countered.

"I will take you."

"I will find it on my own," I repeated with a little more force. I was a woman alone in a city I didn't know. I'd never seen this soldier before this morning. I squared my shoulders, visually becoming more aggressive.

He inclined his head in agreement. "As you see it. Yoav wants you to meet him at the tavern by the gate. The Honey Bee."

Israelites had taverns?

"Go in, identify yourself to the owner, then he will show you where to meet Yoav."

"*Todah*," I said, shouldering my jar. It was my tardy excuse slip, should I need one. As I set out, I noticed the soldier followed me at a distance. It was a little unnerving, but people were on the street. I was certainly safer now than walking the streets of Dallas at night or Istanbul during the day. I might not get this chance again—and working in the harem was making me increasingly antsy.

As I pushed through the crowd, jar on my shoulder, I puzzled through why he would follow. Had I been single, I might have been in danger. Because I was wedded, anything, whether rape or seduction, would be adultery because the definition of adultery rested on the female.

It was less of a moral law and more of a—I gritted my teeth at this—property issue. A man had to know that his children were his. However, everyone knew that I was married. Since I didn't think this soldier would risk being stoned to death for raping a married woman, I looked for another reason.

Why was this guy following me? I lowered my jar, then ducked into an alley to check my theory. He walked past, looking around with his eerie blue eyes. There were dozens of women carrying stuff on their shoulders and heads, moving through the streets. I watched as he hurried a little to catch up with a woman whose jar looked like mine. I slipped out of the alley and followed him.

Only when she turned down a street did he notice she wasn't me. I about-faced, knowing that he was looking all around him now, wondering where I'd gone. It was kind of fun—certainly more so than fetching and carrying dozens of garments to whiny women!

After a few more false tries, a couple of times of losing him and being sighted, I realized I had a major problem on my hands: I didn't know where I was going. I didn't know my way around Mamre. It was getting closer to evening; the streets were emptying.

The soldier had said by the city gates, so I followed some day merchants who would stay outside the city. Through pure luck I managed to overhear two Mitanni discussing the lentil soup that was served at The Honey Bee. My jar had grown heavy, despite being empty.

I attached myself to them, walked in the tavern, and was told I had to leave my jar outside. Hoping it wouldn't be stolen, I complied, then approached the bar. The man looked me up and down, then jerked his chin toward the back of the room.

I walked through a curtained doorway.

"*Shalom*," Yoav said. Avgay'el sat next to him.

"*Shalom, adon, g'vret.* You wished to see me?"

"You lost my man very well," he said. "This lets me know you are who I look for."

I said nothing, though I wondered what he meant. *Play poker, Chloe. Don't let him know what you are thinking.*

"*B'vakasha*, seat yourself," he said with a wry twist of his lips.

B'seder, Yoav, I too remember when the roles were reversed. I took the stool that was the room's only choice, my glance moving between Dadua's second wife and his second in command. Wasn't it unusual for them to be here? Alone? Together?

I've become a busybody, I thought.

He leaned forward, the black curls by his ears falling forward. "Your husband is an Egyptian scribe, *isha*?"

"He is," I said.

"And you, a 'goddess'? What else besides? Do you spin gold from straw, a secret you forgot to tell us?"

"*Lo.*"

He sat back. "I know from our dealings in Ashqelon that you are no stranger to strategy," he said. "Tonight you have confirmed that. You are aware of your surroundings, you know how to blend into the light and shadow. How is this?"

I glanced at Avgay'el. Her eyes were dark, but kind. Or was this "good Israeli/bad Israeli" they were playing on me? "Why do you want to know?" I asked. "What lessons was I supposed to learn by your man following me through the city?"

"A city you do not know," he said. "Among a people to whom you do not belong. Yet you disguised yourself with a jar, covered your hair and ears so that no one would give you a second glance."

I said nothing. There had been no forethought on my part. He was giving credit where it wasn't due, but I certainly wasn't going to tell him.

"Who are you? What are you?"

"You said it yourself. A 'goddess.' "

His green eyes sparked. "*B'seder.* Keep your secrets," he growled.

"*Todah,*" I said sarcastically.

He raised his brows at my tone of voice, reminding me that I was a slave and he was my master. *Geez, Chloe, come on!* "Forgive me," I said, totally not meaning it.

"Look at me and say that."

I raised my eyes to his; they were almost the same color as mine, though I doubted mine could be as expressionless as his were. For some reason, just as he had in Ashqelon, he really irritated me. I gritted my teeth, refusing to look away. He didn't either. Another stare-down.

Even if my eyeballs fell out onto the table, I refused to blink first. He must have felt the same way. We were focused on each other, neither willing to give in. My eyes started drying out, tearing up. Yoav's bottom lids squinted, then filled with tears.

"*Ach!* You two are children!" Avgay'el said, exasperated. "This will accomplish nothing, Yoav. Slave, *isha, ach,* what is your name?"

"Chloe," I said, not breaking my gaze. The woman should know, since I worked beneath her nose day in and day out.

"Klo-ee? Very well. You both win, now stop it."

Neither of us would look away, despite her words. Tears streamed down my cheeks, as down his. Avgay'el slapped his shoulder. "Yoav ben Zerui'a, your children act older than you! Stop it."

His eyes bugged in outrage, but he refused to look away. I started to giggle; I was staring down a Bible character! He started to chuckle. Avgay'el slapped him again. I was laughing in earnest now. She waved her hand between the two of us, then moved to stand there.

My focus was distracted, and my eyes snapped shut. "Well, praise

Shekina!" she said. "You two . . . *ach!* Look, Yoav, all this time you have wasted!"

I was rubbing my eyes, which were streaming with tears.

"There was no waste," he said. "I learned more about Klo-ee than if I spoke with her for an hour." They had changed into another dialect, but still I understood. Was I supposed to? Did they know I did?

"*Isha*," he said, turning to me. "Do you want your freedom?"

THE DESERT

"*Todah*," Cheftu said distractedly to the slave. The other slave, he reminded himself. Until the gold was dug up, loaded, and given to Dadua, Cheftu was nothing more than a slave, despite his missing ear chains.

He looked out on the landscape. Not even a lizard crawled beneath the blazing sun, no breeze stirred, and the very air smelled sulfuric.

Squinting against the light, seeing into the distance, he saw that it made no difference; there was nothing but the same terrain.

The Salt Sea stretched beside them, blue green water that reflected the sky. No fish swam in its waters, no animals lapped at its shore. Chunks of rock, fantastically shaped crags of salt jutted up from the waters, littered the shoreline. Even the breeze carried the sting of salt in it.

For one more day they would walk through the blazing heat beside these waters that offered no refreshment. To his west, the hills were distant and flat topped, riddled with rocks, homes for mountain lions and wild goats. And brigands.

Cheftu looked back at the assembled caravan: seventy of the finest families' sons, thirty of their slaves, one hundred donkeys, a handful of priests, N'tan, and himself. Prime plucking for a team of brigands, especially on the return trip. Once again he considered that bringing the gold through the desert was not a smart way to transport it, not unless they had an army escort.

The sun would soon set, and they would walk some more. In an effort to acclimatize the men, especially those from the cooler hills of Jebus and the Galil, they were walking at night. It also made the lack of wine and sex less apparent when the men woke at dusk and fell asleep at dawn.

Cheftu wished his body and mind were so easily retrained. He could be nearly dead and would still want his wife, not solely for physical release, but because his home was with her, within her. He sipped some beer, lukewarm, then got to his feet, pulling his thoughts from Chloe. Something unsettled him about this journey; something wasn't right.

His gaze raked the far hills, washed in the dying light. They were being watched, but by whom he didn't know. He wished he had a blade; but only freemen did.

"I will give you one," N'tan said, stepping beside him, discerning his thoughts.

"*Adon*," Cheftu acknowledged the *tzadik*. Nathan, of the Bible; it was too much to believe at times. "How may I assist?"

The prophet twisted his beard with long brown fingers, his eyes narrowed against the sun. "What is your name?"

"You know my name."

"Chavsha is not your name, Egyptian. What is your name?"

Cheftu felt a prickle of nerves but said nothing. He might have been called on his falsehood, but he was unwilling to share the truth. N'tan waited in silence.

"When you give me your name, tell me how you came to be a slave in Ashqelon, then I will entrust you with a blade."

"That seems an unfair price, *adon*," Cheftu said coldly. "Trade my spiritual defense for a physical one?"

"It will reveal which world you fear most," N'tan said, turning to walk away.

"What is *your* true name, *adon*?" Cheftu asked, irritated.

N'tan turned to him. "If you are who I think you to be, then you know my name. You know my family, my forebears. If you are not, then I will not reveal myself to you."

Cheftu stood rooted, looking at this slightly built and dark-eyed man with long, curling hair and long curling beard. N'tan half smiled. "See what is, not what you hold to be." His smile vanished at Cheftu's confused frown. "Move out, slave."

Cheftu picked up his belongings and stepped onto the path that would lead to his freedom.

WASET

RaEm stared at the counting chart. It was hopeless. There was no food for Egypt. There was barely food for the royal family! Crops had failed nationwide. The floodwaters had barely dampened the soil. Without the tears of the Nile, there was no black land, only the encroaching red of the desert.

She had found old storehouses, sealed with the cartouche of Amenhotep. When the doors were opened, soldiers had picked up torches and preceded her.

Into emptiness.

Nothing remained. Not a stalk, not a kernel, not a seedling. There was no food.

Akhenaten had said aye, of course they had eaten it. RaEm swallowed hard, recalling that he was Pharaoh, she was here on his sufferance; even though she was co-regent, it was a status that could change any moment. *Aii*, how could this have happened?

Instead she had pledged her body to him in yet another letter while her mind sought of a plan, a path. Once she would not have cared if everyone around her starved and died, as long as she was well. Then she had woken in another place and time, terrified of being in the dark, covered in blood, fearing for her life.

The pouch on her back had yielded nothing that she understood. A box that spoke, but how had the person gotten inside it? A thick pad of papyrus, but much better hammered than she'd ever before seen. Something oblong that smelled like food and proclaimed to be a "5th Avenue." Though she could read the words, they meant nothing.

Every nightmare had come true when she'd opened a round, flat case. From inside it, a *kheft*, a demon, had stared at her, red hair waving like flames around a face whiter than the papyrus, with bulging brown eyes beneath bloodstained brows.

Now, safely in Egypt, RaEm touched her skin, assuring herself: brown. Her head was shaved, but her brows were black. She was safe. Temporarily banished from Akhenaten's side, but safe.

Then, however, fearing she was in the afterlife, she had shrieked, thrown the circle away, and cowered in the darkness, waiting for the bite of fangs and nails.

"It's okay," she'd heard in her mind as she'd trembled violently. Nothing had happened. She'd peeked over her arms. The *kheft* hadn't come after her. Hugging the ground, she had crept up on the round, flat case, trying to see if the *kheft* was still in there or if it had flown free. She saw nothing except the ceiling and a light shining in from a distant opening. After she had circled it, realized it was safe, she'd reached out to seal it—

The *kheft* had returned! It stared boldly at her. RaEm screamed, clipping the case shut, sealing the demon inside. Then she saw her skin. The demon had poxed her! Spots of brown and reddish pink ran up and down her arms. She looked at her legs; they too were covered! "HatHor!" she had screamed.

RaEm never felt a part of Chloe's world. Even when she learned the box that talked was a CD player; the 5th Avenue was a candy bar for "snacking"; the pad of papyrus was Chloe's sketchbook; and the "demon" she saw was none other than her own reflection in the mirror of an Estée Lauder compact—still, she was lost.

Slowly things had begun to enter her mind, but they were hard to comprehend, for she had no rational memories, no way to link what she heard to anything that she already knew. Everything was bigger, complicated. Even the people, the emotional memories she had, confused her. Eventually she had found her way into Chloe's life, but it was months and months before she began to understand The Future. She'd never thought of "the future" before . . . there was no future, only the present and then the afterlife.

Trapped in a hospital bed, surrounded by confused doctors who asked questions she didn't know how to answer—"Why are you in Egypt?" "Where is your father now?" "Pick up this pencil and draw for me, please"—had made it worse. Her nightmares were awful; she awoke screaming every time she closed her eyes. When she woke up, however, the nightmare was real. She had become a *kheft*.

Finally the nurses tired of her. They "turned on" the black box in the ceiling and left her alone. There was no way to turn it off; she couldn't even reach it when she stood beneath it. So she'd begun watching Sky TV.

When finally she'd realized what had, impossibly, happened, she'd stepped hesitantly into the world. Now that she had more images, more knowledge, and understood the little bit of Chloe Kingsley who remained in her mind, she could grasp what was being said or done.

She never felt at ease. Her very skin repulsed her. She tried to find Egypt in the dark-eyed people who now lived in the Nile valley, but Egypt was lost. Terrified to leave the red and black lands, RaEm had swallowed her pride and begged forgiveness from Phaemon, the lover she'd tried to murder, the man she'd pulled through time with her.

At least she wasn't alone.

There were fabulous things about the future. Electricity, neon, cheese that came in so many different flavors. Condoms. High heels. Magazines. TV. Nothing was hers, though.

RaEm looked over the empty audience chamber. Empty because this was a feast day for Amun-Ra, the outlawed god of Waset. She was seated on the throne of Egypt. The crook and flail fit in her hands. Hatshepsut had sat here; now she did. It was hers. Egypt was hers. RaEm had to preserve it or it might vanish and she would be left alone again.

But Egypt's murderer was RaEm's beloved, her lover, her brother. She considered her choices again: her lover or herself?

CHAPTER 8

MAMRE

THERE WAS NO DIRECT TRANSLATION for my words: *Duh!* Also, it probably wouldn't be the best etiquette. So I settled for a complacent nod.

"You heard *haMelekh's* challenge a few weeks ago," Yoav said, getting up and pacing. Out of battle attire, wearing the one-sleeved tunic dress of the Israelites, he looked as though he might rip through the woven fabric and gilded fringe, he was so beefy. "Whoever gets into the city of Jebus wins the position of *Rosh Tsor haHagana* forever. I want that position."

Big surprise.

He turned to face me. "You will get this position for me."

That was surprising. "Me? How, how can I . . . ?" I looked at Avgay'el. Her dark gaze was calculating, which made me wonder what she got out of this, why she was here.

Yoav turned away, pacing the room again. "Blind and lame can get in," he said.

The hair on my neck rose. He wasn't going to suggest they blind and deafen me, was he? Instinctively I stepped back.

"Put your eyes back in your head," he said, glancing over his shoulder. "I know rumors of a waterway that runs from outside the walls to the main city well."

"A waterway?" I repeated, trying to understand him.

"A woman, only a woman, will be allowed to the well," Avgay'el said to me.

I remembered the jar I'd carried all afternoon. "What has this to do with me?"

Yoav ran a finger over his mustache. "You are a woman, a clever woman."

My cheeks heated, even though I knew he was using his flattery for a reason.

"Moreover, I have what you want." He faced me, legs braced, shoulders straight, his body a perfectly proportioned specimen. "Your freedom."

"I do not know what you mean," I said, trying to appear calm.

"When your husband returns, he will be free."

I said nothing.

"This is a chance for you also to be free."

"You want me to go into the city of Jebus?" I said. "As a well woman?"

"*Ken.*"

"And do what?"

"Give me the city."

"I'm going to overpower the guards? Open the city gates?" I hoped my tone of voice revealed my disdain for his plan. "One woman alone, you must be mad!"

His green eyes flashed at me. "Be wary what you say, *isha.* Your tongue will land you in trouble if you aren't."

You're a slave, Chloe. Slave. S-l-a-v-e. Think of all those harem women with their petty demands, all those pitted dates. Slave! Behave like one! I bit my tongue. "What would you have me do?"

"Go from the well, down through the waterway, and lead us in."

"What kind of waterway?" I repeated. Were these sewers we were discussing?

"The well, drinking water."

"What if I get caught?"

Yoav shrugged. "You are no tribesman, so they will not suspect us. If anything, they will cast a fretful eye toward the Pelesti. It is no matter." He unsheathed his knife, pausing to let the lamplight flicker over its bronze blade and stone-encrusted handle. "If you don't get me the way into the city, the Jebusi will kill you as a Pelesti spy. If, however, you don't get me the way into the city, I will kill you myself."

"So: You will kill me if I try and fail, and if I try and get caught, I'm dead. But if I don't try, then you will leave me alone?"

He exchanged a glance with Avgay'el. "Once I assure myself that you won't betray me, *ken*."

My skin turned goose bumpy beneath my dress. "What assurance could I give you?"

Yoav slid his blade into its sheath. "I cut out your tongue."

I started trembling all over, uncontrollably. "You . . . jest? Surely?"

He spread his hands, palms up. "I must protect myself. I have *yeladim*."

It was hard to believe he was a father, yet could cut my tongue out with no compunction. I spoke slowly, for my tongue suddenly felt thick and swollen. "If I get in, then I get set free?"

"If you get in and let us in, *nachon*. You are free."

"You don't give me much choice," I said wryly. This was unbelievable.

He sheathed his knife. "Of course I do! Yoav ben Zerui'a is no uncircumcised pagan. You can continue slaving with the expectant mothers, the nursing mothers, the women in their cycle, for every day for the rest of your seven years in slavery."

"Tongueless," I said.

He shrugged.

"Why me?" I demanded. "Why not another woman?"

Yoav glanced at Avgay'el, then back at me. "You are not a woman of our tribes, it is apparent in every move you make. Also, you are not a . . ." His hands moved through the air as though he were pawing for the word. "You lack a femininity. You are as a widow, capable of handling her husband's affairs, not needing a man's help." He looked troubled. *"B'Y'srael . . ."*

In Israel, the lexicon scribbled on the chalkboard.

". . . our women leaders have had this sense, this ability. All have been as widows, from the great D'vora, the judge, to Ya'el, who went against her husband's wishes. Even Yefthah's daughter seemed a woman alone when she went into the desert."

I had no idea who these people were, and I certainly wasn't a widow. And just because I could scale a wall and hit a target didn't mean I wasn't feminine. I glowered at him while I tried to recall that he was an ancient man, fairly progressive for his day and age, but he still had a long way to go. However, was he an idiot? Did he really think I could get into a city that four armies had been incapable of invading? "Let me understand."

"B'vakasha," he said, giving me the floor.

I fought to keep my tone respectful. "You want me, a Pelesti slave, to open the city of Jebus, so that you, the same highlanders who sacked my sister cities, can sack another? You think that I, because I lack femininity and carry a jar of water, can persuade these Jebusi to let me into their well, their sole source of drinking water, then somehow find my way through the city, and return that same way with an army at my heels?"

His gaze moved over me slowly, appreciatively. His dialect changed again; another one I understood, but that Avgay'el did not. "There is nothing lacking in you, *isha*. It is that you know how to manage yourself. You can think. You can hide when someone is following you. You know to be wary of strangers."

His eyes met mine again. "But it is not because you are anything less than comely. In fact, you will need a disguise." He said the last in Hebrew, or Akkadian, or whatever this common *patois* was. "That is another task for Avgay'el."

"Ata meshugah!" I shouted at him. Crazy as a bedbug, that was what he was!

"Is that a refusal?" he asked, his hand going to his blade.

I was trembling, trying to figure an angle but too scared for clarity. "Why do you do this?" I asked, turning on Avgay'el.

"I want my own palace," she said. "I want to stop hearing about the wonders of this city and how Dadua's *nefesh* longs for it. I want the constant beseeching prayers to stop. I want him to have his dream so we can get on with our lives."

"*HaMelekh* is nagging you to death, so you'll pay any cost?" I choked out.

"*Nachon!*"

"Never mind that it might take my life and the lives of these soldiers?"

"You have choices," she said.

"Dying or being mute!"

Her gaze dropped.

Use another tactic, Chloe. "Why support Yoav? Why not one of the other many *gibori?*" I asked. They were all jockeying for this position of *Rosh Tsor haHagana.*

Avgay'el glanced at Yoav. "No one has ever been more faithful to the heart of my husband's desires," she said in her melodious storyteller's voice. "Yoav knows what Dadua wants, even when Dadua claims he doesn't want it." She looked back at me. "Yoav has earned this position already. He has won it through blood."

This was way too bloody a place for my comfort.

"It was not"—she seemed to search for the words—"the most honorable action for *haMelekh* to make this a, a competition among his men."

"*Lo.* They should be comrades at arms, not at each other's throats," I said, trying to be reasonable in the midst of this insanity.

"You've served as a soldier," Yoav said flatly. "With the Ashqeloni?"

My look toward him was not respectful. "What is the plan?" I asked. Did I stand a chance? Certain muteness or optional death? "Do you even have a plan?"

"You will go with two of my trusted men to observe the city. You need to find where this waterway comes out."

Reconnaissance, *b'seder.* "You don't know where this passageway is?"

"*Lo,* that is part of your job as a spy."

My father would be so proud. "What if I can't find——" I didn't even finish the statement; I didn't need to because he immediately reached for his knife. Apparently not finding a way in fit into one of the categories. Choice: mute or dead. "What if there isn't one?"

"You are a clever woman."

That was beginning to feel more like an excuse than a compliment. I licked my lips, taking another deep breath so I didn't scream again. "*B'seder*, then what?"

"Then you will go into the city as an itinerant well drawer."

"This is a common thing?" I asked.

Avgay'el shrugged. "Common enough. Perhaps you should say you are a widow."

Fair enough.

"You will be Pelesti, fleeing from the cities because we destroyed them," Yoav suggested.

It was always good to keep one's lies close to the truth. "*B'seder.* What reference is the blind and lame?" I asked.

"The curse that Abdiheba, the present king, lays on those who try to invade him."

I waited. Was there more?

"Do these things upset you?" he asked.

"That I must betray a people in order to have my freedom? Or that he lays a curse against me—I, who am already cursed by slavery and separation from my husband?"

Yoav exchanged a glance with Avgay'el. "I did not know you pagans revered marriage so much. So: Have you sacrificed your children?"

I blinked, stunned. "What?"

"The Jebusi worship Molekh," Yoav said, then spat. "They sacrifice their children at the full of the moon. Are the Pelesti the same way?"

"Uh, Dagon never wanted anything other than crabmeat," I said. That and the odd tightrope-walking virgin.

"Then why don't you have children?" Avgay'el asked.

"We . . ." I looked down, thinking furiously. Lie or tell the truth? Or embroider on part of the truth? Or fix part of a lie? "We have not been married long," I said hesitantly. "At the first, we lost a . . . baby."

"Poor *isha*. May Shekina bless your womb for this victory you give the tribes," Avgay'el said with genuine sympathy. I nodded, while hoping that God wouldn't make me infertile for that mockery I made of women who had suffered the loss of a child. Yes, I had miscarried once . . . but . . .

It hadn't been exactly the way I'd portrayed it. *Ach!*

Avgay'el stood up abruptly. "I must return. Dadua will wonder where his dinner is."

Yoav looked at me. "Have you decided?"

I recapped the situation as it had been explained to me. My role would be a Pelesti widow, working her way across the country by drawing water for hire. "Will I be safe?" I asked. "Do the Jebusi honor the same laws that your tribes do?"

"*Lo.* You will have to defend yourself," he said. "That is one of the reasons I selected you." His green gaze raked me. "Avgay'el will disguise you so it will be less of a stumbling block."

"So I figure out the rest on my own?" I asked. There didn't seem to be much of a plan.

"Go do the reconnaissance. I will meet you there in a few days and we can discuss options and actions."

I rose. "I'll accompany you, *g'vret,* if I may?"

Yoav was squinting at me, as though he could see inside me. He spoke to Avgay'el. "She will leave at dawn, day after tomorrow."

"Yoav, that is *Shabat* morning! She cannot walk that far! It is a stoning should she do so!"

"She is my slave. She will do as I command." He looked at me. "However, to keep you from *avayra goreret avayra* I will have you leave after dusk on *Shabat.* You can walk through the night."

Avgay'el *tch'*d, then hid her face, hair, and the enormous trademark stone on her wrist, beneath a cloak. I slipped mine on, covering my ears and hair. Just two swaddled women to wander back to the palace. We walked in darkness and silence.

"Before you leave, we will make you a protection," she said.

"*Todah, g'vret.*" But how will I protect myself once I'm there? Could I get away from Mamre tonight? Tomorrow? Where could I go?

Dead or mute; these were considered options?

The trek would take us most of the evening. Since Yoav had the city of Jebus under observation 24/7, as part of a presiege stakeout, we would see soldiers on their way home after their weeklong shift. Some training in my mind noted that these posts were therefore empty for at least four hours once a week. Did the Jebusi know that?

There was no talking, just walking. At about two A.M. in the middle of our trek, we met up with the others. Total silence was maintained, just gestures of greeting as each tribesman passed. I kept my covered head down, my eyes averted. Yoav didn't want anyone to ascertain his plan for getting into the city because they might steal it.

My mind was completely blank by the time the sun rose. The colors passed through the spectrum so rapidly, I hardly had time to appreciate them. The sky turned red, then pink, with tendrils of gold etching the clouds, then the sun was fully up, pouring light onto the white stone city of Jebus.

Zion, Jerusalem the Golden, City of Peace.

Whoa.

It was built of reflective stone, so it picked up the colors of the sunrise. High on the hill, it seemed showered in golden light. Below us we saw the circumscription lines on the hills.

History was in the making.

Seeing how it was surrounded on three sides by steep valleys, with a mesa rising behind it, I realized for the first time how secure this city was. I had not been here before, and Father never discussed Jerusalem as a destination, only as the plum of negotiations.

All of the many tiny kingdoms around here had tried to oust the Jebusi. Despite the city's many gates, no one had ever conquered Jebus. For one, it was impossible to approach unseen; for another, the Jebusi seemed to have an endless supply of water, food . . . and patience.

Our handpicked team of twenty of Yoav's men fanned out, two of us per lookout. My partner, Dov—of the sheep-jesting fame—and I had a post observing the back of the city and the mountain, since Yoav thought we might be able to do better work out of sight.

People were already standing in line to get through the city gates. Some were there to sell, others to buy, still others to see King Abdiheba. Most of them were there seeking permission to cross Abdiheba's land into upper Canaan. It was the on-ramp to the King's Highway, which led from the Salt Sea straight up to Mitanni, then into Assyria—twentieth-century Arab enclaves.

According to Yoav, Dadua said the pagan tribes—the Amoni, the Amori, the Keleti, the Edomi, Moabi, Alameda, not to mention the united tribes who were Dadua's cousins—were watching how the tribesmen handled the attempt at Jebus.

A victory over the Jebusi would establish Dadua's supremacy over the remainder of the countryside. No battles would be necessary, for the other tribes, impressed by Dadua's primacy, would be open to negotiating.

We pitched our goatskin tent, which was nothing more than a few poles with a fleece thrown over them to give some shelter, then Dov and I took turns observing. How often and for how long were the gates unlocked? Did anyone ever leave through the wall? Over it? Under it? Were any of the windows, built high into the ramparts, ever unmanned? Dov and I watched silently, alternating which of us walked the perimeter.

As dusk began falling we saw the gates fill up again, this time with people going outside. Unlike most cities, Jebus did not allow those who were strangers to pass the night within the enclosure. To stay overnight within the walls, one must be vouched for by a citizen in good standing. Thus an invasion from within had been impossible.

Or at least improbable.

Craftsmen, merchants, and families began pitching their tents on the slopes beside the road into the city. Tonight Dov and I would mingle with them, selling hot food—which another part of the team was preparing—while listening to their tales from inside the city's walls.

While it was yet day, for the tribes didn't consider night to have fallen until one could see the first three stars, the Jebusi closed the gates. The clang and clatter as the gate's bar fell into place was audible from our perch. As rehearsed, we joined a few others, all in different clothing, to hike into the visitors' tent city.

The humor was that those visiting the city knew they would be approached by spies. It had been happening for too many years, by too many different branches of Avraham's far-reaching seed, for them not to know. Consequently those waiting outside the city bartered their knowledge for food.

A merchant would begin discussing an underground path one of his customers used for storage, then abruptly ask for free seconds on dinner. Fortunately, it was such a joke that everyone knew all the tales of Jebus. They had become the original urban myths.

It reminded me of the story about men in prison who had memorized each other's jokes so that a guy would just shout out, "Number fifty-two," then they would all laugh, since they knew the punch line.

My job was to pour out the gruel we were giving away under the marketing tool of calling it "soup." The comments—teasing, seductive, ribald, humorous—were endless since it was obvious I was female. Dov stayed close to my side, ignoring the gibes about a third wife, the joys of making love in early summer in the forest, et cetera. Fortunately it was dark, so my blushing was hidden. Having learned nothing new, we headed back to our outpost. We would divide the night, me sleeping the first watch and him sleeping the second.

It might not have been a tent by my standards, but I slept. My only thought was for Cheftu's safety. The next thing I knew, Dov was waking me up.

He snored. Loudly. I found myself on the edge of an outcropping, far enough from him so that I could actually hear the sounds of the night, watching the city. I heard only a few rustlings and growls, but no movement. I squinted at the window in the city wall, watching it until I thought I saw movement: the square became dark, then light again. Someone had walked before a lamp, I reasoned. Walking generally meant awake, so that was not the way in.

An impregnable city. If I could come up with another plan, could we skip the "waterway or die" program Yoav had suggested? I wanted my freedom; what a delight to tell Cheftu that as soon as he was freed we could leave, since I'd won my freedom, too. I couldn't even consider how it would feel for Cheftu to come home and hear I was dead.

I refused to be dead. There must be a way, a less dangerous way. Why didn't *I* have the Urim and Thummim right now?

I looked out at the city again, pondering another way in.

Would the Trojan horse routine work here? No—the gate was too low, too narrow. Not even a horse and chariot could make its way through—even if the tribesmen had them. They would be a hindrance in the streets of Jebus, which Yoav said were twisty, with many flights of stairs. Would oxen and cart work? Certainly not.

Maybe Yoav was right. Maybe water was the only pathway in.

When Dov awoke, I told him I was going to go look at the stream. He nodded, then told me where to find it. I picked up my bulky water jar, then started downhill at a slope of at least forty-five degrees. I alternated between jogging and sliding. I was sweating before I'd gone an eighteenth of a mile.

It was hot for this June day!

By the time I reached the valley floor I was aching and exhausted— hiking muscles were different from date-stuffing muscles. Now all I had to do was climb up the other side, at a similar incline. Where was a taxi when you needed one?

Above me the pilgrims to Jebus were stirring, while another band of spies was trying to buy information with breakfast.

The empty jar rested on my shoulder, as awkward as balancing an elephant, while I picked my way along. The hills were almost solid rock. Olive trees, turning silver and then green in the wind, clustered on the hillsides.

I found the tiny stream, noting it flowed straight for a distance, then vanished into the ground like a drain. Feeling eyes watching me, I spent some time lifting the jar from my shoulder, submerging it in the water. As I held the clay container so it could fill, I looked around, wondering what to do next.

The jar was now too heavy to move. It was a millstone. I tried kneeling beside it and lifting it. No way. Looking around, both embarrassed and concerned that I was blowing my already flimsy alibi, I dumped out some water and tried to lift it again.

It was still as heavy as granite. I poured more water out, then tried hefting it up from a different angle. No luck, though I came very close to dropping and breaking it—which would have been a blessing.

How did these little women do this? I'd carried backpacks for years. I skied, I climbed, I could even do the butterfly stroke. But this, this was beyond me. Apparently I didn't have the right muscles for doing an over-the-head lift with the weight of a small dinosaur. Or maybe I just needed to rest.

I left the jar standing on the ground, half hoping someone would steal it, while I followed what seemed like the logical path for this underground stream. Perhaps it would pop up again? I had canvassed around half the city when I suddenly stopped. I glanced up, noting that I was standing directly below a guardhouse built into the wall, though the guard couldn't see me from this angle. I cocked my head, listening intently.

Running water.

Strolling leisurely in the shadow of the walls, I walked and listened. The sound grew stronger, then fainter, then strong again. It was getting positively loud as I turned around another side of Jebus. I couldn't see much, just enough to note some huge stones across a faint rise. Guarded by very large, very scary-looking, yellow, faux dogs.

I dropped to the ground. This must be it!

After sucking on my finger, I held it up in the air, checking the direction of the wind. I was downwind, which was why the dogs, which weren't exactly dogs, tied to the wall, weren't barking. A definite sense of victory surged through me. Maybe the Jebusi weren't as protected as they thought?

The yellow dogs looked vicious. In fact, they looked a lot more like wolves than dogs. I closed my eyes for a moment, trying to recall any Egyptian artwork featuring dogs. With the exception of Anubis, the jackal-headed god of the dead—wait, those were jackals!

As though he heard my thoughts, one of them turned my way, slowly moving his head as though he felt me. My faith in his rope wasn't strong, so I began backing up, flat against the earth, while memories of officer's training camp ran through my brain. Once out of the jackal's visual range, I stood up, pressing myself against the stone out-cropping.

There was a point of entry! Despite myself I was excited. I'd dis-covered the secret!

I was halfway back to my tent, going around the other side of the city, when I saw the same setup: jackals, stone, the sound of water. Were they both ways into the city? Or was one a decoy?

Which was live and which was Memorex?

My enthusiasm evaporated like sweat in the desert as I trudged back to camp.

Only when I got there, soaking wet and breathing raggedly, did I recall the jar of icy water on the valley floor. Dov snorted in disgust when I told him, then left me alone. I fell asleep, leaning against a tree.

Day three of my week's recon, I watched Dov practice with his sling-shot. He posted a branch forty paces away, then in five quick tosses he hit it. The wood was struck with five perpendicular shots as evenly spaced as a Singer sewing machine's stitches. The guy wasn't much for conversation, but wow, was his aim good. Antsy to do something and knowing my area of the wall was already under surveillance, I decided to try the slingshot.

Easier said then done.

Dov refused at first, claiming it was the skill of the Binyami tribe alone. They were the ones who wielded slingshot and bow. He repeated this reasoning until I picked up a bow and proved my marksmanship. Then I asked again. Reluctantly he agreed.

I had no intention of using the slingshot as a weapon; it was just a way to take up some time and enjoy the gorgeous windy weather while learning something from these people. The thought of how hard the rock must have been thrown to become embedded in Goliath's head made me feel a little nauseated.

The slingshot was a pocket of leather at the end of two long thongs. The plan was to hold the stone in the pocket while swinging it over your head until it gained velocity. Then you released one of the thongs, letting the stone fly to the target. Split-second coordination was required; this was not a bow and arrow.

I dropped the stone the first time and it bounced off my head, which, needless to say, smarted. Dov hid a smirk, though I sensed he was not surprised. It took some getting used to, holding the strings tight while swinging it. I knew that centrifugal force held the stone in when it swung fast enough, but I knew that only because it was the same concept that kept me from falling out of a loop-the-loop roller coaster.

The sun was getting hotter, and the breeze had died. Once again I swung the sling around and around, listening for its whistle. "Now!" Dov shouted. The stone went flying twenty cubits to land somewhere downhill in the rocks. Dov sent me to find it since smooth and even river stones were a precious commodity. I tried again. Then again. My determination grew each time I messed up. I could get this skill down, I just needed more practice.

My arm was aching by dusk—again, different muscles from stuffing dates. Fortunately it wasn't our night to creep around the city, so I fixed bread, he fixed some kind of stew, and we ate in silence, watching the lights. Are you well, Cheftu? I wondered.

WASET

RaEm held her wife's small hand in her own capable brown one. Meryaten's face was screwed up with pain as she panted and wept. It was a false labor; it would have to be a false labor, for there was no way under the Aten that the girl could truly be pregnant.

Cursing herself for drawing this upon her shoulders, RaEm murmured encouragingly to Meryaten while her mind processed the newest information from the Delta.

Plague had entered Egypt, was traveling down the Nile, taking with it the souls from bodies too long standing. Poor food had weakened them, a sickness of the heart when their gods were taken away had drained the marrow from their bones, now the plague was there to lay them out.

Meryaten screamed, arching her neck. Pharaoh's elderly physician stared at the space between the girl's legs, as though he had never seen a female before.

"Give her something," RaEm said. "She is in pain." *From what, I have no idea.*

"She has refused the poppy, My Majesty," the old man said, peering into the darkness. "I do not see a babe's head."

"Well, of course you don't!" RaEm burst out, then caught herself. "She is not due for some time yet," she amended. "Give her the poppy whether she wants it or not."

"My Majesty—"

RaEm turned toward the girl again. The grip on her hand had weakened. Sweat droplets moved across the newly fourteen-year-old's cheeks, and her forehead was scorchingly hot. For a moment RaEm felt real fear. Perhaps this was more than just Meryaten's imagination? "Touch her skin," she commanded the physician.

He laid a wrinkled hand on her forehead. "*Ukhedu,*" he said dolefully. "The battle is strong."

"What do you mean? What can be done?"

"*Aii! Ukhedu* has entered her body, it eats her up inside. We must pray and light incense."

If Cheftu were here, he would have an actual medicament, RaEm couldn't help but think. Strange that she would of a sudden think of him. "Is there anything we could give her? An herb? A medicine?"

"*Aii,* since it is *ukhedu,* it is a spiritual battle. Best you inform Pharaoh, living forever! that the Aten needs to see to her needs, since only he speaks to the god."

RaEm couldn't help but feel a challenge in the old man's words.

"You are dismissed," she said through gritted teeth. Meryaten screamed again, gripping RaEm's hand so tightly that she winced.

Tiye came in a moment later, touching Meryaten's forehead. "The child has been poisoned," she proclaimed.

RaEm's head snapped up. "What do you say, Mother?"

"Poisoned. Her belly is swollen but empty, her skin is hot and dry." She turned to Meryaten. "Child, where does it hurt?"

"My . . . my belly," Meryaten whispered. "They put a knife in me, to make me believe. I want the Aten, I want my father, I want my mother." Her voice was ragged, drifting in and out of RaEm's understanding. Poisoned? Meryaten had been poisoned?

Akhenaten's voice rang in her ears: *Keep my daughter happy.*

"Make her vomit," RaEm said, rising abruptly. "Whoever did this, his head will decorate my doorpost! She cannot die."

Tiye looked up. "She already feels it. The poison has done its work, all that remains is—"

"Nay!" RaEm shouted. "She will not die! She cannot die! Either help me or leave!"

Tiye's eyes narrowed. "You really do love her, don't you, in your own, odd way?"

RaEm halted, realizing that her behavior fed the fiction that Meryaten was her beloved bride. "What did you think?" she snarled. "Now get me something to make her vomit."

"It is too late."

RaEm strode to Meryaten's couch, pulling the girl upright despite her whimpering. "Shush, my beloved. You are going to feel worse, but then you will be all better. You have to trust me."

"*Aii*, Smenkhare . . ." She sighed, leaning against RaEm's linen-covered chest.

RaEm called for slaves, who held up the body of the child. With the girl's head in her left hand, holding her mouth so she wouldn't be bitten, RaEm stuck her finger down Meryaten's throat, gagging her.

At first Meryaten regurgitated only acid, but then came the food, masses of it. RaEm was disgusted but relieved. The girl had suffered only from indigestion? What had possessed her to eat so much food? When Meryaten's stomach was empty, the slaves cleaned the couch and the floor, then RaEm laid the girl back down. She was weak now, but her body seemed to be cooler.

"What shall we do with, uh, this, My Majesty?" the chamberlain asked, gesturing to the pots with Meryaten's stomach's contents.

"Feed it to the dogs. See if they sicken."

Tiye stepped to RaEm's side. "Go and bathe, My Majesty," RaEm's deceived mother said. "Know that I have never seen a greater display of filial love." Her voice broke. "My mother's heart swells with pride at your actions."

RaEm escaped.

Cheftu looked over the port side, out at the wild expanse of Midian. They had been docked for days now, negotiating with the local shepherds and merchants for the supplies to outfit the seventy for their journey to the mountain.

Har Horeb. Cheftu shook his head in chagrin. How his generation thought it knew everything, that no other minds had ever been so advanced. What arrogance!

Having seen the Sinai, grasping the knowledge of how many people left Egypt with Moses, only a fool could imagine the Sinai would offer enough food and camping ground. It was simply too small, too overrun with Egyptians, for a people who were fleeing.

The Sinai had at least twenty thousand slaves and probably another ten thousand soldiers, and that was now. Cheftu felt the weight of dozens of gazes on his back. Those Egyptians were watching them closely. Would word get back to Pharaoh? How was N'tan intending to get this gold back to Mamre?

Or would Dadua be in Jebus by then? Did he know the way to get into the city was through the *tzinor*? At least it was according to Scriptures—though no one knew how to exactly translate the term. Water spout? Sewer? Drain? There was so much he didn't know, couldn't comprehend. What had the *tzadik*'s cryptic phrases meant? Why was it so vital to know Cheftu's real name?

He rubbed his eyes and sighed. Ach, *Chloe, ma chère, are you still bored safely grinding grain?*

"Egyptian!"

He turned at the word. N'tan refused to speak to him as anything other than slave or Egyptian, not even acknowledging the name Chavsha. How Cheftu longed to be free again, to walk where he would. Perhaps the holes in his ears would heal, given the chance. He loathed that sign of ownership on his body.

More, he loathed the ownership of his time.

N'tan beckoned, and Cheftu went to him. "We have the guides, the asses, the provisions now," N'tan said. "We will go in three different divisions." He lowered his voice, looking over Cheftu's shoulder. "I grow concerned that the sight of so much wealth might cause one of the seventy to transgress."

"A man's heart is an uncertain thing," Cheftu commented.

"Gold is enough to inspire covetousness and murder. And any manner of actions: *Avayra goreret avayra.* So: We must lessen the temptation for them."

"Hence, we split them up?"

N'tan nodded, then shrugged. "It is the best plan I can fathom," he said.

"Which division will I travel in?" Cheftu asked.

N'tan looked him over appraisingly. "You will lead the first group."

Cheftu inclined his head, acknowledging the compliment though he never forgot this man was his owner. "*Todah rabah*, for your confidence in me."

"Even if you are an idolater."

Cheftu kept his gaze focused on the ground, unwilling to react despite the insult he felt. Why should N'tan say anything different, from what he had seen? Cheftu knew *le bon Dieu* knew the truth; wasn't that all that mattered? "Will we have a guide? Or should I know the way?"

"You worship many gods, Egyptian?" N'tan asked.

Cheftu stood in stony silence, ignoring the *tzadik*'s gibes.

N'tan sighed. "The guide will take you."

"What if something should happen to him? If he should fall ill? Or run away?"

N'tan chuckled. "I assure you, nothing will happen."

Cheftu's sense of foreboding grew. One should never make those types of absolute statements. It was unlucky. "I would feel better knowing," he said. "It—"

N'tan turned cold. "The guide will lead you, slave. You will leave at the new watch. We will join you, the first thirty-five men, then the second thirty-five men, within the next two days. *Maspeak!*"

It was enough; the conversation was finished. Cheftu allowed himself to be dismissed, then stared into the desert from the ship. He had the stones—from them he could learn whatever he needed to know. But he needed a blade. In order to get one he would have to break one of the laws and steal one. However, if he didn't, did he dare just go out there unprotected? Unwitting?

Were the stones enough?

AKHETATEN

RaEm TUGGED ON HER MOURNING KILT, staring for a moment at the way she was dressed. She was Smenkhare, the bereaved husband returned to Akhetaten to bury his beloved. Damn Meryaten's *ka* for her frailty. How many more days of grieving would RaEm have to endure for that weak, manipulative little child? At least under the Aten it wasn't as many days as under Amun-Ra. Soon the business of the court would start again.

She leaned forward, bracing her elbows on her knees. The business of the court was an antic's quip in the city of Akhetaten, good only for a laugh.

The reality, RaEm had realized, was that Akhenaten never concentrated on business. He cared nothing for the country, only his impersonal deity, the Aten. RaEm had read the letters from the outposts of the empire. For fourteen years they had pleaded for intervention. Now it was too late; some new authority prowled the hills of Canaan. Egypt had lost her empire. The power had shifted away from the red and black lands.

Though RaEm loved Pharaoh in a way she'd never felt about anyone, it pained her immeasurably to see Egypt dying. The agony of watching all that Hatshepsut, her sole friend, and Hat's father, Amenhotep, had gained slip through Akhenaten's fingers like Nile water was almost too much to bear. The position RaEm had fought and killed for would cease to exist.

Akhenaten cared about nothing outside this city; to him Akhetaten was the length and breadth of Egypt. He had declared that there was no need to go beyond the cenotaphs he had set all around the city. Tiye did what she could in Waset to keep the nobles on Pharaoh's side, but it was better that he stayed in Akhetaten. Truthfully, he was not welcome anywhere else.

Outside of this enclave, Egypt had rejected her king. The populace was stricken with a pox, a plague that was killing in the hundreds; Inundations had been poor; every border was struggling against marauding sand crossers. Egypt was dying. In the Egyptians' eyes Pharaoh was at fault; he was to blame. He'd turned his back on the gods.

It was bitter to realize that for all her scheming, now that RaEm had gotten here, sat on the throne, held the crook and flail, it meant nothing, for now Egypt was nothing. May the gods curse Meryaten; she had died, making that avenue to the throne undependable. Though Smenkhare was still co-regent, even he was suspect with all of the bad fortune the country was experiencing.

RaEm threw off her crown. It was beautiful, but it was heavy. It left marks on her brow. What would Hatshepsut do in her position? A country runs on goodwill and gold, her Pharaoh had ofttimes said.

RaEm barked a laugh into the emptiness of her chamber—the two things that Egypt didn't have.

Heat beat against the walls. It was the Season of Growing, but already it was too hot. There was not enough water, and the Aten had been too powerful. The emmer would die in the field, just like everything else. She put her head in her hands, the fuzz of her shaved head ticklish against her palms.

Amun-Ra, have we offended thee? she prayed. Mother-Goddess HatHor, are you angry with us? These were words she dared not even breathe aloud, for Akhenaten would turn from her. Without the delights of his voice, his body, she would die. Though the heat of him was enough to scorch her to her roots, still she had never loved life more, never so wanted what she couldn't have. She craved the part of him that only the Aten possessed.

The Aten, an obscure god who cared nothing for agriculture or the state of the country; who was this god? Were the old gods protesting the forgetfulness of the house of Thutmosis?

Gold and goodwill.

There was no repairing the rift between the house of Pharaoh and his people. Only his death would be an acceptable gift. There was no goodwill on either side. Akhenaten considered them nothing, and they considered him a madman unworthy of the double crown, as was anyone he selected.

However, if she didn't rule, who would? Plenty stood in line for the throne of Egypt: Horemheb, the salivating Commander of Ten Thousand; Ay, the overtly loyal servant to the throne; not counting assorted cousins whose palms itched to feel the flail. But none of these cared for Akhenaten. Not a one would allow the Aten to continue. Even little Tuti, the rightful heir as Akhenaten's littlest half-brother, was less than faithful to the Aten and his brother's vision.

Therefore we get gold. RaEm was not going to lose this crown, this control. It meant little, but she would hold on to it, build it up. She would defeat those who would bury Akhenaten with their power lust.

With gold we could purchase grain for the populace from another country, she thought. With gold we could buy goodwill. Then, perhaps, we could reopen just a few temples, as a gesture of peace. The gold would allow Egypt to purchase what had once been hers for the taking: relationships with the powers of the north and west.

RaEm would not lose. Not this throne.

"Why do you sit in the dark alone?" Akhenaten asked from behind her. She closed her eyes, willing her body to rise to meet him. She turned to him, smiling. He was naked, erect, his eyes gleaming. "Open for me," he said.

Sighing inside, she accepted him obediently, driving his passion. It was such a position of power to feed his lust, for like this she controlled him. Like this she ruled the highest ruler in the land. Emphasizing her authority, she dropped him to his knees. "Give," she said, licking him, "me——"

"Aye," he groaned. "Anything you want."

She took him deep. "Swear it."

"Any—anything. I"—he was gasping—"anything you, you wan—"

"Swear it on the grave of Nefertiti," she whispered low. For a moment he stopped, his eyes cold; RaEm feared she had gone too far. She pleased him with another finger, this one with a ring, sending his passion higher. Instantly he was returned to the plane of lust. Quickly she finished him, letting him pour into her.

As he was rising from the floor, he looked at her. A hard, calculating look. "What do you want so badly?" His smile was not kind. "What made you take me with such purpose?"

"My first purpose is always to bring you pleasure . . . My Majesty," she said.

He lounged back on her couch. "Your second purpose?"

"I want the army."

"A pharaoh won't satisfy the fire between your legs?"

RaEm bit the inside of her lip at his intentional crudeness. He was Pharaoh. Anything she had could vanish tomorrow if he so much as thought it. "My Majesty is all I need in my couch," she said. "However, I think to exercise them."

He sat up. "Exercise for what? What is the purpose in that?"

Because no matter what happens, I want Horemheb and his men on my side, she thought. "It was just a whim," she said, curling into him. "Still, can I have the army?"

He lifted her chin, kissed her lips. "You can have anything. You already own the heart of Pharaoh. In truth, you shall bear the titulary of Nefertiti; you shall be known as Smenkhare Neferhetenaten."

His voice speaking those words was more than she had ever dreamed. The seduction of his mouth, his mind, was effortless and lethal to her. She looked into his wonderful misshapen face and knew that she would die for him. And when he died—as he must, for Egypt could not survive under him—she too would perish.

CHAPTER 9

I ADJUSTED THE VEIL OVER MY FACE as I looked up at the walls of Jebus. Dawn had broken, now the Jebusi were open gated and ready for business. Adjusting my hobo pack, I shuffled forward with the rest. The *serenim* sat at the gate, which formed a small room. As in Ashqelon and Mamre, one had to first get past the city fathers, then the actual opening into the city was at the side. Consequently you were in a blind before you entered the city's streets. Each person was halted, questioned, then either accepted into the city for the day, given traveler's accommodations on the testimony of a citizen in good standing, or rejected.

"You. *Isha.* What is your business in Jebus?" The Jebusi conveniently spoke the same language, even a similar dialect.

I held up my business card—the detested water jar. The soldier was broad, muscled but not fat, his uniform was neat, his beard combed, his armor gleamed. His professionalism was not encouraging.

"Speak!" he said gruffly. "You draw water?"

I nodded.

"What are you, mute?"

This was the tricky part, I wasn't mute, but I did have the wrong accent. Though it felt Dickensian, I spoke in "low" Akkadian. "A widow, sir, traveling to her family. Alas, they are poor and I have no dowry." I kept my eyes downcast.

"Sorry, *isha*," the man said. "You are from the coastal plains?"

I nodded once.

"How did your husband die?"

"The highlanders," I said, spitting on the ground, "destroyed my family, they took my father, my brother, and my husband." It was no effort to sound vitriolic. All I had to do was recall Takala-dagon, Yamir . . . and Wadia, whom I'd probably never see again.

The man conferred with the other soldier—another well-groomed, disciplined-looking soldier. Blast. But maybe these were just the soldiers used in the front lines? For appearance sake? "Who was your husband? How did he die?" the second soldier asked gruffly.

I told them my story, received my pass to enter the city, and joined the group that had passed inspection.

The guardsmen packed us sojourners into the first room, then led us through the smaller gate, one at a time, until we stood blinking in the light. I felt a tremor of elation at getting in. Inside Jebus.

The city was made of stone, which was still cool from the night. A drainage ditch of sorts ran down the middle of the street, paved on either side. The houses were clumped together, atop each other, and stairs were everywhere. The city started at this level, then climbed upward, attached by small flights of stairs, ridge after ridge after ridge, to the top. I could see trees poking up all over the city, smell the first opening honeysuckle and rose. It was white, it was clean, and it was beautiful!

This was Jerusalem?

I didn't say that because I thought it would be less, but because so rarely do things really live up to their PR releases. Stonehenge is small, the Tower of Pisa doesn't lean that far, and the Parthenon is scattered across the Acropolis like a jigsaw puzzle.

Jerusalem truly *was* beautiful.

The merchants weren't trading yet; it was early even for them. I stumbled on the dew-slick stone but kept moving forward. It was an effort to jerk my mind from the curling leaves of ivy that adorned the walls, the turquoise blue sky above me, the empty ache within me, to the city. The reason I was here. *Duh, Chloe. Waters. Wells. Dead or mute. Wake up.*

Where was the well? Women would group there. My gaze moved beyond even more well-trimmed, well-polished soldiers, toward the women. For some reason the place felt odd. Something was missing, maybe? I walked on, figuring I was still in shock to be in Jerusalem.

Streets were tangled in each other, so that soon each step became a community effort as people began to join in the bustle. Men, women, both those wizened and those in their prime, filled the thorough-fares—but something was missing. Keeping my eyes sharp for congregating females, I pressed forward.

Stalls began opening up, offering wares from the sea, the mountains, the desert, the lands beyond the desert. Merchants started their business day, drawing people away from the clump moving through the streets. Hawkers commenced shouting, the same sales calls you would probably hear on these very streets from now till 1996.

A *souq* was a *souq* was a *souq*.

Something was missing. It was an eerie absence that went beyond the daily ache of wondering about and praying for Cheftu. Something was bizarre.

I looked around; maybe it was because this was my first day at being an acne-covered and freckle-spotted overweight brunette?

We were still walking up; I could feel it in my legs. Once we passed the market, most of the people had filtered out, so that there really wasn't much of a crowd. Soon I was walking down a street, almost alone. How did I go about selling myself as a water woman when I couldn't find the bloody well?

"Isha bay'b'er!" someone called.

The call came again before I realized someone was trying to get my attention; she was calling for a well woman, even though it sounded like "beer." I stumbled around, thinking they could add "graceful" to my list of shortcomings. Balancing the jar, which felt like a small sky-scraper on my shoulder even after a week of practice, I looked up at a grouping of stone buildings. Their doors and windows were black compared to the brightness of the day. I searched for the source of the call.

"*Isha!*" the voice said again. I finally saw a tiny woman. She was bent almost double, supporting herself on a cane. I stepped closer, so she beckoned again. There was something vaguely familiar about her. Not in her stature, but in her shiny crow black eyes.

A frisson ran up my spine as I inclined my head respectfully.

"I need water," the tiny thing said, her voice strong. "If you also grind my grain, you may share in my bread. Speak up, girl."

"*B'seder,*" I said, swallowing my bad accent.

"Do we have an arrangement?" the old woman said.

I nodded, and the old woman, whose face was hardly visible, frowned. "*B'seder.* Now go, get some water," she muttered. "It is foolishness for men to design where wells will be, since we women have to live with their silly plans, because we carry the water. Many of us in Jebus can no longer dip our jars, much less haul them up the walkway. We are too old here," she said mournfully. "No youth." Then she sniffed, fixed her bright gaze on me. "Do you know where the well is?"

I shook my head—as if this were not the reason I was here!—and the woman began with the directions:

"Turn toward the city gates. Pass Rehov haLechem, K'vish Basar, and Rehov Shiryon." My lexicon flashed pictures in my mind: these were the streets of the foodstuffs, the butchers and the bakers. My stomach growled at the thought, while a Dallas version of similar establishments passed through my mind. La Madeleine, Ozona's, and . . . the Swiss Army Knife store?

"On your left side you will see a small house with a metal grate. Pass through the grate and you will find yourself in a corridor." These sounded like directions out of *The Thousand and One Arabian Nights!* "It is tall and long, very cool, which feels good in the afternoon. It slopes downward until you get to the steps. Walk down those carefully, they are very slippery." Her beady eyes gave me a once-over. "You should be wary, even though you are young." She sighed again, sad. "We have no life in Jebus. No young, no calling in the streets, playing in the parks." She sighed again, then turned to me. Apparently the directions weren't complete yet.

"The steps turn in on themselves until you reach the level of the water. There is not much room to stand, and very often there is a line.

Be patient, then return to me. As soon as I have my water, you can get back to the well if you need to, make some more wages."

That whole trip more than twice a day? I'd need provisions! Wow, talk about inaccessible. I just hoped I didn't get lost. Maybe Yoav's plan wouldn't work? Of course, it had to, or I would die—and I didn't doubt his threat. With a sigh I picked up my water jar and left, walking back toward the gate.

Sunlight was beginning to fall on the city, bleaching the upper stories, casting warmth onto the cold stone. I glanced at the sky; it was important I be the only one at the well. Could I beat the women? Or should I wait until late? No, that would cause too much speculation.

Picking up my pace, I followed the directions carefully: through the *rehovim*, the streets. Armorers; past the butchers and bakers; a sharp left, through a heavy gate.

On the way, I saw not one child.

Wait a second. That was what was missing, or rather who was missing. After drowning in *yeladim* of all ages, now I saw only adults. No kids? How was that possible? Why would a city not have children? So intent was I on my thoughts that I walked right past the guards.

"Halt!" one of them called. I kept walking, focused on the lack of offspring.

"Halt, I said!" he shouted, chasing me.

He stepped in front of me, and I had to fumble not to drop my jar. I kept my gaze fixed on the ground; Jebusi women didn't have the freedoms tribeswomen did.

"Are you working here today?" he asked.

I nodded.

He tapped my jar.

"Are you filling water for the village women?"

I nodded again as he thumped the jar. "Are you hired by the village women?" He thumped my jar. I began to fear for my jar.

"*Ken!*" I shouted, moving my jar out of thumping range.

"Be sure you are gone by dusk," he said, turning away. I heard him mention "Pelesti riffraff" under his breath. He turned back around. "Work as quick as you can," he said. "I'll be awaiting you."

Dismissed, I continued walking down to the well. This site was guarded quite heavily. This was not good news. Were all the soldiers fit and able? I hadn't seen a doughnut-and-coffee-swilling one yet. They were undefeatable this way; inside the walls, with primo armor, weaponry that was wielded by people who knew what they were doing.

Could I swing this deal?

The stairs to the well spiraled downward, murky and clammy cold. With every step I felt the muscles in my legs screaming protest. Carrying forty pounds of water on my shoulder, while walking uphill on the way back, was going to be murder. I groaned at the thought that I'd set myself up for days of this.

Even with practice I was never going to feel the same.

Women passed me heading up, some alone, but mostly traveling in threes. Jebusi women wore what I'd always considered biblical dress: no style, little color or pattern. They were sackcloths with sleeves simply tied around the middle.

One of the things I'd noticed about the tribespeople was that they were fashion plates, both male and female. Women didn't wear veils and the fabrics they used were bright and well woven. Most significant, especially after Egypt, clothing was individualized.

I reached the bottom step, blinking in the darkness. I knew by the sound of water that the well was here. Women before me in line filled their jars. I could barely see them since the room was lit by only two torches. We danced around each other as each group or person filled their jars, then climbed back up the stairs.

A Jebusi soldier, seated comfortably beside the well, whittled away, sparing us the occasional glance. The lazy weasel!

As my eyes adjusted, I saw the layout. A platform of wood, approximately two feet by four feet, capped the well. This wooden cover was fixed into the stone with copper bolts as thick as my wrists. Within the framework of the large wooden covering, a smaller aperture was cut—the hole for drawing water. You could close this opening and never know there was a well.

The really bad news was that the inside space was maybe eight inches square—even a healthy rat couldn't make it through that! I noticed that there was a separate bucket for drawing water, then you poured it into your receptacle of choice before hauling it upstairs.

There was no way someone could get up from the water source into the city.

I was a dead woman.

My eyes filled with tears as I thought of how I'd have no choices— I had to go to Midian, meet up with Cheftu there. I had to sneak out tonight, before they knew what I was up to. Oh God; I set my jar down before I dropped it.

The girl standing in line ahead of me was about six months pregnant. I watched her struggle with the jar, but her belly was too big to hoist it. The other women ignored her, which angered me. I stepped forward and picked it up, groaning as I helped her adjust it on her shoulder.

"Todah," she whispered, not meeting my gaze.

I murmured that it was nothing and edged out of her way. The townswomen had fallen silent, watching us. My heart was in shock; my arms already hurt. I just kept staring at the small opening; this was the entryway? Even if I dieted for a year, I wouldn't fit through. The desire to wail was almost uncontrollable. Wacky as it was, I'd almost talked myself into thinking I could do this, invade the city.

Laboriously I filled my jar, bucket by bucket. As I had seen women do and as I had practiced, I knelt on one knee, my back straight. Then I edged the jar up my arm and onto my shoulder. Forcing my knees not to buckle, I got to my feet.

This was only half-full? I staggered away from the well. This was agony.

I hoped my copious sweating didn't melt my disguise off, literally. Not that it mattered.

I was a dead woman.

AKHETATEN

THE PRIEST STOOD before Smenkhare again: the high priest of an out-lawed god, the god who ironically was going to outlive them all. Things had changed so quickly. Plague, ostensibly, had taken away the high priest of Aten and also Akhenaten's granddaughter, who had been borne by his daughter.

These double deaths, so close to Pharaoh, had convinced even the most loyal followers of the Aten that Akhenaten had offended the sun god. This city in the plain was emptying like water trickling from a cracked jar. Each time one looked up, there were fewer citizens than be-fore. RaEm's beloved's dream was dying; Pharaoh was killing her dreams also.

The priest was here. Time was running down.

"What lies do you come to spew this time, Horetaten?" RaEm knew he hated when she changed the nomen in his name from Hore-tamun to a more fitting name for this court: Horetaten. However, it was a more realistic way for her to behave with an audience of courtiers.

"I see my"—he cleared his throat—"Lord Smenkhare is as gra-cious and forgiving as ever."

"What part of my ruling and reigning as co-regent of Egypt, liv-ing in the light of the Aten forever! does your feeble brain fail to com-prehend? Address me properly, Horetaten."

He bowed his head. "My Majesty. I see the Aten has blessed your nature so that you are even more compassionate than I recalled."

"Should you ever seek forgiveness, you might find me so. Why are you here?"

"You know the seasons. Pharaoh, officially, should prepare to sail the barque down for the god's holiday."

RaEm glanced at the courtiers and nobles, all bored, watching this scene that they had seen many a time with priest after priest. The former religions of Egypt had not ceased in trying to lobby for their deities as consorts, or courtiers, of the Aten. RaEm wished for wine. "He no longer acknowledges that god."

Horet dared to step closer to the throne, lowering his voice so that even the scribes couldn't hear it. "Egypt will no longer acknowledge him." There was no venom in his gaze; instead his eyes were imploring. RaEm felt the blood in her body chilling. Was this the day? Could nothing else be done?

She took a cup of wine and sipped, hoping the high priest was here for other reasons, not the one she feared. There had to be more time; she didn't know, she hadn't found the answers they wanted!

Horetaten was unflappable. RaEm had a good mind to imprison him, just to see his color change. Such an action would be foolish, petty even. She finished her wine, feeling it flood into her veins, ease her fury.

With a wave of her hand she dismissed the roomful of soldiers, nobles, maids, scribes, courtiers, and slaves.

"What do you seek, Horet?" She heard the edge of exhaustion in her tone. Indeed, between spending the night sating Akhenaten, then rising at dawn for prayers to the Aten, before devoting the day to audiences in hopes of straightening out the kingdom, interspersed with endless feasting, drinking, and carousing until Akhetaten returned her to bed for his pleasure, she spent most days at tears' edge.

The last thing she needed was more intrigue. The wives schemed, the children plotted, the soldiers had their motives and plans, the nobles had theirs. Akhenaten remained a giant child, playing in the sand castle he'd built, with no understanding of how his people loathed him. Nor did he care.

As a priestess in Hatshepsut's Egypt she had thrived on the gossip and scheming of the court. Then, however, Egypt had been healthy, at peace, rich beyond imagining, full of ideas, beautiful people, and power.

Now Egypt was riddled on every side with skirmishes, poor beyond bearing, tolerant of only one idea, and lacking beautiful people. Power was an illusion. The sport of palace life was gone; all that remained were the realities of hunger, poverty, and illness. "Why are you here?" she repeated.

"My Majesty," he said, affording her the title she was due, the title for which she had paid blood, "Waset calls for a new ruler, a new king to lift the burden of these poisonous years from us while yet there is time."

No longer were his words couched; there was no delicacy in handling the situation now. RaEm felt her fear grow. She clenched the crook and flail in her hands, forcing her breathing to be even.

Always, Waset had ruled Egypt. There dwelt the nobility from generations before. There resided the hundreds and thousands of priests and soldiers. There were the temples laden with gold, filled with magic and secrets. There, the lifeblood of Egypt flowed between the land of the living and the City of the Dead. Akhenaten hadn't been able to change that, at least not for long.

"I grieved for you at the death of Meryaten," he said.

RaEm shot him a quick look—did he guess? She bowed her head.

"It was a valiant, brave effort to extend the Aten's reign," he said. "But it failed. There were no children, and Egypt needs new blood. Stronger, healthy blood."

"There is only the boy," RaEm said, weary beyond endurance. "With only his sister to wed."

"How many years is he?"

"Seven."

"She?"

"Eleven."

Horet sighed. "I love Egypt, My Majesty. I was not one of those who fought when taxes to the temples were cut. Nor did I protest when my brothers in the priesthood began spending more time at their homes instead of serving the god, because there were no worshipers and no gold." He crossed his arms. "The temples had grown too powerful. Decision making had been taken from the court of Pharaoh and placed in the back gardens of the priests." His brown eyes were open. "It was not right." He glanced up. "Amun sought for Ma'at to be restored."

Horet gestured. "This pendulum swings to the north, then to the south, before centering on the navel of Geb, the earth."

RaEm sipped from her glass, only to realize it was empty.

"Pharaoh, living forever! swung too far," Horet said, a little more metal in his tone. "The time has come to center Egypt once more. She is ravaged." He stepped forward, dropping to his knees, bowing on his face as he should have done but had chosen not to. "I love these red and black lands more than any woman, more than any god." He looked up again, his cheeks wet with tears. "I would be nameless in the after-life—"

RaEm gasped.

"—rather than have her bleed further."

"Do you know what curse you lay on yourself?" she whispered as she glanced into the shadowed corners of the room. "Nameless?" It was the greatest fear of an Egyptian to have no name, no identity, before the gods. Nameless meant that one would be destroyed, consumed by the Devourer. Then one's deepest self would wander, weeping and lost, throughout eternity. It was a heinous end.

"I will do anything to turn Egypt from this cliff of destruction," he said.

RaEm's heart thudded in her breast. Egypt, the land of her roots, that she knew in her blood, whose soil she ate, or Akhenaten, the man she adored, body, soul, and mind? "How much time?"

Horet looked away. "Months at best. The nobles have returned from Akhetaten to Waset. The power base of Pharaoh's support is gone."

She agreed silently.

"There is one below me, an avaricious man whose hatred of Pharaoh knows no bounds. He would strike even at me, if he knew I were here."

She nodded once. "Would gold ease the pains?"

"Ease them only, My Majesty. It would only postpone the inevitable."

"Aye, I understand, but we need the time for Tuti to grow, and perhaps—" However, RaEm realized, Akhenaten would never change.

There was no possibility of his becoming more rational, more reasoned.

Was there the chance that she could reign as Pharaoh alone?

He nodded thoughtfully. "Were they better fed, the diseases would not claim so many. Gold could also be used to restore some of the smaller temples."

"Aye, opening them again would soothe . . ." RaEm fell silent. Her very words were a betrayal of Akhenaten. But it must be done. She closed her eyes, unable to stop the few tears. Horet waited in silence. She sniffed for a moment as she regained control.

"Gold could bandage many of Egypt's wounds," Horet said. "Where is it?"

RaEm sighed. As Sky TV would say, that was the million-dollar question. The mines were picked almost clean, and the gold in the temples was not accessible. The treasury was empty, and no tributes had arrived, save piddling trinkets. Egypt had lost her throne as a worthy power. For twenty years she had ignored the world.

So the world had moved on.

"I don't have it yet."

He threw up his hands in disgust. "I cannot hold back a tide of fury on mere promises!" He glared at her, stepping back and pacing—daring to turn his back on her. "For a moment I thought you understood, that you agreed! That was our agreement, *haii?* Egypt is dying! Murdered by this, this . . ." He spun on his heel.

"The people are starving. The temples are ruins. We've lost sons and brothers and fathers to endless skirmishes that aren't even acknowledged as battles!" He turned to her. "I come to you, to plead for the land Pharaoh is sworn to consider above all other concerns. And you mock me!" He was crying again, tears streaming unchecked down his cheeks. "It would mean my life were I found here, speaking with you. I am the only pebble holding back the river, woman. Build me a corvée, or we will all drown."

RaEm got off the throne. Her kilt, carefully shaped to fit becomingly on the chair, fell into a mass of wrinkles with her movement. She stepped down one step, a jeweled foot resting by her footstool.

Carefully she laid her more delicate versions of the crook and flail on the throne, then looked down into his eyes. "I will get you gold. I do not know where, but I have heard rumors." She ground her teeth. "More than you, if one word of this conversation were repeated, then I would die. Drawn and quartered after spending a week in an ant pit, I assure you." She stepped down again, still taller than he. "Keep the river from overflowing for a few more months, I beg you. I will provide the gold."

He looked at her; RaEm thought of the mess that tears could make of kohl and feared she looked more of a specter than a co-regent of the living god. "Tuti's marriage to Akhenespa'aten can be announced by time of flooding," RaEm offered.

"It will not put off the need for gold," he warned.

They stared at each other. He was a young man, though the lines of worry had creased his cheeks, drawn grooves along his forehead. His brows were dark, as were his eyelashes. Again RaEm felt no personal interest emanating from this man. His gaze was limpid and pure, that of a child's.

"You are worthy of the double crown," he whispered. "For you love Egypt more than your own heart."

RaEm wanted to laugh, then weep. *Aii*, Hatshepsut, my friend, the illness of character I teased you about now apparently infects me! RaEm was exhausted, trying to guess what would be said or done about their meeting. "I must have you flogged," she said softly.

His eyes widened for a moment, then he nodded. "Since the last priest was stripped naked and made to swim back to Waset, I guess I should consider whipping a . . . lesser sentence."

She stood in silence. If he were not beaten, then questions would abound. If this priest left without a mark, it would be too obvious that they were in collusion. Already Akhenaten would be asking for details that she had yet to invent. "Have you felt the bite of leather before?"

He smiled wryly. "Only by my old schoolmaster, who claimed the ear of a boy was located on his back. The more often he disciplined us, the better we would hear."

A common Egyptian belief, RaEm remembered. "When you feel it, breathe out, from your belly. Listen to the way that I breathe and join it."

"Will you be the one wielding the whip?"

She bit her lip, turning from him. It seemed so long ago, those many men and women. Lords and ladies who would eat of the poppy or the lotus, drink too much, and then beg for her whippings. How it used to excite her, thrill her. Even the sailor on the ship, whose body she had striped with blood before using him, excited her. Pain, blood, they had seemed such rare, precious samples of the edge of life. "Do you want me to be?" she asked.

"I trust you," he said. "You will do what is necessary for Egypt."

"Slaves!" she screamed, spinning. As the doors flew open, Horet was seized by both arms. His expression of bafflement was quickly hidden. "He is to be flogged!" she yelled, pointing at him. "He dared to bring his talk of Amun-"—she spat—"Ra, that outdated, puny god of Waset, into the chambers sacred to the mighty Aten!" One of the overseers quickly pulled out his whip, testing it on the floor as RaEm paced, ranting.

"You fool!" she shouted, snatching it from the man's hands. "Why test a whip against the tiles when you can test it on his back? Turn him!" she shouted.

The priest was spun around as though he were on a spit. The leopardskin was torn off his shoulder, his kilt untied, revealing his pale, trembling backside. RaEm lifted the lash and brought it cracking down on him, careful to exhale as the reverberations traveled up her arm. He'd gasped, increasing his torment.

She struck him again, then walked over and pulled his face back by the skin on his neck, like a cat. "Polytheistic cur!" she said, spitting on his cheek. Beneath her breath she admonished him to breathe with her. Tossing him away, RaEm returned to her scourging position and, alternating arms, beat him soundly. Welts of red were interwoven like a basket pattern on his back.

But he'd breathed with her. Though he was in great pain, he had decreased it considerably.

"Give him his kilt and throw him back to Waset," RaEm said, perching herself on the throne. Her clothing was damp with sweat, the crown sliding on her forehead. "Nay! Wait, bring him to me!"

What do they see? RaEm wondered. They watched Smenkhare

with wide eyes as the priest was thrown before her, his hands shackled behind him so he fell on his face. She picked him up enough to see into his eyes. Did they see his skin go white when she whispered to him? Pressing her foot against Horetaten's forehead, she kicked him off her dais, then called for wine.

The high priest was dragged from the room, then she dismissed the many slaves, soldiers, and scribes.

Where was gold?

She'd sent informants to every sector of Egypt, hoping that some untapped vein of gold would be found. A hundred men combed the Sinai alone. She drank another cup of wine to ease her fears. Would she be found out about today?

Would Egypt be given the chance to live?

Help me find gold, she prayed to the Aten. If you are real, give me the gold. Show me where it is. Save Egypt.

JEBUS

ONCE I'D DEPOSITED the water with my employer, thus earned my wages—some bread, some salt, some wine—I hoisted my jar to set about exploring the town. Ostensibly I was drumming up more water-drawing business. In reality I was both doing recon and trying to find alternative routes in . . . and out. On that hill, right outside the gate, I knew that some soldiers awaited me.

However, Jebus had lots of gates, though you were admitted in only through one. I could sneak out though, then head . . . *Where, Chloe?* I forced myself to focus on the reconnaissance. *Don't give up yet, there may be another way.*

The thought of facing half the territory of Israel alone with no money, as a fair-skinned woman, on foot, was terrifying.

Recon was many things, or so I'd been taught. Learning how many men are quartered, what their weapons capacity is, their level of readiness and awareness, seeking out those who are disgruntled, all these things are part of it. A huge amount could be learned through observation.

Not that I'd done this before—just taken a class or two, with a required text. I'd also listened to Mimi's passed-down tales of the War Between the States.

The biggest difference I noticed between Jebus and Mamre, aside from the weird lack of kids, was the presence of blood and idols. In Mamre, for all its mud, life was pretty hygienic. Here, blood ran in the streets. The butchers worked in the open, even letting flies sit on the meat. The men paid no attention to the coagulating blood they stood in or left the meat in. Granted, I'd grown up in countries where buying meat meant standing in an open-air market and pointing to a swinging carcass, but the way these vendors handled the meat made even my skin crawl.

More than that, the scent of blood tinged everything. It coated the inside of my throat and nose, and it seemed to almost tint the air.

The next thing I noticed was the *teraphim*. I'd seen them in Ashqelon, but none in Mamre. Statuettes ranging from the size of a bottle of fingernail polish to the size of a German shepherd dog filled shop after shop. Some of them were stone, but most were clay.

There seemed to be two basic models: Ba'al, brandishing a lightning bolt while wearing a crown that looked exactly like an upside-down bowling pin; and Ashterty, the mother-goddess, sporting a sixties flip hairstyle and a strategically placed flower or two on hips wide enough for twins.

Another shop had crude copies of Egyptian gods, though the fineness of the original design managed to glimmer through. Could I make these, sell them? I wondered frantically.

Focus, Chloe, focus.

I passed two rug shops that were side by side, with their works hung on the doors. Thickly woven wool dyed in shades of blue and green, woven into an indiscernible mass, hung next to rugs in yellow, orange, and a putrid red. The next salesman had the upscale stuff: rugs in yellow but interlaced with a bluish purple.

"You like, *isha?*" the rep said to the woman standing in front of me. "It's very fine, the purple is from the Keleti, taken painstakingly by beautiful women like yourself, from the sea creature, then mashed." He stepped closer. "This mollusk is what makes it so rare, so desirable. Come, see, I have another," he said, flipping through his merchandise.

The next example was orange with an even more faded shade of purple. Watching her expressions from the corner of his eye, he stopped when he sensed her interest.

It was a game.

She pursued her lips.

"You want to buy?" he asked her, elated.

She shook her head no, then left.

Like any decent salesman, he chased her into the street, screaming the discounts he would give. Except that it wasn't in terms of coinage, but rather of trades. For a horse, he would give her the purple rug. For the yellow-and-purple one, though it was robbery to him, he would let her have it for only two asses and a chicken. His final offer was for the purple-and-orange rug. Such beautiful colors together! What a bargain for only three doves and a donkey!

She was gone by the time he'd finished his tirade.

It seemed so commonplace, so everyday normal. Did they know the highlanders prowled outside the city? That David, God's favorite David, wanted this place and sooner or later would get it? Were we all pawns? Was it all some plan? What was I doing here? As my feet turned me onto the Rehov Shiryon, the Street of the Armorers—bronze weapons, since only we Pelesti had iron, I felt as though I were drowning in my fears.

Concentrate on eavesdropping, Chloe. Think! Grateful that everyone seemed to speak loudly and clearly, I meandered down the wide street.

The combined heat of the forgers with the heat of this summer afternoon made the stone walkway shimmer. My nostrils felt singed after only a few moments. This was an important street; weapons were built here. The clang of working metal pounded through me as I counted the weapons, then the armor, then how many men in uniform I could see.

One guy, probably not much older than eighteen, was hammering horseshoes. Sparks flew with every strike of his tool, leading me to wonder just how many horses they shoed. However, the horses weren't quartered here—so I couldn't steal one—the city gates weren't big enough.

Did they sell them to someone else? Mentally making a list, I walked on. Spearheads, sword blades, arrowheads—all were laid out, displayed for sale. It was hard to tell if they were copper or bronze from this distance. Because it would be suspicious, I didn't step closer.

However, the count in my head grew. Jebus was one well-stocked city.

A quick stroll around the perimeter of the walls showed me that the foundations were in great repair, each guard tower was manned by three men, and despite the many gates, each was guarded by three soldiers. If these people ever managed to build a portcullis, Jerusalem would never ever be conquered!

Still not a sight of a child.

At dusk, with the rest of the travelers, I went outside. My employer had been willing to let me stay in her courtyard, but her younger, savvier son suggested otherwise. Under the distant but watchful eye of Yoav's soldiers, I slept.

MIDIAN

Cheftu looked around them. He was convinced they were lost. It had been almost four days of travel, and they should have found the mountain in two. Yet they were nowhere near anything. All that stretched around for miles was sand, soft, supple, endlessly undulating sand.

The majority of the slaves had traveled in the first crew, to prepare the camp for their masters. Cheftu had been bidden to look around, see if he saw any signs of gold at the foot of the mountain.

Not only was there no gold, there was no mountain.

The guides refused to speak to the slaves or to him. They led by gestures, they stopped and went as they felt the urge. Cheftu touched the stones against his waist; he'd prepared them for use, if needed. Then it had dawned on him that he already knew the pathway the Exodus from Egypt had taken, because he knew the Bible.

In the still of the afternoon, when they were all supposed to be resting in the heat of the day, he had scribbled down those things he could remember. According to Holy Writ, the Hebrews had traveled for three days without water after the crossing of the Red Sea. Then they found water, bitter water. Moses and God intervened, and the water was healed, made sweet, and God told them that he was a God Who Heals, Yahwe Yi'ra.

Then they arrived at an oasis named El'im, where they camped.

They left El'im and started into the desert. The Bible said it had been one month since they had fled Egypt. It had been one month since Pharaoh had cornered them against the sea; he knew because he'd been there. It still gave him chills to realize these words were true, transmitted correctly through the ages. Why did Chloe have such a problem understanding the validity and reality of the Bible, the existence of God?

Manna and quail fell to the Hebrews in the desert. Then Moses incorrectly struck a rock, after they had traveled to another spot, but still God gave them water. The Amalekites—the Amaleki, as they were called—had attacked, only to be defeated by the tribes.

Shortly afterward Moses was reunited with his family, most especially his father-in-law. He was the one who suggested Moses delegate authority. Then he returned home, and the tribes entered Sinai, to camp at the foothills of the mountain of God.

Accordingly, Cheftu's group should have passed the springs of bitter water, Mara springs. Palms, seventy of them, should be on the horizon, somewhere.

Unless they were lost.

Cheftu turned onto his stomach, feigning sleep. He slipped the stones from his waist sash and whispered to them, "Are we lost?"

"Y-o-u a-r-e i-n t-h-e c-o-u-r-t-y-a-r-d o-f Y-H-W-H."

As the last letters clicked over, Cheftu knew he would wear shoes no longer.

He was walking on holy ground.

AKHETATEN

"WE MUST MAKE the pronouncement," RaEm said softly. "Egypt needs to know who the next ruler will be. It is the way of Ma'at."

Akhenaten pulled away, his sweaty skin detaching from hers. "Still you mention these outdated"—he looked over his shoulder—"outlawed gods."

"Ma'at is an ideal!" RaEm protested. "Not a deity."

"Egypt is new, now," he said darkly, looking away.

Inwardly she sighed. Pharaoh was becoming more difficult by the day—and his days were growing shorter. "Beloved," she purred, her hand on his back, still red from her nails. "Times are uncertain. This is a safe thing to do."

"The Aten asks that we believe, even when things seem uncertain. There is to be no other way."

"See it from another perspective," she said, trying again. "If you announce that Tuti will be pharaoh next, it gives a sense of continuity to the reign of Aten."

He was silent a long while; she felt his breaths beneath her palm. "To announce Tuti pharaoh will be to deny my own seed," Pharaoh finally said. "The Aten wants a child of my own flesh to sit the throne. Not some little brother, not the son of Amenhotep Osiris."

"I am your brother, and I sit the throne," she said.

Akhenaten shrugged. "You are my son-in-law—" His voice caught, and Pharaoh spent a moment weeping silently for his daughter. "You sit beside me."

Meryaten, the little brat, RaEm thought. There had to be another way out of this problem. She had told the high priest of Amun-Ra that Tuti's ascent would be announced; it must be done. Egypt must not die.

Her place on the throne, in history, must continue.

When in doubt seduce him, she thought. RaEm was leaning forward to reengage her lover when they heard footsteps running in the corridor. Akhetaten had a near silent palace. Who would be running? Why?

Outside they heard a scuffle, then a rap on the door. RaEm looked about for a slave, but none were hovering. They were terrified of her. Sighing, she drew on a wrapper and flung open the door.

The messenger immediately fell to his face, quaking. "What interrupts the rest of Pharaoh, living in the glorious light of the Aten forever!?" she asked.

"Sightings, My Majesty! As requested."

RaEm stiffened. She felt Akhenaten's interest behind her. "Report to the kitchens for refreshment," she said, dismissing the man. The messenger scurried backward. RaEm motioned to the guard, gave him her instructions, then closed the door.

"What sightings?" Akhenaten asked, suspiciously. "Do those cursed priests of the outlawed god sneak across the desert?"

The one way to get Pharaoh interested in the workings of his kingdom was to want to keep them secret, RaEm thought with a sigh. "I asked the soldiers to keep a watch on those who passed by our copper mines in the Sinai. That is all."

His dark eyes searched her face, then moved over her body. He looked at her again. "How many soldiers do we have in Sinai?"

"Several companies." *Not near enough to defend our interests there.* "Most of them work the slaves."

"How many slaves?"

RaEm shrugged. "I have no idea." *Not enough, though.* "A few thousand, perhaps?"

"Why do we need copper?"

She had to fight to keep her expression from revealing how stupid she occasionally thought he was. Did he imagine that the country just ran itself? That Egypt needed nothing from other peoples? That all services and products were produced in Egypt?

Mayhap in Hatshepsut's or even Rameses' time—which was yet to pass, she had come to realize—but not now. "We must crown Tuti," she said, returning to the original conversation.

"He's a child, not old enough to be with a woman. Besides," he said petulantly, "Akhenespa'aten should be my wife!"

"She is also your daughter, and the only woman who bears the king-right, still living."

"*Aii*, Meryaten," he said beneath his breath. For a moment he was silent, then he rose up, his thick thighs streaked with the seed he would never let her body take. "I will get her with a king."

RaEm blinked as she tried to understand his words, to comprehend what he was saying.

Pharaoh lifted his kilt from the floor. "If you tell me that a king must be crowned, then I will take Akhenespa'aten to my couch until she is pregnant."

Tears immediately rimmed RaEm's eyes. "You are leaving me?" she asked, her voice thready.

"You tell me this must be done for Ma'at," he said. "I tell you that Ma'at is a dead god, that Ma'at has grown into being an understanding of candor. However, I concede your point that Egypt must realize this dynasty will continue. Since you"—he snickered—"failed in this duty, it is up to me. The next generation of Egyptians will have known nothing save the warming love of Aten. They must have a king of my blood to lead them."

RaEm's hands were fisted so tightly that she felt the half-moons now carved into her palms. The bite of hurt was the only thing keeping her upright. "I love you," she whispered, words she had never said and meant. Words that had previously been uttered solely for manipulation and power.

She had no power now. "Please . . . please don't do this. Don't leave me." The thought that she was begging was repulsive, but the idea of life without him was worse.

Akhenaten's look was cool, his rich voice flat. "Go to your copper mines. When you return, Akhenespa'aten will be expecting. I will take you again, then, should I desire it."

RaEm felt the blow, just as surely as she'd felt his hand on her flanks and buttocks, time and again. "As you wish, My Majesty," she whispered.

He crossed to her, his kilt rumpled, his belly sagging. Lines were etched in his face, carved on both sides of his womanly, mobile mouth. His shoulders sloped, his arms were thin, but she loved him. Every line of his body, she knew. Every way to tease him, tantalize him, but it hadn't been enough. I'm doing this for Egypt—she wanted to shout it, to have her actions vindicated by the gods, to be explained to her lover. He bent to her, kissed her. "I also care for you," he said. "Hurry back to me."

Then Pharaoh was gone.

RaEm stared at the closed door, then called for slaves to bring her wine and the messenger. Wine first.

"Majesty?" she heard a moment later from the doorway. Immediately she picked up the symbols of kingship, trading them for her cup of wine. She inclined her head, as there was no scribe or chamberlain to transmit her messages.

"A spy from the copper mines in Sinai, My Majesty. Here to see you," a slave said.

It was beneath her to speak to this man, but she had no choice. "Bid him enter."

The slave backed from her presence. A moment later another man entered the room. He was darkly tanned, young, with a glitter in his eye that said he could be used. He prostrated himself, awaited her word.

"Rise," RaEm said softly.

He did, sharp dark eyes looking out from either side of a beak of a nose. He'd just come from the barber, and he had nicks on his neck and chin. His kilt was fresh, if out of style. No jewelry, just a plain copper blade at his waist.

"Speak."

"My Majesty, I was among those sent to inquire about gold."

"There is a new vein?"

"Vein? Nay, nay, My Majesty. There is a ship sailing from Midian." Was the man addled? "Ships often do."

"This ship sails from the mount of Horeb."

"What is that? How do you know this?"

He glanced down. "My people were Apiru, My Majesty. Gold lies in Midian."

"A vein? An untapped source?" Who ruled Midian? Could they be bought or vanquished? "Speak!"

"*Aii* . . . an untapped source, My Majesty."

"Speak!" she barked.

"The Apiru buried much Egyptian gold in the mountains, My Majesty. The ship that sails is from Jebus in Canaan." He must have sensed these names meant nothing to her. "The Apiru returned to their homeland, Canaan, during the reign of Thutmosis Osiris the Great. Now they seek their gold, to take it also."

"Where in Midian?" Where was Midian? "Can we beat them there? Better yet, can we let them get it, then take it from them?"

He scratched his nose, then shrugged. "Aye, My Majesty. They have already dug it up. If a contingent of troops sails"—he ticked off numbers on his fingers—"within three days, we should be able to strip them of it before they return to Jebus."

"Make it so," RaEm said, quoting Sky TV. She'd liked Jean-Luc Picard, he was shaven headed like an Egyptian. He'd ruled the entire starship *Enterprise*. A reasonable and a powerful man.

That was the sole point of agreement between RaEm and Chloe's sister, Camille.

"Make ready the way. I will come with you," she said. I will take Tuti, and we will both come with you, RaEm thought. We'll leave Akhetaten, this city of rejection, and win the heart of the army by traveling with you.

He bowed, then backed from the room.

Thank you, HatHor, she breathed. For this I will build you a temple of gold. Just let me feed my people first. Don't let me be alone.

MIDIAN

IT HAD BEEN SILENT with the slaves for days. They all walked in a reverential quiet through the slippery, sucking sand. Cheftu took up the rear now, to prevent stragglers. All were able-bodied, but none tried to flee. Beneath the cavernous sky even slavery seemed a comfort, a place to go, a way to belong.

They halted at once, forming a wall of men. Cheftu pushed through the group, noting that they had been climbing a small brown hill, unnoticed amid the sand. He rounded a curve, then looked up.

The mountain rose like a bulkhead from the desert floor. Twin peaks, charred black, were silhouetted against the blue sky. No people, no animals, just the mountain. Did they have any right to invade the space of God?

The guides motioned them down the hill. The guides themselves would not go, they would not step over into the valley of the Amaleki or onto the Mountain of God. Cheftu took the asses, with their remaining provisions, thanked the guides, then started down the hill to Har Horeb—Moses' mountain.

As they crossed the plain, a few scraggly bushes and trees rising from the dry earth, the mountain grew larger. By dusk they were at its foot. It had been forty years since the last group of tribesmen had been here. Still, a few signs of their stay were clear. The encampments were visible, with rocky cairns designating how the tribes were to be positioned. The slaves, many of them tribesmen, set to re-creating the camps. Cheftu walked the base of the mountain, looking around. Postings, sloppily etched in stone, declared that to touch the mountain was to die, while every twenty cubits or so was a smaller cairn, a boundary marker.

Cheftu felt the blood leave his face when he saw the altar to the golden calf. There, carved in the side, was a crude rendering of the goddess HatHor being worshiped. Where would the gold be? he wondered. But a shout kept him from looking. The first division was arriving. Apparently Cheftu's guides had directed them straight across the desert, not using the same path the tribesmen and Moses had used.

Where had God eaten *b'rith* with the seventy?

At night, after the first group had arrived, dined, and rested, N'tan stood before them. The mountain glowed blue, millions—or "bullions and bullions," as Chloe would say—of stars filled the sky. The moon was small, casting little light on N'tan. He led the men in psalm after psalm, punctuating the night air with shouts of *"Sela!"*

Cheftu felt the cadence taking over, sweeping through his mind so that any action seemed normal. As a body the men followed N'tan, standing between each of the boundary stones. Cheftu felt as though he were outside his physical form, watching as forty men scrabbled in the dirt.

He'd been digging for a while, clawing at the ground in his spot between the cairns, when he felt something. Fabric? All around him men were finding wrapped parcels buried in the sand. Grasping it with both hands, he pulled. The bulky object came out of the ground so suddenly that he fell backward, the thing on his chest.

With shaking fingers Cheftu fumbled with the cloth, tearing at it with a lust he'd thought alien to him. It crumbled in his hand around a solid shape. In wonder he held the find up to the blue light of the mountain.

An idol, a statue of pure gold, its face cut off.

"'Do not make cast idols,' Shaday proclaimed," N'tan said from behind him. "Does it look like one you have worshiped, slave?"

Cheftu turned back to the sand. Essentially they were clearing a trench the original *zekenim* leaders had filled with the gold of the Egyptians.

N'tan knelt beside him, spectral in the blue light of Horeb.

Cheftu's perfect, albeit slow, memory finally recognized him beneath the long hair, the beard, the youthfulness. "You are an Imhotep!"

The hauteur vanished from the *tzadik*'s face. "And you are the Traveler, the nomad throughout my family's lives." His eyes were wide. "The Pelesti goddess, she is the other one?"

Was it that Cheftu was influenced by the light, the mystery, and the miracle of this place, or was he hearing and understanding what N'tan, biblical N'tan, was saying? "You are an Imhotep?" he repeated.

The answer was in the man's bones, his eyes, the shape of his body. How many thousand years had it been? How many allegiances had the Imhoteps sworn? The court of Aztlan? The many courts of Egypt? "How is it you are a Jew?" Cheftu asked. N'tan's confused expression told Cheftu that he'd spoken French. In fact, "Jew" probably wasn't even a term yet. "You are of the tribes?"

"You are a worshiper of the One God," N'tan rejoined.

A shout drew their attention, and Cheftu turned. Beneath the waning moon the pile of treasure was growing. Heaps of bracelets, statues, votives, candlesticks, incense burners, the glittering mass was being added to as the men moved through the sand.

The wealth was dazzling, gleaming, spellbinding. The splendor of a pharaoh's tomb could not be so rich. All this *le bon Dieu* had seen fit to gift the Israelites with. Talents and tons, gold and bronze, studded with turquoises, carnelian, jasper, jade. Ornaments of silver, figurines of ebony. The mountain of gold grew in the shadow of the mountain of God. The men were progressing further, hauling huge items, samovars and wheels—gold-plated wheels from Pharaoh's fallen army—statues, breastplates, collars, armbands . . . Cheftu's mind was going numb in the presence of such magnificence.

"We will talk, you and I," N'tan said, rising from his crouch. "I must get as much from these men tonight as I can. The ditch surrounds the mountain." He held out his hand to Cheftu. "My name is Imhotep, from a long line of Imhoteps, though we are called Yofaset, a less Kemti name, as befits a member of the tribes."

Cheftu rose to his feet. "My names are many, but only one is the man I have become." He bowed. "Cheftu *sa'a* Khamese of Egypt."

"Together we shall find a pharaoh's treasure for a freeman's king," N'tan said.

They knelt in the blue light and continued to dig.

JEBUS

I'D BECOME A COMMON SIGHT around Jebus; in fact, I'd even learned to carry my jar on my shoulder—at least half-full. Once again I descended the steps, glancing at the guards but staying somewhat quiet, withdrawn. After all, wouldn't that be how a woman in my position would really behave?

They were there, the village women. A few nodded at me, though no one spoke. As a foreigner I was last in line, always. As I was lifting the bucket to drop it through that impossibly small hole that still spelled my death, I heard a sound behind me. Turning, I saw it was the same girl I'd seen the first day, the pregnant one.

Her face was streaked, as though she'd been crying. Then again, the lighting in here fell under the category of "indirect," so I could be wrong. After my four buckets' worth of water, I was ready to leave. Shouldering my jar carefully, I turned around.

She was crying. Her face was in her hands, and she was shaking silently. I glanced beyond to the guard. He was whittling, studiously ignoring us. Although it seemed inane, I leaned forward and whispered, *"Hakol b'seder?"* Is everything all right?

Immediately her tears ceased. She looked up, seemingly startled that I had spoken to her. Or surprised to be caught weeping? *"Ken, ken,"* she said, nodding her head fervently, not meeting my gaze. Her hands moved protectively over her stomach. I stood there for a moment, then shrugged and wished her a good day.

Halfway up the steps—which I loathed with a passion—I heard footsteps behind me. *"Isha?"* she called. *"Isha?"*

Balancing myself and jar carefully, I turned around to face her. "My name is Waqi," she said. "My husband is a merchant, away. Would you . . . care to share bread with me at zenith?"

"How much water do you want?" I asked. By now I knew that Jebusi women had a cagey way of asking for my services, usually as a friendly overture.

"*Lo, lo.* For company," she said. "I will send a slave for water."

I blinked back tears. How long had it been since I had talked to someone who wanted to be with me, not just for what I could do for them? "*Todah,* I would like that."

"My house is off the square on Rehov Abda," she said. "I will see you there."

As I walked up to the residence on Rehov Abda I saw that there was much I hadn't understood. For one, Rehov Abda was the equivalent of Dallas's Highland Park; wealthy, ritzy, and appearance oriented. Even the slaves had attitude. Second, Waqi's merchant husband was none other than the bronze monger for most of the artisans. They were living high on the hog.

What on earth did she want with me? My feeling of insecurity grew as I was shunted from the front door to the back door by a long-eyed Assyrian houseman. Once at the back door, I was made to sit in the courtyard and wait.

Suddenly this reminded me of the part of advertising sales that I hated: the waiting. It had been about an hour with me lounging in the sun, wondering where Cheftu was, when I heard a shout from above me. "*Isha!*" It was the woman. She waved, then disappeared inside.

Moments later the door was thrown open. "I did not know you were here!" she said, glancing at the sheepish Assyrian beside her. "Come, come, wash your feet, have a refreshment."

She seated me on a stool. As I was leaning over to unlace my sandal, she *tch*'ed. A slave dropped to her knees. She unlaced my sandals and gently bathed my feet while another slave offered me a cool drink, some form of yogurt, and a cloth for my face.

I couldn't wash my face or my disguise makeup would wipe off. I blotted a little, then watched the slave dry my feet. Waqi awaited me, the other slave said. Would I be so good as to follow her?

Up the stairs we went, dark, narrow stairs in a dark, narrow house for all of its wealth. Rugs covered the floors and walls. Samovars, now empty, were on every landing. Lamps, both in stands and handheld, littered the place. We emerged on the roof, where a low table lay, surrounded by bright cushions.

It reminded me of Dadua's home.

"Please," Waqi said, "sit, eat."

In the sunlight I could see that she was young. Really, really young. Maybe fifteen? She was also unhappy; her eyes were swollen from so much crying. Rarely did she move her hands from their protective place over her belly. We ate lunch in near silence, steamed grain, vegetable patties, salads of cucumbers and onions in vinegar and spices, and wine.

"You might want to water your wine," I suggested, "since you are—" I gestured toward her stomach. To my horror, her eyes filled with tears. *"Hakol b'seder,"* I rattled on quickly, "a little wine won't be that bad for you, but too much, well, it's not good for the baby, although I'm sure yours will be fine and all . . . I mean . . ." *Shut up, Chloe.*

She was sobbing, silently. I threw down my bread, crossed to her, and took her in my arms, hugging her. The woman clamped on to me, crying as though her heart were breaking. "My people are from another place," she said through her tears. "My father did not know what it would mean for me to be here. He didn't know. He would never have agreed to the marriage. . . ." That started a whole new cycle of crying. Poor kid, I thought, stroking her hair.

"I can't believe the women endure this," she said. "I try to think of how to avoid it, but I can't. Where would I go? What would I do?"

Questions started chasing themselves in my brain.

She pulled back, wiping her face and trying to smile. "Would you like halva?" she said, offering dessert in a falsely bright hostess tone.

You're a slave, Chloe, I reminded myself. I moved to my side of the table again. Another slave showed up, presented us with the sesame-seed paste flavored with honey, and left again.

"You live outside the city?" she asked.

"I do."

"It must be wearying to travel back and forth through the gate all the time."

It certainly is, especially when I'm interrogated every night on my progress by Yoav's soldiers. "Ken."

"My husband will be gone for a few more weeks. I . . ." She fought for composure, "My time is soon. I have no family."

I nodded.

"Would you care to move in with me? There is another room on the second floor. It is not luxurious, but it has a pallet, a nice breeze. You, of course, would be my guest, though if you still wanted to sell your services, I will understand."

I couldn't believe she was offering me a room! "What of the guards?" I said.

She shrugged. "My name is Waqi bat Urek, wife of Abda, the first cousin to the king. There is no problem."

Rehov Abda.—The street was named after him.

I set down my piece of halva. This was ideal! I could stay with her while I tried to find a way to escape the city alone or a way to invade it with an army. *Talk about betraying hospitality, Chloe.* I sighed. "It would be too much trouble. I couldn't take advantage of you."

She laughed, a rich, real sound. "I ask for your companionship, *isha.*—What is your name?"

Don't give your real name, Chloe, names have magic, I heard Cheftu say. "Takala."

"Takala, how pretty."

I smiled, feeling sick to my stomach.

"Takala, I ask you to live with me not because of generosity. My time is close, I would like having a woman nearby, more than a slave."

"What of the women at the well?"

She smiled sadly. "My people are Assyrian, despised here. However, in the tradition of both peoples, the woman of the household gets the water. It shows the honor of a home, a family." She looked away. "Even unwelcome at the well, I would not so disgrace my family by sending an underling for water. It is not done. Also," she said, looking up at me, "I worship Ishtar, goddess of childbirth, love, filial emotions. They worship Molekh." Her tone was sharp. "I would not have such a woman at my childbirthing bed."

Ideological differences, I thought. *Ach,* the more the Middle East changed, the more it stayed the same. *"B'seder.* I will stay with you," I said.

Waqi smiled and clapped for slaves.

"This is perfect, *isha,"* Yoav said, smiling in the darkness of the tent. "You have an excuse now, to stay." He slapped my shoulder. "How long do you think it will take to get us in?"

I'd conveniently forgotten to mention to him that the opening to the water well was basically nonexistent. Call it self-preservation. Waqi had about two more months to go, two months for me to plan, to buy time, to wait for Cheftu's return. "About three months?"

Yoav's look was calculating. "The end of summer?"

I shrugged. Sure, why not.

"How will we contact you?"

"Contact will blow my cover," I said. "It will be a fragile thing, living with people all the time."

"Isha," Yoav said, "we will stay in touch with you. You will not be out of our sight, ever."

I looked into his glass green eyes. How many cities had he sacked? How many people had he killed? "Why do you want this job?" I asked almost before I realized the words were coming out of my mouth.

Even he looked startled. Then ruminative. "Dadua is my uncle," he said slowly, "though I have more years than he." He smiled at some remembrance. "Dadua was always a wiry, fiery-haired child, running wild, singing at the top of his lungs. He charmed the women in the harem almost from birth, he ran mental circles around his father's cronies, he insulted his brothers with such cleverness that it was days before they realized it." Yoav looked at me. "Dadua was the essence of life, the purest divine energy, like the Shekina powers of Yahwe."

"I thought Shekina was a goddess?"

"*Ach!* The women have said so, but Yahwe, he is everything. Male and female, dark and light, joy and tears." Yoav shrugged. "The women pull Yahwe's powers over the night, over the body, and give these skills a name, Shekina. But the Shekina of Yahwe, the energy, the *nishmat ha hayyim*, can never be separated from its source."

"If you believe in *nishmat ha hayyim*, the divine breath, then how can you remove it from so many people? If life is sacred, how can you kill for a living?"

"Because Dadua, to protect that part of him that is the Shekina glory of Yahwe, cannot."

"Dadua doesn't kill?"

Yoav laughed, throwing back his head. The lamplight flickered over the muscles in his throat and chest, muted the scars on his face. "Dadua has killed, no doubt. However, it pains him to do so. When he loses that pain, when killing is a job, then the glow of the Shekina will fade." Yoav shook his head. "Y'srael would suffer, we would all lose something pure, something beautiful, if Dadua became as we are. Ordinary, Touchable."

"So you take that blood on your hands and head?"

"*Ken,*" he said. "Dadua is a man and a king, but to Yahwe he is the most precious of children. We who are Dadua's family must protect that innocence. He doesn't transgress as we do."

"*Ach!* How can you say that? He's an earthling!" The translations of some words were weird.

"He is. But he doesn't know lust, hatred, murder, in his flesh. He is like bronze that never tarnishes. For this purity, I will bathe in blood." Yoav looked at me. "The land must be claimed, there is no doubt. Those of us who love him must do it, and count the lost lives against our own souls, not his."

I stared at him as silence gathered between us, looking into his clear green eyes. This was David's henchman, and he had the purest motive I could imagine for wholesale slaughter. Did that make it better? Forgivable? I didn't know, but I felt suddenly unworthy to judge. Had I ever loved someone that way? Even Cheftu? "I agree with Avgay'el," I said quietly. "You do deserve to be *Rosh Tsor.*"

He got to his feet, holding out his hand to me. I took it and he pulled me up. "Your husband is still in the desert," he said. I suddenly realized how close we were standing, how his eyes had darkened, how warm the tent had become.

I suddenly realized that my hand was still in his. I removed it. "*Todah*, I appreciate your telling me."

We stood in awkward silence. "Good. We'll contact you, Klo-ee."

"*Laylah tov*, Yoav," I said to his back.

He turned around. "*Lo*, tonight begins the Sabbath. *Shabat shalom*."

CHAPTER 10

My CHANCE WAS TONIGHT. I'd kept careful count of the days since I'd met with Yoav. The day after the Sabbath was when the soldiers left the city open for four hours. That was my window of opportunity.

The moon was full tonight, which would make for easy travel. I felt dishonest leaving Waqi, who really was a dear and deserved better. But if I stayed, I'd have to betray her, and Shamuz at the well, and Yorq, who sold me bread. These were real people, this wasn't a game, it wasn't a push-button war. I just didn't have it in me to betray them.

So I was sneaking out of town. My hobo pack was tied as I watched the streets from my room. There was a lot of activity tonight, lots of people with small lamps scurrying to and fro. Sadly I threw on my cloak and slipped down the stairs. The wind was blowing; it was a wonderful feeling, buoyant, free, as though it could sweep you up and set you anywhere in the world.

I would have given most anything to have Cheftu's hand in mine, to be enjoying this evening with him. After closing the door behind me, I made my way into the street, blending with the shadows, I hoped. As I walked I noticed dozens of bobbing lights, a steady river of them flowing down from the city's dung gate. People were going into the valley? At night?

That was weird. Most ancients rose with the sun and retired with its setting. Days were long and hard; they needed their rest. Not to mention there were usually a lot of fears about things going bump in the night. What was going on? We couldn't all be fleeing the city.

I exited the dung gate, stepping around the trash piles—since that was the reason it was called the dung gate—giddy. I was free! The wind blew my cloak back from my face, whipped my skirts around me, as I walked down the steep hill. Looking back, for I would never see Jerusalem again, I paused a moment: it seemed as though the city glowed with the points of a thousand fireflies; lamps in windows, torches affixed to the walls; braziers burning at the gates. The air was heavy with honeysuckle, roses, and herbs.

I picked my way through the growing darkness, being careful of the rocky terrain. The night was mostly silent, and the dozens of lights I'd seen had apparently vanished. The deeper into the valley I got, the less the wind played with me, the more potent the flowers smelled.

As I bypassed the path that headed straight down, in favor of the road that led to Yerico, I heard what sounded like a shriek. I paused for a moment, then took the southerly trail. When I changed direction a stench hit me. It was a sickly, roasted type of smell. It blocked out the citrus, the honeysuckle, even the faint smell of evergreens from the hills.

Fanning my face, I walked faster, rounding a corner. Then I saw the source of this odor.

A fire burned at the bottom of a narrow ravine about fifty feet below me. A cluster of lamps—those missing people?—were grouped a few feet from it. What was up? A low hum, which sounded as if it were from *Carmina Burana*, rose up to me on the pathway.

Curious, I walked down a ways, getting closer. My eyes were adjusting, moving from the darkness to the brilliance of the flame.

As I watched, people clustered around the fire. A lone individual approached, then handed an object to someone else. I squinted. The smoke, the stink that clogged my throat, the weird singing, were surreal.

As I watched, the second person, the one who accepted the hand-off, threw something into the fire. Something tiny. The first person was gone.

Were they burning trash? It stank badly enough. I covered my nose, breathing through my mouth, as I watched. I joined the throng, trying to figure out why trash burning would draw such crowd. Beneath the singing I heard hysterical sobbing, begging, though the words were indistinct. As I drew closer, I saw the fire wasn't in a cave, but rather in the belly of a large, ugly statue.

Another person approached, handed the thrower something small. Something crying. A tiny thing.

The hair on my arms stood on end.

"No," I gasped in English. "No!" I clapped my hand over my mouth, whether to keep from vomiting or shutting myself up didn't matter. As I watched, another one went up into the flame. Two men held a woman back, a screaming woman. The wind shifted so that I heard her words: "*Lo!* Not my baby! Not my precious lamb! Curse you! *Lo*, not my baby!"

They sacrifice their babies, I heard Yoav say in my mind. *I don't know how the women endure it,* Waqi's words haunted me. *If only my father had known—* Omigod. This would happen to her?

Trying not to draw attention to myself, I continued down the pathway, horrified and stumbling, unable to fathom what I had seen. Someone walked before me, thankfully empty-handed.

A shrouded figure approached, handed the thrower a baby, then backed up as the murderer raised the child over its head, screaming to the heavens, then threw it in the fire!

The person before me crumpled to its knees, repeating *"lo"* like a mantra. I was shell-shocked. Surely not, surely I was not seeing this. The images didn't even compute, though the smell of immolation, which I had the sorrow to recognize, was choking me. Very real.

I almost tripped on the woman in front of me. She squawked, and I looked down. She was trying to get to her feet but was too bulky to do so. "Waqi?" I whispered.

She looked up, horrified. "You are one of them?"

"Lo, lo," I said quickly.

More screaming, more pleading, behind me. I didn't know what to do. Could I rush the priest? Waqi had to get out of here; I was leaving town . . . Oh, dear God.

An infant's scream rose to the heavens, submerged in the chanting of the people.

"For your protection we give you blood.

"To save ourselves, we feed you our flesh—" The song was horrible.

I went to Waqi, helping her up. "Why are you here?" I whispered.

"I had to see it, I had to know. I would rather take my own life than watch my baby die." Her face crumpled, tear tracks gleaming in the light. "His first three wives didn't survive the grief."

She was Abda's fourth wife? "Let's get you out of here," I said. "You can leave him, tonight."

She shook her head. "My pains began this afternoon. My baby is coming."

There were not enough curse words in my vocabulary. All I could hear in my head was Prissy's disclaimer from *Gone With the Wind.* "Is there a midwife? A wisewoman?" I asked her.

"If she comes, they will know. . . . The only protection is to pretend I lost the child."

There were logistical nightmares with that, but it didn't matter. "We're going back to the city," I said, pushing through the crowd, pulling her with me.

"They'll know, they'll know," she insisted.

I put my nose to hers. "If you try to have the baby alone, you will die. So will it. If you call a midwife, have some assistance, maybe we can sneak you and the baby out of town, but at least there will be two of you."

"Where were you going?"

"I was running away."

"From me?"

"*Lo,* you have been nothing but goodness to me. I have—"

"You aren't merely a well woman, are you?" She was leaning on me, her fingers interlaced with mine. As the pains came she would grip my hand, but she gave no other sign of discomfort.

"*Lo,*" I said. "I came to spy."

Her hand tightened on mine as she slowed her steps for a moment. Her breath was a little ragged when she spoke again. "For whom?"

"The highlanders. They want your city."

She gasped, practically breaking my fingers. I felt her legs trembling next to mine as she fought to stay upright. I looked at the city that I'd thought I'd never see again. It was about fourteen light-years away.

"Do the highlanders have children?" she asked, walking on.

"By the hundreds," I said, adjusting my grip around her middle in case she fell.

"I wish they would invade," she said. "I would give them our city." Her grip tightened, but her pace didn't break.

"Why do they have this practice?" The smell of charred flesh was in my nostrils; I could no longer smell the roses even though we were approaching the city.

"Protection. Every child that is given to Molekh becomes another of the demonic guard the city has. That is why the city has never been invaded." She dropped to her knees, whimpering.

I looked around us; we were at the edge of the garbage dump—not the place to have a child. "Come along, Waqi, only a little farther." Was there a guard around? Someone to carry her? While she caught her breath I searched the walls, the dump, the trees beside us. "Help us," I called out. "Please, someone?"

Waqi shrieked, silencing herself almost immediately. I was on my knees beside her. "What is it? Worse pain?"

"My water," she said. "It broke."

I stood up, looking around. Nothing moved, not a sound. Smoke from the valley was clouding the night sky. Switching to the dialect that I'd heard Yoav use on occasion, I spoke loudly, my voice carrying. "You say you watch me. I need your help. For the love of Yahwe, assist us!"

Was it only my imagination, the sense of eyes on me? No response. I knelt beside her. "Put your arm around me," I said. "I'll carry you."

Draping her left arm over my shoulder, I stood up. She was tiny, but she was also pregnant and half-unconscious from the pain. We were halfway through the dump when he stepped out into the path-way: the soldier from Mamre, the one who had followed me through the city streets before my first meeting with Yoav. I didn't even know his name. Without a word, he picked her up.

"Waqi," I said, still holding her hand. "What shall we say to the guards?" The Mamre soldier didn't look Jebusi; maybe Pelesti?

"No guards tonight," she whispered. "It is the night of Molekh's moon. They, they—" She screamed again.

"Isha," he said to her. "Press your face into my cloak, *b'seder?"*

Waqi turned into his chest. "Lead quickly," he said. "She can no longer hold her legs together. The babe is almost here."

We burst through the door of the Rehov Abda house. The Assyrian took one look at the situation and led us to Waqi's chambers, invoking Ishtar all the way. The soldier laid her on the pallet, looking at me. I stared back. "No midwife?" he said.

"The baby will be sacrificed," I said. Waqi was soaking wet, so the Assyrian—whose name was Uru—and I stripped her and bathed her skin, then covered her in blankets. Her thighs were smeared with blood. I felt ill—what could we do? The soldier had his back to us while he worked something in his hands.

Waqi screamed as we put another cover on her. Uru rushed to her side, speaking to her in a tongue I didn't know. "Where do I go to find a midwife?" I asked them. "It's the only chance."

The soldier turned around, aiming his spectral blue gaze at her. "I've delivered sheep, cows, donkeys. I can deliver this child, save it from this bloodthirsty god."

I looked at Waqi, who was lying sweat soaked and quiet. "What is your name?" she asked.

"Zorak ben Dani'el."

Waqi closed her eyes, balling the sheets in her hands. She should be breathing a certain way. I'd seen that on TV, but I didn't know how. The contraction passed, and she spoke to him. "Deliver me."

Zorak turned into a commander. We were running with clean linens, hot water, wine, an iron knife, lamps, all orderly placed in her room. He wrapped his side curls tightly around his ears and washed his hands in wine. Labor lasted forever, but she was tough. She screamed only rarely; mostly she caressed her stomach and smiled in between the agony.

Periodically Zorak would pray, then look between her legs and tell her they had more time. The night was utterly black, the moon behind a cloud, when he announced it was time.

Bricks were brought in, and Waqi was walked from the pallet to crouch on the bricks. I was assigned her left side, a slave girl her right hand, and Uru stood behind her, rubbing her neck and down her spine with scented oils. Zorak sat in front of her, massaging the insides of her thighs and her belly, speaking to her in a low, calming voice, staring up into her eyes.

Waqi never looked away from him. When the pains came, she kept her eyes open, locked in his gaze as we held her upright and watched the mass of her belly undulate. Uru sang softly, strange words to a sweet melody.

Sweat ran down Waqi's body like shower water. Strangely enough, my revulsion had faded as I watched this teenager talk to her baby, staring into the eyes of a stranger who was going to make it all happen. It was humbling.

Then suddenly she screamed and screamed again, almost fighting against us. "Put her down," Zorak said, so we lowered her into a squat. The other slaves moved closer, giving as much light as they could. Zorak spoke to her, smoothing her stomach, Uru spoke to her, even I did, telling her she was doing a great job, that it was going to be *b'seder*, just to keep breathing.

Her body trembled, we almost dropped her because she was so slippery with sweat, and then . . . this sphere of blood slid into Zorak's hands. It was gross; it was incredible!

It was a moment before the baby wailed. Tears streamed down my cheeks as I realized what had just happened. A child was born before me.

We cleaned up everything. Zorak removed the afterbirth, wrapping it and handing it to a slave, who left the room. Then he handed the iron blade to Waqi, who said a prayer as she cut the umbilical cord. Uru and Zorak rubbed the child down with salt, while the slaves changed the linens everywhere. The other slave and I washed Waqi, then rubbed oils on her thighs and belly and breasts. It should have felt strange, touching another woman, but instead it felt protective, unified. What her body had done, mine could do, and that was a bond.

The child was a boy. Zorak handed him to her. "He is beautiful," he said. "Just like his mother." He kissed her forehead and stepped away. Waqi was oblivious of us all. She touched the baby's face, kissed every inch of him that wasn't swaddled, then set him against her nipple.

He was, of course, a fast learner, because he was also the most beautiful baby in the world and would be the smartest, I had no doubt. Within minutes he was suckling away. Waqi leaned back, her expression utter bliss. I glanced over at Zorak, who was still bloodstained, and saw that he was crying. Uru touched my arm. "*Isha*, let us give her some time."

We all slipped out, leaving mother and child enraptured with each other.

THE DESERT

CAREFULLY ARMED, the hundred men walked through the Arava valley. Cheftu's gaze was on the gravel plain when all of a sudden he saw a reflection on the dirt, a moment's flash. Only training kept him from stumbling, betraying what he'd seen—the glint of sunlight off metal. He continued walking but now focused intently on his surroundings, listening to every sound. Behind him, carefully packed beneath foodstuffs, clothing, and a dead goat, was the wealth of Hatshepsut's Egypt.

It was a desert, but unlike Midian, there was no undulating sand, no herds of camels running wild. It was a brutal, rocky environment where only acacia trees and wild grass lived. Caves honeycombed the hills on both sides. Periodically they saw a goat or a wildcat. Hyenas cackled in the distance, and gazelle herds left their tracks, moving back and forth across the salt flats.

Sweat broke out on his body at the same rate that it evaporated, since it was so dry. Given the urgency of their return, they were walking throughout the day, an uncommon practice. An insane action this late in summer. Ahkenatan should try this, Cheftu thought. More of his "Aten" than even Pharaoh could endure.

Walking in the sun, covered in cloth, monotonously placing one foot before the other, made his mind a blank. Which was why he hadn't noticed they were being tracked.

N'tan stumbled up beside him. "Do you sense it?" Cheftu asked in an undertone.

"We're being watched."

Cheftu casually scanned the hills, the acacia trees, the rocks, as he had been doing. "I cannot see them."

"Nor can I."

"Should we keep walking?"

"Do you think animals or men?" N'tan asked.

Cheftu resisted the urge to laugh. Animals would flee this great a caravan. Only the human animal would try to attack this many people. "Definitely men."

"*Ach!*" N'tan said. "We are close to the edge of the Salt Sea."

"How close?" Cheftu asked.

"By dawn, if we kept moving."

Which would be better? To keep moving and hope to outrun, or outfinesse, whoever was following? Or to camp as they had been doing, and prepare for a battle with the dawn? "The men have what weapons?"

"Bronze swords. A few have Pelesti blades."

"We'll divide up, into three divisions again. Split their attention."

"What of . . . the treasure?" N'tan whispered.

"Tonight, under cover of darkness, we will bury some. The bulk of it."

"Leave it?" N'tan said, shocked.

Cheftu resisted the urge to lick his dry lips; that would just dry them further. He fumbled in his side pouch for a small rock, his sucking rock. He'd learned that a pebble beneath the tongue kept moisture in the mouth and throat. In moments he had enough saliva to swallow, ease his speech. "We will send one division ahead, with some gold and the men with bronze blades. They will take the path through Midian, then into Yerico around Jebus to Mamre."

"The other two?"

"One will stay to fight, ostensibly those who are buried will account for the disrupted soil."

"We will kill them? Then bury the gold with them?"

"*Lo.* Whoever is stalking us will kill them. We will bury the gold with them, cover it with stones in the fashion of desert burials, then return for it later."

"Do you think that will prevent the brigands from digging up the bodies and the gold?"

Cheftu's gaze perused the far wall of caves; were they in there? How many? From which people? "If they are Egyptian, they will not disturb the bodies." I hope, he thought. "Our other choice is to hide the gold in those caves—somehow."

"According to your suggestion, what of the third group?" N'tan asked.

"They will go straight to Mamre, bring reinforcements."

"We do this under cover of night?"

"*Ken.* Tonight."

N'tan squinted into the sky. "We shall be stopping in about another watch, then. I will tell the others," he said, falling out of step.

Cheftu walked on, his eye on the ridges. One gleam would tell him what he needed to know. If it were Pharaoh, there would be armor. If it were other tribes, he would hear them calling to each other, using the sounds of the desert.

Another watch would betray them, whoever they were. Regardless, they would get the gold to Dadua. David would have his gold. Cheftu would regain his freedom.

Cheftu walked on.

I UNDERSTOOD HOW the French Resistance must have felt. On the outside everything appeared to be the same, but I knew differently. The women moving through the streets of Jebus were no longer strangers, they were my fellow spies; the men who smiled and behaved so kindly were the same men who demanded their children burn to protect their hides. They had become the enemy. Yet to an observer, nothing had changed.

Behaving as though this were any other day, I walked to the well. "Coming early today, are you? A new jar?" the first guard commented.

I shrugged. "*G'vret* Waqi wishes a bath this morning."

"*Ach*, the wealthy!" Chuckling, they passed me on. A few women passed me on the stairwell. Everything was going according to plan.

The same guard I'd seen every day was on duty. "That cough sounds worse," he said as I doubled over with the force of what was in my chest. Blearily I nodded. I wasn't faking the cough; I had a cold, which I'd gotten somehow. Instead of being in bed with *Marie Claire*, my remote control, and a pint of Ben & Jerry's—always good for what ailed me—I was going to lead the invasion and betrayal of Jebus.

Adrenaline would have to carry me through.

Between my hacking and coughing, it was taking forever to fill my extra-large jug. I looked over at the guard. "Is there any way to open this aperture bigger? I'll"—I sneezed—"be here all day if I don't."

"Who told you?" he asked suspiciously.

I sneezed. "Waqi. She wants water, a lot of it."

"Bathing? In the middle of the week?"

I shrugged. "The babe is due."

He hopped off his throne and went to the wall. There, tied to a hook, were ropes. With a few tugs he had levered up the entire wood platform, disclosing the natural opening, which was about twelve feet wide. My excitement welled up with another sneeze.

"Hurry along," he said, watching me. Though I had gotten stronger, I still couldn't lift a full normal-size jar after filling it. Which made this huge one impossible, especially since I kept sneezing. Exasperated, he carried the full jug for me, up the steps, passing women on their way down. Did he notice the looks we gave each other?

At the top of the stairs I tripped myself, rolling back down, trying not to bash my head too badly. The guard shouted for help, then ran to the top of the stairs to get someone, leaving my jar on the step. In seconds the women who had just passed us were helping me up. Another woman took my cloak; we had already painted her face to look like mine. Sadly, she was bruised already.

She lay down in my place while I hobbled and ran down the stairs. The other women clumped on the stairwell, blocking the guard's way back down.

Moments later I was staring into the depths of the dark water from my bucket perch, both ropes in my hands, the whispered "Good luck" wishes of the women in my ears.

I realized that tunnels of dark water should be terrifying; however, my particular experiences had prepared me for this exactly. I had no uncertainty that I'd find a way out, nor was I frightened that I'd stay underwater too long. After all, during my time in Aztlan I'd survived a bloody complicated labyrinth, not just once, but three times. This should be a piece of cake.

Cold cake. I sneezed again, felt my nipples pebble beneath my dress from the chilly updraft. My hands were shaking so much that I could barely work the ropes. Voices, the guard's, the women's, floated down to me. Now or never.

According to the women, I would be submerged for only a few seconds since the well was more of a pool. When I got into it I could swim out—hence the reference to "lame"—since you could move through water even without using your legs. If I followed the current, it would lead me outside to where one of the contingencies of Yoav's soldiers waited.

If the women's words could be trusted.

Geronimo, I thought, releasing the ropes. The flax raked my hands as I plummeted toward the water. First its iciness grabbed my dress. I hissed as it touched my legs, then my belly. With a giant gulp of air, I was in the dark wetness.

Allowing some inborn sense of direction, not to mention the water flow, lead me, I quickly found my way to the drain at the bottom of the well. Things were going great—I was pretending to be a stick of wood, seeking the way out—when I got stuck.

I was holding my breath, submerged in a cascade and wedged in like a cork. Stone cut into my shoulders, tore at my breasts. Real fear grabbed me as I struggled. Nothing moved; my ears were aching from the water pounding me from above.

Oh God, oh God. The urge to sneeze was growing; my lungs were burning. I felt my legs swinging free in the passage beneath me, while water was building up behind me. I could see nothing and wondered briefly if this were it. Had my vanity done me in, or was this a plot on the women's part?

My nose was itching, and I inhaled automatically, gagging on water.

And sneezed so violently that my body ripped free. I dropped like a rock into the passageway beneath me, the backed-up waters cushioning my fall. Water closed over my head for a moment, then I was on my feet. Hurting, but standing in waist-deep water.

I walked in total darkness for about a hundred paces, hearing nothing except myself sloshing through water as I headed down a gentle hill. I moved slower, sensing the passage widen out. There just possibly might be someone standing guard. I didn't sense another presence, but I was cautious.

Suddenly the tunnel turned, while simultaneously changing grade. With all the grace of which I am capable, I fell, slid, and crashed into a shallow sunlit pool. I surfaced, sputtering, instantly sobered by the sight of covered corpses lying at the water's edge.

One of the *gibori*—Abishi, I think—greeted me as he hauled me out of the water. He wrapped a cloak around my shoulders. "What happened to those men?" I asked, wiping my face.

"They are Yoav's spies. They got caught and fought with the Jebusi guards." Abishi looked away, and I noticed that he'd been crying. "Would you like to see them?"

I paused but didn't want to look. I didn't want to recognize the few faces I associated with living and laughing soldiers with the bloodstained bodies lying next to a water source. Had any of our guys won? "Do the Jebusi know we are here?"

Abishi's expression was resigned. "Not yet, but they will by the next watch."

His words made my blood go cold. These women, this small group of women, had risked everything to help us, to buy freedom for themselves, to have the right to keep their children. "Then let's go," I said.

"Yoav has planned two attacks on different sides of the city if we need the distraction."

"The man loves strategy," I said.

"*Ken,*" he said, then looked at me with concern, his gaze moving over my body. "*Isha!* Were you attacked? Are you healthy? Do you need wine? Bread?"

I sneezed, shaking my head. I bet I did look a fright. Unwashed, slippery, running makeup, ratty clothes, hair dye. Yikes! "The drain attacked me." I didn't even want to see what wounds I'd sustained; the cold was numbing, a feeling that probably helped about now. "You aren't going to fit well," I said, gesturing to his shoulders. "The passage is very narrow. Take only the smallest men and let's go." How long had it taken me to get here? Time in the water had no sense of passing. The sun was still shining outside, the birds still singing on this summer afternoon.

"Is there anything—"

"*Lo.* Let's go."

Wading through the utter darkness of the spring was cold but also surreal. Outside it was bright and happy, beneath the city we were planning on killing.

However, my conscience had been somewhat assuaged because Waqi had asked me to invade. Then other women—I don't know how they learned—began bumping into me in the market, whispering, "I'll help," or, "Count on me." The city's women wanted new rulers, new laws. It wasn't all of them, I was certain, but a very vocal minority, led by the queen. They wanted a chance to see their children live.

The caveat was that I negotiate their freedom. No *herim* or *hal* for this group. No slavery, either. Yoav was desperate enough that I thought he would agree. Zorak thought so, too—Zorak, who had become less my shadow and more of a guardian angel for Waqi and the little, still unnamed, one.

The men behind me were silent, only a few shallow breaths betraying the dozen soldiers slogging through the water. My sandals—I was surprised I still had them—tugged at my feet, giving the feeling of walking in flippers. The farther we progressed, the deeper the water got, moving up from our calves to our thighs to our waists. Shivering and wet, I led the men up the dark passage. We dared not use any light, but in the midst of the darkness I felt the walls, the ceiling, the mass of earth, weighing down on us. The sound of falling water attested to the presence of the shaft.

We were well inside the city walls. Was everything going according to plan?

After adjusting my dress so that it covered my knees, I began the laborious process of climbing up the duct. I'd rock-climbed before, but never through the middle of a waterfall, with no gear, and in a dress! Beneath me the soldiers lined up to shove my body through. The stones tore at my hands, while water cascaded straight onto my head as I blindly fumbled upward, always upward.

The channel narrowed; we'd never be able to make it through. Clinging like a barnacle to the wall, I slipped my knife from my waist, using the haft to chip away at the limestone. Just losing a few inches would make such a huge difference!

Bits fell onto the men beneath me, then a large section dropped. I winced as I heard the surprised shout at impact. After I carefully tucked my knife back, I continued to climb. Squeezing through was still tight but doable, especially with a prod from below. I barely had time for a huge gulp of air before I was in the pool.

Lungs bursting, I surfaced. I treaded water for a moment, waiting to read our prearranged signal. It was still silent here; we were several dozen feet beneath the city yet.

The soldiers popped up in the pool around me, each gasp signifying another of our group joining in. It was amazing how much and how well I could see in the darkness. The rope and bucket bobbed on the surface of the water, the mouth of the well shone a dim square of light between us. The smallest square.

We had to take the other route; this one was being guarded.

As we watched, the bucket was lowered, only voices and shadows discernible above.

Trying not to splash, I gestured for the men to follow me. We would swim to the source upstream, for the water moved downhill from here.

This was where it would get hairy, since no one had taken this particular pathway in a long time, Waqi had said. As I surface-dove, a remembered phrase slowly saturated my mind, soothed me. *The waters will guide, they will purify, they will offer salvation.* The words off the time portal in modern Egypt for a traveler of the twenty-third power.

Okay, Chloe. Remember.

While the soldiers waited and watched the well covering, I swam to the far end of the pool, feeling around on the stony wall for an opening. The water ran through this well pool, then down the drain we'd just come up. Which meant it came from somewhere above us, but just how big was the "faucet"? Finally I found it, a two-by-two channel of total blackness filled with rushing water.

I gestured for Abishi to hand me some rope to tie us all together, me in the front, him bringing up the rear. Blind and lame in a big way, I thought. I closed my eyes, resting them from the masses of water that threatened to wash away my eyeballs.

We were moving uphill, breaths held, our bodies being torn and battered by the icy, flowing water. I saw spots behind my closed lids, and my chest was completely aching, burning, when I noticed the channel had widened enormously. The water level had dropped.

Half swimming and half walking while clinging to the rope, we moved upward against the current. Then we began dog-paddling at a 60 percent grade as the passage narrowed again, pushing the water almost to our chins. I barely heard the sounds of the dozen soldiers above the roar. Then we were walking level again, the water at our thighs.

I would have missed the opening had I not been running both hands along the wall. A crevice, with a breeze. I halted, feeling the next soldier come to a stop just behind me. Craning my head, I looked out—daylight! We were close!

Now how did we get out of this channel and into the streets? This was the part none of the women had known.

Seeing no other alternative and realizing that the Jebusi were now noticing some guards missing, which meant time was running out, I tied my skirt around my thighs, then squished myself through the crevice. I gritted my teeth as the stone abraded my skin. Fortunately I was tall and skinny and could slip through sideways. Also, I could probably make an excuse for being there, if I got caught. A tribesman would be spotted in a millisecond.

I wedged myself through the five-foot-long crack-style shaft, halting for a moment at the mouth of it. Would I be ambushed? I waited two, maybe three minutes. No one. Was that to lure me into a false sense of security?

After five minutes I hissed at Abishi to walk on through the water. I was safe, and I would meet him at the mouth of this thing, wherever that was. Please God, let me find the source.

I dropped immediately onto all fours, watching and alert. I heard nothing out of the ordinary—not yet. To my north I saw a mansion. I knew the tunnel ended inside it in the courtyard there; that's what I'd been told. So far, the directions were accurate. If the queen had cleared out the rooms, as she'd promised, then I'd be okay.

If not, then this could be the worst part, for no one was there to help me. I was on my own. *Oh God, please don't let me get caught.*

Surveying the front of the house, I saw no guard dogs, just an older man slumbering on the front stoop. It was the Mediterranean siesta hour, and the sun was hot, drying me almost immediately. No one was moving as I skirted the front in favor of the back doorway.

It would be open, right? I pushed against it, then harder, enough to feel the catch of metal. The door was bolted from within. Damn, she hadn't gotten to the doors. Backup plan? I walked around, looking at the windows. They were high and narrow. And barred. Great.

Scaling a house wall in broad daylight was not smart, but I didn't know what else to do. Beneath me soldiers waited; throughout houses in this city women waited. I sighed and unwound the rope from over my shoulder. It took me six tries before it looped around the wooden bar in the clerestory window.

Grinding my teeth against crying out when the rope cut into my already agonizing palms—which inspired me to shred part of my dress for protection—I climbed up and slipped in between the wooden poles.

The courtyard was painted floors surrounding a large pool. But every inch of wall space was covered with shields—stunning dress armor, made of gold and silver, adorned with semiprecious stones. There must have been more than fifty of them. A waterfall cascaded from the side of the house into the pool. Sunlight played off the water, then reflected onto the shields, giving the whole room the sense of being submarine. I watched, mesmerized, as it roared into the mirror surface of the pond, drowning out any other sounds, filling the warm air with a brisk chill of spray. Then it dawned on me: they'd built a house into a mountain!

Holding my breath, I dropped to the courtyard floor, rolling and rising, watching. Waiting. I was safe, since no one could hear me. But would they see me? I waited a moment more. Apparently the queen had done this part of her job. I could see a man dozing before what must have been the storerooms. There were no animals at all, an unusual thing for this day and age. A man's ass was treated better, certainly fed and watered better, than his children. Especially in a city without children, I reminded myself. Another moment of waiting.

Nothing.

After pulling up the rope, I approached the pool, keeping to the shadows.

I couldn't see the bottom, which was good since there should *be* no bottom.

As I tied the rope around one of the supporting pillars, I stifled a sneeze, the sound lost under the rush of the waterfall. I hoped the rope would be long enough. The flax in my hand, I took a deep breath, then surface dived, feeling for the bottom, then the "drain."

As I suspected, just as before, the tunnel went down, through a narrow passage, then . . . I fell, water all around me. Unlike my last fall, this one was not cushioned by a pool. I dropped about six feet, then landed on a rock that was jutting up from the streambed. My screech indicated to Abishi and company that I'd arrived.

He splashed through the water, racing to my side. "Up," I said through gritted teeth; I hurt! "In the royal harem, in a courtyard." I winced as I got to my feet. "It's on the eastern side. The gate is slightly downhill."

"You are coming with us?"

I stifled a sneeze. "I will join you and the women at the gates. Remember your word—no raping, no pillaging, and no women killed. We wait for everything until Yoav arrives."

Abishi's voice got sharper. "It was not my promise, but I will hold to it."

"They are betraying everything," I said softly. "Don't punish them for helping you."

Aching from the series of falls I'd taken, in addition to the general misery of a cold, I backtracked to the fissure and squished myself through. The city was strangely silent; people should have been up and moving now, for it was approaching sundown.

I had an unsettling feeling that something had gone wrong. Where was everyone? Walking downhill toward the main gate, I saw no one, I heard no one. What was up? There should have been people on their way to market, women on their way to the well. Jebus was a ghost town.

You made it this way, my conscience whispered. *You are to blame.* Somewhere above me I heard the cry of the *shofar,* then a roar of men. Inside or outside? I didn't know, but I ran to the main gate, which was still barred. It would take at least ten of us to lift that piece of wood. Within in the city I heard a scream—"We are betrayed!"—that was suddenly silenced.

Nothing. No one. This was getting downright eerie. "Hello?" I called. "Anyone here?"

"*Isha!*" Yoav called from the other side of the gates. "Open the gates!"

Suddenly I knew this was my chance. I had the city; it was up to me to give it to him. "Only if you take a solemn vow, Yoav."

"What?" Only in this language it was very abrupt: *Mah?*

"Promise *hal* will not apply."

"*Mah?*" He didn't sound pleased. "Open the gate, *isha. Akchav!*"

Now, huh? "Promise on the name of the Most High," I said.

"Open the damned gates!"

"Assure me that these women will not be punished. They have helped you get the city, you must spare them."

"This is not the time to discuss this, Klo-ee," he said.

I looked over my shoulder. Three women had grouped, wide-eyed and shaking. "*Akchav* we discuss this, Yoav. No *herim*, no *hal*."

There was a pause. "*B'seder.* Open the gates."

"No slavery, either." The group had grown to about seven.

We were back to his shocked "What?" "Where is Waqi?" I asked one of the women softly.

"With the queen, in the palace."

"What has happened?"

"We passed around a sleeping potion. Most of the men are asleep."

Yoav was banging on the door. "Your promise on God's name, Yoav," I shouted to him, speaking softly to the women. "And death to no men, except the soldiers."

He yelled in anger, outrage. I knew this wasn't the tribesmen's way.

"It is not the Jebusi way to betray their loved ones," I reminded him, looking at the growing group. "Only men who are soldiers die."

Another five women came running down the street. "The high-landers," they shouted right before the soldiers I'd led through the *tzi-nor* burst onto the street. I grabbed one of the women's knives and held it up menacingly. "Promise, Yoav," I shouted through the gate. Abishi halted, quickly taking in the scene.

"Yoav!" he yelled.

"Get that crazy woman to open the gates!" Yoav bellowed back. "This is becoming a farce!"

Abishi took a step closer. "Stay back," I said, waving my knife. "I know how to use this." I did—carving turkey. "Promise these women will be safe, well," I said. "All they want is the freedom to have and keep their children, their nonmilitary husbands. No more sacrificing to Molekh, no sacrificing as *hal*." I watched as he wiped blood from his sword.

"*Isha*, Yoav is going to gift Dadua with the city. These are not his assurances to make."

"I don't care what the rules usually are. Promise, Yoav," I shouted again. The thoroughfare was growing crowded with watching women.

Zorak, who came through the water with me, though I hadn't known it, yelled over to Yoav. "She is unreasonable, Yoavi. We must agree, I fear." Abishi turned to him, glaring.

I heard muttering and tried to imagine what it looked like on the other side. Suddenly I saw the arrows rain down just as I heard the cries from the first hits. Jebusi guardsmen from the towers were lining up on the wall, aiming into the city. In haste I opened the gate, the women and some soldiers helping. Behind me I heard the sounds of battle, of shrieks and groans.

We lifted the bar and pulled as the soldiers on the other side pushed. "Promise, Yoav!" I shouted into the men. "Promise, promise, promise!"

He grabbed me by the upper arms, glass green eyes glaring into my face. "Damn you, I promise."

"On—"

"*Ken! Ken!* On the name of the Almighty!" Then he pushed me away, fighting into the crowd.

Movies had not prepared me for really being in battle, seeing people swinging swords with the intent to kill. No choreography and no tasteful blood. The sounds were awful: the sucking of a blade being pulled out, the thud of bodies falling to the dirt-and-stone path. I hid in the fading shadows of the gate enclosure, watching the soldiers pick the Jebusi men off the wall, so that they fell in front of us, splattering on the ground.

Through it all, with every drop of blood, I heard my voice in my head: *You did this. Because of you, Chloe Bennett Kingsley, this is happening.* Had I totally screwed up history?

Bloody late to be thinking about it now, *isha*, I responded to myself sarcastically. Then it was too much, the sights, the sounds, the smells. I vomited on the ground, dizzy and guilt-stricken.

The fighting moved from the gates deeper into the city. The women vanished into their homes like a flock of sparrows into the sky. I huddled in the night.

Sometime in the darkest moments before dawn, the unearthly cry of a ram's horn echoed over the city and through the valley. By that signal, I knew that Abishi and Yoav had the citadel. The *shofar* had sounded. Jebus was open.

Was I a betrayer? Or simply a woman with her back against the wall? The women had asked me, they had forsaken their husbands. Or was I rationalizing because it had been either me or them and I knew that Jerusalem ultimately went to Dadua? Had it happened this way? Had I taken some other person's place in this story? Had I messed up history?

Or was history like Cheftu said, just people muddling through every day, with only time and perspective to decide which event was significant?

I didn't know, I couldn't think. My body was numb; I leaned against the stone, panting with the effort. My sneezing was unstoppable, I was bruised and cut in a dozen places; I just wanted to go home.

Home where?

Home with Cheftu, I amended; location and time meant nothing to me.

As dawn tinted the stone, soldiers swarmed through the streets. The bodies of the men who had fallen in battle were laid out in the valley.

Wrapped in wool and sneezing spasmodically, my dozen or so cuts scabbed over, I watched as the men separated the townspeople.

Dadua was arriving soon. He would be entering the city on the back of a donkey.

Apparently a mountain prince, *nasi*, rode an ass up a hill into his city.

A king, *haMelekh*, commanded an army from a chariot. Therefore, while Dadua was *haMelekh* over all the tribes, because he led them in war and directed them from a horse-drawn chariot, here he was *nasi.*

There was no sense of king and prince being in a hierarchy or that you had to be a prince before being a king. They were two separate categories. A prince, only of a mountain kingdom. A king, only as a war leader.

Consequently, the Pelesti were kings because they rode in chariots with horses. Dadua was *haNasi* of Jebus because he entered on a donkey. My brain throbbed in counterpoint to my bruising as I tried to grasp this concept that upended my whole lifetime of understanding the prince/king relationship.

Standing tall in the midmorning light, the remaining men and women of Jebus met the new *nasi.* Yoav stood at attention, bloodstained but proud, surrounded by his soldiers, who were bearing the gold-and-silver shields I'd seen. We watched Dadua ride up the hill, astride the donkey. Though his feet almost dragged the dirt, still there was a humbling majesty about him. Gold shone from his helmet, throat, and greaves.

This was *David.*

The donkey, white and clean, drew through the gated enclosure to stand in the shadows. Yoav walked to Dadua, the city and soldiers watching. "*HaMelekh* Dadua ben Yesse, I gift you this city, this dream of your heart and desire of your *nefesh,* to be yours always, a seat for the dynasty of Dadua which *el ha*Shaday will continue into forever."

The donkey was a little nervous, prancing back and forth, pawing the ground. "As I step into this city, this gift of your loyalty, I tell you, Yoav ben Zerui'a, that you will be *Rosh Tsor haHagana* until breath leaves your body," Dadua responded.

"Thy will be done," Yoav said, bowing.

All around us the men cheered, Dadua looked our direction. I wondered if he considered the cost of this. If he knew how well Yoav loved him, the price he paid for Dadua to have what he wanted but not to be tainted by the task of getting it.

Dadua rode into the city amid the cheering, and we all dropped to our knees, bowing our heads. Today he looked like royalty. He dismounted and walked before us, an impressive figure in his iris blue girdle and cloak, a jeweled dagger at his side, the sun shining off his armor.

"Jebusi," he cried out. "I mean you no harm. Your ruler Abdiheba is dead, Jebus is no longer your city. Forever after, this city is mine, peopled with my *chorim* and *giborim.*"

Friends and associates, the lexicon provided. Even I figured out that one.

"Jebus is a new city today," he continued. "A city of ancient promise to my people. It belongs neither to the tribes of the north: Zebulon, Asher, Y'sakhar, Gad, Binyamin, Efra'im, Manasha, Naftali; or to the tribes of the south: Yuda, Reuven, Tsimeon, Dan. It is a new place, the City of Dadua, Qiryat Dadua."

Though I'd been expecting it, I was still breathless. David. Israel. Jerusalem. *Oh, Cheftu, what you wouldn't give to be here right now.*

The crowd was silent, stoic. The women, whose fathers, brothers, and husbands were either sleeping or slaughtered through the women's doing, stood stalwart. They held on to each fiercely, narrow eyed and questioning, listening to this man who had conquered the Pelesti. "I invite you to stay, to join with us in making this a city of promise. Two conditions I demand be met." I glared at Yoav; had he told Dadua the promise made?

There was a nearly audible intake of breath. I watched, waited.

"The first is that the laws of our God be obeyed. He is the only God of our people, he will be the only God of this mountain. He is himself higher than these hills. Above us"—Dadua pointed to a plateau rising to the north—"I will build a house for this God, a place on earth where he can rest among us. No other gods will be tolerated in this city, within these walls or on this mount. Ever."

The Temple Mount, oh my God. The Temple Mount? That had been the cause of almost all of Jerusalem's troubles since the dawn of time, at least according to my father.

Was *this* where it began?

Dadua's expression became cold. "No longer will the sacrifice of *yeladim* be permissible. No longer will you feed the belly of Molekh in the valley, with the seed of your loins. There will be no other God in Jebus, save *el ha*Shaday.

"The second condition is this: Our custom offers protection to the widows and"—Dadua stumbled here, since there were no orphans—"*ach*, those who dwell among us. Should a man of our tribes approach you, wishing to take you as wife or concubine, you must know what is right. He is obliged to provide for you for a full month. During this time you are to observe mourning for your family, your losses.

"Shear your hair, allow your nails to grow, know you have the security of a month's protection to honor that which was lost. If at the end of this time, if he wants you still, he may take you to wife by knowing you. He will give you children, which you will not destroy."

I looked out over the women. We really are the stronger sex, I thought. Men have the easier task of falling bravely in battle. Women have to start over, join the enemy in bed, give him children, forsake old ways and adopt new.

Had it been worth it? Were they exchanging old shackles for new? My gaze moved over the male merchants, the farmers whose lives had been granted. Did they appreciate what their women had done? Would they honor the new regime?

"If after that time, that month, he no longer wishes to marry with you, he is obligated to let you go free. He cannot sell you, for he does not own you." Thank you, God, I thought. No slavery, no *hal*, no *herim*. I breathed a sigh of relief as his words sank in. "You and your possessions are free and may leave."

But he gets to keep your house, I thought. Sneaky, Dadua. Really sneaky.

"Should he persist and take you to wife, because you are taken under duress, he may never divorce you. You are protected by the laws of the land, by the honor of these tribes. You will worship our God; walk in our ways and be our people. Your children will be reared in the ways of Y'srael, they will worship Shaday, they will marry within us."

Dadua looked at the masses, then raised his glance to his men. In unison they said, "Thy will be done."

He bowed his head, acknowledging their acquiescence, then spoke to Yoav: "As you will."

Zorak went directly to Waqi, pulling her into his embrace, kissing her. He was tender and sweet, the expression I'd seen in his face when he delivered her child only intensified now.

The women were picked like fruit, gently, carefully. There were no bawdy comments, no groping. The women whose husbands were still alive stayed close to their spouses, ignored by the tribesmen. It was silent, efficient, and strangely impersonal. I made sure to stay in the shadows.—I didn't want to be mistaken even if someone was willing to overlook my painted complexion. Then I touched my face, realizing that my paint, the protection of looking as though I had extreme acne, was gone.

As dusk fell, the gates were closed. Dadua had taken possession of his gift city, and he would sleep in his new palace tonight. Qiryat Dadua—my head was spinning.

In Egypt, walking through the temples during the day, I'd sworn I could hear the voices of the dead. They were telling me their stories, of how beautiful it had been. They pushed my pen to draw it, but I'd been unable to.

Then in Kallistae, with the wonders of the Aztlan empire, the sense of magic in the air had been nearly tangible. It was no wonder that our stories of gods and legends were born here. The hills were raised by mysticism.

Here, however, I sensed what I'd never felt in either of those two places. With the night wind blowing my sweat-damp hair, the stars scattered above, tonight for the first time I felt holiness.

Was it that the air was that much clearer? Was it because I was so highly elevated?

Or was it because Jerusalem, under any name, really was the foot-stool of God?

PART

IV

CHAPTER II

IN LESS THAN THREE DAYS Dadua, his multiple wives, and his perpetually-in-motion children were moved into the city. The traveling men returned two weeks later, on the hottest day we'd had yet.

We didn't see them first; we smelled them.

For a moment I thought I'd returned to the time when this was a city of Molekh, because the burning of human flesh and the carrying around of dead and rotting goat have a similarly pervasive, nauseating odor, which wafts across miles, up hills, and through stone.

We women were sitting innocently in the courtyard, fanning ourselves, drinking lukewarm cucumber-and-yogurt drinks, and gossiping. Apparently some young thing had caught the eye of *haNasi*. But who was it?

A slave? Someone's daughter? Shaday knew that from nowhere princes and their eligible daughters were showing up. The compacted city had become a glorified bed-and-breakfast of royal rejects. Had they been lurking in the hills, just waiting for the outcome of the battle? Not two days after Dadua moved into the city, some desert king and his beveiled daughter had shown up with ingratiating smiles and laden donkeys.

However, between Mik'el, Avgay'el, Hag'it, and Ahino'am, did Dadua need other wives? Mik'el and Avgay'el wouldn't stay in the same room together; Ahino'am forbade anyone else to wear the deep red she favored; I was convinced Hag'it was bisexual, and the children fought with each other when they weren't running.

So who was the young maid? The speculation was all-consuming.

To this end, Mik'el was paying the guardsmen at Dadua's door for information on who came and went; Avgay'el was paying the mushroom to see which slaves entered his private quarters and how long they stayed; Hag'it was paying the kitchen help to count the cups and plates used, to learn if he were eating enough for two; and Ahino'am was eating enough for two, because she was still nursing.

Since Gerber's wasn't yet invented, three or more years of breast-feeding was common.

It was *Yom Rishon* dinner, and each of Dadua's wives had prepared her specialty dish. The afternoon before, since we couldn't work on the Sabbath, clothes had been selected and discarded, jewelry had been traded, hands were hennaed. I had longed for the simplicity of the millstone, of grinding flour to make bread. Though I wasn't a slave, I was in the harem, so refusing was awkward.

Waqi had invited me to stay with her, but Zorak and his mother were there for the month of her "mourning" before Waqi and Zorak made their relationship official. Just seeing them together, their longing glances, accidental touches, made me yearn for Cheftu. Then again, most everything did.

The roof was decked out, and the temperature had dropped finally so that a wonderful, perfumed coolness permeated the dining area, lit with a perfect sphere moon. I stood with most of the other women while the men ate. Rarely, if ever, did the family eat together. For the men it was a huge social outlet, for the women it was a massive drain on time and energy. Consequently we would eat later, after they did.

It was while we stood there that the hideous smell blew over us. Then away.

In some ways the Middle Eastern culture is similar to that of the American South; I think this was why my father was so at ease in both societies. Mimi taught me that the ultimate role of southern hospitality was to keep your guest feeling comfortable and wanted. Nothing was to interfere with that, hence the lack of confrontations in my family.

Saudi customs were the same. Nothing was to make the guest feel ill at ease. Nothing negative was mentioned; no sore spots were prodded. "Ignore the unpleasant," was the motto.

As the horrific odor blanketed us, that mentality held. No one said a word, though we all reacted by choking, gasping for breath, wheezing. It was awful. Then the wind shifted and the air cleared.

The hodgepodge of foreign kings, princes, and nobles all pretended they hadn't smelled a thing. Dadua's eyes were watering, but he said nothing. Silence settled uneasily on the tables, so the *gibori* Abishi passed him the *kinor*. "Sing us a song, *adoni.*"

Dadua didn't look up; he plucked a few strings, testing them. Around him the air filled with unspoken hope as we watched.

The breeze changed again, flattening us with the smell. There was nothing, polite or not, that could be said. It was unignorable. "By Shaday, what is that?" a woman asked, tears streaming from her face.

"They return!" we heard shouted from the gate. "N'tan returns!" The *shofar* sounded. In chaos we left the palace and raced to the heavily guarded gate. The stench was awful. It was the men; it had to be. Darkness was fully on the land, so we each held a torch, stretching down the road so they would have a path to walk up into the city.

I tried to squint through the night, to see my husband. But I couldn't; I felt as though I were going to hurl. "Is that the men?" someone else asked.

"What have they done?" Avgay'el asked, her nose buried in her hands, tears streaking her perfect oval face.

Abiathar, the high priest, stepped forward. Though he wasn't in his uniform, he was impressive. "N'tan?" he called out.

"Ken?" We heard the voice from the night.

"You must be purified before you step into the city," he shouted. "You stink!"

I couldn't believe all the rigmarole the men had to go through before they were allowed in the city. Washings and shavings, prayers and debriefings . . . I was going nuts, pacing throughout the night, waiting. Finally I climbed up on the gate, looking out over the valley, waiting for my husband to be released to me.

At midnight Dadua went out to the men. The acoustics weren't very good, so I had no idea what was going on. I finally sat down on the walkway between the towers, huddled against the wall from the wind, and slept. On the edges of my consciousness I heard sandals against stone, time and again. "Chloe?" I finally heard.

I woke up from a dream, opening my eyes to see the face I loved best. "You're back," I whispered, holding my arms open for Cheftu. As sleep faded and the reality of the day penetrated, I reacquainted myself with his scent, with the feel of his body against mine. "You're back," I said again, almost crying with wonder that he was here with me. "How are you?" I asked, but didn't move because I didn't want to lose contact with his flesh.

"Perfect, now," he said.

"Did you get it?" I asked. "The gold?"

"*Ken, chérie.* Enough gold to sate a pharaoh."

I opened my eyes to see that the sky was brightening. "How come we didn't see this gold when we were with the Apiru?" I asked. "We were part of the Exodus!"

"It was carried alone, gathered from everyone before we left. The grieving Egyptians were more than willing to pay the Apiru to leave by then."

I pulled back to see his face. For a moment I just wallowed in his beauty. Thick brows met over a knife-blade nose, his jaw was squared, his lips full and sensual. "What do you look at?" he asked, his eyes crinkling at the corners with laughter.

I reached out, touching his clean-shaven cheek, and saw the humor fade from his expression. "It's been——"

"Too long," he said as he pulled me into his arms, then pressed me against the stone wall, his mouth against mine, devouring me with kisses. He gripped my jaw, opening me wider to him. Raising my thigh around his leg, his hand running from my ankle, he hiked up my skirt. With some fumbling, a few stifled giggles, he dropped his kilt.

There, in the morning sunlight, he held me in his palms, my legs wrapped around his, as he slowly lowered my body onto his. My eyes closed as all I felt, all I knew, was Cheftu. The sun poured light onto us already, as though an oven door were opened while preheating.

I felt his shoulders flex and move beneath my palms, his palms beneath my bottom holding me carefully, powerfully, our legs linked together and the fullness of him within me. He was my universe, the only reality for this space in time. Slowly, steadily, he stoked the flame higher and higher. I asked for more, I begged for speed, but he tortured me, making my skin burn from the inside out. Sunspots filled my vision, burning me, enflaming me, until I combusted, sagging in his arms, the two of us collapsing, trembling, against the wall.

"What was that all about?" I asked a moment later, still breathless.

"*Ach*, well, you want to have children," he said. "I refused to do it as a slave, but now"—he shrugged—"my freedom is real." He turned his head, smiled at me though his eyes were closed against the sunlight.

It took a moment for his words to sink in, then I sat bolt upright. "You're free!"

The holes were still in his ears, but they were bare. He smiled, his eyes still closed, but his whole demeanor eased. "*Oui, chérie.* We have a home, I have employment, we are in the beginning of the rise of the people Israel . . . I thought we should start our family."

I swallowed the tears in my throat. "Didn't want to waste time, didya?" I teased.

He pressed my face against his chest, hugging me tightly in total protection. I sighed, listening to him. His voice was serious as he answered me in English. "Never do I want to waste a moment with you, *ma* Chloe."

We sat that way until we heard a very loud, very obvious clatter of metal on stone. "*Merde,* soldiers," Cheftu said as we disentangled. The sun was blazing onto us, baking us in this cleft of white reflective stone. I tugged down my hopelessly wrinkled skirt while Cheftu adjusted his kilt.

Then he looked at me, probably for the first time in broad daylight. "Your chains!" he exclaimed. "Where are they?"

I grinned. "This Cinderella didn't wait for the prince," I said jokingly.

Another clatter of sword on stone, a loud cough. "We should leave so that poor man stops abusing his weapon," I said.

"I will not move until you tell me what this is about."

Smiling, I shrugged. "I won my freedom. Official today."

"What is this? How?" he asked. "You are amazing to me, *chérie*. Today you won it?"

"*Lo*," I said. A young *gibori* walked by, looking out to the valley, whistling. I glanced back at Cheftu. "However, when Yoav heard that you were here, that Dadua was meeting with you, he sent for me."

Cheftu crossed his arms, raising a brow. "And?"

We'd met in lamplit darkness. I had smelled wine before I'd stepped inside the enclosure. "You are a slave no more," Yoav had said. He didn't sound or look intoxicated, but he'd been stripped down to his undertunic. Muscles bulged and flexed in the flickering light, softening the craggy features of his face. "So come, let me unchain you."

There was nothing untoward in his words, but the tone of his voice was suggestive. I stood there, wanting to be chainless when I did see Cheftu, but afraid of stepping that close to Yoav. I knew he wouldn't touch me, I knew I wouldn't touch him, but it was an awkward and scary feeling being so aware of him. I was married. Not only that, I was happily married! What was my problem? I'd swallowed, which had sounded loud in the darkness.

"We owe you a debt," he said, stretching in his chair. "I do. Never could this city have been breached without your cooperation."

"I'd hardly call my part 'cooperation.' Your methods are more like blackmail, *adoni*."

He chuckled and shrugged. "I do what is necessary to serve my liege."

"You got what you wanted, *Rosh Tsor haHagana*."

His green eyes met mine. "I cannot have what I want."

I swallowed again, feeling the heat of my chest and my face.

"I will not take it. *Avayra goreret avayra.*"

"What does that mean, transgression begets transgression?"

"*Ach, isha.* You are such a pagan." He picked up a tool from the low table beside him. "Sit here and I will tell you about my people."

The tension was dissipated, but I was still nervous. I sat on a stool before him and gingerly pulled out the chain. Through everything I had had it, but I'd grown used to it, the weight, the feel. It was like having long hair or an elaborate manicure. You just adjusted. However, this was no slavery like I'd ever heard of before. He pulled up the metal links, a slight tug on my ear, and then I heard the small hammer as it hit.

"*Lifnay* Dadua there was Labayu. *Lifnay* Labayu was made king, we were ruled by judges. From the time of *ha*Moshe in the desert until Labayu, the tribes were divided and each had its own group of judges, then judges above them, and so on."

The sound of metal on metal was a rhythm to his story.

"So when the tribes were reentering the land, Achan was one of the soldiers sent to conquer the city of Ai. The battle was a defeat, though it should not have been. Achan was a brave soldier who led the attack. The judge at that time inquired of Shaday the reason why we had lost. Shaday said he couldn't help us when we had broken our agreement with him. We were instructed that taking the land was a holy task, *herim.* Not for us to rape and pillage like the uncircumcised do. *Ach,* well, after some divination it became clear that Achan had taken some booty from a former battle."

"So what happened?"

"An example had to be set; *avayra goreret avayra.*"

There was that phrase again: transgression begets transgression.

"Achan, with all his belongings and family, were taken outside the camp. Because the transgression was against the community, causing us to lose the next battle and many lives, the community exacted judgment on him."

"Uh . . . judged how?" I asked, though I had a sinking feeling inside. After all, I'd grown up in the Middle East. Justice was a bloody draw.

The metal fell free. There was hushed silence. "Achan, his family, and possessions were stoned to death."

"Stoned?" I repeated.

"And the remains burned. Whenever you see a mass of piled stones outside the city walls, it is a marker for one who transgressed against the community and was punished by the community." He sat back. "You can remove your own chains."

I pulled them through my ears, which felt curiously airy with those huge holes, and lightweight without the press of metal. "I still don't understand. Why does transgression beget transgression?" My back was to him. He was leaning away from me so that I felt the heat of the lamp on my skin. My hands were trembling.

Yoav sighed deeply. "You tempt me," he said bluntly. "If I were to take you, that is adultery. However, as you say, my position is *Rosh Tsor haHagana.* I have the ear of the king. You tell no one. I tell no one. The next time I want something that is not right, I think to myself, I committed adultery and no one knew. If I steal this treasure, or I tell a falsehood about this man, or I cheat, who will know? I got away with it before."

I was motionless, listening, almost afraid to remind myself that I was here.

"Perhaps it is a small thing, but from it my pride grows. I come to think I know more, I know better than Shaday. It infects my *nefesh* so that the laws, they become suggestions. When I transgress and there is no punishment, I transgress further the next time. And the next. In time, I have a tree of dishonesty growing up, poisoning the air and the earth of the land." He shifted in his seat. "Transgressions pollute the land. This pollution will cause the land to vomit us out."

The tenor of his voice changed, became resolute. "I sacrifice my blood for this land, for my tribe. No less will I sacrifice my desire for it."

I had risen and walked out of the lean-to into the night air, down the outside steps, not stopping until I stood on the wall's walkway, blown by the wind, looking out where my heart was. *From tiny acorns big trees grow,* I heard Mimi say. *Don't even plant the seed.*

I looked at my husband. "He shared the story of Achan's curse, the concept of transgressions growing from one thing into another, until everything was corrupted. Then I came here, waited for you."

His eyes sparked; I knew he knew what I hadn't said. The wind blew at my hair, and again I felt the emptiness of my ears, the sense of freedom. He reached out, his hand on my neck, cradling my head. His thumb touched the hole. His pinky finger would probably fit right through it. I didn't want to look at him, the expression in his eyes was too raw. I gazed off into the valley.

"Chloe?" he said. I met his gaze reluctantly. "I will never leave you again. This I promise."

"Nothing—"

He cut me off. "I know that. I know you." I'd looked away again, and he tilted my face to his. "I was remiss to you, not fulfilling my duties."

Inexplicably my eyes filled with tears. "You don't—"

Cheftu kissed me, hard, rough. Despite the sun and the heat I felt goose bumps all over my body, I wanted this man again. I wondered briefly if the soldier was walking the entire length of the wall or just this space. "I do," he said against my mouth. "I need you. I need to touch you and to hold and listen to you. My duty is to love you, to provide for you, to make love to you."

Was it any wonder that I loved this man? He laid claim to my mouth while he seduced some part of my heart, that absurdly female sliver of me that wanted to be hit over the head and dragged back to a cave somewhere—by of course an intelligent, sensitive, gentle man— and profoundly "claimed."

My body was pressed against his, I felt his arousal, but he was working some other magic as he talked to me, kissed me. We stumbled back into a pocket of shade and he held me, his hand on my head. "No, Chloe," he said in his distinct, accented English. "Never again will I leave you."

Vine-tending season was upon us: all of us. I'd never experienced team-work in the same way. The "land" everyone always referred to became an entity to me. Not a god, but more like a relative, someone you take care of, nurture, and support. Consequently I found myself out in the vineyards till all hours, with Cheftu and most every other tribesman and slave, pinching back buds, training vines, and pruning.

I would never, ever, take wine for granted again.

The good part was that in the evening many of us would gather on rooftops, usually Dadua's, eat dinner, and listen to stories. The cool wind would refresh us, the laughter would rejuvenate us, and after our escapades tangling with near death, psychotic people, and natural dis-asters, Cheftu and I appreciated our new lives.

Housing in the city was still iffy. People moved in and out on a daily basis: Jebusi giving up and leaving for a Molekh-friendly place, tribesmen moving in with their children, wives, and armor. The city streets were still stained from blood in places, but I chose to look away.

One night, not long after Cheftu had returned and we'd been freed, we were sitting on Dadua's roof with Zorak and Waqi, who were now wedded, and assorted others whose names were still foreign to me, when Dadua announced he'd written a new song. "This commemo-rates the brother of my *nefesh*, Yohanan, fallen in battle." The tune was plaintive, even more of a minor key than tribesmen's music normally was. Across the still roof his notes rang, his voice rich with emotion. My stomach growled—the women hadn't eaten yet—but I could not leave. It was no wonder this all became history. Dadua played the last chord, and we sat in silence—savoring the final note.

"What beauty flows from the mouth of the king!" someone shouted from the stairway that led up from the courtyard.

We all turned, wondering who had spoken.

"What passion for his fallen brother! What compassion for the lost of Y'srael!" An older man stepped forward, with curled and braided hair and beard flowing down his body. Though he was aged, he was still very handsome.

"Who are you?" a *gibori* asked, crouched and ready to defend Dadua if need be.

The man pried a scroll from his waistband and handed it to the *gi-*

bori. "I bring a message from the master of Tsor, Hiram. It is a message of peace for your most esteemed poet-king, Dadua."

He was speaking our dialect. True to type, the *giborim* settled back to watch. After all, this might be entertaining as a story.

One of the younger *gibori* took the scroll, then unrolled it. The other soldiers joked with him, for almost none of them could read. The young soldier stared hard at the page, ignoring the gibes of his fellows. In the end he rolled it up and delivered it to Dadua.

He looked at it, no expression on his Rossetti-perfect face. "My scribe will read it," he said calmly. He looked up. "Chavsha, are you here?"

Our eyes met and Cheftu rose, walking to the king. He was dressed like a tribesman, he even was growing a beard, but he still moved with the feline elegance that Egyptians seemed to have.

"Thy will be done," Cheftu said as he bowed, his arm across his chest as though he were serving Pharaoh. Dadua didn't flinch. He handed Cheftu the scroll as though they had done it a thousand times. I was torn between laughing hysterically and dropping my clay cup. Who was Dadua fooling? I looked back at the messenger.

He was tall, his neck and shoulders still straight, unbowed by age. His clothing was a tunic, moderately bright and patterned. He was standing in partial shadow, so it was hard to see details. But he had presence, undeniably so.

"To Dadua, ruler on high: Greetings, my brother, from Hiram, Zakar Ba'al of Tsor, your exalted kinsman," Cheftu read.

"Who does this Hiram think he is, grasping after being a son of Avraham, calling himself 'exalted brother'?" a *gibori* commented.

"He's not circumcised!" another said.

"It's just poetic language," Abishi explained. "He knows they aren't brothers. He simply says that to make his requests more pleasant."

I watched the messenger as the *giborim* spoke. He seemed amused, though it was hard to see his face. Bangs covered his forehead, and the rectangular shape of his beard disguised the rest of his face. However, I had a weird feeling. Something about his nose, maybe?

The men quieted, and Cheftu continued to read. "As you are now living in Abdiheba's abode, you have learned he was no creature of comfort."

"We don't need a pagan to tell us that!" one of them shouted. Cheftu glanced up, his face in profile. He was so beautiful with short hair, though his sidelocks were growing out again.

I heard a small cry and turned. The messenger had staggered and was being seated by one of the *gibori*. The man had turned ghastly pale, visible even in this light. They wet his lips with wine. He stared at Cheftu with wide eyes. "Have I misspoken, *adoni?*" Cheftu asked when the rest of us turned to him to see what the messenger was seeing.

The man closed his eyes, shaking his head. "Please," he said after a moment. "Continue."

Dadua had said nothing. Probably in a real court, he would be above speaking to this man. I thought his silence now was more because he was suspicious. Tsor, from what I remembered of my mental map, was pretty big on both the economic and social scale. Why would they be here? Or why would the Zakar Ba'al not show up himself?

It could be a plot to get inside the city and betray us the way I'd betrayed the Jebusi. I glanced over at Zorak, who was ignoring the byplay and staring longingly into the darkness. Maybe betrayal was more a definition of perspective and less an absolute?

Cheftu looked down and continued reading. "He, Abdiheba," Cheftu reminded us as he continued to read, "believed that physical pain ensured battle victory. An interesting but unnecessary ritual, I think. Reports claim that you are a man of strength, graciousness, and art. To this end, for the cumulative result of peace and trade between our peoples, I propose this:

"The man who has delivered this message is my master builder and architect." Cheftu glanced up at the messenger, and we all turned to him. Tears streaked his face. Was the man in pain? His eyes were still closed, and he was breathing rapidly. His hands were fisted in his tunic skirt. Something was niggling at me. Cheftu kept reading.

"He and the crew with him will build you a palace of Tsori cedar—"

The tribesmen gasped.

"—with outbuildings and governmental offices, as a symbol of my faith in you. Yours is a strong, young nation, biting the ankles of the Pelesti. I wish to see its growth."

I looked at Dadua. His gaze was focused on the messenger; had he even heard that incredible offer? Cheftu resumed:

"If perhaps *ha-adon* cares for his new palace, he will see fit to allow my caravans and those under my protection to travel through his fair valley from Egypt. Allow my architect to build your palace while you consider this exchange. I look forward to seeing my brother face-to-face one day. Your god's blessings on you. Signed, Hiram, Zakar Ba'al of Tsor."

Our heads swiveled as though we were on a single wire. This older man was the chief builder?

"Impossible," Dadua said. We turned toward him en masse. He rose from his chair. "Tell Zakar Ba'al we appreciate his offer, but we are not accepting of it."

Cheftu glanced from one man to the next. He frowned faintly as he looked at the messenger. Did he have the same strange feeling? *"Adoni,"* he said. Dadua turned to glare at him. "As *adoni's* scribe," he said, accenting the "scribe," "I would suggest we offer this man residence for the night and discuss this matter when he is rested."

"He will not stay in my city," Dadua said. There was no belligerence in his tone, he was matter-of-fact. Cheftu glanced at the messenger again. The man was looking down, almost as though he were cringing from view.

My strange feeling graduated to hinkiness, which was the sense of someone not only walking across your grave, but doing jumping jacks on it.

Cheftu was doing some fast talking, persuading Dadua to let the man stay in one of the watch houses. Women began oozing from the rooftop, going to prepare a place for this man, ousting some family to sleep in the groves tonight.

"There is no need," the messenger said suddenly. "We have our own accommodations." He bowed. "I will seek *ha-adon's* face tomorrow, perhaps?" Unlike before, when his voice rang out, now he was almost slurring his words. Had the man had a stroke? Should Cheftu examine him?

Apparently I wasn't the only one with this thought. N'tan stepped forward and offered to check him over. The messenger reacted almost violently, backing away, excusing himself. The *giborim* had tensed up, drawing imperceptibly closer to Dadua.

The messenger turned to go, brushing past the women. For a second our gazes connected. His eyes were haunted, naked, as though his emotions had just been sandblasted. Pain and joy were mingled before he looked away.

The group sat in silence as we listened to him beat a not so old retreat down the stairs and the street. Several *giborim* followed. How had he gotten into the city, anyway? Had anyone asked that?

Dadua turned to Cheftu. "What did that mean?" Like many people who had lived without, he was suspicious of anyone who gave with what seemed to be unflinching generosity.

In this case, I would say suspicion was warranted. There was something about those eyes. . . .

"If I understand," Cheftu said, "his crew will build you a palace, outbuildings, and governmental offices."

Dadua was wary. "For the price of traversing my kingdom?"

Cheftu shrugged. "Also, probably space for his crew to live."

"Impossible," Dadua said again.

Abishi leaned forward. "*Adoni,* we need new homes for our people. Now, it is fine. Tribesmen and Jebusi are in their summer homes in the fields and vineyards. Soon it will be winter, though. Colder than we are accustomed to. Then where will everyone live?"

Dadua frowned. "I will not have a pagan and his crew in my city! It is foolishness!"

Yoav spoke slowly. "Agreed, *adoni.* But there must be a way."

"Could we extend the city?" N'tan said. "Let him build somewhere outside the walls?"

"We couldn't protect it," Yoav said.

"North we could," Abishi interjected. We all looked at him.

"He speaks the truth," said another general I didn't know. "Between here and the Jebusi threshing floor, there are plateaus that could be extended."

Abishi spoke again. "*Ach,* because they are between the lower gates and the threshing floor, no one could access them."

"But no one would be within the city walls," Yoav clarified.

Dadua speared Cheftu with a look. "What say you?"

"They are trading in kind," Cheftu answered. "They have nothing else to give you, nothing of tremendous worth. Building outside the city walls would solve a variety of problems for you. Moreover, they would bear the cost of the materials and labor."

"All you need do is let them travel through the tribes' lands," Abishi said.

"We could even escort them," Yoav added. "It would keep the *giborim* in condition between their assignments with the Pelesti." His gaze scanned the crowd for a moment. I watched Cheftu's face harden. The man didn't miss a trick.

Dadua yawned. "I will think on it."

We all said, "Thy will be done."

"If you will stay with us, you must follow our laws," Dadua said.

We were roasting, all jammed into the makeshift audience chamber. Abdiheba, with the exception of his harem's quarter's waterfall, had had no sense of the aesthetic. Everything had been built for a siege.

I shifted uncomfortably at that thought.

The messenger inclined his head. "*Ha-adon*'s will be done," he said. His voice was timid again. Perhaps that initial booming tone had been only for show?

"When will you begin?" Cheftu asked.

The messenger looked down, mumbling his words. "Tomorrow, *adon.* We will clear an area tomorrow."

"How long will this take?"

"You will be dwelling in your palace three months hence."

"Forgive me, father, but that is impossible," Abishi said.

The messenger turned to him, his eyes snapping. "Two days ago your liege claimed building at all was impossible. Now you say that constructing a building in three months is impossible! I do not think this word means what you think it means." He turned back to the throne, Cheftu, N'tan, Dadua, and Yoav.

He moved . . . familiarly. I frowned, trying to recall where I'd seen him or someone like him before.

"Your palace will not be completed, but you will be able to live in it by three months," the messenger said. Did anyone know his name? Did anyone else think it strange that we didn't? Cheftu's warnings about revealing names rang in my head.

"How can such an older man . . . ? But how can you build? I cannot even see how you would carry wood!" one of the soldiers commented.

"He's an overseer," someone else said.

The messenger looked at the first soldier, giving me a chance to see his face for the first time. I shivered internally. There was something familiar about him. Not the age or the coloring, but the boldness of his black gaze, perhaps. "A wise query, my large friend," the messenger said. "Perhaps all is not seen with the eye, however." He smiled, flashing big white teeth. My sense of familiarity grew.

He straightened a little, glancing my direction. His dark eyes were almost bottomless, lashed thickly. Mostly unlined. This old man wasn't quite as old as he appeared; either that or he'd been using Estée Lauder way before I was born. He turned back to Dadua. "Have you decided where you want to dwell, *adon?*"

Dadua was watching with narrowed eyes. "My reluctance is great to receive a gift from a ruler I do not know, nor do I know his gods," Dadua said. He wasn't buying any of this.

"Would you like to live above the city?"

N'tan spoke. "We will consult with our god, see where the palace should be built."

"Your god is an architect?" the messenger said, his tone almost sarcastic.

"Shaday built the heavens and the earth," N'tan said coolly. "How are we to call you?" he asked the man.

"Hiram, the same as my liege," the man responded, drawing himself up.

Cheftu's eyes bugged for a moment, then he looked away, fiddling with some papers. That name meant something, but what? We hadn't met a Hiram before. Was it historical?

"Your king worships Ba'al?" N'tan asked.

The messenger was looking a little bit put out. "My king worships no god, *adon*. He believes the earth is fruitful unto itself. He believes the sea and sky will stay in their places. He trusts there is an unknown deity who will one day be revealed, but until that point, he will not worship falsely."

He shoots; he scores! That response removed this king from the category of "idolater" neatly, enabling Dadua to pursue a relationship with him. Shaday forbade covenants with unbelievers. "Tell me of your master's palace," Dadua said.

"May I sit, *adon?* Nothing more, It's just these old bones grow weary."

Dadua not only had him seated, but offered wine and bread.

Interesting. No salt. Growing up in the Middle East, I knew that an offer of salt and bread was a banner of protection for as long as the food remained in the visitor's system—which was estimated at three days. My father always made a point to refrain from emptying his bowels until he'd left a place.

My mother had complained about this, said it wasn't healthy. He'd said it was his job. She'd made dark comments about doctors. He'd kissed her. Argument over.

The messenger was finishing his second glass of wine, seeming to savor every drop, uncaring about his audience. What a poseur, I thought. He wiped his mouth with the bread, then ate it. The *giborim* stood in the close near darkness, watching this like a play.

"My master's home is exquisite. Ashlar . . ." Hiram rattled on about the wonders of the palace. He waxed eloquent over dressed stones, polished cedar, handcrafted ivory windowsills, furniture carved and emblazoned with "images of royalty."

Dadua was leaning back, completely unmoved. I looked at Cheftu, who was distractedly spinning his scribe's brush with one hand while staring at the floor. Was he even listening?

"What do you see for *adoni*'s palace?" Yoav asked.

The messenger smiled, a grin that was devastating, a smile that would make angels weep, he was so gorgeous. He might be a hundred, but he could still model. That face, those teeth. He was perfect.

He's gotta be gay.

Then I realized who he was.

My skin turned to ice. No way; it wasn't possible, was it? I looked as Cheftu, who was still frowning and spinning. Maybe I wasn't seeing clearly; maybe I was tired; maybe I was hallucinating.

"*Adon* has a large family?" Hiram inquired.

Dadua's voice swelled with pride. "Four wives, eleven sons."

"*Ach!* A fine family. And servants? I ask because I must know how many rooms and stairwells are needed."

Avgay'el spoke: the way she and Dadua tag-teamed was something to see. "One hundred."

"*Ach!* Enough to keep all comfortable." Hiram belched. "Fine wine. My cup is dry." A steward hurried over and poured more into the man's cup.

I was right! Omigod, omigod. I could barely make myself stay still. Only knowing that every single eye in the place was on me kept me from running, screaming, from the room. It couldn't be . . . it couldn't be! Surely the world was bigger than this?

Not this court! Not this time, please, no? I glanced at Cheftu again. He hadn't realized who this Hiram was. Perhaps he would be led astray longer, by the beard, or the bangs, the apparent aging.

The messenger recovered himself to sell his images to Dadua. Terraces and private courtyards, tiled floors and tinkling fountains. Gold-inlaid furniture—at a discount, because his brother was a furniture maker and this wasn't part of Hiram's offer—then he smacked himself on the head. "*Ha-adon,* I must plead your forgiveness!"

Suddenly the room was tense. What had he done?

"My master sent a gift, a present. *Ach!* What a worthless old man am I!" He turned around and whistled. Nothing. He whistled again. Still nothing. The *giborim* had switched from leisure mode to alert. A few hands were resting on the hilts of decorated knives.

The doors flew open and a bulky thing was carried in on the back of a giant. The roomful gasped, both at the thing and at the giant. He took it off his back, with people all around ducking so he didn't take their heads off in the process, and set it down. With a strangely graceful gesture, he pulled off a cover.

We all gasped again.

It was a throne, a graceful chair, flanked with two huge winged lions. The whole thing was white, it glowed. Grapes and pomegranates were picked out in gold on the arms and legs, etched into the . . . my God, it was ivory? The giant had left and now returned with a matching footstool, upholstered in zebraskin.

Now I knew how endangered species got that way.

"*Ha-adon* asked about the beauty of the palace, the quality of the work," the messenger said. "I offer you an example."

I scooted out of Dadua's way as he left his wooden chair with hand-embroidered cushion. He circled the thing first. It was elaborate, far more majestic than anything he'd probably ever seen. Even the Egyptians would be impressed, I had to admit.

The giant kept coming in and going out, bringing other, bulky pieces. While we watched he unwrapped and assembled them. "What is that?" some *gibori* finally shouted out.

"I show," he said in a low voice. Then he picked up the throne—with Dadua in it. The *giborim* almost rushed him, but he sat Dadua down again and moved away from him. He'd slipped something beneath, a dais of sorts, and now was assembling more dazzling pieces of craftsmanship.

Only these pieces weren't white, they were black, shiny and emblazoned with more gold. He kept working, moving into the crowd, which dispersed rapidly. Finally he stood up. It was complete?

A series of seven long steps, lined with smaller winged lions, climbed to the throne.

It was . . . wow!

"Do you care for my master's work?" the messenger said. "Do you wish to accept his gift?" I looked at him again. It was so obvious, I wondered that I hadn't recognized this man right away.

Of course, without the bull's blood and exploding mountains he was a little out of context. Cheftu glanced over at me, caught by my expression. He frowned but didn't understand my mouthings and looked away.

Dadua rose regally, swept down the stairs—which were facing the opposite direction of the messenger—and went to the man. Head high, he invited the messenger to stay outside Jebus and complete the project his master had bade him. Dadua offered his soldiers and his populace to aid the architect as he saw fit.

The hospitality here was extended only as far as military coverage could back it up. Very wise, Dadua, I thought. The messenger is a wily old—it staggered me to think of how old—snake.

"As a token of my gratitude for your visit," Dadua said, "I will send your Zakar Ba'al a collection of shields gathered from our battles."

Shields? The ornamental shields or ordinary shields? I wasn't impressed.

Neither was the messenger. "That will be an honorable token to carry my master . . . up the King's Highway."

"I shall give you escort," Dadua said.

Check and mate.

"My gratitude," he said.

It was him. It was! How in the hell . . . ?

Dadua turned to his *giborim*. "May *el ha*Shaday bless you and keep you, make his face shine upon you, and be gracious unto you."

We all said, *"Sela."*

I didn't see Cheftu again until that night. Our times of privacy were few and far between since we were still living in the improvised palace and working in the fields. "Do you know who he is?" I asked hurriedly. We had only moments before we were due on the roof.

He kissed me, but for once it wasn't distracting. "Do you?" I asked.

"But of course, Hiram. It is in the Bible."

I opened my mouth, then rethought. If Cheftu didn't recognize him, maybe I should say nothing? After all, we didn't need to revisit that time in our lives or our relationship. *"Nachon!"* I said enthusiastically.

"Who did you think he was?"

I smiled and kissed him, concentrating on being distracting. However, one thought raced through my mind: It's been a thousand years, and he's still alive.

The elixir works.

The day after they received permission from Dadua, the Tsori started building. Wisely Dadua had placed them outside the city, where they would build their "quarter." By day they came in and beefed up the hill on which Dadua wanted to build his palace, making terraces of stone and filling them in with dirt, then building higher. By night they worked on their own quarter.

Within a week they opened the first floors in their quarter for business. In the Tsori section of town, one could buy a Philadelphia cream cheese knockoff, a blue glass plate to serve it on, the linens with which to set the table, and the company of a man or woman to enjoy it with you.

Tsori craftsmen quickly started a series of government offices in the lower city, sandwiching the Jebusi quarter between the *giborim* and the taxman. The Jebusi had built the city with beautiful stone, but they'd built it for war, for insularity. Though I knew why there were very few windows and tiny dark rooms, I hoped the Tsori did it better.

We were enduring the blast furnace heat of summer. Working from dawn until just after zenith, we then retired to the shade of the groves, or a courtyard, or, if really blessed, a house.

One of those days I was sitting motionless, perspiring, when

Cheftu poked his head around the corner. "*HaMelekh* requests us," he said.

"Do I get a bath first?"

He smiled. "Are you hot?"

I plucked at the long-sleeved, high-necked gown I wore, then lifted the headcloth off my neck. Because of my pasty complexion I almost had to wear armor to work. "I'll never be cool again," I groused.

He held out his hand. "What are you harvesting now?"

What weren't we harvesting? The summer produce and summer heat came together. The grapes continued to ripen; peaches, pears, and plums were almost falling off the trees; cucumbers, onions, and leeks needed to be gathered. Lettuces were picked every day. Lemons and limes, but no oranges. Had they not been discovered yet?

The olives were ripening, the pomegranate bushes were covered in red flowers, the figs were swelling with sweetness.

I followed him—it was too hot to hold hands—through the court-yards, out into the street, and down a series of thankfully shaded steps. Qiryat Dadua was silent under the blazing sun. "Egypt must be miserable right now," I thought out loud.

He flashed me a puzzled look, then walked on.

Zorak was standing guard. He greeted us both and let us in.

Déjà vu all over again, I thought. Dadua and Yoav were sprawled out on the cool floor, engaged in another round of a board game. Avgay'el, her hair tied off her neck, her arms bared, was slowly weaving. She kept nodding off in her battle with the afternoon heat. Ahino'am was sitting against the wall, a child asleep on her chest. N'tan was cross-legged on the floor, whittling. No lamps were burning.

Yoav glanced up, looked at Cheftu, then me, then back to his game. N'tan saw us and sprang up. "Che-Chavsha," he said. "And Klo-ee. Welcome."

We were bidden to sit, offered wine, and then Dadua turned away from his game. His hair was in a ponytail, and he lounged in only a patterned kilt. His sidelocks were twisted around his ears, and he was barefoot. His olive skin gleamed with sweat, but on him it looked good.

"Chavsha," he said, "I understand from N'tan that you were invaluable in the desert. Indeed I have found you so in my court. Therefore, I would like to offer you the position of scribe, officially."

Was I the only person who saw, literally saw, the pulse in Cheftu's throat race? Graciously my husband inclined his head. "I consider it an honor, *adoni*. Thy will be done."

Those black eyes turned to me. "Yoavi says that although you lived as a pagan, *isha*, you have the *nefesh* of a tribeswoman." I felt a blush beginning. "However, it is for your diplomatic expertise I invite you to join *G'vret* Avgay'el as a lady-in-waiting, also available to give advice on matters of the court."

Lady-in-waiting? But these are the years before NOW, Chloe. At least you are out of the kitchens! Would this get me out of the seasonal fieldwork? Either way there would be no more millstone. "I consider it an honor, *adoni*," I said trying to hide my smile. After all, this was the Bible. "Thy will be done."

Two others joined us. One was a new seer, from the tribe of Gad, another was a prophet who had been living in the Negev, eating locusts while he prophesied. I darted a glance at Cheftu, but he was too stunned to pay attention.

Dadua sat up so that Ahino'am could stuff some pillows behind him and refresh his wine cup. Slaves attended to the rest of us. Again I was impressed by the wheel of fate; a month ago I wasn't important enough to be in this room; now I was invited.

"Egyptians have been sighted traveling to us. The Pharaoh Smenkhare, I've heard," Yoav said to me, not meeting my eyes.

"From the west there is activity among the Pelesti, *isha*," Abishi said.

"She is *g'vret* now," Dadua corrected his general.

"*Tov, todah*," Abishi said, chastened.

"What activity?" I asked. Surely Wadia wasn't planning anything?

"We don't know, but if it continues, we will have to squelch it."

Shit, I didn't legitimately know enough about being a Philistine to know what they were doing. Please, Wadia, don't do anything foolish.

"Why would the Egyptian pharaoh be traveling here?" Dadua asked Cheftu.

"He is the co-regent of Pharaoh, not the actual ruler," Cheftu said carefully. "As for why, as Hiram has demonstrated, *adoni* is in a powerful position. Egypt uses the King's Highway also. I would imagine that Pharaoh, or whoever is traveling, seeks an audience with you to be certain those transportation rights will remain."

A cooling breeze blew through the windows. One thing about Jebus, no matter how hot it became, about four or five o'clock in the afternoon it would cool down. Avgay'el, who had been snoring softly at her loom, woke up and started weaving again. From within the courtyard sounds of Dadua's children floated in. The boys were fighting, but then they always were. Their mothers didn't help.

"*G'vret*," Dadua said, "you speak Egyptian, so you will be in charge of any needs this Egyptian might have. He travels with an army, so he will not be invited to stay in my city. However, I will provide both a welcome feast and entertainment. That is how it's done, *nachon?*"

His insecurity was endearing. "*Nachon*," I said. "Thy will be done."

The prophet and new seer sat down as I was dismissed. "Chavsha, kiss your bride, then return to keep a record of what we say," Dadua said. "*Ach*, Yoavi, tell them of the house."

Yoav looked straight at me, his green gaze blank. "*HaMelekh* has gifted you with a house in the lower *giborim* district." He turned to Cheftu. "Your belongings have already been moved." His smile was conspiratorial. "It will be a dinner meeting, so you have a few hours to collect your tools, scribe Chavsha."

"*Todah, adoni*," Cheftu said, rising up.

"Serve well, Egyptian," Dadua said.

"Thy will be done."

I stood in the corridor, waiting impatiently for Cheftu to finish one last thing before he joined me. "We have a house!" I squealed as soon as the door was closed behind him.

Zorak grinned. "Dadua takes care of his own," he said.

"Tell Waqi I will see her at the well tomorrow," I said gleefully.

Cheftu greeted Zorak and took my hand, silent as we left the temporary palace. Once outside we heard the sound of tools on stone coming down from the Milo, the area where the Tsor were building. A fine coating of white limestone dust hung in the air, covering everything.

My husband still hadn't said a word as we walked through the streets, which were just now waking up for the remainder of the day and night. The sun's heat was strong yet, but the breeze had shifted so that it cooled and refreshed. I loved this city.

He took my hand, still silent as he wandered through the narrowing streets. The lower *giborim* quarter was not luxury, but it would be ours! "We belong!" I whispered.

"You are excited about your new home?" he asked.

"Well, duh," I said in English, smiling. "One correction: Home is with you, anywhere. But I'd love to see our house."

We went up and down, through narrow streets overhung with laundry, then up a flight of stairs.

He opened the door. "Welcome, beloved," he said.

"This is our first home," I said, a little giddy.

"Oui."

I stared at him expectantly.

"Are you going to go in?" he asked.

"It is bad luck for the bride to step over the threshold; she is supposed to be carried."

"Ach! A bride?"

I crossed my arms. "I am a newlywed still. If we added up the time we've spent together in the past three years, it probably hasn't even been a year!"

He picked me up, wincing. "If I had known this, last night I might have loved you a little less, uh . . ."

"Enthusiastically?"

He chuckled, then stepped over the threshold, kicking the door closed behind him, shutting us into the darkness of our own house. "Never without enthusiasm, *chérie.*"

I kissed him, perched in his arms. Our first home. Not quite Coca-Cola, but still momentous. *I* certainly felt like crying. I wiggled free. "So let's see this place!"

It was long, narrow, and dark. Resembled an overgrown coffin. We walked to the back, then I saw the prize of the place. "It's a room with a view!" I shouted. We were a section of the city wall. Our balcony was the parapet, with a view of the fields, the valley, the mount opposite to our right, the Tsori construction upward to the left. "It's wonderful!" I launched myself at him, covered his face in kisses. "We have a home, beloved! We belong somewhere!"

"You, *G'vret* Klo-ee, belong with me," he said.

That was when I noticed the heavy gold seal around his neck, flat on his smooth chest. "Scribe Chavsha?" I said, touching it. "Your seal of office."

"The same."

"So what did they tell you that I had to stand in the corridor?" I asked.

Cheftu was watching me with a half smile. "Dadua reminded me that now we are participating members of the land. Therefore we have certain duties." He reached out a long arm, snaked it around my waist, and pulled me to him. Our feet were touching, and I felt his knees through the fabric of my skirt. A cool breeze blew from the balcony into the house. Our house. I was elated; we even got the breeze!

"Those are . . . ?" I asked a bit breathlessly, because he was staring at my mouth.

"We participate in the feasts and festivals. The New Year begins in a few weeks, then the Day of Atonement and the Sukkot."

"*Nachon,*" I said softly. "No yeast in the spring, for what, Pesach?"

He touched my nose with his finger. "You are growing spotted."

Immediately I covered my nose.

"It's cute," he said.

"It's from working outside." We were talking, but the energy between us was getting stronger, narrowing onto each other. I licked my lips, and he groaned. "Did Dadua say anything else?"

"*Ach, ken.* The most important task in the land."

"*Avayra goreret avayra?*"

He kissed the tip of my finger, and that made me whimper. "*Lo,* the most vital task in the land is this." He leaned closer to me, his breath warm on my skin. His lips hovered above my ear. "Be fruitful and multiply."

My laugh turned to a gasp. "Ooo, Chavsha, thy will be done."

CHAPTER 12

THE EGYPTIANS ARRIVED.

How my father would have been laughing to see his little girl as a liaison between the throne of Egypt and the stone-throwing David. I'd been given my own kitchen to supervise for the Egyptians, and I'd inherited the mushroom to grind my grain. A few Pelesti women and new brides among the Jebusi rounded out my diplomacy team.

The Egyptians didn't actually come up into the city, but rather camped on the far side of the Kidron valley in a sprawl of white tents, pennants, and soldiers. They lounged like cats in the shade but made no move toward the city. It would be up to us to initiate contact.

I was with Avgay'el, brushing her hair, which was what ladies-in-waiting did, when Yoav entered. He greeted her, then me. "There are two hundred Egyptians on the hillside," he said, pacing, fretting with his side curls. "Another thousand camp in the Hinon valley, still another thousand at the foot of Har Nebo."

"Have they done anything?" I asked, still brushing.

"*Lo.*"

"What sources do they have for water?"

"They're digging wells."

So they intended to stay for a while, and they realized that Dadua would not be opening up the city to them. "What do the pennants say?"

"Smenkhare, living in the Aten," he said, "forever." Someday I was going to ask him about his education. A tribesman who was literate was impressive; one who spoke and read other languages was almost unheard-of. "The tribespeople are ostensibly gathering the olives, but in reality watching the Egyptians," Yoav said, chuckling. "It's better than having spies. Instead I have grandmothers who make up in observation what they lack in eyesight."

It would be interesting: the Israelites with their brightly colored clothing, sashes, and fringe and long curling locks, next to the Egyptians, who were sleek, clothed only in white and gold, with painted eyes and straight hair.

"Should we send a message asking Pharaoh if the view is good, and by the by, why is he so very far away from his flat land and his many gods?" Yoav threw up his hands.

"How is the audience chamber coming?" I asked. "Will it be ready in the next few days?"

Yoav shrugged. "It could be. I will speak to Hiram."

"Then we will send an invitation to Smenkhare inviting him to present himself in court to *haMelekh* Dadua and his court." I looked at Avgay'el. "Can we do this in the middle of the harvest season?"

Dadua's wife smiled. "Whatever he needs, give him."

"Then excuse me, *adoni, g'vret,*" I said, and hustled out of there.

Fortunately *Shabat* was between the time that Smenkhare arrived and the time that . . . Hiram of Tsor arrived. *Shabat* afternoon's peace was torn by a shout from the wall. Someone was approaching the valley gate. It was close enough to walk, so Cheftu and I joined the throng that watched, bemused.

"He approaches! He approaches!" we heard shouted from below. Criers stood on the road, calling out, pointing.

Who was arriving?

"Hiram comes! Hiram Zakar Ba'al comes!"

I eyed the criers and put them down to a marketing ploy; they weren't Jebusi or tribesmen. Obviously they were part of the team to make Hiram—did the Tsori have any other names?—seem a big man.

"By the power of Shaday, what is that?" someone, a genuine citizen, shouted. We peered over the rocky wall to the mountain road opposite us.

Hiram of Tsor, Zakar Ba'al, traveled in great comfort—not to mention style.

"*Zut alors,*" Cheftu breathed. "What is that thing?"

"An . . . elephant," I said. Granted, it was a dwarf elephant, or it wouldn't have been able to get up the hills, but still, an elephant? Riding guards was a band of . . . women? They were hard to discern, but they didn't look like men. One shifted her shield, and the crowd gasped.

Holy shit!

"Are those Amazons?" Cheftu asked me.

"In Israel?" I said in English. "I didn't know elephants had ever even been in the Middle East," I said. "Much less warrior women." Yet in the back of my head, in my mother's softly proper British accent, I heard mention of pygmy elephants from Africa. Was Israel Africa? My head was spinning, watching this group grow closer. On the back of the elephant was a little Quonset-style hut, swaying to and fro with the motion.

Just seeing that made me feel a little seasick.

This colorful team was approaching the walls. "Smenkhare's audience is tomorrow," I said. "But Zakar Ba'al isn't going to give us much choice if he just shows up at the city gates."

Cheftu looked at the sky. "It is a full watch before *Yom Rishon* begins," he said. "It will take him some while to get across the hills on that creature, though," he commented. The elevation was nowhere as steep as the Kidron valley or Hinon valley side, but they were already encamped with Egyptians and not much of a pathway. North of us, in the new, unenclosed section of town, the Tsori rested through this day, as did all the tribesmen.

"He's out of luck," I whispered in English. "He'll just have to wait."

After a while watching the Amazons and the elephant navigate the hills grew old, so we returned to our house. The minute the *shofar* sounded that night, however, we raced toward the audience chamber. Soldiers flew down the stairs with us, as we all hightailed it to the palace. We burst into the new throne room.

Chaos.

Avgay'el was in high dress, her hair trailing into the hands of a Jebusi serving girl, who was trying valiantly to braid it, while keeping up with Dadua's wife. Dadua had been wet on by his son, so he was dabbing frantically at his one-shouldered tunic while Shana screamed for another.

N'tan rushed into the room, his white clothing bloodstained.

Shana screamed at him, "You! What are you doing? What kind of *tzadik* is covered in blood?"

"I was casting omens," he shouted back, pulling off the tunic and scrambling for another. It was like backstage at a fashion show!

The *zekenim* leaders adjusted their cloaks while slaves scurried around, trying to create the illusion of wealth and plenty, and the *giborim* helped each other with armor.

Honestly, if the man was riding an elephant, he would know full well that Dadua was neither wealthy nor did we have plenty. He was the one building the palace.

However, this was marketing, which I understood.

Therefore we scrambled for the illusion.

Zakar Ba'al arrived less than an hour later. What did he see? I wondered. We stood in form: wives, children, soldiers, private guard, and attendants all dressed in red—assuming that since he was from Tsor, his people would be in royal blue—with gold.

We were in the new audience room in the upper city. It was a spacious chamber open to the sky, though linen curtains tied with elaborate tassels, which had been finished only the day before, canopied the space. The cedar ashlar walls gleamed, having been polished with beeswax while they were being placed. Dadua's throne and dais commanded center stage, with the rest of us lined on both sides. A blind musician—why were they always blind in ancient times?—strummed softly in the corner. I did a double take when I saw that Cheftu was seated cross-legged on the floor, a quill and scroll in hand. The scribe Chavsha winked at me before tucking his sidelocks behind his ears.

Though he hadn't recognized Hiram the builder, I knew Hiram recognized him. I was completely out of the recognition loop, because my red hair and pale skin served better than any disguise. What was that man's angle? I wondered.

As we waited for the royalty to show, I checked on the slaves. They stood at the ready with wine jugs and cups, baskets of fresh figs and grapes, pickled cucumbers, and grilled Ashqeloni onions to offer for refreshment.

Everything was clean, primped, primed, and polished. Let the games begin.

First the Zakar Ba'al's Amazons entered. They looked like stars from a B-movie about bimbos and aliens. Their clothing was skimpy, they were gorgeous—but they had only one breast, which along with their scars was bared to the eye.

There were twelve altogether. Each woman stood with her hand on her weapon, her legs apart. They looked aggressive, even mean. More than that, they were silent, gesturing to each other with the briefest of hand signals. Deaf Amazons?

Next were the servants. They were pierced and tattooed like punk rock teenagers, though nearly naked. They fell onto their faces, evenly spaced between the twelve Amazons. It was a good thing the new room was large, because all these people never would have fit in the old one.

Then the three body servants entered, young men, wearing peacock feather skirts. That particular shade of azure brought back a wealth of memories from Greece.

The whole group hit the floor in sync as Hiram Zakar Ba'al appeared in the doorway. I stared, thunderstruck. That deceptive, manipulative rat, I thought.

I looked over at Cheftu. The color had drained from his face. In fact, he looked as though he'd eaten too much squash; he was sort of yellowish green. One of those peacock feathers could have tipped him over in shock.

After the glamour of his entourage, Hiram himself was rather understated. His dark curling hair was very short, his beard was closely clipped, his clothing was nearly somber, his makeup and jewelry were restrained. Two things made him shattering. One, he wore a coiled serpent around his neck—not a gold representation, but the real thing.

And two, I knew his eyes. I'd seen them more recently in his masquerade of being the Tsori master builder. What was his reason for all of this? What had happened to the white hair and beard? I watched him walk forward, the gilded fringe of his skirt rustling faintly above the noise of the musician. Dadua's court said nothing, just observed him silently.

His eyes were fixed on Cheftu with such intensity, I was surprised that the air hadn't incinerated.

When I'd seen him as Hiram's messenger, when I'd avoided him as such, I'd been amazed that he was still alive. I'd also felt a petty amount of glee that he had aged. Apparently the aging had been merely a costume.

Dion still had the looks and bearing of . . . well, the Prince of Darkness. Satan was allegedly the most beautiful of all God's creatures. There was a strong possibility that Dion might have been, might *still* be, Satan.

Unwillingly I looked at Cheftu. His dumbfounded gaze was on me; even the blind musician could see this triangle. *"G'vret,"* someone whispered, "the Egyptians are here."

Of course they are, I thought. "Check our stores, refill the wine jugs," I instructed, while Dion's despised voice recited the greetings of one king to another.

HaNasi welcomed the master of Tsor, his speech fluid even though his eyes were cold. Dion inquired about the health of the king, which N'tan answered. Cheftu seemed intent on taking minutes of the meeting. What was he thinking? I at least had known Dion was alive, but how did Cheftu feel?

There was another rustle at the doorway—the Egyptians—and a child entered, throwing white flower petals on the floor. Her youthlock, ringed eyes, and copper skin made it obvious she was from the Nile valley.

A squadron of Egyptian soldiers with long painted eyes, white kilts, and gold armor followed her, trailed by three priests with shaved heads, wearing leopardskins, filling the air with incense.

As the hostess, I was counting people and guessing how much they would drink. The slaves were milling about, serving wine to the *giborim* who were present—fortunately not that many—and the assorted minor kings who had attached themselves to Dadua.

"The Crown Prince of Upper and Lower Egypt! The Glory of the Aten at Dawn! He Who Rises in the East, He Who Reigns with the Aten!" and on and on the bilingual chamberlain went, announcing this person. Others from Hiram/Dion's entourage had slipped in, advisers, seers, nobles, the hangers-on with whom every king traveled.

They all needed wine.

"He Who Loves the Aten," the chamberlain continued, "Tutankhaten!"

I almost fell over. If I'd been carrying anything, I would have dropped it. No way! I must be hallucinating or dreaming or both. I watched as a little boy was carried in on a little-boy-size golden throne. I recognized his beautiful face instantly because I'd grown up seeing it! This was the boy-king of Egypt!

Tutankhaten? Tutankhamun? David and Tutankhaten?

Not even Cheftu would recognize this significance. This was my piece of history alone. I picked up counting again while the formalities were exchanged. Tutankhaten was a child, not even in puberty yet, his voice high but strong. Then he stepped aside, and the chamberlain started reading a new list of titles: Pharaoh's honorifics.

Smenkhare was announced.

I looked back to the doorway. Gold glittered on him everywhere, from the diadem on his shaven head to the eye paint on his eyes to the . . . *he* had *breasts?* I waved away a slave's question while I stared at the androgynous person before me.

Of course I knew from my sister that controversy raged among twentieth-century Egyptologists as to whether or not Akhenaten had been male or female, straight or gay, a transvestite, a cross-dresser, or the victim of some obscure illness that gave men breasts. Since Smenkhare was a cousin . . .

But that face. The features were all wrong for Egypt. His nose or hers, or whatever, was more Greek.

Something shattered, and I looked away. Dion, as Hiram, stared at Smenkhare the same way he'd stared at Cheftu two months ago. I looked at Cheftu, who was intently focused on his work, not that there was anything to write, since no one was saying anything.

The court was agog, because while this creature had small but still apparent breasts, he/she also displayed an impressive bulge in his/her kilt.

Of course, that's because I saw only in silhouette.

"Greetings from Pharaoh, he who reigns in the Aten forever!" the chamberlain, now acting as translator, said.

"Egypt welcomes Dadua ben Yesse to the realm of rulers." Even the voice was hard to tell. Male or female? The *giborim* were mystified, defensive. The Amazons ignored him/her, and Dion's expression didn't belong on the face of a man who'd lived a thousand years. It was too surprised. What did he see?

Cheftu looked up, and his mouth dropped open.

Curiosity was killing me. I edged around the crowd, keeping pace as Smenkhare advanced into the chamber. Tall, tanned, and wiry strong, the legs were covered by a long kilt, but the arms were a woman's?

Dadua looked revulsed as Smenkhare approached. Cross-dressing just wasn't done in this court. In fact, there were religious laws against men and women dressing alike. I slipped to the side behind Avgay'el, from where I could see out.

A woman stood there, dressed as a man. Despite the lack of curly black hair, I knew that face!

I'd worn it, after all. My world was tilting; she stepped forward, elegant, graceful, and distinctly predatory.

She was Sibylla, the seeress whose body I'd inhabited in ancient Aztlan; she was Dion's aunt and the body Cheftu had known as mine. Gold glistened on her dark skin, while her almond-shaped eyes glittered maliciously at us all. "Pharaoh himself is far too busy to visit, to welcome." She stepped farther into the room.

So, my racing mind reasoned. You have your body; the spirit of Sibylla hasn't had a body in a while. The Egyptian body was destroyed in Greece. Which leaves two spirits and two bodies. I was one of them—in my own body. Which left a missing body and spirit.

"I AM his beloved, Smenkhare."

The court gasped.

The ancient, time-traveling priestess RaEmhetepet, wearing the skin of the Aztlan seeress Sibylla, masquerading as Smenkhare, Pharaoh's male co-regent, gazed at the court in whole. Please don't look at me, I thought. Please don't see me.

"She blasphemes!" one of the *zekeni* shouted. "She must be stoned!"

He was immediately muffled by his brothers; one did not even jest about stoning Pharaoh. RaEm and Dion eyeballed each other; I noticed the heat in the room had risen.

All of my lives were gathered in one place. I craved a cigarette with every fiber of my body. Cheftu still stared, stunned. Dion glared. RaEm was . . . Pharaoh?

Dadua sat on the throne, regal, motionless. "I bid you welcome, Smenkhare of Egypt. For the sake of my tribesmen and my god, I must ask that you refrain from using his name."

RaEm was wearing the blue helmet, the war helmet. A faint line creased her painted brows. She really did look great—considering I knew what that particular body had been through, that was impressive. "I AM unaware of your god, *adon.*"

I was impressed; she was speaking whatever language this was: Hebrew? Akkadian? Pelesti?

N'tan smiled faintly. "Our god's name *is* I AM."

Suddenly it made sense! No wonder I had never been able to say "I am." It wasn't just a statement of identity; it was a statement of eternity, the perfect name for an unfathomable deity. I AM was a clause of perpetuity: I was that I am that I will be, endless and immutable.

"Neither are we to use Shaday's name to swear by, to take oaths with, to cry in less than prayer and supplication," N'tan added quickly.

I thought of the many times "god" punctuated my thoughts. Since I hadn't used his proper name, was I safe?

"When your gods Amun-Ra, HatHor, Ma'at, when these gods faced our God in Egypt, your priests asked the name of our God," N'tan said.

"Amun-Ra is himself unknowable," RaEm said stiffly. I marveled at how sexless but beautiful she looked. Did everyone know she was female? Or . . . I was confused. "But the Aten rules now. Only the Aten," she said.

N'tan shrugged. "It is no matter, Pharaoh. Here our God is known as Shaday. You will refrain from using his name." There was a lot of steel in N'tan's voice. I cringed; he was telling Pharaoh what to do? More than that, he was telling RaEm what to do?

Surprisingly enough, she inclined her head. "I will strive to honor my hosts."

Then it dawned on me: I was the liaison. I would see her face-to-face. I bit my lips to keep from cursing out loud.

"What brings you so far from the Nile?" N'tan asked.

"It is the time for tribute, for sharing with a new brother in the family of nations," she said. "To welcome Dadua into suzerainty with Egypt."

We all stood very still: Egypt was demanding a payoff in return for leaving the tribes alone.

N'tan stood very tall, looking like a prophet. "We are honored by"— he sounded as though he were choking on the words—"mighty Egypt's interest and will certainly gift My"—he coughed—"Majesty before he returns to his fertile river home."

RaEm moved her eyes over the people, cool and calm, every inch a pharaoh. Hatshepsut had taught her well. "I will enjoy your cool hills this summer and will delight in returning to Kemt with this budding nation's offerings to Egypt."

After a long silence Dadua spoke reluctantly. "You are invited to stay. My palace is still under construction, but every effort will be made for your comfort." Mimi would have docked him hospitality points for his lack of enthusiasm. Then again, his house *was* under construction. "Our celebration of the New Year begins day after tomorrow."

RaEm raised her chin a notch. "I wish you well on its eve. Do you celebrate?"

Dion was glaring ferociously at RaEm, then glancing at Cheftu. I felt like laughing because Dion anticipated that I was she and expected Cheftu to react to that. Meanwhile RaEm knew what I looked like as me, but Dion didn't. So she was also looking at Cheftu, probably surprised that he was alive and casing him to see if I was around.

And I had to feed and entertain all these people.

"It is a month for celebrations," Dadua said. "In weeks we will bring the totem of my people into this city as its new home."

"I have heard of this marvel," RaEm said.

"Then you must of course stay," he responded coolly. "As you are also invited, Zakar Ba'al."

Dion bowed his head just a fraction. Modern business power plays were managed by who spoke first. Now, they were using the degree and angle of head inclinations in the same way. In my time, he who made someone wait carried the power. Here, he, or she, who bowed his, or her, head the least seemed to broker it.

Dadua was holding his own well, especially considering he didn't have the experience of his fellow rulers. He really *was* a Bronze Age Bible character. RaEm had played around in the twentieth-century world. I guess Dion had lived through the past millennia. They both had a right to more polish, but Dadua was recognizably a king.

How had RaEm become Pharaoh? I was dizzy with questions.

Avgay'el touched my hand, speaking from the corner of her mouth. "Is dinner ready?"

Hysterical laughter bubbled up. She had an immortal—make that two—three time travelers, the founder of the nation of Israel, and twelve Amazons in this audience chamber, and she was worried about dinner?

"Klo-ee?" she repeated my name.

Yep, she was worried about dinner. "Thy will be done," I said on my way out.

The New Year (*Rosh*—first; *ha*—the; *shan'a*—year) began with the *shofar* blowing. Each family would eat sweet things, pray to Shaday, and prepare for the Day of Atonement.

Cheftu was cracking nuts and eating the meats as we sat on our balcony, watching the sky darken with night. It was our first moment together alone since the weirdness that was a transvestite RaEm and Hiram Revealed had showed up.

"She's Pharaoh?" I commented, still amazed.

He grunted.

"Has she said anything to you?"

"*Lo*, though there has been no time, with the feasting, the harvesting, the preparing for the day, and the return of the totem."

"Has he?" I asked, though my tone was a little arch.

"*Lo*, nothing."

I leaned my head back, looking up at the stars. "Why are we here? Just how screwed up is history that RaEm is on the Egyptian throne? My sister the Egyptologist would completely freak out at how we've messed up the past with this crazed ancient Egyptian!"

"Do you not like being here?"

"I'm with you, but you must admit it's kind of odd. Nothing is blowing up, no one is sick. There are no fires, no locusts. In fact, I don't know what our purpose here is at all."

He looked up. "Perhaps simply living?"

I sighed, antsy. "Perhaps."

"Dadua just completed negotiations for the plateau above the Tsori Milo," Cheftu commented. We could see it from our balcony if I leaned out really far from the southern corner of the window.

"More land for us to inhabit?"

Cheftu's gaze sharpened. "Is there an 'us'?"

"You and me," I said. "Just you and me."

We harvested the olives by spreading linens beneath the trees, then using long poles to shake the branches so that it rained olives.

RaEm and Dion sat on opposite hills, alternately seeking audiences with Dadua. RaEm wanted gold; Dion wanted access. Dadua gave RaEm some gold; he assured Dion of escorted access. Still they sat sprawled over the mountaintops, their entourages mingling in the city, growing lax under the summer heat, glowering at each other, trying to get more out of *haMelekh.*

Cheftu wrote: letters to Abdiheba's old vassals, demanding tribute; documents that created a formal state with a governing structure; and transcriptions of N'tan stories. Around him the Tsori built the city of Jerusalem.

Avgay'el was pregnant again. Mik'el never showed up for anything, ever. The mushroom sprouted breasts, and somehow her teeth began fitting in her mouth. The heat of summer faded into Indian summer— though pre-Indian, it seemed a strange statement. And every night Cheftu took delight in trying to impregnate me.

It was *Shabat* morning, in the courtyard of the under-construction palace, where we all still were after the evening's storytelling and feasting. The court—*giborim,* wives, priests, seers, and the ever-present minor nobles—were lying about in the sunshine like cats. My head was on Cheftu's knee as we lazily munched grapes, listening to some musicians plink and pluck.

From inside the palace there was a shout; doors slammed against walls, then another shout. Running footsteps, then Dadua stepped into the sunshine. The *giborim* were just getting used to treating him like royalty, affording him the protocol his station demanded, but there was a delayed reaction before we all knelt.

"I have heard from Shaday," he said without preamble. This was news; Dadua had been mournful because Shaday had been silent. "He has told me how to build his house," he said.

God's house? What would that be? I wondered. Not a church or a synagogue—omigod. Suddenly I was fighting the urge to shiver and run. God's house, on the Temple Mount? I swallowed.

Dadua unrolled a sheaf of papyrus. "I dreamed, then drew the plans." Motioning for us to step forward, he began to describe the House of Shaday.

"It must be finely wrought from cedar and gold," he said. "A temple that shows the most beautiful side to the world, but encases Shaday."

I looked at the plan. It seemed fairly small, compared with Karnak, where Amun-Ra was worshiped, or Knossos, home of the mother-goddess, but very elaborate. "It will be a permanent Tent of Meeting," he said.

Dadua was pointing to the drawing. "The outer court is here, where the sea and the fires are."

The sea was a huge basin of water. Huge. Sitting on the back of life-size bronze calves. The fires were at the top of ziggurat-looking buildings, a place for sacrifice. "This will be the outer court, where those who are not tribesmen, but who believe in Shaday, may come to be close to his glory."

His finger moved to the next enclosure. "This will be the court for women to worship. Here and here," he said, moving his finger to the left and right, "will be storage rooms for the Levim priests." The next space was the court for men, then for priests only, and finally only the high priest would enter the room with the Seat of Mercy.

"The two pillars from the current tabernacle will front the building. The whole thing will be from limestone and cedar, the interior walls coated in gold, then etched with pomegranates and the winged lion of my tribe."

I watched the raised eyebrows among the *giborim*. With those emblems he would be making a clear point.

God's House. The Temple in Jerusalem. David went on to explain that this Temple would not belong to any one tribe; it would be the property of this city, which was the possession of Dadua. The strategic position of Jerusalem would be not only in bridging the tribes of the north and south, but also in housing their holiest relic. Dadua would not only be king, he would be comptroller of the faith.

He showed another piece of papyrus filled with his passionate but illegible writing. "These are the outbuildings, the priests' offices." He indicated how they would link through an underground passageway to the governmental offices below.

"What does this symbol mean?" Yoav asked, pointing to a repeating character.

"Covered in gold," Dadua said.

The whole Temple was going to be gold.

We looked at the Temple drawings in silence. I wondered if these tough soldiers realized how this building was going to change everything. Had they brought back enough gold to do all of this?

"What say you, N'tan?"

"Most excellent, *haNasi!* This beauty is sure to please Shaday. These plans will be simple to execute. However, there is a great deal of gold needed."

Dadua met his prophet's gaze until N'tan bowed his head. "Thy will be done."

The Feast of the *Shofar*, or New Year's, segued into plowing season, interrupted by the Day of Atonement. Solemnly we stood on the walls and parapets and streets of the city, watching as a priest tied a red sash around the goat's neck.

One goat was sacrificed before the totem in Qiryat Yerim, coating everything in sacramental blood. We didn't see that part. Another goat, the one with the red sash symbolic of the tribes' transgressions, was sent into the Hinon valley to live with the garbage. He was the inspiration for the term *scapegoat*. The rumor was that if Shaday forgave the tribesmen their offenses, the red sash would turn white miraculously.

Nothing was eaten on this day. We didn't bathe or dress ourselves, as an outward sign of the internal realization of how we needed to strive after god. Although Cheftu and I weren't tribesmen, we followed the ritual.

The next morning the tribesmen were back to plowing and I was back to avoiding RaEm, Dion, and the entire surrealistic mess. RaEm wanted more gold; Dion—was just watching and waiting. He hadn't sought out Cheftu, so maybe he had changed?

At dusk the *shofar* blew, summoning us to the city gates. Dadua stood above us, the dying sun creating a ruddy nimbus around his head. Abiathar, the high priest, stood to one side, Dadua's wives to the other. I was beside Cheftu.

"Good people of Jebus," Dadua said, "my friends, my family, my *giborim*. The vines grow heavy with fruit all around us, all about us *el ha*Shaday blesses our efforts throughout the land. In worship of him I have decided that the city of Jebus will no longer be known by this name. No more will the gods, the traditions, or the bloodthirsty rituals of the Jebusi be commemorated.

"Tonight Jebus is reborn as a city apart from the tribes. A city fought for and won by myself and the *giborim*. It will be called Tziyon. This is the name *el ha*Shaday has himself given it."

What did Tziyon mean?

"No longer a part of Binyami or Yuda, but a royal city.

"Tziyon will be a city devoted to peace, to the worship of *el ha*Shaday. I will open her gates to any who seek to share their wisdom, knowledge, or skill with the tribes. Artisans may journey from any land to rest within her gates. Craftsmen from any tribe will be welcome at my table in exchange for their training. Scholars, scribes, and seers are forever after invited to stay for study, discussion, and to educate each other and us."

I was floored. He was talking nothing less than a Bronze Age renaissance! No wonder David had gone down in the history books. Especially *the* history book.

He continued speaking. "The quarter once known for its prostitutes and idol shops will become an avenue of actors."

Actors? But the lexicon in my brain said, *Actors = philosophers = thinkers.* In this language there was no term for something as sedentary as thinking, no concept of an action with no visible end result. There were no verbs that didn't actually move.

"Already we are gathering scrolls from every country and culture to be stored here, available to any who seek knowledge."

"A library?" I said to Cheftu, speaking over the starting cheers.

He nodded, grinning.

Dadua pointed out where the new market would be; how the Street of Merchants would be expanded; where the new sectors of the city would be with new housing going up—literally—from here.

This was going to be one hopping place, I thought. An open call for artistic types in a city that was already bursting at its seams. "Above us," Dadua said, "I have purchased the Jebusi threshing ground, and there we will place the Tent of Meeting and totem. Tomorrow."

The shouts were deafening.

Tomorrow the court and the country would travel to Qiryat Yerim by cart, along with most of the other tribesmen who could make it, and escort the Seat here, where it would stay forever. By moving the Mercy Seat here, Dadua was creating a theocracy. Both government and religion would be served by the same bodies and ruled by the same laws.

Cheftu and N'tan would be leaving right after dinner, along with the other priests, seers, prophets, et cetera.

Since Dion and RaEm were both still here, I was still on the clock. Smenkhare—who plagued us all with constant demands for more, whether it be food, wine, or Dadua's gold—and Dion—alternating his costumes between Hiram the king and Hiram the contractor—were camped out. Dion was observing the building of the city's addition from his mountain outpost; Smenkhare, RaEm, was lounging opposite, thinking of new ways to indebt Dadua to her. Tomorrow night an even bigger feast—this one with stuffed quail, since they were easy to find as they migrated south—was my responsibility.

"So to Shaday, who gives more than we ask, who shows unceasing *chesed*, be these blessings on you and your families. May he make his face shine upon you and give you peace."

As though choreographed, the first three stars shone in the sky.

"Tomorrow" had begun.

I joined the parade route with Zorak, Waqi, and the baby. We were part of a larger group that included Yoav's wives, Abishi, and his new Jebusi bride. The pathway down from Jebus was packed. People already had their positions on the road, where they were indulging in tailgate parties even without tailgates. Wine flowed, music filled the entire eight-mile journey, and the general mood was feverish and anticipatory—just like Mardi Gras, despite the polarity in motive.

Yoav and the *giborim* stood as an honor guard before the walls of the city, while the ramparts themselves were already filling up with people. The closer we got to Qiryat Yerim, the more densely packed the way became. People, all drinking, singing, and dancing, filled the roads, the hillsides, the valleys. If we hadn't been VIPs, we might never have gotten close. Still, it was hours before we arrived.

I saw Cheftu across the way, standing at N'tan's side. He smiled at me and toasted me silently with his wineskin. The mass stood before a barn-like structure where the Mercy Seat had been kept since it was sent back from the Pelesti two decades ago.

We waited. Priests milled about in their best. Any moment now the doors would fly open, and with a shout the Mercy Seat would be pulled forth. Or so I'd been told.

The crowd inhaled sharply as the *shofar* sounded. Slowly, beardless Levim boys pushed open the doors. The people held their breath. According to Shana, who thought I was still an ignorant Pelesti despite my free status, no one had seen this totem of the tribes for the past twenty years. N'tan, even as a *tzadik*, had glimpsed it only once.

Rumors and legends had grown up around the Mercy Seat in the years it hadn't been used. It caused plague, it fought other deities, the *elohim* on it portrayed how Shaday felt about his people.

How that was possible, I couldn't guess.

The mass craned forward, curious and demanding. This was *their* totem. They wanted to see it, to see if its magic worked, to learn if the tales were true. It would be a formidable weapon. The conversations flew around me as the wagon rolled out.

The Seat was a rectangular gold box. Standing on its top were two winged creatures, *elohim*, embracing each other beneath the swoop of their combined wingspan. God was purported to sit enthroned between the *elohim*. The sun was blinding on the cover, the actual place where Shaday dwelt when he stayed with the tribesmen.

I blinked, dizzy. Was I having a Paramount movie flashback?

The gold-plated cart was being pulled forward at a majestic pace by two white oxen, garlanded with flowers for the occasion. The shock wore off the throng, and the noise level grew exponentially.

The Be'ma Seat, the Mercy Seat. Only I knew it by another name, famous for being lost, famous for fictionally being found: the Ark of the Covenant.

How could anyone sit between the *elohim?* I wondered. They were in such a cli— I frowned, looking at the golden statues. Hadn't they been hugging? Now they were facing each other, male and female figures, holding hands.

I could have sworn—

The oxen walked forward, the Ark wobbling on the flatbed of the wagon. I frowned; wasn't the Ark supposed to be carried on poles? "What is in it?" I asked out loud.

"Within it, according to *tzadikim,*" the man next to me said, "are the original stones of the Commandments. The ones written in Shaday's own hand. *Ha*Moshe threw them down—"

"You know he was in a fury," someone else added. "But how could they know? Our forefathers had been slaves for centuries!"

"Our forefathers were worshiping an idol."

"We'd been Mizra—"

"*Ach!* Silence yourselves," some woman said. Strangely enough, every-one fell quiet as we watched.

After a moment the first man, who was a bit older and more edu-cated, edged closer to me, answering my question. "Also inside are Aharon's budded rod, which proved *el ha*Shaday had chosen the Levim as high priests forever. Last, it contains a jar of manna, the honeyed food of the desert sojourn."

My helpful neighbor also explained that God had designed the Levim robes: they were to be white, with bells and pomegranates on the hems, embroidered in white and gold. They wore turban-type head cov-erings of blue or white, depending on their position.

"There is the high priest," Zorak said to us, "Abiathar." The man walked by solemnly, his breastplate sparkling in the sunlight. "Those stones each represent a tribe," Zorak said. I looked at the high priest's or-nament. Twelve etched gems were set onto a metal chest covering, in three rows of four.

The tribespeople were drinking and laughing as they watched the Ark trundle by.

"The ruby on the breastplate is for Reuben, topaz for Tsimeon, beryl for Gad, turquoise for Yuda, lapis lazuli for Y'sakhar, emerald for Zebu-lon, jacinth for Efra'im, agate for Mana'sa, amethyst for Binyamim, chrysolite for Dan, onyx for Asher, and jasper for Naftali," Zorak said in a rush. I looked at Waqi, but she was focused on the baby.

"Memorized that?" I teased.

"Everything must be memorized," he said, watching the street. "We are to be a nation who remember."

"*Sela!*" said my neighbor.

The people were throwing wreaths of flowers before the Seat, showering the priests in petals and praise. A woman danced seductively in front of the Ark, welcoming Shaday in a tone and manner that sent shouts into the air. Undulating before it, her smile wide and her gestures unmistakable, she looked more like a pagan priestess than a worshiper, but what did I know? Dadua's smile was fixed, the finery of his crown and clothing as impressive as the priests'.

CHEFTU WATCHED THE WOMAN: though she was lovely, she did not stir him. Her style of rejoicing seemed rather inappropriate to welcome the presence of the living God. Beyond her he saw Chloe, smiling with her friend Waqi, drinking wine underneath the still-hot sun. The mood of celebration was contagious. Even the priests were laughing, jovial.

Dadua rode behind the Mercy Seat in another gold-covered cart, waving at the people, accepting gifts of wine and kisses. This was the first day of officially recognizing Jebus as Tziyon, capital of the tribes, his own city. It was a day of celebration.

A day of idolistic celebration.

There seemed very little difference between this and the many Egyptian rituals of which Cheftu had been a part. The Be'ma Seat was being worshiped much as a statue of a god. The people were wild with their senses as they escorted *their* Ark into *their* city. They walked and danced beside the oxen.

N'tan stood beside him, watching the Seat pass. He glanced at

Cheftu. "Why do you frown? Is this not the day that the stones admonished us to bring in the Seat?"

"You've never seen other lands, have you?" Cheftu asked.

"Nor other times," N'tan said, tipping back his wineskin. "Why do you ask?"

Cheftu watched the milling, dancing, drinking horde, aware that he could be in any of the times and places he had lived. Human nature did not seem to alter with the passage of years. "Shaday admonished you to keep separate, did he not?" he mused. "Ways to remember this were to not wear or use interwoven fabrics, grow no intermingled orchards, tolerate no mixing of milk and meat?"

"*B'seder,*" N'tan said impatiently as they moved forward, pushed by the bulk of the viewers, all sweating. It was a long walk back to Jebus, Tziyon, but it was eased by the glee and abandon of the moment.

"*Ach,* well, these things are all examples. Daily reminders that you are to lead lives separate from the uncircumcised, *nachon?*"

N'tan was smiling, staring at the Seat. "It is covered in gold. It is beautiful, *nachon?* Won't it be perfect in Dadua's temple, the most precious stone in the richest of settings?"

Cheftu looked at the Seat, frowning more. Had it looked that way before? The male and female gold statues on the cover were positioned on the far edges of the piece, leaving at least a cubit and a half between them. He looked away. There was something familiar about this, though he couldn't remember what. His gaze met Chloe's again. Across the stream of people she blew a kiss at him. Cheftu caught it and returned it, smiling. He was faultfinding, he admonished himself, why wasn't he enjoying the day?

Because . . .

The procession was moving slowly, making its way through the press of raucous tribesmen as they neared the huge threshing floor of Kidon, the last stop before Tziyon. It was uphill from there to the city, but the tribesmen seemed not to notice. All around, the hills were terraced with vines, sprinkled with the red of pomegranates, rich with the bounty of the land. It was beautiful. But they are admonished to be a different people, Cheftu thought again. Perhaps, though—

The crowd crashed to a halt.

A slip.

A slide.

A Levi reached forward.

"Lo!" the people screamed.

Fire exploded from the sliding Seat with a mighty *zzzzp.*

The Levi fell to the ground, screaming, clutching his arm. "I burn! Help me! Help!"

The oxen tried in terror to get away, and the Seat slid farther.

Gasping, clawing his chest, the priest writhed on the ground.

The Seat fell with a jarring thud, flames shooting out from it.

In mass chaos the people fled, trampling each other, screeching with fear as they raced away from the totem. Cheftu fought his way to the Levi's side, dragged back by the bolting crowd as they tried to escape the Seat. Finally Cheftu broke free and ran to the man, kneeling beside him. The oxen bucked, edging the Seat farther up on end, two corners of it wedging into the dirt, the cover sliding. Tribesmen and -women screamed and cried, threw themselves on the ground, and raced for the hills, fleeing Shaday's wrath.

Cheftu's hands moved over the man's body, ascertaining what was damaged. Bits of bloody foam flecked the priest's lips. His hair was on end, and scorch marks streaked his chest with black. Cheftu closed the dead man's staring eyes, then he looked up. Only seven people—no Chloe, thank God—the frantic oxen, the instrument of death, and the resultant corpse were left. It was eerily silent.

"To touch the Seat is death," N'tan whispered. "I thought it was a punishment we were supposed to enact."

"Looks like Yahwe took that decision from your hands," Cheftu said, his nostrils filled with the smell of burned flesh. He glanced up at the box, sitting at a seventy-five-degree angle in the road, erroneously named the Mercy Seat.

N'tan took a step forward. "Stay back," Cheftu said.

"This man—"

"Tzadik," one of the remaining priests said, "you are not to touch the dead. You are a priest."

Was that yet another gibe at the religion of Egypt? Cheftu wondered.

"What happened?" Dadua asked in stunned voice, running up from his cart, Avgay'el behind him. He knelt beside the body, also not touching it, staring into the man's face, eyeing the Seat askance. "What happened?" His wife touched his shoulder as she tried to calm him.

"Shaday struck him down," N'tan said slowly. "The penalty is death."

"He was trying to keep it from falling!" one of the priests burst out.

"What exactly occurred?" Dadua asked, turning to the young man.

"The cart, it must have hit a rut." The priest gestured toward the Seat. "The Be'ma began to slide and, and . . ." His face crumpled. "He tried to keep it from falling! That was all. There was no . . . he didn't . . ." He buried his face in his hands. Dadua embraced him, glaring over the youth's shoulder.

Cheftu looked at the body, remembering what happened. What had that sound been? That *zzzzzp* sound? Then the man had fallen, clasping his arm and chest, crying that he was on fire. Where had the flames come from? The ground where the Seat was cantilevered was now black, also scorched. Cheftu backed away from the Seat. What was it?

"Why would Shaday do this?" Dadua asked. "*Ach*, he accidentally touched—"

N'tan spoke in monotone, his eyes closed, his hands outstretched. "We were welcoming Shaday and the Seat into our midst as though we were the focus for the occasion."

"You were acting like pagans," Cheftu said, crossing the arms of the corpse in the position of death.

"We were excited!" Dadua said angrily. "We were delighted to have him among us again! There was no evil intent!"

"The Egyptian is right," the *tzadik* said. "We were focusing on the Seat like an . . . idol. It is not our possession, it is the residence of God."

They all glanced toward the Seat, sitting in the dirt, surrounded by a starburst of charred land.

N'tan turned to another of the remaining priests. "Get some women to prepare the body."

The man, white-faced and shaking, nodded, then ran.

"What did he die of?" N'tan asked Cheftu, crouching beside him.

"See those marks?" Cheftu said, pointing to where the priest had raked his chest, clawing at his garment. "See his face? How his features are drawn down?"

N'tan grunted.

"I believe his heart seized up," Cheftu said. "However, I have no explanation for this." He turned over the corpse's hand, his blackened hand. "Or the fire. Or how his hair is still on end," Cheftu said. "More than one thing happened. A stroke when he realized he'd touched it? Or perhaps . . ." He turned the hand over again. "I do not know for certain." He looked up at N'tan. "Who was he?"

"My uncle Uzzi'a."

The words popped into Cheftu's brain at that, the Bible story of the failed entry of the Ark of the Covenant into Jerusalem. Why couldn't I recall it earlier? he wondered. Perhaps I could have said something, warned them. He looked at the body, the marks on a man who was trying to assist. It made no sense.

"What does Shaday want?" Dadua said to them all as he paced a safe distance from the Seat. "Can we not be like other people, worshiping our God in joy?"

"That is exactly right," N'tan said. "We cannot be like other people."

"We are to have no joy? No celebration?" Dadua asked, his voice rising.

His second wife looked at the Seat with calm eyes. "Perhaps our joy is to have a different motive."

Cheftu coughed, hoping he was doing the right thing. "In Egypt we carry our totems on the priest's shoulders." He pointed toward the Seat. "Perhaps that is what those rings are for?"

Soldered onto each corner, both upper and lower, were gold rings. Substantial gold rings. "If we carried it on our shoulders, we would be exactly like the pagans," Dadua said in frustration. The smell of seared skin still hung in the air. What had burned Uzzi'a? The box appeared to be nothing but gold.

Cheftu covered the body as Dadua stared at the Seat, then shrugged hopelessly. "I know not," he said. "N'tan?"

The *tzadik* shook his head. "We know not to touch it," he said. "That has been passed down. To touch it is death."

Everyone took a step back from the Seat, as though reminded. Cheftu looked at the *elohim*. "N'tan?" he gasped, staring in horror.

"*Mah?*"

"The *elohim?*"

The *tzadik* looked up, then screamed, throwing himself facedown into the dirt.

Dadua stood stock-still. "Then it is true," he whispered. "When we are in disfavor it shows among the *elohim.*"

Cheftu stared at the box, at the figures that had been on opposite ends of the cover but facing each other. Now they were each turned away. The inlaid eyes of the female were focused in the distance. *The statues had moved!*

Dadua spoke, his voice heavy with despair. "How can I dare to bring this box into my city, knowing it may kill someone who was only trying to help? How can we please such a God?"

Cheftu stared at the Seat, noticing details about it. Etched into the sides were depictions of winged lions, symbols and letters, grapes and pomegranates. The top was ajar, allowing a small space no wider than his finger. As he watched, something black flew up and away. A tiny black thing. Then another and another.

"The top is off," he said.

"Only Abiathar may touch it," another priest said.

"Get him," Dadua commanded.

As Cheftu watched, the little black things continued spiraling out of the opening. His skin was crawling. What were they? What was alive inside the Ark of the Covenant? He was grateful that Chloe wasn't in range of whatever device this was. It shot fire, and it was infested. He noticed people starting to slap themselves as they stood around, talking, watching the Seat.

One of the black things landed on him, a vivid dot on his white tunic. Hesitantly Cheftu picked it up, examining it in the late afternoon light. A flea. The Seat had fleas?

"In the desert, *ha*Moshe ground the gold of the Egyptian idol, then made those who had danced and defiled themselves before it, drink," N'tan said, continuing his conversation with Dadua.

"But Uzzi'a wasn't trying to defile it," Dadua reasoned. "He was trying to help, to protect the Seat. He was no pagan; indeed, he was a hand-picked priest in good standing. But Shaday killed him," Dadua said. "Is there no tolerance?"

The *tzadik* looked away, closing his eyes as though trying to see something in his mind only. "We think motive overrides action," N'tan said, his tone entranced. "We think the wrong thing, done for the right reasons, will be accepted." The prophet opened his eyes. "It won't. Shaday is mercy, but he is also justice. We forget the latter."

As though they heard their names called, the stones shifted against Cheftu's waist. The mercy and judgment stones. Would they be of use now? Cheftu squashed the flea, then another.

Abiathar came huffing up the road, his skirts lifted, his white chubby legs moving slowly. He halted when he saw the Seat. "The top is off," he breathed. "On your knees, all of you! This is blasphemy! You court death!"

The group, now numbering about twelve, fell on their faces. Cheftu heard nothing aside from the pounding of his heart. When he looked up again, the high priest was adjusting his breastplate. The hair on his head was standing up, and his white clothing was spotted with tiny black dots.

The fleas.

Dadua spoke to them all. "I will give Uzzi'a a state funeral. It is a bitter thing to be a lesson used by Shaday to teach others."

Dadua arranged for the Seat to stay in the barn of Obed, a local Jebusi farmer, until the king knew what to do. "I cannot risk the people of the city," he said again and again.

More priests had rejoined the group at the Seat, so Abiathar directed them to edge some of Obed's scythe poles through the rings. Warily they lifted it. Everyone waited to see if lightning flew from the *elohim* or if another person was struck down. When nothing happened they carried it into the barn carefully. One of the priests began to remove the scythes, but Obed motioned to leave them.

"But you won't have scythes," a priest said.

"The Seat has brought plague to those who touch it, *ken?*" Obed asked.

Dadua nodded.

"I'll get new," he said. "My body is uncircumcised, as is my household, yet we will honor the Seat of your God."

"We will give you them," the priest said hurriedly, glancing at Dadua.

Dadua looked over at the Seat, speaking in an undertone to N'tan. "Can we leave it here? Will it kill them?"

"I do not worship Molekh," Obed announced.

N'tan looked over at Cheftu, who shook his head. Did Dadua see their communication?

"*Lo*, this household will be fine," N'tan said dismissively. "We who touched the Seat, however, we will pay."

Dadua's color faded. "The death of a priest is not enough?"

"We sinned as a nation. We are admonished to live separately, to honor God above idols and legends and nature, to honor him with our lives."

The realization hit Dadua. Cheftu watched his face change, the anger and indignation fade to shame and brokenness. "I led them in pagan practice," Dadua moaned, falling to his knees, stricken. "I tried to make us as other nations! I led them in believing the Seat was an artifact, not the home of the living God!" He picked up clumps of dirt and manure, rubbing them on his face, in his hair, and onto his iris blue clothing. "Shaday, Shaday, I was wrong! Forgive me for blaspheming your holiness!"

"Are you sure we should leave the Seat here?" one of the priests asked. "Should we not try to take it into the city?"

"And endanger more of my people when the sin is mine alone?" Dadua asked, his face streaked with brown. "*Ani haMelekh.* The responsibility is mine, as is the punishment." Tears overflowed his eyes. "We need, I need, to know more of *el ha*Shaday. I need to be forgiven for my pride in marching the Seat before the other rulers to impress them. I need to remember that the Seat, the Tent, the practices, are for God, not for us."

N'tan's black pointed brows rose in fury. "You did this for pride? To impress the pagans of Egypt and Tsor?"

"I was wrong, I was wrong." Dadua was sobbing openly now. "I thought nothing I could do would err, but I was wrong."

"*El ha*Shaday looks on you with favor, as no man has ever seen, but he is still God, beyond the mountains, beyond the sea, beyond the stars," N'tan raged. "He is not controlled by us."

A point made abundantly clear today, Cheftu thought.

"He is immortal and invisible; we are earthlings formed of dirt!"

The *tzadik* spun on his heel, leaving. Dadua beat his head on the dirt, startling the animals that were being led away, drawing sympathetic glances from the priests.

"As the deer thirsts and pants for flowing water, so my nefesh thirsts after you. My nefesh longs after you, Shaday, the living God. When can I meet with you? My tears feed me as I hear men say, 'Where is your God?' I remember these words as I pour my nefesh before you. In my youth I joined the tribesmen, leading the procession to where your house resided. With joy and thanksgiving, we were a festive group."

"There was no joy, no thanksgiving, today," another priest said. "It was ownership, even lust." He dropped to his knees, wiping dirt on his robe, crying out. *"My nefesh is downcast and disturbed in my guf, my flesh. I place my hope in Shaday, I will praise him even now, for he saves me, he is my God."*

Cheftu watched the priest and Dadua speak in words Cheftu knew as the psalms, though now they seemed genuine pleas to God, not written and poetic. *"Even as my nefesh is downcast, I will remember you,"* the priest said. *"Through the Yarden to the heights of Hermon. Deep calls to deep in the roar of the waterfalls, the sea has swept over me.*

"By day el Shaday directs his love. At night I hear his song in me, a prayer to the God of my life."

Dadua beat his breast, shouting at the roof, prostrate before the Seat. *"I say to you, Shaday, the rock of my life, why have you forgotten me? Why do I mourn, why am I oppressed like an enemy?"*

His voice cracked as he raised up, his hands in the air. His next words were from a throat raw with weeping, a soul torn. *"Why is my nefesh downcast? Why this disturbance? I will trust in God, I will believe in his chesed. I will praise him, for he is God, my God."*

Dadua cried quietly into his hands, a shattered man. Avgay'el's expression was pained, watching her husband. The Seat glowered from behind him. The other priest knelt a few cubits behind the king.

Before Cheftu closed the door, leaving Dadua, Avgay'el, and the Seat, he looked over his shoulder.

The *elohim* were embracing.

He fled.

PART

V

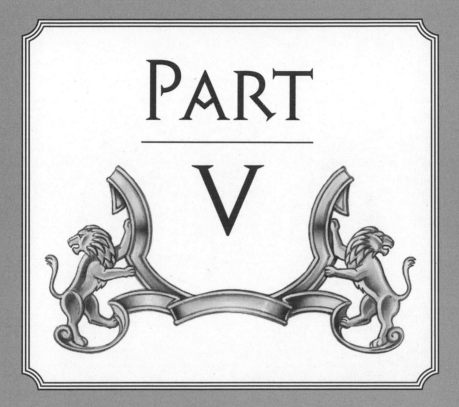

CHAPTER 13

RaEm motioned the fan away. Lazily she reached for a grape, then ate it as she squinted against the sun. The tribespeople were hiding in their homes from their own god. She chuckled at that. Tuti played in another tent, surrounded by soldiers faithful to her, the little brat. Her spies had confirmed that the beautiful, arrogant ruler of the tribes was sitting in the dark, covered in filth, pleading with his god and shunned by his priests.

And Cheftu, damn him, somehow had the ear of the king.

If the king had just been in the dark alone, she might have gone to him. As it was, she would wait. There was no need for her to roll about in manure. The game board lay before her, half the pieces moved. She sighed, her hand floating above them.

"I will play the hounds, if you will indulge me as jackals."

His accent was thick, foreign. RaEm rolled over to see Hiram looking down on her.

He was perfect, dressed in a simple blue kilt, his hair free, no makeup save eyes ringed with kohl. Simple, fine jewelry adorned him. "Zakar Ba'al, I believe?" she said slowly.

His gaze was calculating. "Pharaoh Smenkhare, the male who is so delightfully female."

RaEm smiled. "Also delightfully co-regent as Pharaoh's beloved."

"Among others?" he asked, peering intently into her eyes, her face. He seemed inquisitive.

"Pharaoh alone is a fortunate man," she said.

He continued to stare, a look completely free of lust, but curious. "And for you?" she asked. "Does a queen grace your throne?"

Hiram laughed, crossing his arms over his chest. "I have many wives, Vena's offspring," he said, watching her carefully. "What man in my position doesn't? But alas, no queen. Perhaps that is because Pharaoh saw her first?"

Though he was flirting, he wasn't interested. RaEm, with wonder, realized that Hiram wanted nothing of her as a woman. Instead of being offended, she was relieved and slightly challenged. He gestured to the game board. "If no one else entertains you, may I challenge your skills?"

She clapped, then instructed the slave to bring another set of cushions, more wine, more fruit, and another fan. Soon Hiram was seated across from her, evenly matched.

"What think you of the news of our host?" he asked after a few opening gambits on the board.

"They are a strange little people," RaEm said.

Hiram rolled the sticks. "Their god Shaday is uncompromising. I know tales of twenty years ago."

RaEm noted his move, then rolled her own sticks. "What happened?"

"Curiously, the Pelesti caught the Seat in battle. They placed it in Dagon's temple in Ashqelon. You have seen the temple there, have you not?" Hiram asked her.

"I have not."

"It is rather amazing," he said. "Beneath the sea they have more worship chambers."

"Beneath the sea?"

"Aye, there is a series of rooms."

RaEm glanced at him. Did he think she was that stupid? "What about the Seat?" She moved her piece, then sat back. "I understand it is solid gold, this totem?"

"Aye," he said, continuing to speak in Egyptian. "A box of gold with two enchanted angels, that you would call *ushebti* and they call *elohim*, affixed to the cover. Twice at the temple in Ashqelon it threw down the statue of Dagon."

RaEm watched him move, then looked up. "How did that happen?"

"It is ascribed to the power of Shaday. The Pelesti determined to return it to the tribesmen since it had killed many of their people."

"How?"

"A plague, with tumors."

"The Ark carries a plague?"

He shrugged. "It bears it. Though how it moves from the box to the people without anyone touching it, I do not know. That is why it is forbidden; in fact, that is what happened yesterday. They say lightning flew out from the box."

RaEm beat him on his final move. She tried to keep the smile from her face. Lightning was in the box? Was this a blessing from HatHor? Or was the Aten proving his existence?

Hiram seemed a bit surprised. "You play to win, My Majesty."

"You speak my tongue fluidly, Zakar," she said. "How is that?"

"I once kept company with an Egyptian scribe," Hiram said slowly, studying his game piece intently.

"As did I," RaEm admitted, chuckling.

"So tell me," he said, lifting his dark gaze to her again. "Have you ever traveled to the islands in the Great Green?"

"You of all people know Egyptians, Zakar. In truth, you recently sent Wenaten, our ambassador, home on the edge of a nervous breakdown from your highhandedness."

He laughed, but his gaze was still intent. "Are you a native Egyptian?"

"Aye, Zakar."

"Please, call me Hiram."

"As you wish," she said. She did not offer her name, purposefully.

They played several more games, in near silence. Slaves entered and lit lamps, then brought food and kept their cups full. Finally he sat back. "Why are you in Jebus?"

"To meet the newest king," she lied glibly.

"We both know that to be a falsehood," he said. "Show me the respect to tell me it is not my concern, but do not think to put me aside with poorly woven tales."

"Then you tell me," she fired back. "Why are you here?"

He finished his wine, set down his cup, and looked at her. His eyes were long lashed and dark. The features of his face were perfectly modeled, from a straight nose, high forehead, and squared jaw to the lushness of his lips, the fullness of his cheeks, the curve of his head. He was exquisite, too beautiful to be real.

She missed Akhenaten, with his woefully misshapen body and head, his piercing eyes and deep, rich voice. Even though he'd thrown her away, she wanted him still. For that RaEm despised him, because now her life was incomplete, with no hope of restoration.

Had Horetamun done his work? Gods forgive her for sacrificing perfect passion.

Hiram was beautiful, but he seemed to have no soul. Nothing gleamed from his eyes. He looked away from her. "My purpose has changed," he said slowly. "Originally I came to build Dadua his palace."

"Why would you do such a thing?"

"I have no army to work my way on these people, so I must be subtle."

"You stage an invasion of carpenters?"

He chuckled. "I build a city that I will know, he will not. Whenever the time is right, I can work with another ruler to take the city. I want Tziyon; I want the location, the streets, the view of the surrounding valleys. Most important, I want the guardianship of the King's Highway."

RaEm couldn't believe he'd just told her his plan. Either he was a fool or considered that she was. "Do you jest with me?" she asked coldly. "I will not be mocked."

He focused on her again, those soulless eyes peering into hers.

"Nay, I do a brazen thing by showing you my full intent. Will you do me the same honor, Sibylla?"

"Gold," she said flatly.

He stared at her for a moment, then threw back his head and laughed. "I lose my wit in these late days," he said. "You are unaware—yet how is this possible?" he muttered. "What did I think to accomplish?"

RaEm frowned at him. "You asked a question, I respected you and answered it. Why do you laugh?"

He sobered immediately. "Forgive me. Dadua has gold?"

"He has a pharaoh's ransom in gold." She smiled briefly. "I have a pharaoh much in need of ransoming."

"So you want the gold, and I want the city."

RaEm laughed. "Aye. Perhaps we should open the Seat, allow it to kill the tribesmen, then I will sweep in and take the gold, you will have a city, free of people."

Hiram laughed. "Use their own magic against them, *aii?*"

"It would be easy enough," she said. "Take over while they are weak."

"How would you get the gold? Not everyone will die with the plague."

RaEm stared into the dregs of her cup. The evening cool was alien, as were the trees, the hills, the dew. She sighed. "Maybe what we really need is the Seat. It is gold, you say. We could just take it instead."

"It is also deadly," he reminded her. "And quite weighty, I would guess."

"I need a lot of gold, whether it be the Seat or some of the wealth in *haNasi's* coffers." She stared into the distance for a moment. "The Seat is important however. They would pay attention to that."

"Hold it for ransom to ransom your pharaoh?"

She met his gaze across the table. "Aye. If this were a real conversation."

He picked up his glass, tapped it gently on the table. "You and I would be in covenant . . . if this were a real conversation."

"And how is that, Zakar Ba'al?"

"I would let you into the city, to get the Seat. You would hold it for ransom, assure me that most everyone will die, then give me the city."

"I would get the gold."

"I would get the city."

She tapped her cup on the table. "You are correct. If this were a real conversation, we would be in covenant."

FOR A WEEK AFTER the Ark shot fire—electrical shocks, I guessed from the stories I heard—the tribes cowered. Because of the terror they skipped the Feast of Tents, Sukkot. The next day I was sleeping, cuddled close to Cheftu, when there was a knock on the door.

He slept through it, but the knocking was insistent. Stumbling to my feet, I put on a tunic and went to the door. "Who is it?" I asked, the door's bolt still in place.

"Zorak," he said. "*HaMelekh* requests you for *G'vret* Avgay'el."

I had no idea why she would need a lady-in-waiting this late, but I braided my hair, tied on a sash, and slipped into some sandals. In chilled silence we walked up through the city, past the guards, and into the Tsori sector, where the palace was being built on the Milo.

"She's sick, Klo-ee," he said before letting me into the women's quarters.

Dadua knelt beside her, and Avgay'el lay on her bed, tossing and turning. Her hair was matted, her eyes tightly shut. I was standing a foot away and could feel the heat of her body. Blood stained the front of her sleep dress, blood that she had coughed up with mucus.

This looked far more serious than just a flu. "How long has she been like this?" I asked, kneeling beside him.

"I woke up because of the heat of her body," the prince of Tziyon said. "She is quite cool usually. Then I couldn't awaken her."

"My husband, he is a physician," I said hurriedly. "I can try to make her comfortable, but he'll know what is going on, what to do for her."

"Chavsha is a physician? Is there anything the man doesn't do?"

I grinned, hoping that Cheftu would forgive me for busting his cover story. Dadua dispatched someone to get Cheftu.

For the next hour I patted down Avgay'el with cold compresses. She hadn't vomited, though she had dry heaved in her sleep. She was so hot, I almost couldn't touch her. Maybe she was just one of those people who ran high fevers? I had once had a roommate who was like that.

The cloth was dry by the third pass.

Dawn came. I was bleary-eyed, then terrified. Avgay'el shivered, coughed, spat up more blood, shrank from light. I tried to keep her hydrated but freaked out when I saw her tongue.

It was coated white.

By midmorning she had faint gray circles all over her body.

What was this? Where was Cheftu?

By midafternoon she was covered in patches of black, with horrible protrusions from her neck, armpit, and bulging out from her groin. Cheftu finally showed up, bloodstained with bloodshot eyes. "What happened?" I asked.

"N'tan's son was a brutal delivery," he said. "His wife didn't survive."

"She's dead?"

Cheftu wiped his face; at least his hands were clean. "Ken. The child is very weak." I stepped forward, and he saw Avgay'el. My husband froze, then knelt by her, not touching her. "Get out," he said in distinct English.

"Why? What? Chef—"

"Dammit, Chloe, get the hell out of here! Take everyone who isn't a priest and get out! Close off these rooms and don't let anyone in."

He'd never spoken to me this way before; I could hear the terror in his voice. I hesitated one more minute. "She has the bubonic plague," he said, turning to me. His eyes were wide, amber, and brown—and scared. "Go!"

"You're supposed to be quarantined," N'tan said. "Chavsha was insistent."

"I was sorry to hear about your wife," I said.

He looked away. *"Todah."*

"Shouldn't you be mourning or something? I can take care of myself, I can even quarantine myself," I said.

"She was not my family," he said in monotone. "I will not mourn her."

"Mah?"

"It is the law."

I was about to rant, but then he looked at me. His narrow, overbred features were pinched, the circles beneath his eyes deep and gray. "How is your son?"

A faint smile touched the edges of his mouth. "Beautiful, a gift from Shaday."

"What is his name?" The questions weren't just polite; I found that I really wanted him to know that I was genuinely sorry for him and happy for him.

"On the eighth day I'll name him."

More customs, more laws.

"G'vret, you have been exposed to Avgay'el, as was Dadua. You need to be set apart for a few days to make sure you don't sicken. This is what your husband says."

Bubonic plague. That was one scary concept. I'd had European history—but weren't rats involved? How had Avgay'el been bitten by a rat? I knew I hadn't, but if it would make Cheftu feel better, I'd take a few days of vacation. After all the busyness of the past days and weeks, it would be nice.

But surely Cheftu was wrong about the plague? There were no rats.

"W<small>HAT CAN BE DONE FOR HER</small>?"

"I do not know, I have no idea where she got this illness," Cheftu said, watching as Avgay'el shivered, soothing her burning brow with wet cloths. "You? How do you fare?" Cheftu couldn't imagine his pain, losing his wife. Childbirth was a very uncertain thing. Was he sure he wanted to risk Chloe, her very life, that way?

N'tan shrugged. "You show no fear around this plague," the prophet said. "Why is that?"

"Nor do you," Cheftu countered.

"*Ach*, well, it has no power over me."

Cheftu turned to look over his shoulder at the *tzadik*. "How is that possible?"

"Anyone who might come into contact with the Seat, in the course of his serving with the Levim, is purposefully made ill so that he never gets sick again." The priest rolled back his sleeve, motioning Cheftu closer. There, barely visible in N'tan's hairy armpit, was a scar—a plague scar.

"You know it is deadly?" Cheftu asked, stunned.

"*Ken*, which is one of the reasons that only the priests of Levi handle it. Only they are made sick each generation." He crouched beside Avgay'el. "She must have stood too close."

"What can be done for her?" Cheftu asked. "This will be fatal otherwise."

N'tan's dark eyes met his. "We can pray, intercede."

How could he still have faith when his own wife just died? Cheftu wondered. "There are no medicines? No herbs?"

"Keep her fever down." N'tan's hand touched one of the bulging, blood-filled buboes on her neck. "She was such a beautiful woman. What a tragedy."

What irony, Cheftu thought. This disease obliterated a quarter of the fourteenth-century world, and yet the Levim purposefully infected their youngsters with it. So they could survive. "What makes the Ark so deadly?" he asked.

N'tan shrugged. "The power of *el ha*Shaday."

Cheftu bathed Dadua's wife with icy water, trying to keep her cool. Her hair was falling out in hanks because her temperature had gotten so high. She coughed up blood, then fell back into her deep sleep, again and again. Though he felt like a grand inquisitor, he made her drink when she could barely swallow, forced her to keep drinking even when she protested that she couldn't take another sip. But she drank, urinated, and drank more. Would it flood the disease out of her body? How had this happened?

She hadn't even touched the Ark. The only thing that could have transferred from the Seat to her body were . . .

Fleas.

I'VE BEEN IMPRISONED a few times. The only tangible differences were that now I hadn't been thrown into this cell, and I was being fed. Other than that, this stone underground room lit by one measly lamp was the same as the others.

The plague?

I was on my second or third day of nonsensical navel gazing when Dadua joined me. A shot of espresso and a pack of Camels couldn't have made me move faster. As it was, I was talking to myself, or rather God, about the absurdity of life, liberty, and the pursuit of happiness. "Are our lives a game?" I asked loudly, blowing off some steam. "We get pulled from time to time, put in situations where we have no choice but to do what you say!" I stared straight up into the face of the unknown. "Do we no longer have free will?"

"What language is that, *isha?*"

I spun around. The slayer of Goliath, the sweet psalmist of Israel, the however many times removed grandfather of Jesus, stood not a foot away from me. "My, my . . . *adon,*" I said quickly, bowing.

"How are you?" He glanced around. "This room is dank enough to be a prison," he said. "How many more days do we spend here?"

I felt a strange sense of peace steal over me. Did Dadua carry a force field with him? "I don't know. How is Avgay'el?"

Dadua sighed. "Still in this life, but very ill."

"I grieve for you."

"She is a good woman, better than I deserve," he mused. Leaning against the wall, he slid down onto the straw opposite me. "What question were you asking Shaday?"

"You, you understood me?" I was shocked. Beyond shocked.

He chuckled. "Not the words, *lo,* but the *nefesh* behind them, *ken.* I recognize the sound of it." He looked at me, a Rossetti in the raw. "What did you ask?"

Why not ask David? I mean, if anyone really knew God, it was he, right? I licked my lips, fighting hysterical giggles. I was chatting up the king of Israel while waiting to see if I had the plague. Boy, was life weird. "I wanted to know if I still had free will."

"Because you were a slave?"

Instinctively I touched the hole in my ear, the hole I rarely thought of anymore. I almost said, "No," then realized that being a time traveler, I really was some form of slave—depending on one's perspective. "Sometimes," I said.

"We are all slaves," he said.

"You are the king, how can you say that?"

"Shall I tell you a story?"

"*B'seder.*"

"First, I brought some wine."

He poured and we sat. I was dazzled to be in his company; I guessed that he was worried sick over his wife.

"A king is also a slave," he said. "When I was no king, indeed I was fleeing the king's wrath, hiding in the caves of Abdullum, I mentioned, on a hot day, how I would love to have some water, cool and refreshing, from the well in my father's yard."

"*Ken?*"

"At that time it was behind enemy lines. A dangerous path to get there, an even more dangerous one to return home."

"Did you not have water?"

"That was it. We did have water. I was longing for the security of home, the refreshment of being with my family, yearning for the years before all this began. That was the meaning of wanting water specifically from that well." He sighed. "So then: Two of my *giborim* slipped through enemy lines, drew the water, then came back.

"It was an expensive trip. They were covered in gore, for they had had to kill several people to get the water." Dadua licked his lips. "I was so humbled, so terrified."

I could understand the humility, but the terror? "Why?"

"I had spoken thoughtlessly. Because of that, they had undertaken this feat that could have lost their lives. Over my frivolity!"

"They were grown men, they made a decision," I reminded him.

"*Ken*, but they had made it because of my longings. I realized then, for the first time, that I wielded power." He drained his cup in one swallow. "Power is as great an enslavement as any ring you've ever worn through your ear, *g'vret*."

"What about slavery to God?" I asked. "How do you know you are doing the right thing?"

"The right thing?" he repeated. "If you do not worship idols, if you are faithful to your family, your tribe, Shaday . . ." He trailed off. "What other 'right thing' is there to do?"

I opened my mouth to retort, but I had no response. Was it really that easy?

"My mother is from the land, a cousin whose father did not go into Egypt," he said. "They do not have the laws that we, the tribes, were given. For her, it is very simple. She doesn't have to worry about the Seat, or cleanliness, or *hal*. Three things Shaday asks of them, because they are not chosen."

"They are . . . ?"

"Show justice, love mercy, walk every day humbly with Shaday."

"That's it?" I asked.

"They are not chosen, so less is required of them."

"More is required of the tribes because they are chosen? Why is that?"

Dadua sighed, poured himself another cup of wine. "Being chosen is an extreme, *b'seder?*"

I sipped my cup, tried to understand. He must have sensed my confusion because he kept talking. "Chosen means you are picked out, you are no longer just part of the mass, but you are an individual." He flashed a smile. "Usually, the only reason someone is selected from a group is for a good end or a bad one. Take, for instance, sacrifice."

"The sheep and goats?" I asked, thinking of the scapegoat now living in the garbage dump outside the gate.

"*Ken.* They are picked out, selected as the best, because their blood must be shed for us. Selection is for a high holy purpose, but not so good for the sheep, *nachon?*"

I laughed. "*Nachon.*"

"Or a group of workmen. The one who is singled out is either the best of the group or the worst, *ken?*"

I nodded.

"So," he said with a shrug. "We are singled out, chosen for a purpose. Sometimes it is to be the best, to show how it is done. Sometimes, *ach*, well, we are the worst example. 'This is how not to be,' Shaday tells the other nations. 'Ignore them now.' "

"How does that—"

"Matter to slavery?"

"*Ken?*"

"Because as the sheep belong to the shepherd and are picked to be eaten or be sacrificed, or as the workmen belong to the overseer and are selected to be promoted or discharged, so a slave belongs to his owner." Dadua swigged his cup of wine. "We are slaves. Shaday is our owner." He stretched out his hand. "The fields and hills, they are not ours." He belched. "They are God's. Every fifty years, no matter who owns the land, it goes back to the very first owner, from when the first tribesmen bought land here. That practice serves to remind us that we are tenants."

He poured wine into my empty cup. "We are here, fed, clothed, housed, and protected through our own wits, *ken*, but because Shaday allows it. If we break his laws, he will kill us." Dadua laughed humorlessly. "Obvious, *nachon?*" He shook his head. "The land will vomit us out. We must guard against any transgression, and that is why."

Avayra goreret avayra danced through my mind. "Is this selection a blessing or a curse?" I asked.

I'd been allowed to see pivotal moments in history. Was that a blessing or a curse? I was sitting here, discussing theology with the writer of the Psalms; was that a blessing or a curse?

He chuckled, poured another cup. "When we were in Egypt as kings, it was a blessing. When we were in Egypt as slaves, it was a curse."

"So when you are the rulers, it is blessing?"

"*Lo*, even ruling ourselves at times we have cursed ourselves. *Lo*, the blessing and cursing come from what we believe of Shaday. If he is disciplining us so that we behave properly because that will bring fruition to us, to the land, then even a curse could be a blessing."

"I think I've drunk too much to understand," I said, my head spinning. I looked at my cup, staring into its depths, wondering how badly I was slurring. "So it is a choice, then, to decide if the wine cup is half-full or half-empty?"

He looked at the cup in his hands, surprised. He laughed after a moment. "*Ach*, because the level of the wine does not change, but our perception of it does? *Isha!* That is a fine lesson!"

I silently thanked whatever self-help book I'd read that in.

Dadua stretched. "We are all slaves, *g'vret*. You may be a slave to Shaday, to live a certain way or in a certain place you would not have chosen. But you are free, if you choose to be."

The next day brought the good news that Avgay'el, while weak, was alive. Also good news was that if Dadua or I were going to get sick, we would have by now. The bad news was that I had the worst hang-over of my life—from getting drunk with the king of Israel.

Lastly, Sukkot, which had been postponed owing to the fire-shooting Ark, was rescheduled. Zorak, who came to free me from my cell, told me that for that feast we would all live outside in tents, decorated with the four species.

"Which are . . . ?" I asked as we walked the labyrinth up to the light. I was amazed when we got to the top, because we were above the city, looking down on the Milo and the gates.

"*Ach*," Zorak cursed. "I must have taken the wrong turn."

I looked over my shoulder and gasped unconsciously. The Tent of Meeting?

"*G'vret*," Zorak said, "I must get you down from here, I don't know what court we are in."

We were inside the tented enclosure, steps away from the actual Tent where the Ark would someday go. I greedily took in every detail. The walls were woven panels, fixed on poles that formed an enclosure around the main tent. Candelabra the height of a man were arranged on either side of the bronze seas that Dadua had shown in his plan. The Tent stood in the center, brilliantly colored, the front patterned with stripes in purple, blue, and red. Two columns stood before it, the only permanent structures in sight. They were as thick as redwoods, fluted at the top with a frieze of pomegranates and grapes.

A wind swept across the plateau; automatically I bent to remove my shoes. In twentieth-century Jerusalem, the Dome of the Rock covered the Temple Mount. Father said those Jews who were devoutly religious wouldn't step onto the Mount, since they didn't know where the altar had been and they didn't want to walk on it accidentally. I understood this feeling. Terror, joy, a sense of awe.

God's Mountain.

How did we get here? I wondered as Zorak led me back down stairs that ran straight up from the city's limestone pits into the inner court of the Tent of Meeting—where the Temple would be.

We got turned around again but eventually ended up on the streets of the city, at night. "When will the feast begin?"

"Look out, *g'vret*, it already has."

Sure enough, lean-tos of palms were sprinkled throughout the city, striping the night with lamp fire. I suddenly felt very lonely. "Is this another of the feasts when the men will go to Qiryat Yerim?" I asked, thinking of how I missed Cheftu.

"*Lo*, Klo-ee, from now on the Tent is here, so the celebrations will be, too. Tomorrow is the progression and official start of the eight days."

We bade each other good night, and I stumbled home, filthy, hungry, and heartsore. My husband was waiting with hot food, hot bath, and open arms. I took them all, but not in that order.

The *shofar* signaled the beginning of the feast. Song drifted through my window, not that that in itself was so unusual, but the volume was. The streets were dense with people, those gathered in from the local tribes, all walking to the hillock above the city. From here I could see the Tent of Meeting, which shielded us from the power of God.

After the last week's display I think we all felt safer with that protection. Within that area was the smaller tent, the home of God. The warm tones of sunset fell on the mesa, coating it with liquid gold. Donkeys and oxen laden with produce, and decked in flowers, were being led up to the Tent. Burdened with cakes and oil and wine, the tribesmen hurried along, their joy stilted as they pondered in fear if their gifts would be accepted.

In some ways it must be nice to know immediately if you were on God's good or bad side. If the rains came, you were. If they didn't, you weren't. No dodging, no wondering, no seeking. On the other hand, repentance wouldn't necessarily have an immediate cumulative effect. The facts were in the soil, the precipitation. Where the boody-trapped Ark came in to play, I had no idea.

The throng bypassed us, since we were pagans and not allowed into the presence of God, singing, "Hosanna!" They were really loud; or maybe for the first time in my ancient journeys I found myself part of the masses. It was unreal that I was hearing it *for* real. Before we knew what was happening, Cheftu and I were caught up in the group, absorbed into the milling, marching tribesmen. We walked uphill rapidly, the crowd's song our rhythm, until we were all on top of the mountain.

The wind had grown stronger, colder; it whipped around us. In a wavelike pattern, the people fell silent as this otherworldly feeling engulfed us. From this promontory you could see all the hills surrounding Tziyon, all of the city. We were raised above the earth, suspended on the platform that was Jerusalem. Above us were only stars.

"We see as God sees," Cheftu whispered as we were separated into groups of men, women, and foreigners.

All around us women were covering their hair. Through the crowds of people I saw the Tent of Meeting, illuminated by a thousand torches. The men left the women and children behind, outside the curtained walls, as they entered into the territory of God.

I pushed through the masses, getting closer to the screens, near enough that I could discern the interwoven pattern of pomegranates, winged lions, then so near that I could hear the tinkle of tiny bells in concert. The music of the bells decorating the hem of the priests' robes.

Don't ask me why I began crying. Not sobbing, but tears streaming down my face. I was *here*, for whatever reason. I was being allowed to observe this. Was this because I'd chosen it? Had it chosen me? Was I lucky? Or unlucky? What else was asked of me, or was my life now ordinary, the drama of time traveling passed? It was already October and still we hadn't found another portal. Was it destiny to stay here now?

"Why is it always the men?" a woman hissed behind me.

"*Ach*, D'vorka, cease with your complaining."

"Still, I wonder. The men always see Yahwe. Why not us? We are the ones cursed with childbearing!"

Obviously these were tribeswomen, not Jebusi, who were thrilled to have morning sickness.

"Shush. We are blessed with childbearing."

Hushing her only served to make her louder. She snorted. "Tell that to my hips! With the birth of Yohan, I swear, my hips have spread so far that one is in Y'srael, the other in Yuda!"

I had to bite my lips to keep from laughing out loud.

"You call that a blessing? My Yuri, he says he can't feel the walls inside me! He says it's like loving a cave! This, this you call a blessing?"

"Shush. Better not to speak of your husbandly relations in the presence of God."

"God? What? He doesn't know what it is like between a man and woman? He knows too well! He knows why Lilith didn't stay with Adama."

The high priest, the stones on his chest reflecting colored light upon the men, climbed onto a platform. He was visible to us all. His presence silenced the women behind me; the power of his office hushed everyone. He offered prayers, solemn and earnest. I imagined that the priesthood was a little nervous right now. We all said, *"Sela."*

"So why aren't women in the Tent?" the woman behind me hissed. "What? We can't repeat like these men?"

"We aren't there because who would take care of the children?"

"Their fathers can't?"

The other woman said nothing; I had to force myself not to turn and see the look I felt her give her friend. *"B'seder.* That was a stupid question," the complainer acknowledged.

The priest said something, and all of a sudden people were passing food toward the front. Before us a man mounted the ziggarut-style stairs and we watched as a sheep's throat was cut. I was a little squeamish—but at least it wasn't a living baby.

We sent the offerings forward: loaves, vials of oil, skins of wine, pots of honey.

"So, the men couldn't do this?" the woman behind me asked her friend.

"You trust your Yuri to handle your loaves, make sure they get to the Almighty without damage?"

"He gets the sheep to Shaday," she said.

"All your sheep do when they get there is die," she said. "They don't have to be in the best condition for that."

"And what, my loaves have to dance a jig for the Almighty?"

"Better them than Yuri!"

They smothered their laughter. I found myself stifling a grin.

Priests, in cone hats and white-and-gold kilts, blew *shofars.* The men chanted in a rumble that seemed to shake the very mountaintop. A sudden gasp silenced everyone. "It is a sign!" someone shouted out. We were craning to see. Abiathar, the high priest, fell to his knees.

"What is it? What do they see?" the woman behind me asked. We were all trying to see what was going on. The high priest hadn't looked up, but the whisper moved over the crowd like wind over a grain field, stirring the stalks. My blood ran cold when I heard it:

The scapegoat had come back, climbing up the hill and walking through the enclosure.

The sash around his neck was still red.

RaEm was seated, mentally penning a love letter that she would never send to Akhenaten, when the message arrived.

"They live in huts tonight. Would you like to see my passages? H."

Hiram's passages. It would sound nearly obscene from someone else, but not from Zakar Ba'al. RaEm told the messenger that her answer was affirmative.

"Then if My Majesty will come with me?"

"Now?"

"Beneath the cover of guests, we can move you from one camp to the other without alerting those who watch."

RaEm sighed. Tuti would have to be cared for tonight. What had prompted her to bring him along, a small boy with the attitude of an emperor? "My slaves will know," she said.

The Tsori stepped a little closer. "Zakar Ba'al sent a decoy for you. She will wear your clothing, if that is suitable to you, while you will masquerade as her for a night."

"Where is she?"

He stepped back, motioned outside the tent. RaEm watched herself walk in—tall, slim, flat-chested, short black hair, dark eyes. Slowly she smiled. The way Hiram thought was very appealing. "Leave us," she said to the Tsori courier.

A while later, the two lackeys of Tsor made their way down the hill, across the stream, around the city, and up the opposite hill. It was nearly dusk when they arrived in Hiram's camp.

RaEm was sticky with sweat; it had been a long time since she had climbed and walked such great distances. The decoy walked her to the servants' tents, for those who watched, which opened into the back of Hiram's tent.

Immediately RaEm was in the presence of Hiram's one-breasted soldiers. They gestured to each other, then one disappeared into another part of the tent. Hiram appeared in the doorway. RaEm did not want to seduce him, but still she wished she looked better. "I have taken the liberty of ordering a bath for you," he said. "After our excursion."

RaEm went from pleasure to impatience.

"To blend with the night I advise blackening your face; thus you would need another bath before returning to your camp."

His plan made sense, but she hated to feel so unkempt. "I will abide by your suggestion," she forced herself to say. "This plan was quite clever."

Hiram smiled, a beautiful, perfectly cold expression. "Shall we dine briefly first? The tribesmen are congregating for dinner."

It was a quick meal of grains and poultry. Then he presented her with dark clothes, makeup for her face. He excused himself. Within the decan he showed up—made as invisible as a shadow at night. His gaze, visible only because of the whites of his eyes, raked her. "You are sufficient. Shall we go?"

"Where are we going?" she asked. It had dawned on her while she dressed that he could be planning to kill her in the darkness of the tunnels.

"You wondered if he had gold, did you not?"

RaEm nodded.

"Therefore I will give you a tour of his coffers. Then, should you have cause to demand, you know what his capacity is." He glanced at her mouth. "It is good to know the other side's ability to meet your needs, is it not?" He smiled again. "Besides, you were bored witless sitting on your mountainside as they scurried around after their god."

"What do you get out of this?" she asked abruptly, somewhat offended that he understood her so well.

He shrugged. "It amuses me."

"Everything amuses you," she snapped. "Did your little Egyptian scribe amuse you, too?"

His eyes burned as he looked at her, and RaEm revised her earlier opinion. He wasn't without soul; he was a demon. "Never breathe a word about that again, or it will be your last."

"My soldiers would simply kill you," she said haughtily.

"I cannot die."

THAT NIGHT IN THE SUKKAH, which Dadua's energetic children had built, Dadua stood up. "I sinned," he said. "In this land, I dared to mingle our neighbors and ourselves." He looked away. "We did not know how to treat the totem, the Be'ma Seat. Along the way we have forgotten the Sages' words. Never again. A scribe will always be there to remind us, to keep us close to the words of Shaday. Just walking on this land is not enough." His voice cracked, but he continued.

"I have made Tziyon into an object. If we worship her, the very soil of the mountain, we will be no better than idolators. But"—he looked at us intently—"if we remember what she means—that our history is our future, that Shaday is giver and creator above all we have or imagine—then we will have created an everlasting ideal. Then Tziyon will be eternal."

You have *no* idea, I thought.

"For this reason, while we seek the face, the favor, of Shaday, we will become a people who know the truths of our God. It is not enough to recite the stories on feast days. We must know every word he has ever said to our people."

I tightened my grip on my cup. It hadn't occurred to me before—which was stupid, it should have—but there was no Bible at this point.

"*Ha*Moshe brought us laws, laws we follow, though we do not know why. For the next week, every evening we will gather and learn why we follow these laws. We will learn how to please Shaday.

"In doing this, may we avoid his wrath."

A hesitant knuckling grew loud. "Additionally," Dadua said, "I have taken steps to structure our city as a royal city. This way, more attention can be given to the following of Shaday. Chavsha the scribe will take down the words of the priests, the *tzadik*, so that nothing is lost. This chronicler will—"

I sank to my haunches, behind the ranks of slaves and concubines. It couldn't be! It couldn't be! But I had memorized the books; it was one of the things I recalled from those lessons long ago and far away. Genesis, Exodus, Leviticus, Numbers, Deuteronomy, Joshua, Judges, Ruth, Samuel I and II, Kings I and II, *Chronicles I and II!* I was dizzy; I wasn't believing this!

"We start a new beginning as tribesmen," he said. "We will build Y'srael and Yuda into a united monarchy. We will be a nation!"

We knuckled in response. N'tan stood up. He was in priestly attire, his golden cap reflecting the multitudes of lamps. He intoned a prayer to Shaday, then gestured to Dadua.

Dadua spoke. "Shaday will do this for us," he said. "It is not the work of our hands, but our obedience to him." He took a deep breath. "Because of this, Shaday's words need to be inscribed in our *nefesh*, be a part of our blood." There was a sense of expectancy. "N'tan will teach us these words, we will breathe them and remember them!"

We knuckled approval as the *tzadik* walked forward.

"Tonight we learn the first law!" N'tan shouted. "Shaday is the only God for the tribes!"

THE MOON WAS BEHIND a cloud, proof that the tribes' god was forgiving them because he was going to send rain. Rain, RaEm shuddered. Nasty, unnatural stuff. The only good part of rain was lightning—which was thrilling. She and Hiram crept up the wooded side of the hill, toward a section of wall with no gates, just homes. Hiram walked to a large tree, felt around on the bark.

It opened outward! A section of the tree was a doorway! RaEm was speechless. "How?" she asked in wonder.

"We hew them out in Tsor, leaving the roots remaining. Then they can be transplanted, easily covering up this," he said, removing a wooden plate. "This particular example is a dirty one, quickly executed. My other work is neater, but . . ." He shrugged.

RaEm looked down the hole. It was darkest black, narrow, and reeked of manure. Hiram crawled into it backward, his long skirts tangling between his legs. He held himself on the edge for a moment, then dropped from sight.

She heard a thud, then silence. The interior of the tree was slightly bigger than her shower stall in modern Egypt. "Are you coming?" she heard from below. For a moment she hesitated. Could she trust this man? He waited a moment longer. "Smenkhare, you remind me of a boy who cannot choose if we wishes to bed a female or be bedded by a male. Decide!"

He didn't shout, but his point was made: Stop wasting time.

RaEm edged herself down the hole, feeling nothing but air until his impersonal touch gripped her ankles. He placed her feet on his shoulders, then she was through the hole. They crawled from a limestone room into another tunnel. There were no lights, no lamps, no candles. She moved through at the sound of his voice.

They walked crouched for a while, then he broke the silence.

"We are within the city."

Almost immediately the environment changed. They dropped down into a limestone tunnel that was tall enough for them to walk upright. Hiram produced an oil lamp and they walked on.

"We're beneath the Rehov Shiryon," he said.

"Can they hear you?" she asked.

"They sit down to hear the prophet about now," Hiram said. "They leave us to invade at our leisure."

THE *GIBORIM* LEANED FORWARD, intent on N'tan. They seemed interested in learning, though I would have said that was like a wrestling team showing interest in needlepoint. Maybe I had judged them wrong?

"Our God," N'tan said, "is a zealous God."

I frowned. I heard he was jealous ... were those words interchangeable or something? I prodded my almost nonexistent lexicon and got nothing.

"Why can we not serve other gods, lesser gods?" one of the *gibori* asked.

N'tan shrugged, his hands upraised. "Why would we?"

They stared at him blankly. I stared blankly, too; it was such an obvious question, but I'd never have thought of it. Cheftu was scribbling down his words. Even he stared, puzzled, at N'tan.

"Let's say you are *haMelekh* of a town, *ken?*" the *tzadik* suggested.

"Ziqlag," the soldier supplied readily. "I rule as *haMelekh* of Ziqlag."

That had been where Dadua first ruled. Everyone laughed as the man drew himself up, adjusting his dress as though it were Dadua's blue robes. Dadua just smiled, watching with a fervent glitter in his eyes.

"You want to defend Ziqlag from the marauding ... highlanders," N'tan said. There was laughter. "Now, you can choose to send a whole division, or you can send a giant, an *anaki*. One man who will fight every single soldier and slay them all. Or you can send seven hundred men who might draw even with the highlanders. Which do you send?"

"The giant. Why bother with all the others when you get the same results with the one?"

"Nachon," N'tan said. "Other gods are nothing but the soldiers. They can be effective, but not as effective as the giant, our Shaday. So: There is no need for another."

"Why did Shaday pick us?" someone asked.

N'tan leaned back, playing with his beard. "Avram lived in a society with many gods. Now look: He yearned for more than just statues and sacrifices. He could imagine a god who could not be portrayed in clay or gold or glass." N'tan raised his gaze to meet the questioner's. "Avram could believe. He could see nothing, yet know it was everything."

I glanced at the audience. Were they getting this? A few looked confused, but the majority nodded. Was I getting this? This was more of Dadua's concept of being "chosen."

"However, we needed to have something else," N'tan said. "Discipline, we needed discipline. This could only be taught through hardship, hence Avram's journey. He had to learn, as now we have to learn, to discern between what is holy and what is daily. This is why we have the law—to show the differences."

The *tzadik* leaned forward. "Shaday selected us, because we are the fruit of Avram's journeys. Because we understand that the universe is Shaday's, but he is not in the trees, or the earth. He is above the other gods, just as the giant is beyond the division."

N'tan was a good teacher. I found myself enthralled.

"So that is the first law: No one but Shaday for the tribesmen." He looked at Cheftu. "Do you have that, Egyptian Chavsha?"

"Nachon!" Cheftu said, wiping his quill.

We were living the Bible.

"Shall we try again? H.," the note said.

RaEm shuddered, remembering how confused they had gotten in the tunnels last night, wandering like lost souls through the pits of the afterlife. Then they had found themselves atop the whole city, looking down on the pitiful little sheds the tribesmen built, from the position of their pathetic tent to their god.

RaEm didn't blame their god for not coming to this city. It smelled like trees, there was no river, no richness to the air, no refreshment for the eye. It was crowded and tall. Did she want to go back into the tunnels and see the gold? Aye, she needed to. Any day now she would hear from Egypt. They would want to know how long the crown prince would be away on his "diplomatic tour."

Any day she would hear her beloved was dead.

She looked at the slave. "Tell your Zakar Ba'al that I will join him later."

He bowed and left. Shivering in her linen shirt and kilt, RaEm stared out at the green trees, the brown hills, and the gray sky. She had to get gold from Dadua, but how? Her finger traced the shape of her leg up her thigh to her seat of pleasure. Sex had always worked before. In fact, she had entranced the pharaoh of Egypt. The king of a mudhill should be an easy task.

Except I don't want him, RaEm thought, hiding her face in her linens. Why did Akhenaten send me away? Why did he make me choose? As the first gentle shower fell on the foreign terrain of Tziyon, RaEm cried herself to sleep.

THE NEXT NIGHT we were all grouped in the sukkah again. We had eaten a little faster tonight, with less wine and conversation. N'tan rose, tugging at his beard. "What was our downfall in the desert?" he asked us.

"We forsook Shaday!"

"We forgot who rescued us from the Egyptians!"

N'tan watched us. Apparently no one had gotten it right yet. "What did our forefathers do?"

"We made a graven image," Dadua said.

N'tan glanced at the king. "*Ken*, we crafted an image of gold, called it our god. To it we attributed our salvation, our freedom. We made it with our hands."

The artist in me perked up. This was always an interesting point in art history. Neither the Jews nor the Muslims went in for reproductions of people or animals. Why was that?

N'tan paced a moment, tugging at his beard. "The Pelesti, they worship who?"

"Dagon, Ashterty."

"*Ken*. The Amori, who do they worship?"

The men spat on the floor. "They serve Molekh."

"*Ken*. What is Dagon ruler of?" the *tzadik* asked.

"The sea? Is that not why his manhood is made into a fish?" someone said.

"Perhaps he is fish to protect himself from Sodomi-style love!" The men laughed uproariously, then trailed off under N'tan's gaze.

I felt myself growing angry. They ridiculed what they didn't know. *Then again, Chloe, Dagon is an idol, he's not real, and he is depicted as a fish. Where is the cause for seriousness there? Why would you grow offended?* I looked over at Cheftu, intently focused on his papyrus, his quill moving over the page.

"And Ashterty?" N'tan asked.

"*Ach!* That lovely goddess fosters love," the Klingon *gibori* said. "She makes the fields grow." I recalled that someone had said he was from Hatti. They worshiped Ashterty there also. How did he get here?

"So what if there is a drought?" N'tan asked. "No rain. What do the Pelesti and Amori do?"

"Ask for more, sacrifice more? Try to get the gods' attention?" someone said.

"*Ken.* But do their gods control *haYam?* The rain? Can they decide to move or do something?" N'tan asked. There was a pause.

"Uh, *lo.*"

"Why is that?"

"They are stone," someone in the back said.

N'tan was standing before us, his eyes closed. He looked like a third-grade teacher whose students insisted Santa Claus would come to the Christmas party. We weren't getting it. Even with, or maybe especially with, a twentieth-century perspective, I wasn't understanding.

"*Ken.* Stone," he said. "Then what is Shaday?"

It was quiet for a long time. What was he asking? What substance was God composed of? What kind of question was that? I looked over to Cheftu. He was watching N'tan, a faint frown between his brows.

"Invisible," Dadua finally said.

I was beginning to understand why he was king; he did know all the answers.

"Why are we forbidden to make an image of him?" N'tan asked.

"Because we don't know what he looks like?" one of the female *gibori* said.

"*Lo.* Because we could only represent certain parts of him. Not the whole of him, so the image would be a lie," N'tan explained.

"Why?" Cheftu asked.

"Because it would be incomplete," N'tan said. "What is Shaday?"

Well, if he were invisible, then maybe N'tan wasn't looking for a composition question.

"Defender of Y'srael, our Yahwe war god," Avgay'el said in her soft voice. She was weak, fragile, but she was sharp, apparently in tune with God.

"*Nachon.* How would we make an image of that?" N'tan asked.

He was asking us to make an idol? Representing God as an image? Reverse psychology this early in history?

"Uh, a hand?" the answer came from the back.

N'tan shrugged. "So we worship a stone hand?"

They laughed, but it was uneasy, uncertain laughter. His point was coming clear.

"We could show him as master of Tziyon?" someone volunteered.

"How?"

A younger *gibori* stood up. He was trembling so that his side curls seemed to be dancing. "We could form him as a miniature of Har Mori'a? Coated in gold."

"A blob of gold would be our God?" someone else shouted in surprise. The boy blushed while his compatriots gibed at him.

"How about a symbol, some letters?" someone said.

"Saying what?"

"His name," came from the back, from the shadows.

"We do not use his name," N'tan said, peering into the darkness. "He is God. To use his name would be to have power over him."

"You claim he used a name when you confronted the Egyptians?" Cheftu said. How he could listen and write, I had no idea. But he was right; that was the claim. RaEm, however, should have made it. She wasn't here. I wondered if she expected us to deliver her food to her tonight? She could just starve, I decided.

N'tan responded. "It is how we are to call him, it is the closest to a name we come. It is not his name, however. We do not know it. We know only I AM."

It fell completely silent.

"There are two reasons we have no images of Shaday," he said. "*Echad:* Because we cannot accurately or completely portray him. Not in letters, or in symbols, or through the finest craftsmanship. Even the Seat of Mercy is merely the footstool of Shaday." He held out his hand. "The second reason is more elemental. We are to be a people who listen, not who see."

"CAN'T YOU HEAR THEM?" Hiram asked. RaEm stifled a yawn. They had been crawling through the passageways beneath the city. It was rotted with tunnels and paths made by the many peoples who had lived here before.

One could get from the palace to the threshing floor, or from the well chamber to the market place. People had openings into their homes and shops of which even they were unaware.

The two royals sat in the darkness, catching their breath before they explored the passageways in the palace. Dadua stored his wealth in the rock, Hiram said.

"So you do this for the city," RaEm said softly. "The Highway of Kings?"

"Aye, I do. That and another reason."

"The scribe, Chavsha?" she guessed.

"Aye."

RaEm scratched at her bound hair. "You never shared how you came to know him, want him with this consuming passion."

"I didn't."

"Nay." It was silent for a while. Should she tell the enigmatic ruler that she had had "Chavsha" many times? That she had taken him first? She remembered the flash of Hiram's furious black eyes when she'd mentioned an Egyptian scribe before. Better not. "We have time now."

Dion exhaled. "I met him when I was young."

"You are young yet," RaEm said. "Were you a child?"

His laugh was bittersweet. "In the deepest sense of the word, aye, I was a child. Cheftu, Chavsha, *aii*, he was such a man . . . such an impressive man."

Attractive, aye, RaEm thought. Gifted, certainly. But impressive? The man had no power, no throne, no gold. What could be so desirable? "But he was married?"

Hiram was quiet again. RaEm prompted him. "It is a complex tale," he said. "Nothing is as simple as it appears."

"This is something I can understand," she said with a laugh.

He looked at her. "Your face is quite familiar to me, though not with those eyes."

"Indeed?"

"It was the face of my aunt, Sibylla. The same aunt who wedded Cheftu."

RaEm smiled. "Sibylla. You called me that before, though I did not recognize it was a name."

"That was when I knew that somehow you were no longer that green-eyed witch."

"*Aii*, are you referring to Cheftu's wife?"

"He likes green-eyed women, apparently. His new wife is the same."

She burst out laughing; he didn't know that Chloe was still here? Was the man blind?

"What makes you laugh, Pharaoh?" he asked.

"If you tell me your secrets, then I will share mine," RaEm offered. "However, if you choose not to, I will keep them to myself."

She felt his gaze on her face, then finally he spoke "We are tools for each other. There is no need for confidences."

You will be sorry for that, she thought. How easy I could make it for you to have your lover. "As you will it," she said.

"Shall we see Dadua's treasure room now?"

"HEARING, NOT SEEING," N'tan continued. "That is how we are to live."

Was this true? I looked toward Cheftu, to see his reaction. His expression was frozen as he wrote, taking down the *tzadik*'s words.

N'tan had our attention. "The first man and woman, where were they?" he asked.

"In a garden."

"*Ken.* What happened at eve each day?"

"Shaday would walk with them, talk to them."

"*Ken.* Your parents have taught you well the Sages' words. *Ach,* so then what did the Sages say about how Shaday looked?" N'tan asked.

We said nothing. There was no description of God in the Bible, I was fairly certain of that.

"What does it say about his words?" N'tan asked after a moment.

"His words created the world. Separated light from dark, the sea from the air," Avgay'el answered.

"*Nachon.* His words." N'tan let this sink in for a while. I was no longer looking down on these ignorant soldiers; I didn't get the point, either. "How did the Sages teach these words? How did they teach the first story of creation?"

There was silence.

"These stories have been taught only to those who know the letters, who can read. Why is this?"

"Because letters and words are holy?" someone shouted, though hesitantly, from the rear.

"*Ken.* So the stories are passed down, generation to generation, through remembering. Remembering exactly the words, memorizing them letter by letter so that nothing ever changes. Letter by letter." Raising his hands in the air, he intoned "*Bet, raysh alef, shin, yud, taf. Beresheth.*"

In the beginning . . . Were all these stories really handed down?

Once, in a philosophy class, the professor had lined us up, then whispered something in one person's ear. We passed the phrase from person to person, until we got to the end of the line. Then the last student announced what the verse was.

It hadn't changed hugely, but it was definitely different. This, he said, was just an example of how nothing written by a human can be infallible. Ever since then, I'd not believed in the Bible. I mean, it had been bunches of thousands of years. If we could mess up a sentence in five minutes through fifteen students, then who knows what the Bible had said originally?

My mother and I had debated this very point when I saw the Dead Sea Scrolls. Their phraseology was the same as the first, oldest version of the Bible. My mother remarked on this, while I scoffed. Who knew? I said.

Needless to say, I was gnawing on my sandal now! If these first books were passed down letter for letter, there would be no cultural connotation to put on it. There would be no subtle substitution of one word for another, for instance "hill" instead of "mount," that could result in a large difference.

So the stories would be—at least in the Hebrew version—I swallowed audibly, basically infallible.

N'tan stood still, solemn. For once he really did seem like a prophet of God. "We are to have no images of Shaday because we are to hear his words, trust his character, rely on belief. Not in our eyes, not in the crafts of our hands. We are created in his image.

"He is not to be created in ours."

Raising his hands over the priests, wives, concubines, and *giborim*, N'tan intoned, "May *el ha*Shaday bless you and keep you. May he make his face shine upon you and be gracious unto you. *Sela.*"

We all said, *"Sela."*

CHAPTER 14

RaEm COVETED. SHIELDS from Pelesti and Jebusi palaces adorned the walls. Incense holders, candles, lamps, all of gold and bronze, studded with gems and inscribed with silver and lapis, were flung into the room. Jewelry, painstakingly crafted and delicate, heavy and majestic, all of it was heaped into the chamber, in baskets. Jars of unguents, perfumes, powders, frankincense, myrrh, wrappers of salt and spices, all of it was stacked haphazardly against the walls.

Hiram opened another room, a room of gold. This would save her people! This would save her throne! This could buy the loyalty of those priests in Waset. RaEm didn't trust herself to touch anything or she would steal it all. Better for Dadua to give it to her. But it was Egyptian; it wouldn't be stealing, it would be reclaiming. She saw yet another cartouche of Hatshepsut. Had these tribes ransacked the royal guard? Armor, all of it gold, chariot plating, even weapons inlaid with carnelian and jasper, turquoise and beryl, was Egyptian.

How was this possible?

"There are three more rooms," Hiram said.

"How much is all of this?" RaEm asked.

"How much?"

"How much is here?"

Hiram sighed, rubbing his face. "Close to one hundred thousand talents of gold, maybe a million of silver? I cannot imagine how much bronze—there is so much it is not even kept here."

They walked back into the first room. RaEm looked at the shields on the wall, the trophies that every mountain prince and plains king took when they vanquished a city. There were at least sixty shields, all metal, most gold. Clews of gold and copper wire and cabling coiled on the floor like sleeping snakes. Boxes and jars, trays and salvers, of gold, silver, and bronze littered the floor.

It was not beauty; it was gluttonous wealth on a scale she'd never imagined. Here, in this tiny kingdom that no one had ever heard of.

"Have you seen enough?" Hiram asked.

She'd seen that there was more than enough. All she had to do was get it to Egypt.

So all she had to do was . . . ?

"The Seat? What about it?"

"I know it is fashioned of heavy gold plate over acacia wood."

Her wrist was in his hand as they walked through utter blackness back to the tree. "It is their most sacred possession?"

"It is."

"It shoots lightning and brings plague?"

"It does."

"I want it all."

His fingers flexed around her wrist.

THE NEXT DAY RAINS BEGAN to fall—the first rains of the season. Soft, gentle, almost like a shower instead of the pelting water I called rain. The women in my kitchen ran from their tasks into the courtyard and danced. They swayed their bodies, spinning and twirling, their faces raised skyward while they sang.

"Your love, Shaday, pours from the heavens, your chesed *is proclaimed from the skies. Your uprightness is unmovable like the mighty mountains, your justice is unfathomable as the Great Deep. You,* el ha*Shaday, preserve both man and beast. How priceless your unfailing* chesed!*"*

I'd never been in a place so saturated with song. They grew more enthusiastic as the rains grew stronger, linking arms and dancing in a circle. 'Sheva grabbed my arm, with the same focus and passion she had showed when discussing *haMelekh*. She pulled me into the group, slave and owner, tribeswoman and pagan, dancing, laughing—I didn't even know why!

But I finally saw the beauty in 'Sheva. She was a dancer. When she moved, her awkwardness, her large teeth, and bug eyes faded away. She grew lissome, gilded. Her body seemed to have no bones, no joints. She seemed magical, otherworldly. Like water, she moved, ripple after ripple of motion smoothing up and down her body.

Though she was a child, her hips knew seduction already.

I was not the only one who saw it; but 'Sheva herself didn't recognize her gift, her talent, the power that she would have over men one day, through her ability to dance.

Later, as I was watching water flow through the courtyard from the portico, pouring grain as she ground, 'Sheva confessed she loved to dance in the downpour.

"Whenever it rains, it seems like the Almighty is sending little footprints of joy on the earth."

I smothered my laughter—"footprints of joy"?—because she was serious. She actually looked happy.

"Sometimes I dance while I bathe, pouring the water over my head and pretending it's rain."

I nodded as I slowly added grain to the millstone.

CHEFTU WASHED HIS BRUSHES, pondering the day, the night. Suddenly he felt himself being watched. Slowly he turned, masking his fear and dismay.

"Greetings, scribe," said the current Zakar Ba'al of Tsor; a former chieftain of Aztlan; the only man who had ever tried to seduce Cheftu, who had attempted to kill Chloe, and who had changed Cheftu's life forever because of his love.

"Dion."

"It's been a thousand years. Still cannot forgive me?"

A thousand years? Cheftu tried to keep the shock from his face. The elixir, then it worked? What could he ask, and what would give him away?

"Nothing to say?"

Cheftu licked dry lips. "What do you want? Why are you here?"

Dion smiled. "I build. This is what I do, what my people do."

"The survivors of Aztlan?"

"*Ken*, though not the eruption you recall. There was a later one, maybe"—he pondered a moment—"four hundred years ago? There is, sadly, nothing left save a smoking crescent shape."

Mon Dieu! That would have been the eruption during the time of the Exodus! The court magi were right.

"It astounds me that we have not crossed paths before. Where have you been?"

For Cheftu the past thousand years had not been measured in years, for he had slipped through them in an eyeblink. However, to tell Dion of the time travel, the portals, the stones, these things would be to present temptation to a man who succumbed each time. "I have been here and there," he finally said.

"As have I. Not many people enjoy the life we do, Cheftu." Dion's gaze was intent. "I was convinced you had died, though no wisewoman had ever been able to summon your shade. But there was no way for someone to vanish as completely. Not even rumor of you remained." He frowned, picked up one of Cheftu's pens. "Yet you appear here, so I know you must have been around. One cannot just appear and disappear from history, can one?"

That's exactly what one can do, Cheftu thought. Exactly. "Why the disguise?" he asked.

Dion shrugged. "Hiram the king could not enjoy the simple life of a worker."

"Why the aging?"

Dion stretched, unwinding the body of a man in his prime: broad shoulders, narrow waist, thick legs. "Hiram the builder has lived for many years. Eternal youth, I have learned, causes two reactions in people. Either they cower in fear at the unknown or they desire it so badly, they would kill to know how."

"You have had these experiences?"

Dion nodded, then narrowed his gaze on Cheftu. "You speak as though we have not lived the same way. What secrets are you holding?"

Cheftu forced himself to not look away. "No more than you, Dion."

The dark man reached forward and plucked a brush from Cheftu's table. "I see you have found another green-eyed woman. Lovely creature."

He didn't know Chloe was still alive. "She is," Cheftu agreed calmly.

Dion stepped closer. "What magic do you work? It's been a thousand years and still I want you. I don't care what you have done, how you have cast my aunt's spirit from her body, or the demon you now let live there. I don't care about the hundreds of green-eyed women you have had. All I want is you. For a thousand years, all I've wanted is you."

Cheftu stared into Dion's eyes. He saw love in them, the selfsame love he saw in Chloe's, so he knew Dion's feelings were true. He saw lust, passion, and doorways to things he could not imagine. Dion had been a friend, a trusted ally, a man he'd respected and admired. At one point he would have given his life for this dark Greek.

Until Dion had played a god in Cheftu's life.

In a moment of extreme terror and manipulation, he had given

Cheftu an elixir purported to grant eternal life. It had returned Cheftu from near death and had intervened again and again.

The slaves beat Cheftu harder because he healed faster. When he should have been dead on the island or in the desert, when he should have gone blind from staring into the sun for three days, when he should have been murdered by the brigands who beset them in the Arava, he was immune. The pain of abuse, the agony of wishing to die, the exquisiteness of torture, were all his with no surcease. And in the back of his mind, every day, was the realization that Chloe did not have the elixir.

Childbirth could steal her away.

She could drown, fall, be felled with a weapon, choke on a bone, and he would be eternally alone. "Nay," he told Dion. "My answer hasn't changed."

"Try it, Cheftu. Just let me touch you, see if you feel anything. Let me taste you—"

"No."

"I can help you," he said. "Gold, power, prestige, anything you want."

Cheftu stepped forward, his expression intent. Dion focused on his mouth. "Look into my eyes, Dion," Cheftu said. "Hear these truths from my lips."

"It's hard to concentrate when I want to kiss you."

Cheftu ground his teeth. "You would not understand the things I want. You do not know my soul, regardless of what you think. Nor do you own me, any part of me, for what you have done." He stepped forward again, aggressive. Dion held his ground. Cheftu was sickened to realize this man was aroused. "My choice to deny you is because I love my wife. Were she, Shaday forbid, to be taken from me tomorrow, my choice would be the same. I love her, a woman whose body is rich and capable of life, whose mind is fertile and challenging, whose spirit invigorates and embraces me." He put his hand on Dion's chest. "You. Do. Not."

Cheftu pushed Dion away, sending the man staggering back in surprise. "Do not corner me again, or lust after me, or think you have any hope with me. No now, not ever. No."

He turned around, rewet his brush, and continued his dictation. "You will regret these words, Egyptian," Dion said. And left.

THE NEXT NIGHT BAFFLED ME. I thought I knew the Ten Commandments. Most Western law had come from these simple but binding pronouncements. I was all prepared to hear N'tan expound on adultery or murder, or lying, when he started in on festivals.

Festivals?

He discussed how the tribespeople were to remember Pesach and the Feast of Unleavened Bread for seven days. Then he said they were supposed to celebrate Shavu'ot, the Feast of Weeks, and Sukkot, the Feast of Ingathering—which we were currently enjoying. For these three feasts, the men of the tribes were to stand in Shaday's presence.

The next law, N'tan said, was simple. "Don't cook a young goat in its mother's milk."

That was it. Finito. Those were the laws of the tribesmen. A bunch of stuff about vacations, the no other god, the no image of god part, then some information about redeeming with blood . . . and a law not to cook a young goat in its mother's milk. I had to fight myself to not scream, "What the hell is that about?" Instead I joined everyone else and said, *"Sela."*

We were walking home when I erupted, "Where are the Ten Commandments? I thought that is what you would be transcribing! The Commandments that N'tan recited, the ones he's teaching the tribesmen, are not the ones I was taught. How about you?"

"Given the difference in languages," Cheftu started.

"Lo. Even the difference in language can't explain why there is no

'Thou shalt not covet,' 'Thou shalt honor thy father and mother,' 'Thou shalt not murder.' "

He kissed the back of my hand, but it wasn't a leading kiss, it was a thinking kiss. "There is the statement about no gods before Shaday."

"*Ken.* Because his name is Zealous, he is a Zealous god."

"The statement to not cast an image of him."

"True. Especially after the disaster of them worshiping HatHor only months after Shaday got them through the Red Sea." How could they have doubted? I wondered. I'd seen the sea part, and my life had been changed forever.

Well, tweaked, at any rate.

Okay, so I was no different. I doubted, too, even after seeing the seas part.

"Then, instead of the laws about friends and family, honesty and covetousness, there are all these laws about sacrifices and holidays," I said.

"Memory is the tool to perpetuating this faith," Cheftu said. "Just as N'tan explained. If they remember Shaday, remember him in all the little ways—from blessing wine and bread before consumption, to keeping their lives separate from foreigners just like they keep apricot orchards separate from pear—then they will remember Shaday more easily in the large ways."

We walked into our still-undecorated, because almost everything was undecorated, house. Cheftu lit the lamp while I went straight to our view.

I didn't doubt the point he was making. That those Commandments were missing, how they were, was my question. "How could they go from being about one thing, to being about another?" I turned to look at Cheftu. He was staring over my shoulder, fixed on some private horizon.

"Perhaps . . . ," he mused. "Perhaps we have it backward."

I watched him, waiting. His eyes were circled with kohl, the little bit of light flickering off his earrings. How could it be backward? This was the Ten Commandments we were talking about.

"These laws formed a group of slaves into an organized army," he said slowly.

"Ken?" I encouraged.

"Perhaps these were the first laws, the first try at the organization."

He'd lost me. My expression must have said as much.

"They came from Egypt, having been slaves for decades. What does a slave do?"

"Slave?" I asked jokingly.

Cheftu raised a brow at me.

"B'seder. They serve, they wait, they—"

"They don't make decisions for themselves," he said.

I fell silent. Slaves don't get a chance to think for themselves. We'd been slaves for only a few months. We'd been fed, clothed, sheltered, told where to be and when. After a few hundred years of that, people would become untrained in making decisions and following through. Not because they couldn't, but because it had been beaten out of them. So the Apiru always had someone telling them what to do: then overnight they were responsible for themselves?

"So they had exchanged an overseer for Shaday?" I asked. Dadua and his theory of Shaday being a slave owner was popping up again.

Cheftu sat on the ledge, pulling me beside him. "Think on it. The first laws were simple, basic. Mostly dealing with sacrifice, because that is something, as slaves, they would have understood and seen.

"Because they lived among people who revered their firstborn, the laws about redeeming one's firstborn, about not appearing before Shaday without a gift, these laws gave them the feeling of worshiping a god who was similar to, though not identical to, their neighbors. It was a familiar pathway."

He kissed my shoulder, then continued speaking. "Other laws dealing with holy days were another concept they comprehended because of their Egyptian heritage. The religious calendar and the taboo against following idols were the first things to learn."

"Because they were foremost in their minds?" I asked.

"Ken. They had recently served HatHor, the golden calf. They had to be told what was right and wrong in what they had done."

I nodded, following.

"These other laws you recite, the ones I recall from catechism, were more complex. They were for a people who had adapted to the idea that they owned themselves."

"So Moshe didn't write those?" I asked.

"Shaday did."

"Then I'm confused," I said in English.

"The first tablets, Shaday wrote them, *nachon?*" Cheftu asked.

The Ten Commandments movie flickered through my brain, the face of the actor replaced with the dark-eyed visage of Moshe, former crown prince of Egypt. Lighting, ostensibly the finger of God, had written the laws on stone tablets. Then Moses had walked down the mountain, thrown down the stones, and broken them.

"According to the Sages," I said hesitantly.

Cheftu laughed, kissing my neck, tightening his arms around me. "*Ken.* That is what the *tzadikim* say. Then after punishing the tribesmen, *ha*Moshe climbed the mountain again, taking down the Commandments in his own hand."

I turned to him. "Are you saying they dumbed them down, second go-round? Just because the people were too simplistic? So the Ten Commandments that I know, the ones my Mimi used to quote to me, these were the first given, but they were too complicated so Moses and God came up with a learner's version?"

He shrugged, the epitome of Gallic nonchalance. "Abraham bargained with Shaday about other things, so who is to say?"

It was a startling thought. "Do you think that the rules Shaday handed, the broken pieces, were the Ten Commandments we eventually got? So the ones the *ha*Moshe ended up reading to the populace are the ones that he received the second time around?"

I couldn't be still. I hopped up. "These laws that N'tan is reciting, they are the ones Moses received second? These are the simple ones, the training Commandments? These are the ones he wrote down?"

Cheftu was silent for a long moment. "It would be reasonable, for the Ten Commandments we know as such were far too complex thought processes for a herd of slaves." He smiled, catching the ends of my hair in his hand. "It would be like Shaday to make two plans, one for right then and one for posterity, yet neither contradictory. These we are observing now, these are very physical commands. Later, the laws become spiritual, they govern our inner selves. Those are the ones you recognize, but both are in the Holy Writ."

I wasn't sure whether I agreed with that or not. "What language did God write them in, you think?"

"One is tempted to say Hebrew," Cheftu said. "The Urim and Thummim are inscribed in Hebrew, so we know it was around. Written by then."

"What did Moshe write his in?" I asked.

Cheftu opened his mouth; just then I felt the kick he did. "Hieroglyphs?" His voice rose an octave, incredulous.

It was another thing I'd been thinking through. "Where are the pieces that God wrote?"

"In the Ark of the Covenant."

PART

VI

CHAPTER 15

RaEm woke up to the sound of a scuffle outside her tent door. Instantly alert, she crept forward. The soldier on duty sighed as his neck was slit. She was panicked a moment until she heard the words of the killer. "I come from Horetaten, My Majesty."

"Did you have to murder him?" she asked, opening the door, gesturing to the body on the ground.

"Aye. It was necessary." When the person stepped into the tent, RaEm saw that he was a she. A young, flat-chested woman, shaven headed and adorned like a priest, but female.

"What is the meaning of this?" RaEm asked.

"Horetamun, I mean——" She stumbled. "He was my master, My Majesty."

RaEm's eyes narrowed. "Go on."

"He was——" The girl inhaled raggedly. "They killed him, My Majesty."

RaEm felt terror. He was her sole ally! Her only tool! "Killed him?"

"The priests of Amun-Ra are on the rise, My Majesty. They seek to destroy the Aten and Pharaoh."

"Tell me everything," she said, gesturing for the girl to seat herself.

"The Inundation was poor."

"This I knew."

"The gold you sent, it wasn't enough."

RaEm winced against that thought. The tribesmen had thought themselves so clever to bury the gold with the rotting corpses. However, RaEm had personally lashed any soldier who would not dig. They had retrieved a lot of gold—armor and weapons inscribed with Hatshepsut's cartouche, a pharaoh none of the soldiers had ever heard of. RaEm had whipped them again, just for that oversight.

But it wasn't enough gold.

Then she had sent the tribute from Dadua, a nice contribution, but not enough to bribe all the nobles, all the priests, who had greedy palms.

"What happened?"

"He was praying to Amun in the god's room. He had dismissed the other priests, so as he prayed he dug out the stones, the gold, the riches that only he would know were missing."

It was a desperate measure. RaEm hoped the god would understand his reasoning was because of his love for Egypt.

"The, the other priest"—The girl wiped her nose with the back of her hand—"he was always jealous. He broke in with the guards and caught Horetamun in the act."

RaEm's eyes closed. She could imagine the scene, the jealousies, the rivalries. Temples were highly charged places for people who lusted for power. He had been kneeling, probably digging at the floor, when the door would have burst open.

"Did they kill him there?"

The girl shook her head. "He was executed."

"*Aii*, Isis, nay!" RaEm whispered. That meant he had endured a week of torture, ten full days of experiencing different "hells" that it was believed his soul would endure once he died.

He would have been covered with honey, left for ants.

His fingers severed and fed to Sobek, the crocodiles, while he watched.

Whipped in strips until he was a mass of blood, then left in the sun.

His tongue cut out, his teeth torn from his head.

Surgically eviscerated as he watched, but kept from dying.

His sex cut off, stuffed in his mouth.

Then blinded.

His body dipped in pitch and set aflame.

Nothing would remain; his name would be removed from every papyri, his seal sealed over, his ashes scattered on the winds in the desert, then his household sold to foreigners into the meanest slavery.

RaEm wept for him. She tore her clothes, beat her breast, covered her face and head in ashes, and sat in the darkness for three days, mourning him. But before she did that, she made sure the girl had gold, clothing, and sent her to Yaffo, to sail for the farthest island.

On the way, RaEm's agents, disguised as priests of Amun-Ra, would overtake her, kill her, and leave the body. The real priest would have trailed the girl. It would not do to have them connect the deposed high priest and the reigning co-regent of Egypt.

However, her death would be quick, painless. RaEm herself would see that she was mourned, her name written in many scrolls so she would live forever.

At the end of three days RaEm adorned herself as Smenkhare, summoned her traveling chair, and set off for the audience chamber of Dadua.

She'd lost her ally; she needed another.

Time had come for action. The golden totem would enter the city in a month. RaEm wondered if Akhenaten had that much time left. If he was assassinated, without her being behind it, then she would be viewed as the enemy also. Her priest Horetamun was supposed to have done it, then given the credit to her, the reigning pharaoh of Egypt. As Hatshepsut had treated her nephew Thutmosis, RaEm would have placed Tuti under house arrest and usurped his reign.

However, her tool had been discovered. She needed to return to Egypt soon, she needed to return with gold, and she needed to return with a triumphant army bearing spoils of war, the image of Egypt long ago.

The time was now; Horetamun had been dead almost a month.

I was standing on my balcony, grinding my own grain, since I had no slave, when the rains began in earnest. They'd been teasing along, sprinkling, a shower here and there. A little squall from cloudy skies most every afternoon. All week long it had been growing cooler. The fields had been plowed and planted; the grapes trampled into wine; the olives preserved; the pomegranates plucked; and the grain harvested.

Now the rainy season began.

It was my time to be "on the straw." As I watched the rain fall, I felt like crying. Which was ridiculous because everything was going well, really well. Better than any other time period I'd been in.

"You need a hobby," I told myself aloud. "One that will keep you from talking to yourself."

I missed my art, the wonder of creating something. Bread did not count as a creative outlet, though I had gotten very good at baking. I heard a knock on the door, so I set down the stone and ran for it. The mushroom stood in the pouring rain, dancing with a smile.

Right, she liked dancing in the rain. Footsteps of God or something.

"Avgay'el invites you to the first carding," she said. "This afternoon."

I stared at her; the girl was becoming a woman. Moreover, she was exquisite when she moved. Did she have any bones in her body? "When?"

"This afternoon."

"*B'seder*, but when?"

"Now."

"Uh, do I need to bring anything?"

"It's a carding," she said. "Are you coming?"

Why not. I closed the door behind me and followed her into the rain.

I plodded along, she danced. Even as she walked, she danced. She was unaware of the glances, the men who stopped in their tracks, reaching out to their friends to see this woman.

Ahead I saw a group of *giborim*. She was a child even though she moved like pouring oil. "You might want to walk normally for a bit," I said under my breath. She danced. They hadn't sighted her yet. One of them was the Klingon. Maybe we could just go around them?

Thunder.

Suddenly the rains changed from a straight, medium shower into a monumental downpour. I looked around for an overhang, but the mushroom shouted in delight. In the fading afternoon light she gyrated, twirled, and arabesqued her ways through the street.

The Klingon Uri'a saw her; I saw his face go slack with lust. Another *gibori* stepped forward, but Uri'a stopped him with his sword— Pelesti iron. They exchanged comments, which I could imagine were on the lines of "I saw her first."

And the mushroom danced on, her face raised. Your childhood is over, I thought. Uri'a watched. Angry at her, angry at myself, I stalked through the deluge, ripped off my head covering, and threw it around her. Then I grabbed her by the shoulders and we marched through the rain. She protested, but I couldn't forget Uri'a's expression.

Avgay'el and Shana needed to know this.

We arrived at the palace dripping wet, runny nosed, and generally gross.

An Egyptian stood in the courtyard, an Egyptian I hadn't seen before. Though he was dressed as a priest, he wore a sword like a soldier. His kohl had streaked down his face; in fact, he was drenched. No one was around. Curtly I told the mushroom to go the women's quarters. 'Sheva glanced balefully at me, then moved on.

"You have been attended, my lord?" I asked in Egyptian.

He was startled at the sight of me; his fingers moved in the air, making the motion against the Evil Eye since I had red hair and green eyes. "Nay, my, uh, lady," he said.

"Whom are you here to see? Pharaoh Smenkhare camps on the opposite hillside," I said, attempting usefulness. His eyes narrowed. I began to think I'd done the wrong thing. "Or are you here to see *haNasi* Dadua?"

"I bring news of a new pharaoh," he said.

"Akhenaten has flown to Osiris?"

"Akhenaten denied the existence of Osiris," he said coolly.

Okay, I was doing really well here. I decided to shut up while I could.

"Is the boy, Tuti, is he with Pharaoh?"

Was it my imagination or did the word *pharaoh* come with a lifetime of sarcasm? I shrugged. I didn't know. I offered him water, then headed to the women's quarters. Once inside, with Dadua's screaming, running children, I sought out Shana, told her of the messenger. Then I told her of the mushroom and Uri'a. She *tch*'d and sent me to the straw.

The children were laid down for a nap, and we were all passed tufts of wool and two pieces of wood: a tool with two prongs, another with only one. I was convinced, between carding wool and kneading dough, I would never have to tone again. It was hard work, and a hard work-out, being an ancient woman.

Was I always going to be one? I touched my stomach and fought back tears. Did I want to be?

"Tell us a story, Avgay'el!" the women demanded. Avgay'el was pregnant, though you couldn't tell. On the other hand, Dadua's newest wife, a foreign princess, was largely pregnant. In one sense it seemed weird; on the other, not. Polygamy, theoretically, seemed acceptable to me; was I becoming an ancient woman?

The skies had opened above Tziyon, drenching us. We could hear the pounding on the roof; the storms had darkened the room. Ahino'am bade the mushroom light lamps. Then I noticed that 'Sheva slipped away. More rain dancing, I thought. At least now she was in the safety of the palace.

Avgay'el picked up her tools and began scraping her cotton tuft, speaking in time to the sound, her voice strong and melodious. "Given the weather," she said, "I think I know which story to tell."

The women laughed. I focused on tearing apart my wool tuft so I could begin carding it.

"The story begins after the First Family had grown," Avgay'el began. "They covered the face of the earth. Now there was a race of giants, *anakim:* sons of heaven entered into the daughters of men. Hero figures roamed the land, men and women of mythic fame."

I squirmed around on my bit of straw, stretching out my puff of wool. Did this mean that the Bible made allowances for those creatures of mythology? Did I even have the same Bible? Somehow I thought if I'd read about God having a picnic, or giants and mythological figures being real, I would have been more interested.

Instead it had seemed like a lot of thous and begats.

I looked around the room, the one nursing woman, the two expecting wives, the four concubines, all in various stages of pregnancy: the begats were pretty accurate.

Avgay'el turned her carders, pausing to look around at us all. "So then: Yahwe looked upon the earthling, for he was growing to be a monster in the land. His imagination created evil thoughts, which grew into bad actions. Yahwe's heart was saddened, as a father whose son chooses an infertile life. 'I will cleanse the earthlings from the land,' he said. 'Human and animal, crawling creature and flying bird. I regret that I made them.' "

The women watched her, sad eyed at the thought of God's pain. I tried to force myself not to make her words fit anything I knew. I wanted just to hear the story and enjoy it for what it was: rainy day in the harem, the camaraderie of women working together, spellbound.

"Noach the Innocent warmed Yahwe's heart, though."

Noah, of course. Why should I be surprised? Rainy weather like this did make one think of arks. I heard her say that God told Noach to enter the ark because he was upright among the nations. "Gather in seven by seven—male and female who are mated—from every clean creature."

Seven by seven? What happened to two by two?

"From the unclean creatures take one male and one female. Seven by seven birds, male and female. They spread the seeds of life across the earth's face."

"I wish he would have left the snakes," Hag'it said. "They could have drowned along with the unclean people. I wouldn't have missed them." The rest of the women laughed. Avgay'el smiled, then turned her carding tools again.

"So: Yahwe said that in another seven days, water would fall on the earth, unrelenting for forty days and nights. In this way he would wipe the earth of all the creatures he had formed from clay. Noach, his wife, his sons, and their wives entered the ark as Yahwe had said.

"Now look: For seven days, then the water falls for forty days and nights. Yahwe shuts the door on Noach. The water lifted the ark, and for forty days it floated above the land. The water consumed everything, wiping the face of the earth clean. The ark floated across the face of the earth. All the high mountains were subdued by the water."

I thought of flying over the Swiss Alps, the snowy peaks that poked through the clouds, easily visible from twenty-five thousand feet. Those heights covered by water? It seemed ludicrous, but my skepticism lever was getting rusty. God seemed to manage well outside my ability to understand or believe. And in the end, did my belief, or disbelief, really change anything?

Avgay'el continued. "The waters rose fifteen cubits above the submerged mountains. The *nefesh* had vanished from the land. All that had walked, or flown, or crawled; all were erased. Only Noach and his company continued to exist.

"Now the rain from the sky was held back. The waters came, so they were going. Now look: The window Noach had built is opened. He reaches out with a dove, to see if the waters have rolled back from the Land."

How many versions of this had I seen in art? From the Renaissance to the present day: the animals' heads poking out of the windows in the ark, Noah releasing the dove, waiting for its return.

But this time I saw what I'd never noticed before. The terrible loneliness of being the only people on the planet; the overwhelming fear of a God who was introspective and flexible enough—in a way—to destroy his creation because it wasn't up to his standards. As though those people and animals had been pots; thrown, glazed, and fired but warped beyond repair and useless. Thus they had to be destroyed.

But for the first time, I understood God. This was a perspective that I could understand. God as a creator—who was less than pleased with his work. How many times had I painted over a canvas? Pitched out a sculpture? Rethrown a pot?

My musing made me miss when the dove didn't return, though I knew already that moment in the story. Avgay'el sipped some wine, refreshing her voice before continuing. "Now Noach built an altar to Yahwe, took from the clean creatures, the clean birds, offering them up: burned sacrifices on the altar.

"Yahwe's heart was soothed; his nose smelled a pleasing scent. He thought: Never again will I pass judgment on the earth because of the actions of the earthling. When they use the gift of my creativity for evil thoughts, it results in evil deeds. Nevertheless, I will never again destroy all that lives, just to destroy him."

I heard the first small voice calling for his mother. Avgay'el finished quickly. "So here they were: the sons of Noach leaving the ark. Shem, Ham, and Yafat. From these three sons, man spread across the earth."

We'd all carded our tufts into strands that would be made into thread. As we handed back the paddles, I saw the mushroom stagger in. She was bloody, her face bruised.

I felt sick, filled with premonition. " 'Sheva," I said, running to her side. " 'Sheva, what happened?"

She said nothing, just stared into the distance. Shana took her arm, shook her sharply. "You! 'Sheva!" but even that brought no result. Avgay'el touched her hair, noting a bite mark on her neck.

A big bite mark. Oh no, no, no, I thought.

"Lift her dress," Shana said.

I was one of the ones who helped. The girl had been mauled. Assaulted in the mud. The women's expressions were all solemn, but no one was weeping. Avgay'el and Shana exchanged glances.

"Carry her into the straw, Klo-ee," Avgay'el said. "Shana will examine her."

I picked her up, slipping my arm beneath her knees. She was so fragile, now catatonic. Someone had abused her? This seemed inconceivable. These people didn't even rape when they sacked a city! I laid her down on the straw, while the women brought wine for her, then lamps so they could see. Hag'it acted as her pillow, cradling the mushroom's head in her lap, brushing her moonbeam-colored hair away from her face. Ahino'am brought heated rags, which we used to gently clean off the mud and blood.

Her dress was removed, and she was wrapped in an animal skin, shivering and teeth chattering. Shana, Avgay'el holding up a lamp over her shoulder, examined the girl. I didn't watch, but I did note that she had just started growing pubic hair. She was a child, no matter what her body proclaimed.

Bruises marred her skin; it was easy to follow what had happened: he'd held her down with his forearm, just above her throat. If she moved, she would choke. A big knee had ended up in her soft belly. What kind of brute were we talking about? Her thighs had been wrenched apart and held. We practically could have taken fingerprints of the assailant!

Shana's small hands were quick. Dadua's sister shook her head sadly, her eyes glittering with tears. "Her maidenhood is gone," she said. "I will tell Dadua."

"What is the penalty?" I asked. I was fairly certain who had done this, who had defiled this poor child.

Everyone looked at me blankly.

"Uri'a's guilty, of this I would swear. I told you how he was looking at her earlier." I looked around the room. "Is there a prison? Will he be flogged?"

Avgay'el frowned at me. "At times I forget you are Pelesti, Klo-ee. There is no punishment. They will be wed."

"He raped her? Now he'll get to marry her so he can rape her at will?"

Dadua's wife shrugged. "It is the least elegant way to get a bride, nachon—"

"What are the other ways?" I asked, still outraged.

"Seduction or purchase," she answered. "How did your husband get you?"

"He asked me."

They gasped. "He didn't pay for you? He didn't seduce you so that you were bound to him?"

"*Lo.* And he certainly didn't rape me!" I looked down at the sleeping mushroom. "She is just a child! Now she will have to endure this behavior forever!"

"This is good for her," Shana said stoically. "Not the experience.— It would have been better had he used soft words and gentle touches,— but she is a slave. He has treated her as a freedwoman. Now she will be the wife of a *gibori*. She will have her own slaves, a home, clothing, children. *Ach*, it is a blessing!"

I was going to be ill. "A rape is a blessing?" I gasped out.

"Batsheva was no one," Shana said.

I knew that "t" and "th" were interchangeable in this *alef-bet*. As were "b" and "v." Presto-chango and omigod, I had been grinding grain with Bathsheba? Surely not *the* Bathsheba? This scrawny, buck-toothed girl couldn't be Bathsheba of biblical fame? Mother of Solomon, the world's wisest man?

"Now she will be a mother, with fine, strong sons."

Why not, Chloe? I looked down at the mushroom—Bathsheba—and realized her days of being no one were rapidly drawing to a close. Didn't David kill her husband to get at her? Suddenly that murder seemed more justifiable.

The perpetrator was already married to her according to the law; now it was a matter of the formalities. Since 'Sheva was a slave, Dadua served as her father. Shana donned a headcloth to approach the king on 'Sheva's behalf.

We covered up her sleeping body, then dispersed.

I staggered through the rain, thinking about God's proclamation that misused creativity was the root of evil actions, the ultimate reason the "earthlings" were destroyed. Yet this kind of imagination was the only thing that allowed a person to grasp the idea of a god, especially an invisible one.

I really *was* going to become a Hindu.

CHEFTU OPENED THE DOOR, sensed immediately that something was wrong. There was no welcoming fire, no smell of something burning, no cheery greeting. It was cold, dark, and in the quiet he heard her tears.

He ran through the house to the balcony. Chloe was seated with her back against the wall, sobbing. He crouched beside her. "Chloe? Beloved?"

She immediately jerked upright, wiping her face. "It's this late? I'm sorry, I—"

She made to get up, but she was speaking English, so he knew she was extremely upset. He pressed her still, his hand on her shoulder. Her face was splotched, her nose running, her eyes bloodshot. He sat beside her, hissing a little as the cold rain touched his body. He needed to change his linen tunics for wool to survive a Jerusalem winter.

He kissed the back of her hand and waited. She stared out the window, onto the brown hillside. "Why are we here?"

Cheftu shrugged. "It is where the lintels brought us?"

She sniffed, rubbing her nose with her hand. "God, what I wouldn't give for Kleenex!"

He didn't know what a "kleenex" was, but he had a makeshift handkerchief. She thanked him and blew her nose.

"We are here, but nothing has changed. I think we probably messed up history, because we kept the people who had done this stuff before from doing it this time."

"Stuff?" he repeated, confused. "Beloved, you must speak clearly when you choose English. What stuff?"

"Jersualem. The Ark. Bathsheba."

So she had heard. Uri'a the Hittite would marry Bathsheba. At some point the Bible said that David would see her bathing, then after a night of passion she would be found pregnant. Attempts would be made to lure Uri'a into bed with his own wife, but they would fail.

David would arrange for Yoav to get Uri'a killed in battle.

The king would marry his paramour.

N'tan, the *tzadik*, would disguise the story and tell it to the king, asking for his judgment. David would grow furious, claim that the man in the story deserved punishment. Then N'tan would utter the phrase that became his legacy: "You are that man."

Bathsheba and David's first child would die. They would have another, who would be Solomon.

Everything was happening, just as Holy Writ said. Not as Cheftu had imagined these Bible stories would be enacted, but it followed the very words.

The very words an Egyptian scribe in the Israelite court reported.

"What about that 'stuff'?"

"Why are we here?" she said, looking at him. "This history is already in place. We weren't needed. This was pointless!"

He looked into the sky, wondering how *le bon Dieu*, if indeed he dwelt in the sky, felt about her comment. "Shall we start with Jerusalem?" he said.

Chloe shrugged. "Sure." She blew her nose again. "It was invaded. We know that."

"You know this from history?" he asked.

She nodded.

"How do you know that you weren't the essential piece to this invasion?"

"Jersalem was invaded by David. You're saying I've always been a part of this history?" Her voice sounded tinged with hysteria.

The concept was staggering, he had to admit. Then again, it made sense in a circular sort of way. "Now look: You talk of destiny, a path that God has made for you."

"You sound like Avga'el when you speak Hebrew," she commented.

He glanced at her and continued speaking. "Then you talk of history, of a path you know was carved." He shrugged. "It follows that perhaps you have always been in this history; perhaps being part of the invasion is your destiny."

"And being a writer of the Bible is yours?"

Cheftu realized that if the one statement were to be true, then the other might be as well. So history was fabricated by the future? It didn't follow Greek, linear thinking, the thought processes of Europeans or, he guessed, Americans. But it had the Byzantine twists of the East, the legacy of the labyrinth, in its reasoning.

It had imagination. It was a creative way to weave history. Was it possible that scores of people were traveling from one time to another? Did people from beyond Chloe's future travel to beyond the past he and Chloe were aware of?

Perhaps they were not as unique as he'd thought?

"If what you are saying is anywhere close to being the truth, then if I weren't here . . ." She trailed off, shaking her head. The rains, which had slackened, started heavily again. "The idea is staggering: no Jerusalem for the Jews? or the Christians? or the Muslims?" She was mumbling to herself. "No Middle East peace knot, but no monotheism, either?" She looked at him. "If there were no Jerusalem, where would the Temple be built? Where would Christ be crucified? Where would Mohammed return to earth?"

Cheftu shrugged. It seemed a ridiculous idea, all of this history perched on one ivory set of shoulders. "Yoav picked you."

"Why? Why me?"

"He obviously knows more of your military experience than I."

"No, he didn't. No one knows of my military experience."

"Will you tell me?" Cheftu heard the hope in his tone. He'd been curious for years, but she never spoke of her modern life. In fact, he knew more of who she'd been from RaEm's comments than from her own. Did she know how amazing she was to him?

"Sure, why not?" Still speaking English, so she was yet upset.

"How did you serve?" he asked.

"Officer in the air force, the USAF."

Cheftu shook his head in amazement. "A military that flies, *mon Dieu*, what wonder! Tell me from the beginning."

"I started high school early because I'd skipped around so many schools. Which meant I started university early. By the time I graduated, I was only twenty years old. My plan was to do a stint, maybe five or ten years, in the air force as an officer."

"Why?"

She chuckled. "Someone from my family had always been in the military. In the English branch of my family we've fought since Cromwell. I'd grown up hearing about the War Between the States from the American side. My father had served in Vietnam. It was tradition, it was important to me."

"But you are a woman."

"You noticed?" she said teasingly.

Cheftu kissed her hand. "A little." He winked. "Did that not present problems for you?"

"Of course it did, but I didn't care. The more difficult it became, the more determined I became. I felt like my family's honor was on my shoulders."

"Did they support you?"

"You must be joking. My father was livid, Mimi cried, and my mother tore up an entire rose garden in her fury. Only my siblings supported me, understood." Chloe linked her fingers with his. "I was the last of us to declare my filial freedom. So . . . I did the training."

She looked away, her gaze seeing some other world.

"I was in Te—the same state where my grandmother was."

"Mimi?"

"She would have loved the way you say that, with the accent on the second *mi*." She smiled at him, her green eyes dark with pain but fighting through it. "You're so French."

Cheftu kissed her hand. "*Oui, madame.* Continue?"

"At the last minute, before finals week, I had a chance to go see her. It was a Friday afternoon; the leaves were changing with the seasons. I let myself into her house. It was a big Victorian, with a wraparound porch." She wet her lips. "Mimi was sitting in the living room, in the dark, crying." Cheftu reached over and squeezed her hand, fighting to understand through her *américain* accent. "She had just heard from her doctor. She had cancer."

"*Mon Dieu,*" he whispered, aching for her. Cancer—that unknow-

430 SUZANNE FRANK

able, unconquerable illness that took so many, for no reason. Even in Chloe's time it was the same? An ultimate evil?

"Well, I was finishing my last semester of university. I'd been on a temporary assignment for the air force, close by. Mimi did chemotherapy, she tried, she tried. . . . But after a year, when I'd been on active duty, it was obvious she could no longer take care of herself. My father couldn't come home, my mom had come back sporadically, but . . ." She sighed. "I went to my commanding officer. I told him that Mimi didn't have long and I wanted to be with her. So we made a deal." She glanced up, smiled. "I haven't bartered often, I'm lousy at it, but for this I fought with every tool I had."

"What was your arrangement?"

"I would leave active duty, go into a temporary retirement, but continue reservist assignments. Which meant that out of the month, I was active for a week and active for a whole other month out of the year." She shrugged. "Most of my skills were computer based anyway."

"Com-puu-ter?" This was a new technology—fortunately he knew that from RaEm. Exactly what it meant, he did not know. However, from RaEm's comments it was re-creating the world in much the same way movable type had.

"New technology, yep," she said, still speaking English. "For this deal, I would serve twice my original time as a reservist, minus what I'd already served as active duty. Eight years." She groaned. "Don't ask how RaEm effected that part of my life. You don't want to know. In a way, I feel guilty. I mean, it is my name on those documents, my reputation. My poor father . . ."

It was complete darkness and cold. Winter was seeping into the stone. Chloe snuggled close to him, sharing her woolen cloak. "Do you think we will ever return to our home times?" she asked. "Do you think we are doomed to wander history? Well, not doomed like a bad thing. . . ."

"Doomed can be a good thing?" he asked, teasing.

"Destined, maybe."

He twined a strand of her copper hair around his brown finger. "Would that be such a bad life, *chérie?*"

"No. Of course not. It would be thrilling, it would be exciting. Provided we survive it."

"Is that not true for every day, in any time?" he asked. "Is anything ever certain?"

"But what about when we're old? I mean, even Indiana Jones retired after a while."

Cheftu sat up, cross-legged. "Who is this Indiana Jones? You mention him from time to time. Was he a mentor of yours?"

She giggled. "There are some gaps we will never bridge, *chérie*," she said. In French. Cheftu felt his concern fading a little; she was feeling better.

"So Yoav did not know of your military experience?"

"Computer skills wouldn't have helped him much," she said wryly. "He knew that I'd had some training, though. I guess it was obvious." English again.

"Then he chose you for that?"

"So if I wasn't here, then maybe, what, Jerusalem wouldn't have been invaded?" She laughed bitterly. "That can't be true."

"Maybe there was another plan. Maybe a thousand other plans, incorporating a thousand other souls," he countered. "If you chose not to, there would be another. But you didn't."

"I've never said this to you before, but Cheftu, you are mad."

"Because you are one woman?"

"I couldn't be this important. I am a mere cog in the machine. I am a modern woman. This is an ancient time. I couldn't be that vital!"

"You are probably right," he agreed. It was madness. "So if not you, then someone else. You probably are right."

"What if I'm wrong?" she asked, edgy.

He shifted, his hand on her neck, slowly rubbing the knots away. "God plucked you from your family to send you back to my time, Hatshepsut's time, *haii?*"

Again she nodded.

"From there he took you to Aztlan?"

"*Ken.*"

"Now, you are here. Already you have moved from being a grain-grinding slave to being a contemporary of Dadua's wives. You have survived remeeting RaEm!"

"So have you," she said with a laugh.

"We'll get to me later," Cheftu commented. "Think on this, beloved. Is not God big enough to keep you from error, should it be that all-encompassing?"

She was silent, her head bowed. "I believe in free will," she finally said.

"You have free choice, daily," Cheftu said. "But *by* your fear of error, by your desire to do what was right, you have chosen to be a tool of God."

"So are we done, then? Do we just retire in David's Jerusalem? Where rape is an acceptable way of getting engaged?" Her voice rose at the last, and he heard the disgust, the fear. "What if we have a little girl?"

His hand stilled on her shoulder. "Is that a possibility?"

She shrugged. "Not this month."

He tipped her face to his. "There is next month, and the month after that. I do not tire of loving you, *chérie.*"

Chloe took his hands in hers, scooting so they sat knee to knee, cross-legged like scribes. "When you look at me I know that the time gaps in our lives don't matter, that our different centuries of origin don't matter. If anyone has ever healed me or has known me, it is you."

Cheftu was reading over the newest missive from Egypt delivered by the Egyptian messenger who didn't want to stay with the Egyptians. Quite odd. According to this document, Pharaoh Tutankhaten now ruled. There was no mention of Akhenaten or the Aten at all. Did RaEm, as Smenkhare, know she had been usurped?

Wasn't Tutankhaten the small boy in the Egyptian camp? More important, wasn't he under RaEm's wing? Cheftu was puzzling over this when he heard a discreet cough. He turned. "N'tan!"

"Chavsha," the *tzadik* said. He closed the door behind him, shutting out the sounds of the Tsori building and the ever-present limestone dust.

The physician in Cheftu noted that the man didn't look healthy. Though he had bravely borne the death of his wife, there was a sadness in his gaze that Cheftu feared would never go away. According to Chloe, women were lining up to see who would be his next bride, but N'tan didn't even glance their way.

There were dark circles under the man's eyes, and his hands were trembling. "Seat yourself, my friend," Cheftu said. "Shall I call for wine? For an herbal?" He walked around his table, and seated himself opposite. "Tell me, what is the matter?"

N'tan plucked at his beard nervously. His gaze was reluctant to meet Cheftu's. "I have erred greatly, I fear."

"How is that?"

"The Temple, the House of God."

Cheftu felt his breath catch.

"Previously, I told Dadua that if it seemed right to him to build a temple, a house for Shaday, then he should. But I dream at night." N'tan shuddered. "Such awful dreams. I do not remember them upon waking, but the message is clear."

Cheftu nodded mutely.

"Dadua is covered in blood. His purpose was to build a people, carve them from the very flesh of our neighbors." Again N'tan shivered. "One of his sons will build the Temple, a man of peace, just as Dadua is a man of war."

Again Cheftu nodded.

"It is an uncertain thing to have the *tzadik* change his mind. Which is why I journey to you."

"Me?"

"You carry with you magical stones." N'tan looked away. "It is written by my forefathers, passed down through the Imhoteps. They tell you the right thing to do. Will you see if I should tell Dadua that he cannot build? Will you be certain for me?"

Cheftu slipped them from his waist, since there was no longer a need to keep them in other, more difficult to reach places. They warmed his hands, twitching when he brought them close together. "What do you ask?"

"Are my dreams real—*lo,lo,*" N'tan said, falling into silence. "Ask if my interpretation of the dreams is accurate."

Cheftu asked, then threw the stones. It was a simple response, quick.

"*K-e-n.*"

"Is there more you would know?"

N'tan smiled weakly. "How angry Dadua will be?" he asked facetiously. Straightening his shoulders, he said, "I do not want to know that, not really. It makes no matter his response. My avocation is *tzadik.* This is the burden of it. *Todah rabah,* my friend."

"*Shalom,* N'tan," Cheftu said as the prophet closed the door.

Cheftu dropped to his knees, the words in his mind as clearly as if the Holy Writ were before him:

"Go and tell my servant David this is what the Lord says: You are not the one to build me a house to dwell in. I have not dwelt in a house from the day I brought Israel up out of Egypt to this day. I have moved from one tent site to another, from one dwelling place to another. Wherever I have moved with all the Israelites, did I ever say to any of their leaders whom I commanded to shepherd my people, 'Why have you not built me a house?'

"Now then, tell my servant David, This is what the Lord Almighty says: I took you from the pasture and from following the flock, to be ruler over my people Israel. I have been with you wherever you have gone, and I have cut off all your enemies from before you.

"Now I will make your name like the names of the greatest men of the earth. And I will provide a place for my people Israel and I will plant them so that they can have a home of their own and no longer be disturbed. Wicked people will not oppress them anymore, as they did at the beginning and have done ever since the time I appointed leaders over my people Israel. I will also subdue all your enemies.

"I declare to you that the Lord will build a house for you: When your days are over and you go to be with your fathers, I will raise up your own son, and I will establish his kingdom. He is the one who will build a house for me, and I will establish his throne forever."

Cheftu didn't know why, or how, but those were the words of God that would pass down through the ages. David's throne was to be es-

tablished forever. He was God's favorite, the incorporation of the divine nishmat ha hayyim, filled with the zeal of Shaday. For these things he was honored.

And through him, all earthlings were blessed. Cheftu's forehead touched the floor as he whispered, *"Sela."* Thunder rumbled outside. It was beginning to rain, again.

THE MUSHROOM, BATHSHEBA, hadn't spoken. We were gathered around her, family as it were, of the bride. She stared listlessly into space. Shana and Hag'it had curled her hair, then made up her face with fragile pinks and smoky grays.

Avgay'el had loaned her a dress of red, for rejoicing. It was embroidered with silver and gold, with tiny seed pearls studded around the neck. A dowry headband with silver coins matched a necklace of silver coins.

She sat.

The atmosphere was forced, but what more could be done? It seemed barbaric to me, but this would be better for her than being a slave, right? After all, Bathsheba had to marry Uri'a, then, well, marry Dadua, because if not, then where would Solomon come from?

If there was no Solomon . . . I didn't know.

Or was it as Cheftu suggested: there were really a thousand ways, a thousand other souls, and if it didn't happen this way, then another avenue would be chosen? I couldn't wrap my mind around the concept of alternative realities; it was too sci-fi.

By making one choice, did we step into another universe of choices? Were they all connected by filaments like a giant web? If I hadn't been there in Jerusalem, would another woman have done it, and I been killed in the battle of Ashqelon instead?

Better I should stick to my assignment of hennaeing 'Sheva's hands and feet. The women were dancing and drinking while I sat with the mushroom. She held her palms up to me.

"*HaMelekh* will see me," she whispered. "Make me beautiful?"

The irony of that statement was almost beyond belief, but I picked up the brushes. She had never struck me as a woman of flowers; most of the henna designs I had seen used flowers.

Raindrops!

Her hands were long and thin; strange that I never noticed that before. They were perfect hands for a dancer, expressive and eloquent. After dipping the end of the henna stick, which was effectively my brush, I drew little raindrops, like tiny paisleys, in streams down her fingers. Then I surrounded them with dots. Now her palm.

"What do you like?" I asked her, my voice soft beneath the sound of women laughing.

"I like the raindrops," she said.

"I did those."

"I like leaves."

Leaves would look too much like raindrops, I thought. "What else?"

"Stars."

I looked at the palm of her hand. The lines in her hands seemed to split into two directions, one going toward her mound of Venus, the other toward the outer part of her hand. I followed the creases, then connected them. It was a triangle, in a rather Islamic, curved kind of way.

"Stars," she repeated.

With the same angle and swoop, I put another triangle over the first. Then, just to fill it out, I drew raindrops flowing away from it. Her other hand was a repeat of the pattern. They looked like Jewish stars, but she was a good Jewish girl, so why not? When I finished we all toasted her once more, then stood as her guard to meet with Uri'a in one of the recently finished cedar chambers, since it was raining outside and cold. 'Sheva wasn't trembling; in fact, she walked gracefully, proudly, her flowing platinum hair in stark contrast with her red gown.

The Klingon awaited her beneath the wedding canopy. Since he had already taken his ease with her, there was not much celebration.

His family, if they were here, didn't attend. Only N'tan, Dadua, and the harem women were present.

It was over quickly, then the feast. We all ate little, drank a lot, then Uri'a picked up his bride to carry her to his home. "Wait!" Dadua cried. "My right as king, *gibori,* is to kiss the bride!"

We laughed. Under normal circumstances this would be jolly. It seemed forced today. Yet I was grateful he had done this, because the mushroom wanted nothing else in her entire life except to have a kiss from the king and dance in the rain. Would history change? Had it? Uri'a set her down, and Dadua took her hands in his, looking into her face.

Was anyone else breathing fast? I couldn't believe I was seeing this!

"Uri'a is a good man. Faithful to me. Be faithful to him." 'Sheva gazed at him as though he hung the stars, the stars that she liked, just for her. "May Shaday bless you with many children," Dadua said. "May those children rise to do good things for the tribes." She tilted up her head, the better to be kissed. Instead Dadua kissed her one palm, then the other.

He frowned at my henna job, then kissed her right palm again. Uri'a picked her up, now boneless with disappointment, and carried her off.

Thunder shook the building. Avgay'el invited me to stay, wait for Cheftu to finish his day's work, in the peace of the women's quarters. I had fallen asleep when Avgay'el nudged me. Her voice was low. "Dadua wants to see you."

I rinsed my face and walked with Shana to a smaller audience chamber. Yoav was there, frowning over a papyrus. Dadua hopped up when he saw me. "Would you care for wine, Klo-ee?"

"*B'seder,*" I said.

"The temple, *ach,* well, Shaday does not want me to build it."

Cheftu had mentioned that; it was completely in keeping with what we knew of the Bible.

"So, I wish to make a uniform that all the *giborim* will wear."

The Egyptians' and Pelestis' professional appearance had gotten to him?

"Yoav," he said, gesturing to the *Rosh Tsor haHagana,* "has commissioned shields from your cousins, the Pelesti, in Ashdod."

I nodded.

"Perhaps you could speak to them, work us a deal?"

I nodded; I was getting better at bartering, and I would take Cheftu. Maybe I could even see Wadia?

Dadua stepped closer to me. I could smell his skin, he was so close. The mushroom would kill me to be here now. "I have sought for an emblem to symbolize Tziyon, our position here." He raised his hands in frustration. "Nothing, nothing comes to me. Not even Hiram's skilled and gifted designers can think of a thing."

"*Ken?*"

"Then today, at that girl's wedding, I see it!"

"See what?"

"The emblem! It is so clear," Dadua cried. "Such a standard for Tziyon, for the united monarchy!"

I was holding my breath.

"This! It is this!" He whipped out a piece of papyrus. There, with far less grace than the original, was my design from the mushroom's hand. Without the swirls, the curves, the angles, it was simply one triangle.

With another over it, upside down.

"It has three points, the sacred cities in the north on one, then three other points, the sacred cities of the south, on the other. They overlap in Tziyon!"

I stared at it. Two triangles that did indeed overlap.

"This will be easy to do! We can put it everywhere!"

I like stars, the mushroom had said. So I made one. From two triangles. Then a man named David, who just started a country, saw it. Liked it. Decided to use it.

Could I put this on my résumé?

"It will be the Shield of Shalem, for this city will be a city of peace, a city of Shaday. It's perfect!"

I designed the Shield of Solomon, also called the Star of David, because I knew that it was the Star of David, because of history. The history that I had just made—sort of. There was nothing to do but laugh. Circular reasoning had become my life.

CHAPTER 16

"I<small>T PLEASES ME THAT YOU</small> have joined in my feasting," RaEm said, reclining.

Dadua, flanked by several soldiers, stood in her doorway. The tents of her people weren't accustomed to the rains, so her soldiers had learned from the Tsori how to cut the trees. Now a wooden shelter covered her tent but darkened it. And nothing could keep out the cold. She shivered, but when *haNasi*'s gaze dropped to her hardened nipples RaEm sent a quick word of thanks to the gods of cold weather.

"Please, make yourself comfortable, *adoni*," she invited, practicing this tongue that was so foreign. However, she'd had little else to do during the heat of summer. "Your soldiers can wait in the comfort of the next tent. My slaves will see that our needs are met."

He had black eyes, not unlike Hiram's, but his were almost too filled with soul. They seemed to point out all the lack in her own. He dismissed his men and joined her. In deference to his ways she had laid a low table surrounded by silken pillows. Incense burned in braziers throughout the room, giving off heat and scent. He lay down opposite the narrow gilded table from her, his body stretched out across from hers.

RaEm poured the wine and handed it to him. "To the unification of our peoples," she said.

He held it to his lips, swallowed, but she knew he drank nothing. "Forgive me, *adoni*," she said, taking the cup back from him. "We are both accustomed to the wiliness of court, are we not?" She drank, wondering how much of the powdered mandrake aphrodisiac was flowing into her veins. "You can know it is safe now." She returned it.

It was a measure of face now; he had to drink lustily or he would be calling Pharaoh of Egypt a potential murderer. He downed the cup, and she heaved a sigh of relief. This would be easy; she should have more faith in herself. He just unnerved her with his steady breathing and his one, frowning god.

With a smile she summoned the slave girls. They were dressed in beads and wigs only, shaved and perfumed, selected because of their beauty and elegant movements. Designed to fire the passions of this king.

His gaze followed them as he conversed with RaEm over the mundane matters of agriculture and court. They were purposefully questions he could answer in his sleep. The girls served him, brushing against his body, refreshing his cup, pouring more mandrake into his already aroused body.

RaEm blessed the gods. It was going well.

The temperature in the tent rose as the evening cooled outside. Dadua was flushed, his eyes bright, his words slurring together. RaEm felt desire filling her body for the first time in many months. The lamps flickered; behind a curtained wall a solitary flute played. She laughed, he jested, their occasional touches grew more meaningful, until she was leaning against his thigh in the middle of a story and he interrupted her.

"Are you man or woman?"

RaEm threw back her head and laughed. This was exactly what she wanted. Her unsteady fingers released the clasp of her gown. Her breasts were shameful to see, but still sensitive. She turned so that she was seated on her haunches before him. He watched her gilded nails move over her body, pinching her swollen nipples. His mouth opened, his eyes focused on her. "What do you think, *adoni?*" she asked. RaEm reached for his hand, placing it on her chest. Instinctively he cupped her, his dark gaze flying up to her face.

His hands slipped over her shoulder to her neck, drawing her to him. His mouth was hot and mobile. He kissed the way he fought, the way he negotiated, the way he did everything: he seduced her mouth slowly. His other hand moved over her bare back, cupping her backside, pressing her against him.

"So how are you the co-regent of Egypt?" he asked RaEm, then kissed her deeply. His fingers were slipping beneath her kilt, finding her warm and wet.

"Pharaoh . . . is . . . my father-in-law," RaEm whispered, praying that he would not stop touching her. It had been so long; it felt so good.

"He has another son?" he asked, suckling her breast.

"His daughter Meryaten," she slurred, feeling the heat of her body, its want.

He froze.

RaEm writhed beneath his hands. "Don't fear, we do not break your laws. She died." Please HatHor, let nothing stop him, she thought.

His fingers were curved inside her. "You were married to a woman?" His voice was sounding clearer.

"It was politics," RaEm said, the haze fading as he talked and didn't touch.

In one movement he pushed her away, dipping his fingers in wine, rubbing his mouth. "You freak! You were wed to a woman?"

Her shirt was off, her kilt around her waist; she was completely exposed. "It was politics!"

"What kind of creature are you?" he asked, stumbling to his feet. "What was I about to join with?" He spat, then wiped his fingers on the table's cloth.

RaEm was furious. "Perhaps you should ask that question, *adoni*," she said. "How would your priests view you being with the pharaoh, masculine, of Egypt? Any slave of mine would swear I had you on your knees, mounting you like a pig!"

He flinched as though he'd been struck.

"No one would dare suggest I was less than a man, no one has that much imagination."

"What are you asking, Smenkhare, if that is your name?"

"You have gold. I want it."

"*Ach!* Covetousness! I should have known!"

"Your fifty Pelesti shields and I will go away quietly."

His gaze raked her up and down. Then he shook his head. "No wonder Shaday wanted us out of Egypt. You are a corrupt, vile creature. Tell what you will to whom you will. I don't fear you."

"You should!" RaEm hissed. "I have more power in this world and the next than you can imagine. I can summon lighting at my will. I can command a thousand to die on a whim. I know the future!" She was shaking, livid, fighting the mandrake, and battling his revulsion.

He laughed. "If you are so powerful, then why do you hold an eight-year-old boy hostage, why do you seduce a man who thinks you are disgusting, and why do need my gold?"

Screaming with fury, RaEm seized her dagger and rushed Dadua. She felt the blade sink into flesh, then she was thrown. Another man spoke, his Egyptian heavily accented. "This is attempted murder, Pharaoh. Unless you want a war, leave this land."

She looked up. The big green-eyed soldier was removing the body of a girl, an Egyptian slave girl, who had a dagger plunged into her breast. Dadua had been felled but not marked. RaEm had killed her own. Her gaze met Dadua's. "If you wish to continue your pretense, you should cover your woman's body," he said.

RaEm looked down. She was naked. Female.

Powerless.

ONCE AGAIN WE WERE GROUPED—this time by royal decree. Where there had been shouting, there was silence. Where there had been drinking and feasting, there was fasting. Where the attitude had been revelry and celebration, there was now reverence and fear.

Where there had been sunshine, now we stood in pouring rain.

Again the doors were opened. Instead of a wagon, the Seat hung from golden poles, carried between the Levim like a traveling chair. The *elohim* were holding hands, the curve of their wings protecting the actual top of the box from the downpour.

I shivered. I wasn't going to pay attention to them. I didn't really want to know if they moved or not. I'd prefer to think I was drunk. Save that no one had had wine.

The blue-and-white-clad Levim stepped forward with the Seat suspended. Moving at a funereal march, they progressed solemnly. The poles holding the Seat were at least ten feet long, three men holding each end, standing well away.

The Ark must weigh a lot more than Indy thought.

Dadua walked before the Seat, wearing the stone-studded breastplate of the high priest and a simple slave's kilt. No crown, no jewels, for today he was a petitioner, not a king.

At the seventh step, Dadua halted. N'tan led out an ox, pure, white, and healthy. With prayers he slit the creature's throat, splashing blood. It soaked into the dirt, mixing with the rain, running between the bare toes of the Levim.

I darted a glance at the two golden figures that graced the top of the box. Were they closer? Don't ask don't tell, I admonished myself.

When the ox was dead, three Levim dragged it away. We all waited in tense silence. Dadua took a step forward, blood spatters washing down his legs in the rain.

Nothing happened.

N'tan blew the *shofar* as the Levim stepped forward. Step together. We all waited. Nothing happened. As a body, the tribesmen exhaled. In a solemn measure the Seat progressed toward Tziyon of God. Another seven steps, then the second ox was sacrificed.

As a group, we moved in time with the Seat. My anxious gaze returned to the statues of *elohim*. Had they moved? Possibly closer to each other? Weren't they only holding hands before? With each advance the tension melted from the scene, though the momentousness of the occasion was tangible.

The weather broke, still cool since it was December, but no longer raining.

As we walked, the Levim boys began singing Dadua's newest composition. We were listening to the debut of the Psalms. I squeezed Cheftu's hand. His gaze did not move from the Ark, but he did squeeze my hand back.

"Shaday is the ruler of this earth and everything on it, this world and those who live on it. He established it from the seas, drew it from the waters.

"Who may climb to the hill of Shaday? Who may stand before the holy place? He whose hands are clean, whose heart is pure. He who does not follow the ways of idols, or swear by those who are false.

"He alone receives blessings from Shaday, is vindicated by the god who saves him. May this be the generation of people who seek your face, God of our Fathers.

"Lift up your heads, you gates. Be called to a higher purpose, you aged doors! Be blessed that Shaday, the king of all glory, will come in. Who is this king of glory?

"He is el Elyon, strong and mighty, the god of the battle, the god of victory."

Dadua sang the verse again, then invited the people to join him.

I was speechless at the beauty of the music. While it contained the antiphonal signature of most Middle Eastern music, the choirboy voices surrounding us gave it an innocence and majesty I'd not heard before.

Tziyon waited on high, the sun breaking through the clouds, frosting the stone with a rosy light.

My God. Jerusalem. Would I ever cease to be amazed at this city, this time?

"Lift up your heads, O gates," the choirboys sang.

Dadua still walked before the Seat, reverent, his hands upraised in praise. He walked there because he refused to let anyone else risk himself, Cheftu had reported. The *giborim* had protested this gesture, but he had ignored them. He was responsible for the kingdom, for these choices, he said. He would walk before Shaday. Any striking down would be done to him.

He was a true leader.

The sun passed behind another cloud, and it was suddenly cooler. The gates of the city, packed with silent, watching tribesmen, stood open.

The Levim halted, Dadua stopped. What were we waiting for? A mighty wind blew through us, a force of air moving over the assemblage into the city. I'd felt that wind before, when I'd time-traveled. Cheftu's hand tightened around mine.

Then, like a Renaissance painting, a stream of light poured through the cloud, piercing a hole directly over Dadua. He stood motionless, his head bowed, his palms turned skyward in submission. The sunlight stream grew brighter, firing the red, green, blue, and orange jewels on his chest, highlighting his mahogany hair into a halo.

We watched as the sun engulfed him. Before our eyes he became gilded—as divine and mysterious a channel as the *elohim* covering the Seat.

In a rush of movement we could only just discern, he was dancing. Not like from high school: in step, back, step. No, like Baryshnikov and Astaire, with a good deal of acrobatics thrown in.

The choirboys began singing again as the Levim stepped forward, the Seat swinging between them gently. Then the crowd gasped as the king of the tribes—Israel—threw off his kilt.

What was he doing? What was he thinking? The king was *naked?*

Dadua danced.

He danced before Shaday with glee. He danced with the same joy you feel at the end of a great day—dancing because you cannot be still. He danced with the freedom of youth, of childhood, rollicking with a friend in the sunlight. Dancing because life is good. Dancing because you have life and blood.

Dadua danced naked—unburdened of the weight of his ego, pride, shame. Unfettered by sexual implication, unclothed to the glory of being human, being made in the image of God, being a creator like God.

Dadua danced naked with God.

We squeezed into Tziyon's narrow, layered streets as we followed the crowd that had joined in the choirboys' chorus, glorifying God, not themselves as owners of the Ark. They were joyful, they were excited, but this time they were focused on the eternal instead of themselves.

Was that the only contrast between this journey and the last? Yet it made every difference.

"Lift up your heads, you gates. Be called to a higher purpose, you aged doors! Be blessed that Shaday, the king of all glory, will come in. Who is this king of glory?"

"He is el Elyon, strong and mighty, the god of the battle, the god victorious."

I darted a glance at Cheftu. Did he believe where we were? When we were? All of us—Jebusi, and tribesmen, man and woman, slave and free—followed the Seat up to the Temple Mount. The colors of the Holy of Holies tent were brilliant against the watercolor sky and limestone platform. Here the Seat would be housed until Dadua, rather Dadua's son, constructed the Temple.

The procession stopped at the woven walls of the Tent of Meeting. The priests moved through the gates, beyond the people. We fell silent, a crowd of hundreds so quiet that we could hear the priests' bare feet slapping against the beaten dirt. The faint scrape of gold poles against gold hoops as the Ark swayed, carried on the shoulders of the Levim, was audible. It passed by me, so close that I could see the detailing of pomegranates and grapes on the rim. I glanced up at the golden figures. Icy sweat ran down my back.

The *elohim* were embracing.

Those status had moved. They had!

Without a pause the priests mounted the steps, the embroidered curtains sweeping closed behind them. Dadua's voice was audible beyond us, still praising Shaday.

"Sing to Shaday, earth! Proclaim his salvation daily. Declare his glory among the peoples of the earth, his deeds of valor and majesty among the nations. For great is el Elyon, he has earned his praise! Above all other gods, he is the most high, the one deserving of the most respect. Before Shaday, the other nations' gods are merely idols; Shaday alone created the heavens. Splendor and majesty are before him, strength and joy flow from his holy Seat. Ascribe to el Elyon, all the goyim, ascribe to el Elyon strength

and glory, ascribe to el Elyon the glory he is due. Kneel before him with offerings, worship his holiness. May all the earth tremble before him!"

Breathless moments passed as the past years flew by me: Exodus of Israel, the fall of Atlantis, and now this? Within the Tent I knew animals were being sacrificed, that God was being welcomed to his new home. I looked up at Cheftu. "Do you—"

Suddenly something indefinable moved through me, through the crowd. I felt as through the red point of a laser had touched me, then passed on.

A shout: "He is with us!"

Like everyone else, I looked toward the Tent. Within its walls was a holy room: God's boudoir. Against the tinted blue sky, lightning flashed from within that room, upward. Stripes of brilliant gold against robin-egg's blue, pillowed by puffs of silvery, iridescent smoke.

Humanity had reached toward heaven. *El ha*Shaday had reached down in response.

Every knee bowed.

God dwelt among Israel again.

When the smoke cleared—literally—every person was given a loaf of bread, a cake of dates, and a cake of raisins. It was a feast day, and the singing never stopped. Those from the outlying areas started their walk home in the early evening. Those from the city made their way to their homes, with a new sense of pride in being a son of Abraham, in dwelling in Tziyon.

It started raining again, lightning flashing in the distance.

RaEm looked through the pouring rain at her soldiers. "Egypt is falling," she said. "They are coming to take Tutankhaten, to take him to Noph and crown him with Horus, Ptah, Amun-Ra, and HatHor. Pharaoh's vision of one god will be lost."

They stood silently, water dripping off their heads, noses. They didn't look away. "They will take us, too. We will die, as so many have died, at their hands."

A few blanched, but mostly they were still. Resigned.

"All we need is gold."

RaEm paced away, the mud splashing up on her fragile kilt. "Gold will solve our problems. With it we can buy position, freedom, and security in the new Egypt. Without it we will be stripped of everything and left to rot as part of the deposed kingdom."

She looked at them, her leaders. Twenty-five men in all, obedient, strong men. Faithful to Egypt. "I know where the gold is. I need your help to get it. You must believe me entirely. There must be no doubt in my magic."

"How could we doubt you?" one of them asked. "You control the lightning!"

There were murmurs of agreement. Good! Her work learning how to manipulate the skies had not gone unnoticed. "I do. Will you trust me?"

"Not against trusting you, My Majesty, but why do we just not storm Noph? We control the regular army. There are thousands of us encamped between here and Egypt. Every soldier would be glad to return home, reclaim the land for Pharaoh."

She smiled. They were so simple, so delightfully sweet. They would storm Noph, Waset, too. However, for the negotiations within Karnak, for those nobles whose names had been a part of the court for dynasties, gold was what spoke. Violence and fear would not work on those who knew she needed them to have any legitimacy.

After all, she would be Pharaoh, just as Hatshepsut before her. Tuti would have a small accident, and she would reign for him. Then he would die after a long, agonizing fight with illness. Smenkhare would be the greatest pharaoh Egypt had ever known.

The wealthiest, too. Never again would she be called powerless by some mudhill king. She looked forward to eviscerating him, then stuffing his mouth with his own sex and setting him afire. Maybe lightning would work for that, too?

"Do you trust me?" she asked them.

"Aye!"

"Will you follow me?"

"Aye!"

"Never question, just obey and act?"

"Aye!"

"Then cover your faces with mud, leave your swords. Tonight we begin our pathway home."

THE *CHORIM, ZEHENIM,* AND *GIBORIM* had followed Dadua (wearing his clothes once more), who wanted to bless his new home while still in the power of Shaday. We were standing in the courtyard's foundations of Dadua's someday palace. The Ark was safely ensconced on the Temple Mount; all was well within the Israelite world.

Dadua's wives stood in a group, watching us as we entered. He waved to each of them. Avgay'el inclined her head, Hag'it blushed and waved back, Ahino'am blew him a kiss as we cheered.

Mik'el, standing on the far side, waited for Dadua's gesture. She did nothing, gave no acknowledgment. Dadua waved again; Mik'el turned on her heel, walked away.

Stunned silence. She had snubbed *ha nasi?* That was never a good idea, but especially not today. When Dadua turned to face us, he was still smiling, but his black eyes were smoldering. He threw back his head, calling blessings from Shaday on his house, his line, his dynasty, and the united tribes of Y'srael and Yuda.

Was I really here? Cheftu and I joined the rest of the group, wandering back to the palace amid singing. We seated ourselves around the table, dining until the night was black, the stars hidden beneath a blanket of clouds.

When the remains of lamb, grain, fruit, and vegetables lay before us, Dadua excused himself. The musicians played, wine flowed; it was a perfect evening. Cheftu had just kissed me, mentioned it was almost time for us to retire to our own house, when we all heard a crash.

"What—" I heard, shouted over the men's stories. We shut up and noticed the rest of our table had quieted.

"It was disgraceful!" Mik'el's voice was easily recognizable. The room fell silent now, listening.

"How is that? The Seat returned to Jerusalem? We are now the capital of all the tribes!" Dadua said.

"*Ach!* A bunch of unkempt, uncouth peasants who still worship stone and marry into the Apiru." We were not even pretending to not eavesdrop.

Silence

"You forget yourself, *isha.* My mother is Apiru."

"No one could forget it. Not after today's display! Where is your dignity? Your pride! What a shame that the throne of Yuda has become such a farce."

Within the room, no one made eye contact with anyone. It was too late to start conversing again; on the other hand, it was too humiliating to listen to this.

"Your slaves saw your nudity!" she cried. "You are the king! No one is supposed to see even your face, yet you show your penis! My father would be shamed! The house of Labayu would be shamed!"

"There is no house of Labayu," Dadua said, his words fast, furious, and very, very loud. "I danced before my God, in the way my God formed me. He chose me over your father, over your brothers, over your entire house of Labayu! I rule as king. *HaNasi* of Tziyon, *haMelekh* of the tribes, is me!"

If anything, Dadua was getting angrier.

"Before my God, I will celebrate as my heart dictates. There is no room for dignity before God; yet I would be more undignified. There is no room for pride before Shaday; still I would become more humiliated. Though you see nothing to admire in a ruler who follows his heart, those slave girls you so disparage will remember the majesty of Shaday, for they realized my nakedness was for him, not them."

Again, silence.

A long silence.

"Begone from my sight, Mik'el. You will never know a man again."

The curtain swept open; we stared at Dadua, he stared at us. Mik'el stood in the shadows behind him. "In the company of this people," he said, "Mik'el bat Labayu is put away. I show *chesed* to her by not invoking her death." He turned to her. "Never enter Tziyon again."

She stepped forward, proud and beautiful. "I would rather be alone than with a king who does not know what it means to be royal."

I couldn't help it; I winced. Was she that stupid? Or did she really have a death wish? Dadua looked at her as though he wanted to kill her.

"For the sake of Yohan, whom I loved, I will only put you away. *Gibori!*" he shouted.

Yoav and Abishi rushed to him. Dadua jerked his head her direction, so they stepped to her sides and took hold of her wrists. Mik'el pulled away; then, instead of walking out the back, she walked through the group with elegant, measured steps. She was every inch a princess.

We were dumbfounded.

A few minutes passed. What should we do? Even N'tan was silent. Dadua finally picked up his instrument, strummed his *kinor*, and began to sing.

"*Praise awaits Shaday within the gates of Tziyon, to you we will fulfill our vows. O you who hear prayers, you will draw all men to yourself. We will seek you out. When we were overwhelmed by the enormity of our transgressions, you forgave us, started us anew.*

"*Blessed are your chosen ones. Blessed are those who live in your courtyards. We are filled with the good things from your house, we benefit from serving at your holy Tent. You answer our requests with mighty deeds, showing righteousness, O God who saves us.*

"*You are the hope from the land's end to the Uttermost Sea. You formed mountains by your power, you are armed with strength. You stilled the roaring angry waves, you overrule the turmoil of nations. Those who live far away have heard of your deeds and respect you. Wherever morning dawns and evening fades, people sing to you.*

"You have enriched the land, stocked the waters. Your chesed flows like a stream to your people, to feed us as with grain. You have ordained the fruitfulness of all things. You drench us, level us, soften us as the land, with the water of your words.

"You bless growth and production. You crown the year with bounty, the market carts overflow with your abundance, the grasslands of the desert are unending; you clothe the hills with gladness. The meadows are alive with flocks, the valleys are filled with grain. The land shouts and sings with your presence."

We all said, "Sela."

RaEm led them through the night, the pouring rain. Their armor was covered in mud; not a gleam of metal, not a spark of shine, was visible. She arrived at the tree and opened it. Hiram's tricks were not as clever as he thought.

Then down, into the abyss and blackness. Only now she had a lamp. Before, Zakar Ba'al thought to confuse her with backtracking, leaving her no visible checkpoints. However, she had felt the softness of the dirt beneath her feet. Every step was an arrow. Now, holding up the lamp, she could easily follow the steps of dozen of workers into the city.

It was a shorter journey when it wasn't intended to confuse.

They passed beneath the dining chamber, the distant strains of Dadua's *kinor* audible. Then through the narrower rooms into the treasure room. "Listen to me," she said to the men. "Take only what I tell you. Nothing more. Not one thing that I do not instruct you to take. Everything is for a purpose, a power that only I know. Understood?"

"Aye, My Majesty," they said softly.

She looked over them, wondering which one would succumb to temptation, which one would not leave the chamber. "There are shields, both gold and silver. Take all of them. Also, there are coils of wire and cables of gold, copper, and bronze. Take those, too."

They nodded, and RaEm opened the door. Though the soldiers must have been dazzled, they were disciplined. They took the shields from the wall, the coils and cables off the floor. RaEm gestured and they left, each man carrying two shields, the coils looped over their shoulders.

She saw him; he was young, nervous. "Halt," RaEm said. He did, his dark eyes going wide with fear. "I instructed you to take nothing, save what I commanded."

"My Majesty! I didn't! I didn't!" he protested.

The other men watched. They had never liked him, she'd seen that in their manner. "Now you dare tell me falsehoods?"

"My Majesty—" He threw himself on his face, blubbering. "I swear by Ma'at, by the horns of HatHor—"

"Now you insult me by swearing by gods who do not live!"

He lay at her feet, quaking. "I did nothing, My Majesty," he said. "I swear, I swear!" But his voice was softer. He knew he was damned.

"Get up."

He shuddered for a moment longer, then she extended a hand to him. A strange expression came over his face as he rose to his feet. He opened his palm to see a golden earring, one of the earrings that had been casually laid beside the coil of wire he had picked up. His gaze met RaEm's. He knew, now he understood. In that moment every ounce of childlike trust faded from his eyes.

What was the phrase from Chloe's world? Life was a bitch?

"You die for Egypt," RaEm said, plunging her blade into his body. He didn't look away from her. His gaze was focused on hers, not allowing her to look away, either. His blood pumped over her hands, hot, splashed on her clothing, her face, but she couldn't turn from him.

"I would have taken both," he gasped. "Stupid to steal only one."

She removed her blade, wiped it on his kilt, and faced the men. "Do you trust me?"

They didn't trust her, but they were suddenly afraid of her.

"Will you follow me?"

They nodded quickly.

"Then come, we have much work to do."

I HAD JUST DROPPED OFF to sleep—again—after making love to Cheftu when someone battered our door. Cheftu and I were sleeping chest to breast, our legs twined together, and we both jumped. "What the hell . . . ," I muttered sleepily.

"I will see to it, *chérie*," he said, getting up and padding away. The person at the door kept banging and banging. I hid my head under a pillow, dozing again. Until I heard something I never thought to hear: Cheftu shouting, "Holy shit!"

I was up, dressed, and at the door in seconds. Cheftu looked at me. "Soldiers surround the Tabernacle!"

"What?"

Thunder crashed outside. N'tan, soaking with rain, was wild-eyed. "That Egyptian has taken the Tabernacle hostage!"

"Smenkhare?"

"*Ken!* It is an outrage to Shaday, to hospitality, to everything!"

"There is nothing about this, not in anything I've ever read, or even heard, about the Bible," Cheftu said to N'tan

I looked at the offspring of Imhoteps I and II. "Would you like wine?" I asked, showing my own demented heritage of southern hospitality. I poured three cups. N'tan told us that after losing two messengers he'd sent to the Tabernacle, he had gone in search of them. That was when he saw the soldiers.

Egyptian soldiers.

"What of the priests? The people who were there?"

N'tan shrugged. "There weren't so many. The seasons, feasting, and sacrificing are concluded. A few stay, rotating their service through the rest of the winter." He chewed on the end of a side curl. "In fact, many of the implements in the Tabernacle have been stored in the lower city."

"What remains?"

"Merely the outer curtains and the Seat."

Cheftu shuddered, muttering something under his breath about a tool of destruction. "What were the soldiers doing?"

"Dismantling the Tent."

"Were they touching the Seat?"

"Why do you ask?" I said.

"Because one woman, standing sixteen cubits away from the Ark, almost died of the plague."

"The bubonic plague is in the Ark?" I asked, stunned in English.

N'tan was watching us both, lost in the language.

"Fleas, *chérie.* I do not know how, but fleas."

"Are you sure?"

Cheftu jabbed a finger toward N'tan, switching back to Hebrew. "They get the priests sick so they can work around the Seat without illness. It carries the plague." He turned to N'tan and asked him to tell me what was received from the Pelesti when the Seat was returned.

"Golden objects, *g'vret.* Tumors."

"Statues of buboes," Cheftu said in English.

"And golden totems of rats," N'tan said in Hebrew.

I drained the rest of my cup in one swallow. "So what's the worry?"

Cheftu stood up, rubbing his face, speaking rapidly. "A slight jarring of the Ark, opening it not big enough for my finger, almost killed the king's wife. Only because the rest of us were, how do you say? immune, we were safe."

I got to my feet. "But if it were opened more—"

"The plague could obliterate the Jewish people."

Was it possible that RaEm could cause the destruction of the Jews? The plague brought on the Dark Ages in Europe. Could it bring on a dark age here? Instead of the glory of Solomon, the darkness of RaEm ruling?

Thunder deafened us for a moment.

It sounded like so much Gothic fiction, but then who would have guessed I'd ground grain with Solomon's mother, or that I'd introduced the Star of David to David, or that Cheftu was the scribe of some Bible stories?

We ran through the rain.

Beneath the black lowered skies, the driving rain, and the bitter wind, Dadua stood. Lightning flashed in the distance, and men and women joined the group, coming from every corner of the city. Water pouring off his nose, slicking hair black onto his skull, Dadua spoke to his *giborim* and us.

"No one will take my city, my Temple Mount, or the Seat of my God. Sound the *shofar*; summon the citizens to the Temple Mount. Egypt wants a confrontation, Egypt shall have one." He turned to Yoav. "Did you not tell me that the Egyptian boy is the new pharaoh? Get him."

"I have him already," Dion, as Hiram, said, hurrying toward us. "I offer my services, *adon*."

Thunder, lightning. I squeezed Cheftu's arm again. Dadua looked at those assembled. "We go to tell Egypt, yet again, to let Shaday's people go!"

PART
VII

CHAPTER 17

W<small>E WALKED CLUMPED TOGETHER</small>, so I whispered to Cheftu in English and hoped that he understood me. "How do you figure the fleas?"

"In the Ark?"

"Yes!"

"Perhaps they live on the manna, the budded rod, I do not know the lives of fleas."

Dadua split us up, to have us approach the site from all four directions. Cheftu and I were to scale the eastern side of the mountain.

This was muddy and cold and completely unbelievable.

RaEm was on the Temple Mount? "Why doesn't God just blow her up?" I asked Cheftu, huffing beside him. We had reached the edge of the plateau. The outer walls of the sacred enclosure were down, and the Tabernacle itself had been dismantled, leaving only the two front pillars of the Ark.

Lightning flashed and illuminated the tableau. I heard Cheftu's hiss. "*Mon Signeur!* Look at that! What is she doing?"

In place of the Tabernacle, the silver and gold shields were circled, angled toward the sky.

"Her blasphemy knows no bounds," my husband said, shocked.

The Ark was the centerpiece of this very bizarre arrangement. The four poles used to carry it were cantilevered upward. What on earth? I couldn't imagine what her goal was.

RaEm stood slightly to the north of her contraption. All around her, Egyptian soldiers were shooting arrows into the air. My first fear was that what would go up must come down, and how to avoid being speared from on high. Then I wondered what she was doing.

Lightning struck closer.

She looked beautiful in a wild, wicked, witchy kind of way. She'd forsaken the kilt of Smenkhare for a white dress, no jewelry, her shaved head gleaming in the rain-slicked night.

Lightning! RaEm had become obsessed with lightning, my sister, Cammy, had said. Nearly horizontal sheets of rain fell as we crept up a goat's path that led to the mesa. Egyptian soldiers stood steadfast, though their eyes were so wide with fear that I could see the whites of them even in this patchy darkness.

Lightning was drawing closer, encircling us. What was she doing? Making the Ark some kind of giant lightning rod? "Oh, my God," I said in English.

Cheftu stopped and looked at me. "Chloe?"

RaEm had definitely used the powers of the Discovery Channel for evil.

"Tribesmen!" she said in best dramatic fashion. It was a good thing she'd learned Hebrew, because a translator would have ruined the whole mood. "The fire drawn from the heavens tonight is at my command! My bidding!" The soldiers continued to shoot arrows into the air. "Using the superior magic of Egypt," she said, "I have constructed an altar to the gods of the desert, the storm. Shaday himself is my slave."

Thunder rumbled around us, drowning her words for a moment. The gathered tribesmen watched in awe. To them she really did seem to have magic. Did anyone else, anyone with power, buy this story?

It was impressive, though. Very.

"My demands are simple," she said in best terrorism reasoning. "The gold I covet for the box you treasure."

"Why doesn't she just take the box?" I whispered to Cheftu.

After all, it was heavily gold-plated; it took a small army of priests to move it.

"The box is nothing compared to the wealth of gold Dadua has hidden. We brought back hundreds of thousands of talents of gold and silver. Wealth that would still be impressive in your day."

Even with inflation?

RaEm continued her spiel. "This sole totem of your sole god will be blown to your god's own throne room, by the power of the gods of the air, the storm, by Ba'al's own lightning."

As if on cue, lightning struck the Mount. Everyone jumped. Static was crackling in the air. I felt my hair rising off my neck. I looked at the poles, the shields, the Ark. "She's going to get lightning to strike the Ark of the Covenant?" I realized aloud.

How? Lightning rods were designed to absorb lightning, to draw it away from other things. Was she drawing the lightning— Suddenly Cheftu jerked me out of the way, saving me from death. I looked down. Where I'd been standing, now there was an arrow, still vibrating from the impact of hitting ground. I knelt beside it. Tiny golden wires hung in spirals from the haft, like Jewish sidelocks.

Lightning and thunder struck almost in conjunction.

"Chloe," Cheftu said over the rising wind, "if that box is opened, cracked, if a tiny crevice appears, it could be a disaster."

"Why?" I asked, still coming to grips with the arrow.

"Plague."

I looked back at the Ark, sitting in the middle of the gold shields. "She has a better weapon than even she knows," I muttered.

"The priests know this," he said.

I chewed on my lip, trying desperately to recall eighth-grade science. "Gold is a conductor," I said. "If lightning hits, it will only blow or burn out that one thing it strikes. She can't generate enough power for—"

"Do you see the wires?" Cheftu said, almost shouting now. I squinted through the rain. "They are connecting everything together, from the shields to the poles to the box!"

"*B'seder,*" I said. "Now, we have problems." One hit by lightning, and if the force of the electricity didn't melt the gold on the spot, then it would transfer the power, eventually or ultimately, going into the box. "Wouldn't the fleas be burned up in a strike?" I asked, shifting my position.

"It takes only a few fleas, then the illness is in the animals, in the clothes and furnishings. The only riddance of black death is to burn the dead and their belongings."

RaEm was giving a list of all the gold she wanted: all the gold N'tan and Cheftu had brought back from the desert, from the Mountain of God in Midian. Egyptian gold, RaEm claimed. She was right, but it was the gold the Egyptians had given the Israelites when they were Apiru, on the eve of the Exodus.

Lightning stuck in the valley to the west of us. Had the storm cell moved away, then? Another volley of arrows went into the air. The lightning would be returning. Somehow she was drawing it. A little bit of knowledge was a dangerous thing.

N'tan spoke from behind us. "What do you advise? What do the stones say?"

"They are dead in my hands," Cheftu explained. "Too much static."

"Take off your shoes," N'tan said, gesturing to our feet. "This is the law on the Mount, dealing with Shaday and the Seat."

Of course, because being barefoot would ground whoever touched the Ark or was within arcing distance. "We have to break the circuit," I said, eyeing the wires through the rain. And the many soldiers standing between us and it.

"How?"

He didn't ask if it would happen, but how? "Do you believe me?" I was surprised.

N'tan wiped water off his face. "Fire strikes from the sky, it burns fields, homes, villages. I know what lightning can do. Somehow she is summoning it. How will it affect the Seat, though?"

"Boom! The Ark is broken into a million pieces," Cheftu said. There was no current translation for "explosion." "Then the fleas are out and the city is infected."

Not to mention that the Ark would be blown to kingdom come. Was that why no one had ever found it? It had been incinerated? If the plague were freed, if the Israelites were obliterated . . . What would that do to human history?

Where did we get the Ten Commandments without the Jews?

Where did we get the Bible, without the Jews?

Where would Jesus come from? Or Mohammed?

If this small tribe were wiped out, would I even exist? Would America? Einstein himself wouldn't have been born. Or Freud. There would be no Middle East peace knot—because there would be no Middle East. No Jews, no Christians, no Muslims. Would we all worship the trees and sky and storms instead?

"You describe an—" N'tan's words were interrupted by a massive lightning flash that seemed to last for minutes, though that was impossible.

More darkness. Thunder closer.

"You cannot destroy the House of our God!" Dadua shouted at RaEm from his perch on the southern end of the Mount. "He is a mighty God! He will not allow it!"

Kudos on the faith angle, Dadua. But God had also made electricity, designed it to work under certain controls. All of those controls were present and accounted for—and under the power of RaEm.

"I reign over the sky," RaEm shouted back. "Your god is nothing! He cannot stand against me! You are nothing. You will regret every word!"

Lightning struck behind RaEm, so close that we could see the lines of her body in silhouette. In a strange way the shields and Ark seemed almost flowerlike, the stamen sticking out of the middle. A deadly flower, to be sure.

"Shall I break through the wire?" N'tan asked, preparing to run by the soldiers toward the Ark. The rain was letting up, though lightning was returning. "Wait, she hasn't completed the circuit yet," I said, squinting. Sure enough, RaEm held two pieces of wire in her hands. I pointed. "If she connects those, *ach*, well—"

"We are roasted?" N'tan supplied.

He didn't wait, but ran. Quicksilver, two Egyptian soldiers attacked him, dropping him onto the muddy ground. We needed to get past them. Cheftu looked at me. "No one else knows what to do," I said, panicked.

Another few *giborim* raced for the center, only to be stopped by Egyptian soldiers. Having spied a slingshot in the waist sash of a tribesman, I borrowed it, loaded it, and waited. "You've had your chance, fool!" RaEm shouted to Dadua.

"You'll kill yourself also!" Dadua shouted back.

"I AM beyond death!" she screamed, holding the wires above her head. The storm cell was directly over us. Standing, I wound up the slingshot until I heard it whistling above my head. With a prayer, I let go. The soldier before us dropped, clearing the path as Cheftu sprinted toward the Ark.

I was right behind him, my footsteps hesitating for a moment. I was in my own body; should anything happen to me, I had no backup skin. I would torch my own. But if something weren't done, the box would certainly blow, disease would definitely be freed, and we would all die—except Cheftu and Dion—anyway.

Someone touched the back of my arm, sending an electric shock all the way through me. I jumped but didn't slow.

Yoav raced for RaEm, sword drawn. That was a plan! As though it happened in slow motion, RaEm reached behind her, grabbed a stick, and pointed it toward him. The much summoned lightning touched the metal-tipped end of the stick and shot into Yoav.

He fell to the ground, twitching still.

"You! Stop!"

The shout came in Egyptian. Cheftu turned, taking a wallop in the belly from the soldier. Two of them were on us. I ducked the spear, kicking high at the next moment. The move caught the man in his chest, knocked him off balance. He raised the blade to stab me, but I spun away, slipping in the mud.

Moments were lit up eerily as I turned back to my soldier. Blood poured from his throat as his head lolled to the side. He'd been struck from behind. My arm was wrenched from its socket as I was thrown out of the way.

Lightning struck again. Nothing was audible over the sound of the now pouring rain. Through strobelike light I saw a man enter the circle of shields and pull them apart. His hair rose, masses of black curls seeming to grow fuller in the seconds he stood there, fighting the modern machinery RaEm had rigged.

She screamed, "Betrayer!" as the lightning struck.

It hit one of the poles, zipped down into the Ark, then out through another pole and around the circle of shields to where Dion stood. It arched through his body, animating him like a marionette, then went into the ground.

Nothing blew. No freed plague.

Dion, for whatever reason, had saved the day.

"Kill them!" RaEm shrieked. I didn't look to see whom she was talking about. I grabbed Cheftu's arm and pulled him, staggering, behind me. Arrows began zinging all over the place, these arrows aimed at people, not the sky. The *giborim* ran forward, brandishing their new Pelesti swords.

The clang of metal on metal battled for superiority against the raging storm.

Egyptian and Israelite fought on the Temple Mount. Cries, moans, and the clatter of war filled the already static air. But with no arrows flying into the sky to draw the storm, it was passing over us quickly. Cheftu and N'tan were moving through the fray, so I dodged and ducked to catch up with them. More priests seemed to materialize out of the fracas as the tribesmen and Cheftu pulled the gold wire off the poles and the priests realigned them.

Other priests were rebuilding the tented Tabernacle, preventing further lightning strikes, protecting their most valuable possession. RaEm hadn't moved the Ark, she had simply torn down everything around it. They dismantled the shields and straightened the Ark, the cherubim on the cover one mulitwinged creature instead of two. I wouldn't think about that. Status didn't move; hence the phrase *as still as a statue*. I was dreaming. Hallucinating.

Dion lay on the ground, still. The Tabernacle was being restructured, the soldiers were fighting, and in the middle of it all was Dion.

I hesitantly reached for his throat, waiting for a pulse. The sky lit up again and again, but as I counted, "One one thousand, two one thousand, three one thousand," all the way to eight, there was no thunder.

Dion opened his eyes, then gasped for breath. This time when the hair rose on the back of my neck it had nothing to do with static in the air. "Where is RaEm?" he asked.

The bitch.

"You tell me."

He gasped. "Beneath the city. Caverns. Hiding." I looked down at this man whose death I wouldn't have mourned and realized that he was never going to die. Neither was Cheftu. I left him and slipped through the battle, looking for the entrance to the caverns. She wasn't going to get away. Not again.

Pausing, I listened for footsteps. None. No other breathing, just mine. Down I went, then farther twisting and turning, following the path. Beneath another man-made archway leading to a chamber. I'd walked through many, unsure if I were walking straight or in a circle. Did I know this room?

Instead I stepped into another space, a different one than I'd thought. I wasn't going in a circle. This place was a maze! I raised my oil lamp and looked around.

From within this stone tangle I could hear the battle above. Had I heard something else? A whimper, perhaps? Rather than returning the way I'd come, I followed the sound through the walls, going farther and father back. Had Dion stumbled on all of this when he was quarrying for stone down here?

I halted, listening. Had I heard a gasp, a moan? I walked a few steps farther. Yes! After turning a few more bends in this snarl of passages, I found her, crumpled on the floor. "RaEm?" I said.

She turned toward me, and I fought the urge to vomit. She wasn't going anywhere. Ever again. "My God," I whispered.

"He is your god," she said, her voice hoarse. "He is your god and you are welcome to him, to your cold modern world and your—" She hissed in pain.

"Save your curses," I said. "You are—"

"Dying. Yes, I know."

She'd been torched; the right side of her body was black, burned. Her hand had become a scorched claw, and she cradled the right side of her face in it. I was glad the light was so bad. Something was wrong, grotesquely so, with her face. "Why?" I asked, staring at her. "You were pharaoh of Egypt. How did you even become that?"

"You know what they say," she said in English. "You're either born into money or you marry it."

"You married it?"

"The brat Meryaten."

I hadn't heard correctly—had I? "A girl?"

She snorted. "Why does that amaze you so much?"

"Because you are a woman? Or did she know? Are you a lesbian?"

"I'm no fool! Of course she didn't know."

"So you didn't consummate the relationship?"

"Of course I did."

My confused silence prompted her.

"You are an idiot. She was an untried child. All I needed was to draw the curtains, extinguish the lights, and do what I would with her."

"Omigod." I stared at her in shock.

RaEm whimpered a little, swallowing her tears. "But then she killed herself, the weakling."

"I'm sorry." Maybe I didn't know the whole story. "That must have been very hard on you?" I said hesitantly.

"It was. Akhenaten was despondent; everyone was so obsequious. It was a great nuisance."

"Why did she . . . ?"

"She couldn't get pregnant." RaEm shrugged. "So she overdosed on a sleeping draught I kept. Which forced me"—she winced—"to pretend she had died of the plague."

Her story took a moment to sink in. "You are sick," I whispered. My skin felt grimy just from being in her presence.

She turned to me, one side of her face flawless and gorgeous, a face I had seen in the water mirror for a year; the other side ravaged, blistered, and peeling. She moved her hand, and I saw that yes, the other side of her face looked like an exit wound, covered in blood. "You are no different from I," she said. "You would have done the same things, made the same choices. Your life was easier, which is why you stand there in judgment."

I stared into her face. "I wish you had a mirror, RaEm. Because this is the truth of you. Rotten to the core, hidden beneath a veneer of beauty." I stood up. "There are no excuses. What made you think you could get away with it? You drove a child to suicide? You tried to blow up the Ark of the Covenant?"

"Don't forget the murders and whippings," she said.

"And you boast about it! What made you think you could do it? What put you above the laws of human decency?"

"I always have."

I stepped back from her. *"Avayra goreret avayra,"* I murmured.

"Don't leave me," she said, suddenly panicked.

I retreated another step.

"Please, not alone. I'm dying. Don't let me die alone."

Another step away from her. "Did that child, Mary—"

"Meryaten."

"Did she have someone hold her hand?"

"You don't understand—"

Another step back. "Do you think—"

"Please don't leave, Chloe," she pleaded.

"Why should I stay?"

"Don't make me be alone, please." She crawled after me, her burned body glistening in my lamplight. Couldn't she feel that physical pain? She was frantic. "I'll tell you where the portal is, just don't leave me."

"You ruined my relationship with my parents," I said. "Though I'm realizing now that was probably a prebreakfast act for you."

"It's here, in these caverns," she said.

"My reputation, my sister, my company. Did you think of no one besides yourself?"

"This is the day, did you know that? The twenty-third power is the ability to move through the portals. It is the compensation for being born on the unluckiest day of the year," she said, dragging her body toward me.

"You wrecked my military career. There is a warrant out for my arrest, should I return to the U.S. I have no modern future."

"When I was initiated as a priestess, they told me about this gift, but I didn't understand. What power we have, Chloe!" She pulled herself another foot closer.

"I can never go home," I hissed bitterly. "I hate you."

RaEm fell with a whimper, crumpled onto her burned right side. Was she dead? I stepped forward, suddenly horrified at my behavior. I'd watched a human being die? I knelt at her side, holding my breath. She was dead?

She whipped over, slapping me silly.

I skidded back, but she was on me. Months of pretending at manhood had strengthened her, while kneading bread and carding wool had weakened me. A burned hand and whole hand were around my throat. "I will not die alone," she said. I was choking; I was going to vomit looking at her, smelling her skin. "You mock me as they all did. They all pushed me away. Akhenaten, but I paid for his murder. Phaemon, whose body will never be found. Hiram, who betrayed me. And your god-loving Dadua, who spat out my kisses."

I fought against her hands, my hearing now humming as we struggled. Her skin was pebbled and stiff beneath my hand as I struggled to push her off me. She sat on my chest, too close to use my legs, too heavy to roll away. "I won't die alone! I won't!" she screamed. Beneath my hand, on her burned side, I felt a tear in the skin—I couldn't see anymore, I felt the heat in my face as if it were going to explode. My hand on her burned side relaxed.

Limpness was stealing through me. No more oxygen to my brain, I thought. I wonder how *this* fits into history.

No! I was not going to die by RaEm.

I gripped the edge of skin and pulled. She screamed as her epidermis peeled off like a glove. Blood spattered me as she howled, holding her arm. I rolled away and crawled for the door, gasping for breath. She grabbed my foot, and every ounce of self-preservation responded.

I kicked her in the face, slamming the cartilage of her nose into her brain with a sickening crunch, and scrambled into the hallway, retching.

I crawled farther, desperately wanting away from that room, her body. The shock hit and I collapsed into a ball, shuddering and terrified. My God, I'd just killed a human being, an earthling.

When I opened my eyes later, I saw a blue spectral glow.

Carved into the bedrock of Jerusalem was a portal. Shining beams of azure, turquoise, and robin's-egg blue filtered around the room. RaEm had said it was tonight; possibly this was the only truth she'd ever told. Now was the choice to go? This was the compensation for being born on the unluckiest day of the year? To travel now? Now? I was too weak to move, too exhausted to care. Now was the time?

I stared, hypnotizing myself, for hours or minutes, I didn't know. I heard my name, one of the many I'd come to own, bouncing through the limestone caverns.

"Chloe, Chloe? *Mon Dieu!*"

Then he was kneeling before me, sweaty but alive. Cheftu looked over his shoulder and swore. N'tan had halted in the doorway. "My people, for generations we have heard of this, to see it is . . ." He trailed off.

"RaEm is——," I croaked.

"We know."

"I killed her."

"She was dying, *chère.*"

"Dion?"

Cheftu sighed. "Vanished."

There was something else, something niggling. "The Ark is okay?" My voice sounded awful from RaEm's attempt to strangle me.

"Sealed, the Tabernacle rebuilt around it."

Then it hit me again: the knowledge, the bizarre understanding I had of science. "Defuse the Ark," I said.

Cheftu glanced at the portal. "How do you mean?"

"It's a bomb, waiting to blow. The fleas could get out any time it's opened, right?"

N'tan nodded.

"Then take them out."

"Tell me how," the *tzadik* said.

Cheftu and I spoke in symphony. "Remove the manna and the rod."

"Why do you say that?" I whispered, stunned.

"Why do you say that?" he asked me.

"It's biological soup. The fleas have something to live on, so they stay and grow. Remove their food and they will die. Why did you say that?"

"Because according to Holy Writ, when Solomon puts the Ark in his Temple, only the tablets remain inside."

It was silent.

"Wheels within wheels," I whispered hoarsely. N'tan slipped away as I stared at Cheftu.

"It is the day," Cheftu said, squeezing my hand.

I looked over his shoulder at the deepening blue glow. "Do you want to?"

He sighed. "It is a hard thing to choose. Here, we have everything."

"Yep. A home."

"More than that, *chérie*, each other." He turned me around, facing him. "And the freedom to worship the One God. Never before have we known that."

I spiraled his sidelock around my finger, weak but needing to touch. "You like being Jewish?"

He smiled, a flash of white in his dark beard. "We are not Jewish, we are living in the Jewish nation."

"You do have an incredible job," I mused.

"You can do anything you want," he countered. "You are a darling of the court."

"But do we belong here?"

He kissed me deeply, completely, holding me up so that I didn't slide out of his grasp. "Do we belong anywhere?" he asked.

The glow was brighter, deeper, now reaching across this white stone room to touch Cheftu's face, giving him an alien visage. "I hope so. It's depressing to think we may never belong."

"*Lo, chérie,* you do not understand me. Do we belong anywhere, I ask, because we can step into everywhere. Not many people can know all you know of the future and not use it."

Witness RaEm.

"Not many people could take in stride changing bodies, learning new societies, new religions, new languages." He looked at me, holding my face so that I too glowed in blue light. "This is our chance. Say it and we will stay. We will live in Tziyon, we will worship the One God, we will raise our children and make love in our fields and travel to other courts, anything you like."

I frowned, shifting my eyes away from his imploring gaze. "Why is it my choice?" From here I could see the etching on the stone, though I couldn't read it. Was that a sign in and of itself? Was this it for our grand time-traveling careers? "Would we get bored here? Is there another war or something we need to be careful of? How do you know all these languages, anyway?" I said, hyperaware but exhausted to my bones. "Do you have a lexicon, too?"

Cheftu shrugged. "No wars that I recall. I know the languages because they are related linguistically." He frowned. "I do not know of this lexicon, however."

I sighed. "What is the point in staying?"

My husband tugged at his side curl. "Somehow, Akhenaten gets a psalm of David and rewrote it. I would like to know how."

"That's easy. They corresponded for years."

"How do you know that?"

"My sister. Sometime in my century a bunch of stone tablets were found, letters between Egypt and places in Israel. It's the first mention of Israel, I think."

Cheftu sat down with a thump. "*Ach,* well, there went my reason for staying."

I chuckled weakly, a raspy sound. The light beckoned. "How can we know?" I mused.

"Any decision we make is not permanent," Cheftu said. "Every year we can stand here and choose again."

"Unless we have kids."

He frowned, repeating my English. "Baby goats?"

I laughed. "Children. *Yeladim.*"

He tugged at his beard. "*Ken,* that would be a hard judgment."

What did I want? Here, where we had everything?

When I'd jumped from 1996 last year into this crazy world of mermaid-goddesses, biblical characters, and firing Arks, all I'd wanted was to find Cheftu and live with him. Could I be sure that I would find him again? If we jumped, would we both make it through? Would we be together or would we have to find each other? "This is the closest thing to forever we have," I said. "We know the answers here; what to do, where to live, where to work."

We stood up and I slipped my arm around his waist, feeling the muscles of his body even beneath his garments. He pulled the stones from his sash and tossed them on the floor. I looked at him, shocked.

"Either way, the method we use for divination should be prayer, not rocks."

I looked at them. "Would they tell us?" My voice was ragged, my throat hurt.

"What is there to know?" he said. "Here is every security. There," Cheftu said wistfully, looking at the portal, "is all possibility."

I took his hand in mine. I didn't need to look at the sky, at the constellations whose placement I knew as well as my own name—Chloe. I believed they were there.

For the first time I could see the space inside the portal, open. Beyond it was risk, mystery, adventure. Beyond it was all potential, both good and bad. The things we knew from history and the things that didn't make it into the books; the chance that we would be together, the hazard that we might not; the continuation of our bizarre destiny or its conclusion. I spoke, feeling the weight of my words. "The hour is here."

Cheftu kissed my hand, then my mouth, and I knew whatever we chose, we would be together.

Ultimately, only that really mattered.

AFTERWORD

Ancient Israel is no more synonymous with modern Israel than modern Judaism is with its antique roots. Largely, the storyline of *Sunrise* was taken from the same garden-variety Bible found in most any hotel room, with a twist of cultural perspective thrown in.

Negative spaces in history are revealed only by the shadows they cast. In the years between the Ark being taken by the Philistines (Pelesti) and it coming to rest in Solomon's Temple, the jar of manna and the rod of Aaron were removed. After that time, the Ark is no longer blamed for plague or disaster. So it seems possible that the priests, at least, knew there was some connection between the two.

Scholars suggest that the Ark was connected with the bubonic plague because the people of Israel were cautioned to watch out for skin eruptions. If anyone did have an outbreak, then he or she was made to live outside the camp so as not to infect the others. However, if the Ark was taken into less than hygienic conditions without strict cleanliness laws, it could be massively destructive.

Another reason scholars think the Ark and the plague are associated is that the Philistines sent along gold reproductions of tumors and rats when they returned the Ark. How would the Ark work as a receptacle for the plague? The bubonic plague originates in the intestinal tract of the flea. Perhaps the fleas lived on the combination of manna and rod within the Ark. Therefore, when those items were removed, eliminating the source of fleas, the Ark became only a religious totem.

The electricity theory stems from the composition of the Ark and conjecture of how much static could build up inside this heavy gold box. Some facts to support the theory are that the priests were required to go barefoot; the high priest's breastplate could have been protecting the wearer when he opened the Ark; and the Temple itself was designed as a giant containment field for the power of the Ark.

Careful readers will guess that Avgay'el (Abigail) becomes the author of the first version of the Bible, the "J" writer. Borrowing liberally from the syntax of the translation, as well as the core stories told in *The Book of J* by Harold Bloom and David Rosenberg, I place her in that position of power and responsibility.

Hiram of Tsor (Tyre) is among the most enigmatic characters in history. Why not make this man, who is the inspiration for the Masonic legend, whose roots go back to ancient Egypt and Aztlan (Atlantis), who is the muse for many of the world's deities, who is also the builder of the Temple, why not make this man be Dion? Eternal, dark and tormented by his own desires, the fallen Greek steps easily into the role created by legend.

There is no logical explanation for Akhenaten's reign when he single-handedly wrecked the Egyptian empire and moved the divine beyond the people's reach, thus becoming the sole priest in the most narcissistic religion this side of Jonestown. Possibly he purloined and rewrote the psalms. He married his daughters and left no sons. Yet, according to Egyptologist James Breasted, more ink has been spilled on this time period than the whole rest of Egyptian history. To have upset Ma'at, charmed the court, married the most beautiful woman, Nefertiti, and remained in power for more than a decade, he must have been extremely charismatic.

Smenkhare is a mystery also. We have the mummy of an eighteen–twenty-two-year-old labeled with that name, but the identity and gender of the mummy have been debated for almost a hundred years. Who knows? As fashion has always been to imitate those in power, I suggest that the androgyny of Akhenaten was such a fad that RaEm could have made a place for herself in the guise of a man—up to the point of marrying Meryaten, who, coincidentally, vanishes from history at the same time as Smenkhare.

One of the eerier experiences of writing this book occurred when

I came across the name of David's Egyptian scribe. It has several different interpretations, one of them being Chavsha. Evidence suggests that David used Egyptian government as a model for his new, unified monarchy. The water spout (tzinor) invasion of Jerusalem may never be explained satisfactorily because we don't know exactly how to translate that Hebrew term. However, after I personally walked through Hezekiah's tunnel in Jerusalem, the fictional possibilities for our heroine, the water route veteran, were too sweet to bypass.

The tales of Saul, David, and Solomon were written in postexilic times, not as a complete historical record, but as a spiritual account, an encouragement to the Hebrews so far away from their homeland and center of faith. Consequently the Bible stories should not be read as a straight-lined, exclusive reality, but rather as soundbites of a larger, sometimes seemingly contradictory whole. With this in mind, I introduced the Urim and Thummim at a time considerably after the first biblical mention. Scholars suggest that several sets of stones served this oracular purpose. For the sake of the story, ancient Aza is called by its modern name, Gaza. Additionally, Ashdod and Ashquelon are reversed in prominence.

Portraying the world of ancient Israel, Akhenaten's Egypt, and Judaism before much of the ritual structure was documented, was challenging. I had to divorce my reverence for the text from the actual historical characters. Despite my Judeo-Christian Western background, I wanted to scrutinize this history with the same amount of detail, look at these cultures' view of the One God, as unflinchingly as I would polytheistic religions. Several books helped develop my cultural angle, enlightened my concepts of this time period, and gave me insight into the humanness of these historical characters.

I've already mentioned *The Book of J* by Harold Bloom and David Rosenberg, which changed my worldview and inspired the syntax; *Pharaohs and Kings* by David Rohl, whose research always fuels my imagination; *In the Wake of the Goddesses* by Tikva Frymer-Kensky, a riveting realignment of what it meant to be female in Bible times; *Ancient Zionism* by Avi Erlich, whose perspective and erudition stunned and awed me; *The Gold of the Exodus* by Howard Blum for the desert story; and the Bible in Hebrew and several translations.

Motivation, cultural perspective, even the weather all influence that solid foundation for our reality that we call *history*. However, every recent fact, every archaeological dig, every newly translated word, lends nuance and shadow to what we know: consequently history is anything but dead. It lives, breathes, and changes with new information and insight. The past is as vibrant and alive as the present, and if we listen, it will teach us about ourselves.

Suzanne Frank
February 12, 1999
Dallas, Texas

ACKNOWLEDGMENTS

Many people contributed to my sanity and to the accuracy of the story, some to both. Heartfelt thanks to Hanne and Sydney for the freedom of the attic and the Derkato myth; Rene, my *chavera* extraordinaire; the Pirate, for pep talks, inspiring e-mails, and thoughtful surprises; Ernie, for exploding eyeballs; Dannyboy, Peter and Tanya, for the photo; Tim, for last-minute electricity; Mister Avolio, for sharing his understanding of music and giving me the heart of Dadua; Dana and Melanie for the treehouse retreat; Michael, for the box and the plague; Martine, for her magical ways; Fabian and La Madeleine for the party; Marianne, for the paradigm shift; Geraldine at Mystery Bookstore for her enthusiastic support; Maxwell Books in DeSoto for their amazing sponsorship; Brent, for his discerning eye; Kati, for a home, a friend, a sister; and Dan, for whom there are no words.

As always, unending gratitude to Susan Sandler and Jessica Papin, who keep raising the bar, challenging me, and cheering me on; to Sona Vogel and to Harvey-Jane Kowal at Warner for keeping me on the true path. Thanks to my parents for my first trip to Israel (and second and third), for creating in me a world without borders, and most of all, for their trust.

Sunrise was a battle I couldn't have won without the steadfast, enthusiastic support of many people, my personal cheering section, (this includes all of the aforementioned): Renee, Mathias, Paul, River, Ira, Joebo, Drue, Barbara W., Kris, Steve A., David El, David C., the Rickster, Elaine W., Jimbo, John, my SMU classes, Sally in SMU C.E., Debi, Michelle and Dwayne.

Todah rabah.